SOUTH LANARKSHIRE LIBRARIES

This book is to be returned on or before
the last date stamped below or may be
renewed by telephoning the Library.

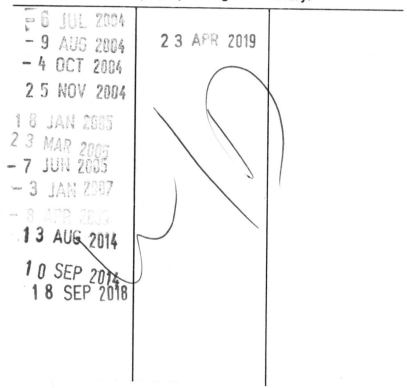
H
Tremayne, Kate
Loveday honour

CH   C40774161%
         18.99

THE LOVEDAY HONOUR

Kate Tremayne

headline

First published in 2004
by HEADLINE BOOK PUBLISHING

10 9 8 7 6 5 4 3 2 1

Cataloguing in Publication Data is
available from the British Library

ISBN 0 7472 6592 5

Typeset in Plantin by
Letterpart Limited, Reigate, Surrey

Printed and bound in Great Britain by
Clays Ltd, St Ives plc

Headline's policy is to use papers that are natural, renewable and
recyclable products and made from wood grown in sustainable forests.
The logging and manufacturing processes are expected to conform
to the environmental regulations of the country of origin.

HEADLINE BOOK PUBLISHING
A division of Hodder Headline
338 Euston Road
LONDON NW1 3BH

www.headline.co.uk
www.hodderheadline.com

To my loving husband Chris for always being there.

To a talented artist and very special friend Denise Kearney.

ACKNOWLEDGEMENTS

To my agent Teresa Chris for being such a wonderful person and for her support and encouragement.

Special thanks and appreciation to Jane Morpeth and Alice McKenzie at Headline – who keep the Lovedays running on an even keel.

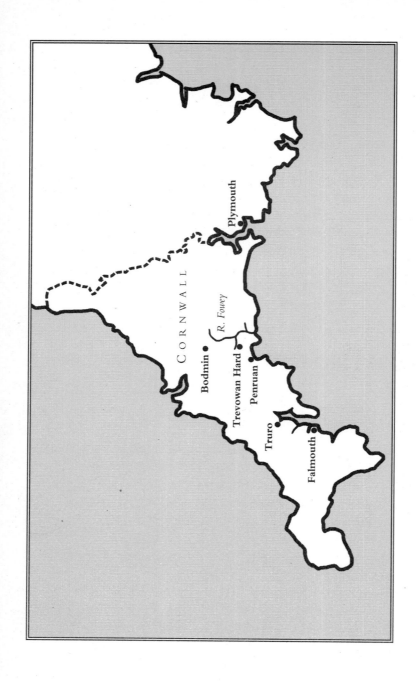

The Loveday Family

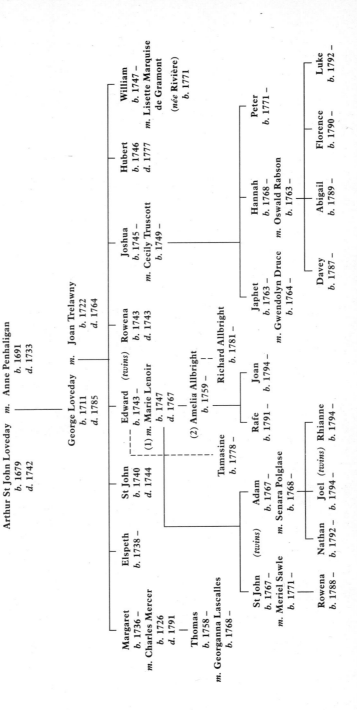

Chapter One

June 1794

'If a man does not have honour, he has nothing,' Edward Loveday declared to his wife. 'I will never sacrifice my honour simply to make life more comfortable.'

Amelia ignored him and stared out of the window of the orangery at Trevowan where they had taken their afternoon tea. Her auburn hair was coiled at the nape of her neck and partly hidden under a lace cap. The tilt of her chin was stubborn and the set of her shoulders uncompromising. There had been too many such strained silences in recent months.

Edward had hoped that the birth of their daughter three months ago would heal their differences. He tried again to ease the tension between them. 'It is time to put the past behind us, my dear. Are you not allowing your recriminations to mar all that has been good in our lives?'

'Scandal is eroding the good name of the Loveday family. How can you make it seem that I am the one in the wrong?' She kept her face averted and her chest rose and fell in growing agitation. 'Since our marriage your family has been linked to one scandal after another. Even *you* have not spared me. Where is the honour in that?'

'You twist my words. Have I not asked your forgiveness for the pain I have caused you? Are these times not difficult enough without your censure?'

'I cannot condone ...' She broke off abruptly and took several deep breaths before resuming in a martyred tone: 'My daily prayer is that no members of this family will bring further shame to our door.'

Edward suppressed a sigh and picked up his newssheet. Where Amelia saw only shame in the actions of family members, Edward himself worried that fate and fortune had conspired against them and that in fact their lives were in jeopardy. These were ruthless and uncertain times.

Amelia's rhythmic tapping of a teaspoon against the bone china saucer soon made it impossible for him to read. He folded the newssheet and put it aside, studying the tense figure of his wife. She was staring across the grounds of the estate, her eyes focussed upon the spire of Trewenna church. Even in her late thirties, she was still lovely; her hair, though streaked with grey at the temples, was thick and luxuriant and her complexion creamy without the necessity for powder.

The annoying sound of the spoon against the cup tested Edward's patience to its limit. He was relieved when a maid entered to clear the tea tray and Amelia relinquished her spoon with a sigh.

The afternoon sun dappled the leaves of hawthorn, oak and elm trees on the hill behind the house and its rays slanted through the glass of the orangery. The sunlight turned the white marble floor golden, and the leaves of the orange trees in their stone urns cast shadows across the carved wood of the chairs and low tables. Edward squinted his blue eyes against the brightness of the glare. His heart was heavy, weighted by worries. He feared for the lives of his son Adam, a prisoner of the French, and his nephew Japhet, accused of highway robbery and now awaiting trial in London's most notorious prison, Newgate.

He reached out to touch a lock of Amelia's hair but she pulled back from him. This coldness between them was hard to bear. He was a passionate man and he did not want a loveless marriage. Honour bound him to the obligations of his past as well as the present. But if he had not yet won Amelia's understanding, how could he hope for her forgiveness? He could not set honour aside but he loved his wife, and was determined that his marriage would not be sacrificed on the altar of family duty.

With so many problems threatening their welfare his sense of

2

honour and duty would be stretched to its limits in the coming months.

Edward was rapidly losing patience with his wife's manner. The gentle, loving spouse of the first four years of their marriage had changed into a bitter, judgemental woman in the last year. This Amelia was a stranger to him. Edward did not condone Japhet's conduct or the circumstances that had led to his own eldest son St John's trial last year for murder – another scandal that had almost brought the family to ruin although St John had been innocent. It had been a testing time, stretching loyalties to their limit. And now this episode with Japhet ...

He ground down his fears for his nephew. He did not believe Japhet was a thief. He was wild, headstrong and reckless but he was no hardened criminal, of that Edward was certain. He accepted the frailties of others, was fiercely loyal to his family and expected no less from his wife.

A fit of coughing made him turn away from Amelia. Pain lanced through his chest and sweat stippled his upper lip and brow. He led a far from conventional life himself. His health had suffered from a recent run-in with excise officers on Loveday land, when they had found contraband hidden by a local smuggler. In the confrontation Edward had been shot and the wound was slow to heal.

'I have duties on the estate that must be attended to,' he announced.

He stood up too quickly, pain shooting through his chest. Momentarily, the room spun around him. He dragged in a deep breath and caught sight of his reflection in the window. His chiselled features were leaner and his tall, slender figure slightly stooped. He straightened his spine. The movement sharpened the pain in his chest and he clenched his jaw to overcome it.

'You do too much, Edward,' Amelia scolded. 'You must put your health first.'

He stared at her lovely face, taut with unhappiness and fear, and his love for her overrode his anger. Amelia had endured much in the last two years, and her tender sensibilities had often been offended. Even indiscretions from his own past had returned to put a further trial upon his marriage. They had taken place many

3

years before he had met Amelia, and he refused to be judged by her because of them, but there was no reasoning with her at the moment. He could only pray that in time she would become more charitably disposed towards the tribulations they faced. He loved her deeply and wanted the rift between them to end.

'You should be resting, Edward.' She sounded more condemning than compassionate. 'You were coughing through the night again. Dr Chegwidden says you do too much. There is a cold wind off the sea. You will get a fever if you go out.'

He disregarded her advice. He could not afford to pander to the pain in his chest and the bouts of weakness that struck without warning. Too much depended on his rebuilding of the reputation of the shipyard which had been damaged at the time of St John's trial. They had lost several customers then, and once the trust of customers was lost it was hard to win it back. It was only Edward's reputation for integrity that had kept the remaining customers loyal to him.

'I am well enough,' he responded tersely. 'You worry too much. And, my dear, you must try not to dwell upon the misfortunes and trials that have beset us. It is the future that is important.' He bowed over her hand and lifted it to his lips. 'I will never abandon my duty or loyalty to any member of my family, but your happiness is of great import to me. You were my rock in the first years of our marriage and have blessed me with two wonderful children. My feelings for you have not changed, my love. I esteem you above all other women. It has been nearly a year since we have truly lived as man and wife. A family is only strong when it is united. Is it not time to set aside our differences?'

Her hand was cold and she drew it away to link her fingers firmly in her lap. Her eyes were filled with tears as she held his stare. 'Whilst your illegitimate daughter continues to live at the shipyard I feel humiliated and shamed. Send her away and I will be a true wife to you again, Edward.'

Her condition was unacceptable. The weight of his burdens pressed down on him. A sharp pain shot through his chest each time he drew a deep breath. Amelia's stubbornness was a bitter betrayal. He knew he was pushing himself past the limits of his

4

endurance, but he had never turned his back on his duty to his family and whatever the cost he would not fail them now.

The sea mist rolled across the gently swelling waves and rose to obscure all but the tops of the stone chain towers built opposite each other at the entrance to the River Fowey. Behind the towers, on each side of the river the hills sloped down to the water's edge, sheltering the harbour from the storms and strong winds that could sweep this coast. In the opposite direction the rolling hills embraced the horizon, their tree-scattered slopes ink black against a milky sky.

Impatience charged the emaciated figure of Adam Loveday as he stood on the quarterdeck of his ship. The chain guarding Fowey harbour creaked as the winches within the towers lowered it to the riverbed. It was frustrating after nine months away from his home to be further delayed by this final barrier, placed there to allow the citizens of the port to sleep in their beds safe from a surprise attack by a French warship.

Adam had dropped anchor whilst the harbour master was rowed out to inspect *Pegasus* and ensure that she was indeed under the command of her English captain. Several months ago word had reached Fowey that the French had captured *Pegasus* and her crew, and that a ransom had been demanded for the release of the men. The harbour master was right to be suspicious. As a prize of war the ship could be used by the French to enter her home port and then turn her guns on her countrymen.

The ragged and emaciated condition of the crew bore testament to the months they had lain in a French prison at La Rochelle in fear of their lives. As the sun broke through the morning mist, Adam lifted his head and breathed deeply to calm the thundering beat of his heart. He brushed aside a long tendril of black hair that had escaped from the leather strip that restrained it. He had been away for so many months. The outward voyage had been to Virginia where he had visited his cousin Garfield Penhaligan's plantation. His brother St John had accompanied him when their father had deemed it necessary for the elder twin to be out of the country for a year or more, to allow the scandal of his trial for the murder of the smuggler Thadeous Lanyon to die down. St John was rightfully acquitted but the old enmity between the families had given rise to damaging conjecture and Edward wanted the gossips to tire of the subject before St John returned from America.

Whilst in Virginia Adam had sold the cargo of furniture he had invested in to other plantation owners, for English furniture was still prized in the old colony. It had been a prosperous venture since for the return voyage he had acquired shipping contracts from tobacco plantation owners to convey their crops to England. But on the return voyage *Pegasus* had been attacked by three French ships and overpowered.

From that voyage Adam had anticipated returning with a substantial profit that would ease the financial burdens of the yard. Instead, he had been lucky to return with his ship and his life. The French had taken the coffer holding the money from the sale of his cargo and also the tobacco he had contracted to convey safely to England. Honour demanded he should now repay its value to the Virginian planters, which would greatly increase the debts already owed by the Lovedays' yard.

Now *Pegasus* sailed past the quay at Fowey where several tall-masted ships were docked; two more were anchored in the river channel waiting to be unloaded when a mooring on the quay became available. The fishing luggers bobbed and swayed in the shallower water and a ferryman rowed three passengers from the landing stage across the water at Polruan to Fowey. Now that the chains were lowered the fishermen would be preparing to set out to sea. From the shore at Polruan the familiar hammering from a boatyard was audible, causing a dull ache of homesickness to rise in Adam's breast. How had the family yard at Trevowan Hard fared? Before he had sailed for America it had been struggling to survive. Several orders for new ships had been cancelled following St John's trial and Adam had hoped to restore their fortunes with the Virginian venture.

Guilt assailed him. He had failed his father and family, but at least *Pegasus* had been retaken from the French. When Adam and his crew escaped from the prison at La Rochelle, their ship had still been moored in the port. The French had repaired her main mast, which had been shattered by cannon fire in the fight before her capture. Unfortunately, there had been no provisions other than ship's biscuits on board, and his men were already weak from the scant rations fed them by their gaolers. The voyage from La Rochelle had taken eight days as the winds had been against them, but they had managed to evade any French ships. At least with *Pegasus* once again in his possession he still had the chance to restore the family fortunes, even if it meant becoming a privateer in order to capture any lone French ships he encountered while England remained at war with France.

A man climbed the steps to the quarterdeck, his swarthy features smug with satisfaction and his black eyes coldly arrogant. 'Cousin Adam, you have brought us to England's shore.' His French accent was obvious. 'You dealt with the harbour master well. It was inspired of you to suggest that I was a French Royalist who had information for your Squire Penwithick to pass on to the Prime Minister.'

Adam regarded his French cousin with little liking. His dark hair was short and foppishly curled and wide side-whiskers emphasised the sallowness of his complexion. Etienne Rivière was immaculately dressed in black close-fitting breeches and a cut-away coat. The ruffles on his shirtfront and at his wrist were starched and pristine white.

Standing beside him Adam felt like a vagabond in the crumpled and stained clothes he had been wearing in prison. Though he had shaved that morning and done his best to get the worst of the stench and grime washed from his shirt and breeches, lack of soap had made this difficult. He was ashamed to return home in such a bedraggled state.

There was a harshness to Etienne's angular face that showed him to be both ruthless and untrustworthy. The Frenchman's glance was mocking as it flickered over Adam's dishevelled clothing. In response he stiffened his spine. The ragged state of his clothing would never make him feel inferior to his cousin. They had been enemies for several years, but for reasons of his own Etienne Rivière had aided the escape from the French prison on condition that Adam allowed him to sail to England with them.

7

'I spoke the truth to the harbour master,' Adam curtly informed him. 'Squire Penwithick will be most interested in any information you can give him. Shortly after the fall of the Bastille in Paris you joined the revolutionaries to further your own interests and have served in the French Army these last years. I advise you to co-operate with our government. There may be those among your exiled countrymen who know you for a traitor. They will certainly suspect you of being a spy for the new regime and shoot you given the chance.'

Etienne raised one brow in disbelief, then shrugged. 'I will talk to your squire. I have no intention of returning to France.'

'Because there is a price on your head?' Adam challenged. 'Your wife and daughter lost their lives on the guillotine. To save your own hide you abandoned them when you joined the army of revolution. And before that you sacrificed your own sister Lisette in marriage to a debauched lecher.'

Rivière's thin lips twitched into a sneer. 'I arranged for Lisette to marry a Marquis when my father wanted her wed to you. I told you when the betrothal was announced that you would never have her for your bride.'

Adam bristled at the insult but in truth it had no power to hurt him. He had never loved Lisette and would have wed her merely out of duty. Her marriage to the Marquis had left him free to marry the woman he loved. But Lisette had been young and innocent and the debauched demands of her husband, coupled with her experiences during the early days of the revolution, had left her emotionally unstable. Her mood swings were volatile and perilously close to madness at times.

Adam resisted the urge to wipe the arrogant sneer from his cousin's face. 'You callously bartered a naïve young girl, and your mother died because of your neglect. You are not welcome in our home. When you land, give your report to Squire Penwithick and then leave Cornwall.'

'I will leave when I am ready.' Etienne's dark eyes were turbulent. 'You cannot stop me seeing my sister. The last news I heard of her was that your family had shut her away in an asylum. Edward Loveday has much to answer for.'

'Lisette despises you for the way you treated her,' Adam flared.

'And you forget, she is now married to my Uncle William.'

'William Loveday is a naval captain with no land or property. He is unworthy of her. How can a mere captain support my sister in the manner she has been reared to expect?'

Adam started forward with his fists clenched. It was rare that he and Etienne met without resorting to physical violence. A short, stocky figure stepped between the two enraged cousins. The man's wavy cinnamon-coloured hair was worn loose and cut short above his shoulders. 'Gentlemen! Would you brawl in front of the crew?'

Sir Gregory Kilmarthen stood four feet high in his socks. Despite the shortness of his figure his voice carried the full authority of his lineage, stemming from a line of baronets unbroken since the days of William the Conqueror.

Adam controlled his temper and nodded to his friend. 'You are right, Long Tom.' He used the name Sir Gregory had been known by when they first met. Long Tom had been an English spy in France and when he was captured Adam had been sent by Squire Penwithick to rescue him. Long Tom's dwarfish stature was startling at first, but it had provided him with an easy disguise, enabling him to travel with strolling players providing entertainment in the cities and secretly send information back to England. Sir Gregory Kilmarthen had the sharpest mind Adam had ever encountered. They had become close friends and he had joined Adam on this fateful voyage.

Adam glanced at Etienne, delivering a veiled ultimatum. 'Trevowan Hard is less than a mile downriver. My cousin will be leaving the ship there and we will not meet again socially.'

Sarcastic laughter burst from Etienne Rivière. 'Indeed not! Your gypsy wife does not mix in the social circles I shall be frequenting.'

At this insult to Senara Adam swung out at his cousin, slamming one fist into his jaw. Etienne reeled backwards, crashing against the railing of the quarterdeck. When he recovered his balance, he rubbed his jaw, his black eyes narrowed with hatred.

'You'll regret laying a hand on me, cousin. I needed your ship to escape from France. Had it been possible for me to get away and leave you rotting in a French prison, I would happily have

9

done so. I have no further need of your family and the limited connections they offer me.'

Etienne swung away and marched to his quarters.

Long Tom looked up at Adam. 'If you are wise you will stay away from your cousin. He will cause trouble. He hates you.'

'It's mutual. I vowed to kill him for the way he abandoned his mother and Lisette. He is a traitor to his family and his homeland who deserves to die. The day will come when he will answer for his treachery. Honour demands it.'

Long Tom did not try to dissuade Adam. A true gentleman lived, and if necessary died, by the code of honour which governed their society.

Chapter Two

As *Pegasus* entered the mid-water channel of the inlet of the River Fowey and could be seen from the banks of Trevowan Hard, the shipwrights raised a loud cheer.

'It be Captain Loveday! Master Adam has come home, God be praised. Captain Loveday be safe!'

A brigantine was moored alongside the wooden dock, pulleys still in place on her deck as the men fitted ratlines and rigging.

As the welcoming cheers resounded across the water, tears of emotion misted Adam's vision. He swallowed hard and dashed them away with his hand as he scanned the dock for signs of his father or wife. The tall figure of Edward Loveday appeared at the open door of the forge. Behind him stood the muscular figure of the blacksmith and his son who acted as his apprentice, and Adam saw that the row of carpentry sheds was disconcertingly silent and empty of workers.

The joy of seeing his father was tempered by the realisation that apart from the brigantine moored by the dock, the two slipways which should have contained keels or partly built ships were empty. In the dry-dock a fishing lugger was having the barnacles scraped from her hull. It was a disturbing sight for the dry-dock was large enough to accommodate a three-masted merchantman. Adam had never seen the place so empty. His heart contracted with foreboding. The yard could not survive if there were no new ships being built. With the farm and estate at Trevowan heavily mortgaged, did his family risk losing everything?

His expression was taut with worry as he ran down the gangplank. He paused to acknowledge the greetings of the ship-wrights then, formality cast aside, hugged his father close. There had been times in prison when he had feared he would not live to set foot on English soil again.

'I despaired of your return.' Edward's voice was gruff. 'You are so thin, I can feel every rib. It is good to have you home safe, my son.'

Adam drew back, appalled to discover that his father too was skeletal beneath his thick woollen jacket. His frame was hunched as though he suffered constant pain. Adam stared into his face. Edward's complexion, usually darkened by the sun, was pale; the high cheekbones more prominent. His long hair, tied at his nape in a black ribbon, was no longer ebony-coloured but badger-grey.

'And how are you, sir?' Adam asked anxiously.

'Better for knowing that you are safe. It has been a troubled winter.' Edward looked over Adam's shoulder and his expression tightened with anger. Etienne stood on the jetty with two port-manteaux at his feet. 'Is that Rivière? What the devil is he doing here?'

'He helped me escape the prison in La Rochelle – drugged the guards. He wanted passage to England.'

'But I had paid the ransom the French demanded. You should have been freed.' Edward's displeasure at seeing Etienne turned to grudging acceptance. 'Though I suppose I should be grateful to the man if he helped you to escape.'

Adam frowned. 'We were told the ransom had not been paid. That was money you could ill afford.' He glanced round the shipyard again only noticing half the usual number of men at work, mostly those who lived in the dozen cottages within the yard.

'You are safe, Adam. That is all that matters.'

A wave of dizziness made him sway and his father's hand shot out to grab his arm.

'Are you ill?'

Adam shook his head. 'There was little food in the prison and we were at sea for eight days with no provisions other than hard tack. The men are weak from hunger.'

'Pru Jensen will give them a meal at the Ship kiddley.' Edward nodded towards the extended cottage that served the yard both as alehouse and general store; the provisions were paid for by the

Lovedays, and the kiddley run by Pru and Toby Jensen. 'You will want to be with your family, Adam.'

Edward tensed, eyes blazing with anger, as Etienne approached him, Long Tom by his side. Edward greeted Sir Gregory courteously. 'I hope that you will stay with us for some days to recover from your voyage.'

'Adam insists that I stay at Mariner's House, and I have a report to make to Squire Penwithick.'

Etienne pushed himself forward, rudely interrupting their conversation. 'Good day, Uncle.'

Long Tom said quietly to Adam, 'I will eat at the kiddley to give you time to be reunited with your wife, joining you later.'

Adam nodded, noting his father's annoyance at Etienne's manner. Edward spoke sharply in reply to his nephew. 'It appears that you were instrumental in Adam's escape from prison. For that I thank you. But you are not welcome here – not after the way you abandoned your mother and sister. If your father had lived, he would be ashamed to own you as his son.'

Etienne flushed and rapped out, 'And has my sister fared better in your hands? Your brother wed her for her money. She had a fortune sewn into her clothes when she left France. She had stolen it from me. You cast her into a lunatic asylum to be rid of her.'

'Lisette was under the care of His Majesty's own physician for a short while,' Edward stiffly informed him.

'An incompetent who could not cure your King's madness,' Etienne flared.

'You are insolent and ungrateful,' Edward snapped. 'But then, you always were. Your sister is no longer under the care of Dr Claver. She is expected to arrive in Cornwall in the next week to await the return of her husband, currently serving with the British Fleet. I do not want you upsetting her. Lisette's mind remains delicate. She suffered most grievously at the hands of the rabble when her first husband was murdered and their château ransacked.'

Etienne remained antagonistic. 'She would have been killed by the mob as an aristo if I had not take her to the convent. Maman had already suffered a seizure after my father's death. I could not protect her.'

13

'Clearly you have no sense of honour or duty.' Edward coughed, his whole body shaken by the intensity of his rage. He controlled the fit of coughing to state coldly, 'I suppose France is no longer safe for you now that the tyrant Robespierre is dead? Nor is there a place at Trevowan for a man who was a traitor to his King.'

'I do not want your hospitality. I have information for Squire Penwithick which will be of service to your government.' Etienne showed no remorse for his conduct towards his own family and his manner was aggressively haughty. 'I have no intention of mouldering away in the country. But first I would assure myself that all is well with Lisette.'

Edward controlled another coughing fit and glared at his nephew. 'Then you must take rooms in Fowey or Bodmin. Send word of your address and I will arrange for a meeting with your sister.'

'You sound like her gaoler,' Etienne challenged. 'In the absence of her husband, I, her brother, am her protector, not you, Uncle. I will take rooms in Fowey until I speak with Penwithick. Have a man row me there. I will wait in the ale house yonder.' He strode away towards the Ship kiddley.

Edward turned away, a pulse visibly beating in his jaw as he struggled to control his anger. His face was unnaturally pale but his expression relaxed as he regarded his son.

'That cough does not sound good, sir.'

'I cannot shake it off in this damp climate. But I am well enough, and greatly eased by knowing that you are safe.'

'Now I am back I can shoulder some of your burden,' Adam offered, shocked by how weary his father appeared.

'There is much to discuss. A great deal has happened in recent months.' Edward grimaced. 'Most of it bad, I regret to say – but more of that later. This is a day for rejoicing. It gladdens my heart that you are safe. And there have been moments of joy too while you were away.' The weariness slipped from his face. 'Senara bore you twins: a boy, Joel, and a daughter, Rhianne. Both are strong and healthy. And you have a sister, Joan, born a month after the twins.'

'Congratulations to you, sir! We have both been blessed.' Adam

14

grinned at his father, but was inwardly impatient to greet his wife and family. He frowned when he saw the door to Mariner's House closed and no sign of Senara in the yard. 'We will speak later. I would hear of all that has happened while I was at sea, and there is much to tell you of my voyage. Now I would greet my wife.'

'Senara left earlier to visit Boscabel. She goes there most mornings to collect the herbs she uses for her remedies, and to give instructions for what work is to be carried out. Little renovation has been done to the structure of the house in your absence, but at least the debris has been cleared from the house and outbuildings, and the grounds have been put into some kind of order. Senara will be back at noon.'

Adam hid his disappointment. 'Are the children with her? How is Nathan?'

'Your son thrives and is into all manner of mischief now that he is walking. Carrie Jensen and a wet-nurse tend the children, and there is …' Edward hesitated and did not meet his son's gaze as he continued, 'Tamasine Loveday has been a companion for Senara while you were away.'

'I know of no Tamasine in our family?' Adam frowned.

Edward stared ahead as they walked past the schoolhouse built for the yard's children by Amelia. Ahead stood Mariner's House. It was a substantial whitewashed stone and tile building as befitted the home of the heir to the shipyard. It had four bedrooms and servants' quarters in the attic. The bow window of the parlour overlooked the yard and there was a dining room and large kitchen at the back. For greater privacy it was set away from the other buildings in the yard.

'I will introduce you to Tamasine,' Edward said, 'and then you must eat and change before your wife returns. There is much to discuss.'

The sounds of a baby crying at the top of its lungs greeted their arrival at Mariner's House.

'Senara, is that you?' a feminine voice called from upstairs. 'Thank goodness you came home early, I can do nothing to calm Joel.'

A harassed young woman, her dark hair swept back and falling in curls to her shoulders, came down the stairs carrying a

15

screaming baby. She looked dismayed to encounter Edward and became even more flustered when she saw the dark-haired stranger with him.

'Tamasine, my dear, this is my son Adam.'

The young woman smiled broadly while holding the baby to her shoulder and patting its back to calm its cries. The little body was rigid as Joel voiced his displeasure and his face was red and streaked with tears. Tamasine hesitated, seemed about to curtsy then glanced askance at Edward and inclined her head in a flustered greeting. 'Senara will be devastated she is not here. And this is no way to be presented to your new son.'

They walked into the parlour and she thrust the child into Adam's arms. Taken aback, he stared down at the red face of his second son. 'He has fine lungs.' He grinned. 'I do not remember Nathan having such a loud cry. Is the child ill?' He held Joel steady, lifting and lowering the baby in the air before him. Within seconds the cries halted. Joel opened his eyes to regard his father in a serious manner, and as the motion continued, gurgled with contentment.

Tamasine laughed. 'My, sir, you *are* honoured. The young rascal has stopped crying. Joel is hale enough, but in a temper that he was left in his crib while Nathan and Rhianne were being dressed. He does not like to be neglected. Fortunately, Rhianne is as placid in temperament as he is volatile. It is a pleasure to meet you at last, sir. You are as handsome as Senara described you, but must have suffered so terribly in prison. You look more like a pirate than a merchant captain.'

The words tumbled out in an avalanche and Adam lifted one brow in query at this young woman who had the blue eyes, high cheekbones and dark hair of all the Lovedays. 'There is no mistaking from your looks that you are one of us, but you must forgive me for I have no recollection of a Tamasine?'

The animation and excitement of her unconventional greeting faded and her forthright stare dropped. 'I am needed in the nursery. Shall I return Joel to his crib?'

Adam handed the baby to her. 'I will change into more suitable clothing. And a meal would be most welcome.'

'I shall summon Carrie to attend you, sir.' The young woman

fled the room in obvious embarrassment.

'What a singular creature!' Adam laughed. 'What side of the family does she hail from, and how is it that she is here and not at Trevowan?'

Edward cleared his throat before speaking. 'Tamasine is my daughter. I did not know of her existence until her mother died last year.'

Adam felt his mouth drop open with shock. He snapped it shut. 'Did I hear aright? Did you say she is your daughter, sir?'

'Yes. And since her arrival, shortly after you sailed, Tamasine has lived here.' Edward's manner became defensive. 'It would be unacceptable for Amelia to have her at Trevowan. To be blunt, Tamasine was to have remained at the ladies' academy that she attended until a suitable marriage was arranged for her, but she ran away and came to Trevowan. I took her back to school but the place was totally unacceptable. Her life there had not been easy. She'd had no contact with her mother's family. In the circumstances that would have been inappropriate.'

Edward looked stiff and ill at ease. Adam was shocked at the unexpectedness of the news, but did not judge his father. Tamasine must be fifteen or sixteen years of age and Edward had wed Amelia only seven years ago. Before that he had been a widower for twenty years after Adam and St John's French mother had died giving birth to the twins.

'Since the school was not suitable,' Edward continued, 'Tamasine needed somewhere to stay until her future is settled. I want no question mark to hover over her reputation. She is known as my ward, the child of a distant cousin who died. It is better that way.'

'Yet you did not marry Tamasine's mother ... or is that an impertinent remark?'

'She was already wed if estranged from her husband.'

Adam remained silent, needing time to digest this information.

Edward extended his hands in silent appeal to his son. 'You must be surprised that Tamasine is lodging in your house? I intended it as no slur upon your good wife. Senara has been most understanding ... In fact, she has saved the situation from being extremely difficult and distressing for all concerned.'

'She would not judge Tamasine for being born out of wedlock.'

17

'Unfortunately, Amelia was not so forgiving. And the circumstances of Tamasine's arrival at Trevowan were unorthodox.' Edward rubbed the back of his neck before proceeding with obvious reluctance, 'You deserve to know the truth ... though it is not easy for me to speak of this.'

'I am honoured that you would confide in me,' Adam hastily reassured him.

'Then you'd best know all of it. Tamasine's mother was Lady Eleanour Keyne. You may recall that she died last summer? She notified me when she was dying of my daughter's existence and requested that I would be Tamasine's guardian and ensure that she married appropriately. I could not refuse. Lord Keyne and Lady Eleanour had been estranged for some years when we met. Lady Keyne preferred life in Cornwall; her husband had his place at Court and had no time for the country. They had four children. When Lord Keyne summoned his wife to rejoin him after a long separation, she was apparently enceinte with my child.'

Edward paused, clearly struggling with his emotions before he went on. 'Lord Keyne refused to acknowledge the child, and she was fostered by a wet-nurse in the country. When Tamasine was old enough she was sent to a boarding school. Indeed, since the death of her husband some years ago, Lady Eleanour feared that her son and other daughters would revile Tamasine and cast her out penniless if she was introduced to her maternal family.'

'It happens all too often in such circumstances, I believe, sir. It is most commendable that you saw your duty as lying otherwise.' Adam felt awkward at the disclosure but his first impression of Tamasine had been of a lovely, if somewhat high-spirited, young woman – just how he would expect a sister of his to be.

'But you acknowledge her as a Loveday when surely her name is properly Keyne?' he observed.

Edward rested his hand on the mantelshelf and stared for a moment into the empty hearth. 'She was baptised Tamasine Loveday Keyne. As you know, Loveday is a not uncommon name among Cornish women. On her unexpected arrival during the harvest feast, Tamasine announced herself as Tamasine Loveday before she collapsed from exhaustion. When Amelia refused to accept her, Senara agreed that Tamasine might live here as her companion. I trust that you will allow her to stay until a marriage can be arranged?'

'Of course.' Adam was too stunned by this revelation to say more. 'I will treat her with all the respect due to a sister.'

'I expected no less from you, which is why I asked your wife to allow Tamasine to live here in the first place.' Edward strode to the door but was halted by another bout of coughing and placed his hand against his chest. His face was pale and strained when he continued, 'Thank you for your understanding, Adam. You will not find Tamasine a burden. She is a quite exceptional girl and I believe that she and Senara have become very close.'

He followed his father to the front door. 'It seems to have been an ill-fated year, sir. I am saddened to see so little work in progress in the yard. And your health? Etienne had heard that you had been shot but that was some time ago. Who shot you? Is it just a cough that you suffer from? I have seen gunshot wounds and know that if infected ...'

'I am well enough,' his father abruptly cut in, obviously reluctant to talk of the matter. 'You have been away from your family for many months. There is much we can discuss later. Senara will return soon and you will want to make yourself presentable for your wife.'

After his father left, Adam ran up the stairs to change into clean clothing and spend some time with Nathan and the twins. His eldest son was sitting on the nursery floor playing with a wooden ship and regarded his father with a frown.

'You have forgotten me,' Adam said with a sigh. He held out his arms but the toddler did not move.

'Ship,' he said, waving the vessel.

'It is a fine ship. Can I see it?'

Nathan stood up and toddled towards him, holding it out. Adam felt his throat constrict with love and regretted the time away while Nathan had grown so fast. He then went over to the two cribs placed side by side. Joel was clutching a silver rattle and banging it against the side of his crib.

'He likes to make his presence heard,' Adam remarked, and looked across at the wet-nurse who was sewing a baby's dress and chuckling.

'He does that,' the woman replied. 'There'll be little peace with that one around.'

Rhianne lay peacefully in her cot. When Adam placed his finger against her hand, her blue eyes bored into his soul. She clutched his finger firmly and gave him a wide toothless smile. That simple gesture captured her father's heart in a strange and powerful way he had never experienced before. He was proud of his sons, but a daughter was someone who roused his chivalrous instincts to protect her from the ills of the world. He understood now why Edward had not wanted Tamasine to lose the security and protection of a family.

When he returned to the parlour, half a roast chicken, some freshly baked bread and a tankard of ale awaited him on a tray. Tamasine stood in the centre of the room, clutching her hands in front of her.

He smiled at her and sat down to eat, breaking off the leg of the chicken and biting into it hungrily.

Tamasine twisted her fingers together. 'You must find my presence here most awkward, Captain Loveday? I do not wish to impose. Senara ... I mean, Mrs Loveday ... has been so wonderful to me ...'

Her blue eyes were wide with uncertainty, but her head was held proudly and there was a defiant lift to her chin. He could sense her vulnerability but she was too proud to show it openly. He admired her for that, and to ease the tension he smiled, speaking between mouthfuls as he devoured the bread and chicken. 'There will be no addressing me as Captain Loveday. Bridie calls me Adam, and you will be no less of a sister to me than Senara's.'

She flushed with pleasure. 'I never hoped for so much. Your father has been most generous in allowing me to stay. I never meant to cause trouble when I ran away from school, only I was so miserable there. And now, for the first time, I have a real family.'

'I hope I do not disappoint you?'

'You could never ...' Tamasine broke off and grinned as she realised that he had been teasing her.

'How old are you, Tamasine?'

'Fifteen.'

'My father explained the reason why you are here. I gather you are not permitted to visit Trevowan.'

'That does not trouble me.' She tossed back her hair again, showing both her defiance and her susceptibility. 'Mr Loveday has been most kind and generous.'

'It cannot have been easy for you,' Adam observed.

'I count myself fortunate.'

The proud tilt of her chin and flash of spirit in her eyes warned him she was not to be pitied. Adam admired her courage and could not resist teasing her a little more. 'I believe that it will prove an interesting experience having a sister.'

There was a cry of joy behind them then Senara ran into her husband's open arms. Her cloak billowed around her as she laughed and kissed him alternately. Adam stood up and swung her round and, heedless of Tamasine's giggles, returned his wife's kiss with passion. The couple had eyes for none but each other and Tamasine slipped upstairs to take care of the children and enable them to be reunited in private.

Senara was breathless as she broke away from Adam's kiss. Her hand caressed his face, her eyes bright with love. 'I missed you so much! And I was worried you would be harmed in that dreadful prison. You are so thin, my darling.'

'And you are more lovely than ever.' Adam breathed in the sweet perfume of her hair and skin. 'Thoughts of you kept me sane these last months. I was mad to leave you for so long. Each night away was torment.'

She pulled absently at the long brown plait that hung to her waist. 'I left early this morning to gather herbs and look no better than a ragamuffin.'

'I like your hair dressed simply. It reminds me of the wild and untamed gypsy I fell in love with.'

She laughed at his teasing. 'You are home again and safe, my love. And much has happened while you were away.'

'Not least the fact I am now the father of twins.' His eyes sparkled with pleasure. 'You have been most productive in my absence, Mrs Loveday.'

'You have seen them already?' Senara's eyes glowed with pride. 'Was it a shock?'

'A delightful one, but as I am a twin myself, as was my father – though his twin sister died at birth – it was not altogether a surprise.' He held his wife in his arms, smiling down into her upturned face. 'Joel was complaining at the top of his lungs, while Rhianne is like a cherub. She clearly takes after her mother. Joel would not be pacified until he was entertained. He has a questing mind. I mark well that he will be an adventurer, that one.'

'Joel will be his own man, of that I have no doubt,' Senara laughed in agreement. 'He already has a mind of his own.'

As though on cue, the child began to cry upstairs, the sound rising to an angry cadence. Senara sighed. 'I must settle him.'

Adam shook his head and continued to hold her close. 'Tamasine and the wet nurse can tend to his needs. I have been too long apart from my wife. Long Tom is tactfully spending an hour at the kiddley; he will be staying with us for a few days.' He kissed her passionately but broke away when he heard his friend talking to Edward outside the parlour window. 'Such a houseful will afford us little privacy,' he sighed.

Long Tom rapped on the outer door to announce his arrival and warmly greeted Senara. Adam introduced him to Tamasine.

'What are your plans, Sir Gregory?' Senara asked. 'I hope you will stay here until you are fully recovered from your ordeal in prison. Both you and Adam look to be in need of several good meals, and judging from your greyish complexions both of you must be suffering from the ailments common after close confinement. I will have you both glowing with health again in a week.'

'I for one would welcome such attention.' Long Tom grinned. 'I will visit Squire Penwithick this afternoon and report to him what little information we gathered while in France – I have offered to take Etienne with me. Your father has invited us to Trevowan tomorrow to dine.' He stared down at his ragged clothes. 'It was fortunate I left a suit and jacket here when we sailed. I could hardly present myself in company thus attired. The French stole all our personal possessions. I will visit the tailor in Fowey later today for new clothes to be sewn.'

'While you are otherwise engaged, Senara and I will visit Boscabel. I have been cooped up in darkness for months and am eager to feel my freedom,' Adam declared to Senara. 'Father tells

22

me work has progressed on the house and grounds. On our return we could call briefly at Trewenna Rectory for me to pay my respects to Uncle Joshua and Aunt Cecily, and then on Amelia and Aunt Elspeth at Trevowan.' He turned apologetically to Tamasine, sitting unusually quiet on the window seat. 'Your pardon, Tamasine. I have forgotten your needs. I would like to spend some time with Senara, but perhaps you will join us tomorrow when we ride?'

'I have plenty to amuse me here,' she reassured him. 'Though I would like at some time to hear of your adventures. You have led such an exciting life.'

Adam noticed that the happiness had left Senara's face. She put her hand on his arm as she said, 'Your aunt and uncle are not at Trewenna. They are in London. Did your father not tell you what had happened to Japhet?'

'Is he in trouble?' Adam frowned. 'Some of my cousin's dealings have come perilously close to the wrong side of the law. Or is it his gambling?'

She took Adam's hand and led him to the settle, drawing him down beside her before she spoke.

'Perhaps I should leave, if this is family business?' Long Tom suggested.

'Please stay,' Senara replied. 'It is nothing that is not public knowledge. Just after Easter Japhet and Gwendolyn Druce were married. It was the most joyous occasion. Japhet had been looking at property and they planned to breed horses.'

'That has long been Japhet's intent, but he's had no capital. I am glad he finally came to his senses and wed Gwen. She has been in love with him for years.'

'We all hoped that the marriage would mark the end of Japhet's wild ways,' Senara continued. 'Joshua married them in Trewenna church. Japhet had vowed to Gwen to put his gambling days behind him.' Her expressive face was taut with worry. 'It was not to be. On the evening of the wedding he was arrested, charged with highway robbery on Hampstead Heath. He had spent several months in London after St John's trial and, determined to win his love, Gwen followed him there. But she arrived too late. He was already mixing with bad company. After his arrest he was taken in a closed carriage to London where he will stand trial at the Old Bailey. He is now in Newgate.'

Adam passed a hand across his face. His stomach churned with sick dread for his cousin. 'I cannot believe how much trouble has befallen our family in the months I have been away. And Father was shot. What happened there?'

'Perhaps Edward would prefer to talk of that himself.' Senara looked uncertain.

'He seemed dismissive of the incident. I thought to pursue it later. Who shot him?'

'Smugglers had been using the cave by the waterfall at Boscabel to store contraband. Edward learned of it and went to check. Excise men were lying in wait for the smugglers. They say your father was shot resisting arrest, which is absurd. Sir Henry Traherne ensured that the charges against him were dropped.'

Senara took her husband's hands in hers. 'Your father is still very ill, Adam. He will not rest and allow his body to heal properly. It is good that you are back. Edward does too much in the shipyard. And now he has all this worry over Japhet.'

'I can assume some of his responsibilities though there is little I can do for Japhet.' Adam grimaced. 'I would have liked to support him at his trial. Curse the French and my damned imprisonment! I was needed here these last months. Father would never have been shot had I not been captured.'

'Do not blame yourself. You could not help being captured. I doubt St John has any such qualms and he is still lording it in Virginia. And Japhet will understand. Your first loyalty must be to your father. Fortunately Gwen has connections in high places. She is determined that Japhet will be freed.'

'If there is anything I can do for your cousin, let me know,' Long Tom stated.

'Your offer is most kind, but you have your own affairs to set in order,' Adam replied. 'We have been away a long time.'

'Gwendolyn has written to say that Japhet is innocent of this crime,' Senara said eagerly. 'And Sir Gregory did so much to clear St John's name ...'

Long Tom bowed to her. 'I enjoyed my work as a spy in France and am not well known in London. I can adopt many disguises in

24

order to gain information. As for my affairs at home ...' He shrugged. 'I spend little enough time on my estate; relations with my mother and sister remain strained. I will assure myself that their needs continue to be met and that all is well there. After that, I would be happy to be of service to your family. Highway robbery is a grave crime of which to stand accused.'

Adam took his hand and shook it. 'Thank you for that. We must trust Japhet is found innocent and that your services will not be required.'

Chapter Three

On the same day that Adam returned to his homeland events in London were coming to their conclusion. A countrywoman at heart, Gwendolyn Loveday hated the capital more with each passing day. She had travelled to London with Japhet's parents, Joshua and Cecily and they were staying in the Strand with Joshua's sister, Margaret Mercer, and her son Thomas who was a partner in Mercer and Lascalles Bank. The family were on their way to hear the verdict of Japhet's trial and the atmosphere in the cramped coach was oppressive.

The arrest of Japhet – a gentleman not to mention son of a parson – for highway robbery had caught the public interest. New pamphlets appeared on the streets every day, salaciously expanding on his affair with Celestine Yorke, his gambling and duelling, but most cruelly declaring him to be a fortune hunter by his marriage to Gwendolyn. Many of these rumours, Gwendolyn suspected, had been paid for and circulated by Celestine Yorke to regain her own hold on public favour. The actress was now playing to packed houses every night, her failing popularity restored.

Other pamphleteers had chosen to turn Japhet into a public hero depicting him as a man with a devil-may-care past who had wed his childhood love. The fact that he had been arrested on his wedding day added to the spice of the story. He was shown as the lovable rogue who may have lived on the edge of respectability by his wild and unconventional lifestyle, but that had all been redeemed by his confession of his love for his childhood sweetheart and his vow to change his ways. Most of those pamphlets Gwendolyn was certain had been written by Lucien Greene, the poet who was Thomas Mercer's close friend.

Gwendolyn had also discovered unwanted notoriety by her marriage and was often recognised in the street now that the trial was in progress. She was reviled by the puritanical, and cheered by those who had taken Japhet to their hearts as a romantic hero. She had to be dignified and strong for Japhet's sake, so she bore it stoically and learned to put a shield around her emotions. Only at night did the façade crumble and she cried herself to sleep. She was terrified that Japhet would be found guilty and she would become a widow before she had savoured the joys of marriage to a man she loved to distraction.

The carriage rattled over the cobbled streets and Gwendolyn stared fixedly out of the window, locked in her inner misery and fear for her husband. Life for her dragged in a weird distortion of time – minutes could seem like hours when the fears were darkest, or a whole day could pass in a blurred haze. Yet she never doubted her husband's innocence. Today the judge would give his verdict. Today she would either become the happiest woman on earth reunited with her husband, or be condemned to a living hell of unrelenting grief. She loved Japhet with a passion that had driven her life – without him she would be plunged into an abyss. Despair rose up threatening to swamp her, her heart clenched in merciless talons of fear.

To keep her mind focussed, she concentrated on the sights around her. The great dome of St Paul's dominated the skyline, but around it the labyrinth of narrow cobbled streets or muddy alleys were claustrophobic with houses teetering skywards, blocking out the sun. Spires and church towers built by Wren or Hawksmoor sat majestically above the ramshackle confusion of tenement houses, taverns, warehouses, and shops. Painted wooden or gilded iron signboards hung above every commercial establishment. From the doorways of shops, pimply apprentices shouted the superiority and diversity of the goods within to entice customers. Above the shop fronts a window would be occasionally flung wide, and a muffled shout of *garde lieu* warned pedestrians to step aside as a slops pail was emptied uncaring of the hapless figures below. Indiscriminately, a maid would beat the dust from a carpet or a wigmaker scatter the surplus powder from a wig over the heads of passers-by.

As the carriage edged through the crowded thoroughfares, fear again threatened to strip Gwendolyn of her composure. To combat it she made herself take note of the commotion in the streets as sedan chairs wove in and out of pedestrians, the bearers knocking aside anyone who got in their way. At the crossroads vehicles jostled for space, and with no driver prepared to give way, collisions were common. Nervous horses would rear, toppling vegetables, coal or milk churns into the road. The thrashing hooves of horses sending sparks up from the cobbles, or crashing down to smash the bones of an urchin's foot or arm as they scrambled in the dirt to steal the scattered merchandise.

In such a mêlée, grimy hands would thrust through the leather blinds of the coach, the whining voice of beggars demanding alms.

The clamour was deafening and the smells from the press of bodies, horses and rotting vegetation in the gutters overpowering. Gwendolyn pressed a nosegay to her face, her hands tight with tension. When she heard a street performer singing a popular ballad, the tears so strenuously kept at bay welled into her eyes. It told of Japhet's exploits, both real and imagined, and of his courtship of Gwendolyn. The end of each verse was the same:

'Is Rogue Loveday innocent and a man of honour, or is he guilty, this man they call Gentleman James?'

Gentleman James was the name under which Japhet was supposed to have hidden his true identity.

Gwendolyn pressed a trembling hand to her temple and breathed deeply to calm the nausea and fear churning her stomach. The courthouse was already in view. The trial had been conducted at the Old Bailey over three nightmarish days and it had not gone in Japhet's favour.

Gwendolyn started as her hand was taken and squeezed by Margaret Mercer who sat beside her in the crowded coach. Japhet's parents, Cecily and Joshua, were seated opposite, together with Margaret's daughter-in-law, Georganna. Margaret's son Thomas and Japhet's brother Peter had ridden to the court on horseback. His sister Hannah had been unable to leave her sick husband and four children on their farm but following Japhet's incarceration she had sent long letters of encouragement to her brother and to Gwen. Gwendolyn wished Hannah was with them now. She missed her childhood friend who had always been so strong and supportive in the days when Gwendolyn had thought she would never win Japhet's love.

'You have been so brave, my dear.' Margaret broke through Gwendolyn's thoughts. 'This has been a difficult time for us all. They cannot possibly find Japhet guilty.'

Cecily Loveday sobbed into her hands; her plump figure embraced by her husband as he tried to comfort her. Joshua, who was several years younger than Edward Loveday, had turned completely grey in the three months since his son's arrest.

The stentorian voice in which Joshua delivered his sermons was a pale reflection of its former self and held a quiver of fear. 'It is a travesty of justice that so much could fall upon the evidence of Celestine Yorke – and she is nothing but a common actress.'

'Celestine Yorke professed to love Japhet.' Gwendolyn's eyes sparked with anger. She had suffered months of torment when Japhet had taken the actress as his mistress and she feared that he would never regard herself as other than a friend. 'How could Mrs Yorke love him and seek to destroy him? That is evil.'

'Japhet was a fool to become entangled with such a woman,' Margaret replied.

At her words Cecily sat up straight, her figure diminutive against that of her husband. There was a fervent light in her eyes. 'The word of a harlot should be thrown out of court. She speaks nothing but lies.'

Margaret shook her head. 'I always feared Japhet's wild ways would get him into trouble. But that Yorke creature has no scruples. She is using the trial to gain notoriety with the populace.'

'Unfortunately, she is not the only one to accuse Japhet.' Joshua spoke wearily. 'There is Sir Pettigrew Osgood, Sir Marcus Grundy and Lord Sefton. Osgood and Sefton declared Japhet had robbed both their coaches on the heath, and Sir Marcus said Japhet had stolen an emerald stock pin from him during an evening of cards at Mrs Yorke's home. Yet the theft was not reported at the time.'

'Osgood and Grundy are the Yorke woman's lovers.' Margaret was heated in her disapproval. 'They dance to her tune. And, of course, Osgood never liked Japhet, since he won the actress's affections.'

Georganna, who had been silent until now, sighed heavily. She was tall and thin and squashed into a corner of the overfilled coach. 'Japhet made a fool of Osgood and now the baronet would have his revenge. Thomas says Osgood is a petty and vengeful man.'

'What do you think of the case against your son, sir?' Gwendolyn sought reassurance from Joshua. 'Is there hope for Japhet?'

Joshua took his wife's hand as he answered. Cecily was looking at him with the same desperate pleading in her eyes. 'The irony of Japhet's case is that he did rob Osgood's coach last winter and Mrs Yorke was with Osgood that night. Japhet confided that much to me. Of course he denies it to the court. The Yorke woman ruthlessly used the incident to garner favour with the public and made Osgood put up a reward of one hundred pounds for the arrest of the highwayman they named Gentleman James.'

'That was all fiction,' Georganna scoffed. 'It proves she is a liar. There was no Gentleman James. Her evidence should be thrown out of court.'

'It does not detract from the fact that the robbery did happen,' Joshua reminded them. 'Though Osgood was in Japhet's company for several months before he recognised him as the highwayman on that night.'

Georganna remained scornful. 'Celestine Yorke was constantly in Japhet's company. Does it not seem strange that she should not recognise him as the highwayman until after she learned that he had married Gwendolyn? It is clear that she acted out of spite.'

'She tried to blackmail him to keep his affection.' Gwendolyn sighed. 'She had recognised him when they became lovers but of course Japhet laughed aside her suspicions as ridiculous.'

'So it is their word against Japhet's,' Georganna announced.

Gwendolyn clung to a fragile hope. 'There was no irrefutable evidence against Japhet. The jewellery taken from Osgood had long been disposed of. And Japhet emphatically denied robbing Lord Sefton's coach. That is the robbery for which he stands accused. I believe him.'

Joshua sighed and shook his head. 'Japhet may be innocent of the actual robbery but he did come by the Sefton jewels dishonestly. The actress says she found Lady Sefton's necklace in a saddlebag in Japhet's rooms.'

Georganna said forcefully, 'Well if that is the case then she kept the necklace for some months before returning it to Lord Sefton – until after Japhet was married. How could Japhet have been so foolish to get mixed up with such a scheming and dreadful woman?'

'This must all be so distressing for you, Gwen,' Cecily sympathised. 'You have always been so loyal to Japhet and I have not heard you say a word against him.'

'I love Japhet despite his faults,' Gwendolyn confessed and lost her battle against her tears.

Margaret took her into her arms. 'You have been so brave. My nephew has much to answer for. How could he have played you false with that ghastly actress?'

A sob broke from Cecily. 'I always feared Japhet's wild ways would bring him to this. Why did he not come to his senses years ago and realise how much Gwen meant to him? She would have saved him from all this.'

'A man cannot always run from his own destiny.' Joshua was only too aware of how the wild blood of the Lovedays could bring ruin and damnation. 'The Lord knows that before I took up my calling I was every bit as reckless as my son. I even ran a man through in a duel. Only then did I see the error of my ways and the good Lord called me to serve him.'

Gwendolyn rose to Japhet's defence. 'Japhet did not betray me with Celestine Yorke. We were but friends at the time that she was his mistress. He did not ask me to marry him until his relationship with the actress was over.' The pain of Japhet's affair with the actress during those months had almost been more than Gwendolyn could bear. She also knew that Japhet was not entirely innocent. It was a bitter irony that he stood trial for holding up the coach of Lord Sefton on Hampstead Heath when that was the crime he had not committed. Japhet made an honest living as a horse trader. He had told Gwen that on the night of the robbery he had been riding across Hampstead Heath returning from visiting a horse breeder to procure a mare for a client. He had heard distant shots and suspected that a robbery was taking place on the road ahead of him.

Gwendolyn believed her husband's story. He had gone on to explain that some time after hearing the shots, a man had sprung out at him on foot, grabbed his mare's bridle and pointed a pistol at Japhet, demanding he give up the horse. Japhet had fought the attacker and been shot in the side. Although wounded, he had managed to overcome his attacker and knock him unconscious. In the struggle his mare's hooves had become entangled in the strap of the attacker's saddlebag. Light-headed from loss of blood and thinking to seize the belongings as recompense for the attack, Japhet had retrieved the saddlebag and ridden off. A quarter of a mile later he had come across the dead horse that must have belonged to his attacker and been shot in the hold-up.

Gwendolyn suppressed a groan of anguish at the memory of Japhet's confession. He had taken a risk that night. In a moment of weakness he had been tempted to solve his financial problems. When Japhet returned to his lodgings and opened the saddlebag he had found it full of jewels and money.

'I sold the jewels,' Japhet had told her, overcome with remorse. 'The stones would have been removed and sold separately and the gold settings melted down, so they cannot be used as evidence against me. I had gambling debts to pay. I would have been arrested and put into debtor's prison. The family was in financial crisis; how could I expect Uncle Edward or Thomas to rescue me from my own recklessness yet again? The sale of the jewels was a means for me to leave London and breed horses in Cornwall. It was dishonest and I am not proud of my actions. But I could see no other way.'

Even though she had been deeply shocked at his confession, Gwendolyn could not turn her back on the man she loved. 'But if you sold the jewels, how did Mrs Yorke have in her possession Lady Sefton's necklace which was taken that night?' She had continued to question him.

Japhet had then looked shame-faced and been unable to meet her gaze, 'On the morning after the robbery I was still dazed from loss of blood from my wound. Celestine came uninvited to my lodging and entered my room while I slept. She must have seen

32

the saddlebag and stolen the necklace for herself. I had no clear idea what items were in the bag, just that they represented the answer to my prayers. She would not have hesitated to steal from me.'

Gwendolyn believed that Japhet's assumption was right. Spurned by Japhet, the actress wanted Japhet punished. Jealousy had made her vindictive.

Gwendolyn now painted on a determined smile. She had fought so hard to win Japhet's love and would fight to ensure that fate would not take him from her.

'Justice will prevail.' Her brown eyes were bright with determination. Her nerves were jagged from lack of sleep and worry, but she forcefully banished her fears. She needed to, or they would destroy her resolve to be strong.

Margaret smiled at her. 'Your courage and strength at this terrible time puts us to shame. Japhet must be so proud of you. He made a wise choice in his bride.'

'Thank you,' Gwen replied. The words meant a great deal to her. Until recent years she had been timid as a mouse and allowed her sister and mother to dominate her. She had changed when Japhet had first flirted with her. To stand a chance of winning him, she knew she had to shake off the bindings of her mother's control. Her determination had brought her to a late blossoming, her true vivacious personality emerging.

When they arrived at the Old Bailey, they had to fight their way through a cheering rabble outside the courthouse. Inside, the building was packed with people eager to hear the verdict of Japhet's trial. Servants, porters and tavern wenches, who had abandoned their work to be here, jostled nobles and gentry. Few had yet taken their seats and Gwendolyn was disgusted by the festive mood of the people, who saw the trial as an entertainment, and not the trauma of a man fighting for his life and his freedom.

Gwendolyn controlled her anger and stood with a regal dignity; she had dressed carefully, choosing a dark green watered silk skirt and matching military-style jacket. Her chestnut hair was curled Grecian fashion beneath a low domed hat that was tilted at a jaunty angle. She knew she did not possess the soft features of a porcelain doll-like beauty, but Japhet had told her that she had striking looks that made her memorably attractive. Her beauty shone from within and was the more haunting and unforgettable. She drew on his words to give her confidence.

Inside the entrance several men surrounded Celestine Yorke who was wearing a dress of crimson silk and a wide-brimmed hat of the same material decorated with black ostrich feathers. The actress's voice was amongst the loudest to be heard as she flirted with admirers.

Then her voice rose to a shrill intensity. 'This is all so distressing. That I, the Darling of London, was so duped ... The man is a knave. He deserves to hang.'

Gwendolyn winced as the actress proclaimed a tale of woe and played on her past popularity. Her temper rose as Celestine Yorke patted the ringlets of her brassy blonde wig and fluttered her eyes at a young lord. He was no more than eighteen and could not take his eyes from the actress's breasts, which were pushed high by her corset, the muslin fichu draped precariously on the edge of her nipples. The actress's face was whitened with rice powder, scarlet flashes of carmine coloured her fleshy cheeks and she wore several black patches. Her fame as a courtesan had replaced her popularity as an actress and her looks were fading.

Celestine placed a hand theatrically to her brow as she thrived on the attentions of her audience. 'How could I be so duped by the callousness of that despicable rogue? I could have been murdered. He was a ruthless blackguard. But I was swayed by his handsome looks. The man had such audacity as to first rob me when I was with Sir Pettigrew Osgood and then seek to win my favours. A man like that has no mercy.' She fluttered her fan in agitation and swayed, falling into the arms of the young lord in a feigned swoon.

'They say there is no fury like a woman scorned.' Gwendolyn shoved aside the press of people in the corridor of the court and bore down upon the actress. It took all her willpower not to strike the baggage for so viciously using Japhet's notoriety to resurrect her fading stage career. 'You revile a decent man because he spurned you. Your evidence was all lies.'

'Oh, the naïve wife defends her spouse.' Celestine Yorke trilled, as she recovered quickly from her swoon and shrugged off the arms of her admirer. She put her hands on her hips and her eyes glinted with battle. 'Then what else would one expect from such a country mouse?'

'And what else would I expect from a trollop with the morals of an alley cat.'

Celestine Yorke curled her hands into claws and lunged at Gwendolyn, who swiftly sidestepped. The young lord grabbed Celestine, appalled that she would brawl in public. 'Miss Yorke, this is most unseemly.'

Joshua Loveday appeared at Gwendolyn's side. 'My dear, this will only upset you and it will not help Japhet. Come, we must take our seats.'

Gwendolyn glared into the malicious eyes of Celestine Yorke. Beneath the thick powder and rouge, the skin was webbed with fine wrinkles. The woman was desperate to revive her popularity on the stage for her rivals were all half her age. Gwendolyn voiced her scorn. 'I pity you. You once dazzled the people with your beauty but it was a shell that coated the evil beneath. The mask has cracked and we see you now terrified of middle age and obscurity. You are vain and incapable of an act of common decency. You could not bear a man to turn from you and sought to destroy Japhet because he did not fall beneath your spell.'

Celestine blanched but quickly recovered her composure. Her laughter was high and false. 'Japhet never spurned me. He adored me, but he was never more than a fleeting fancy. I was taken in by his charm, but he was a pauper and no better than a vagabond – a rakehell and a gambler.' Celestine ran a salacious hand over her hourglass figure, her glance disparaging upon Gwendolyn's slender form. 'Japhet was a slave to his passion for me, humbly accepting the crumbs of my affection. What was his attraction to you – other than your money?'

'Japhet loves me. That is what you cannot bear.' From the corner of her eye Gwendolyn saw Sir Pettigrew Osgood flush scarlet with anger.

'Gwen, my dear, this will not help your husband. The woman is not worth it.' Joshua tugged gently at her arm. 'We must join the family.'

Her anger was justified and it had brought relief to Gwendolyn to tell the actress what she thought of her. She did not regret her action.

Gwendolyn had heard Japhet's account of his affair with the actress. On a night of desperation he had robbed Sir Osgood's coach and seen the actress for the first time. Japhet had been smarting from the unkind words Gwendolyn's mother had hurled at him when she had caught the couple together in an embrace. Lady Anne Druce had accused Japhet of being a fortune hunter, a blackguard, a womaniser and a gambler. For years Japhet had sought pleasure where he could find it, and without an income had funded his lifestyle by his success at the gambling tables. He had succumbed to the charms of countless beautiful women. During those years Gwen had never judged him. She had loved him for as long as she could remember and had never thought she would be blessed by winning his affection. Yet Japhet had fallen in love with her, of that she had no doubt.

Now as she regarded the cruel face of Celestine Yorke, who had whored her way to fame and fortune from a life of poverty to reign for a short time as the Darling of London on the stage, Gwendolyn knew with utter certainty that Celestine Yorke had lied to destroy Japhet, because he had forsaken her.

She held the actress's stare and accused, 'How did you come by Lady Sefton's necklace? And why did you not return it at once if you knew the owner? It was some months from the date of the robbery until you returned it with this fantastical story.'

'I do not have to answer to you—'

Gwendolyn cut the actress short, proclaiming, 'And what of Sir Marcus Grundy, did Sir Marcus not state that he had lost the emerald stock pin at a gaming party in your house when Japhet was present? Could it not equally be possible that you stole the stock pin? Your greed for jewels is legendary.'

Colour flooded the actress's face. 'How dare you, a plain country mouse, so malign the Darling of London?'

Gwendolyn had spoken in the heat of fury but knew her words had the ring of truth. Her intuition gave her greater confidence; she had found the key that would ensure Japhet went free. She gently removed Joshua's hand from her arm and spoke calmly and clearly. 'I think the woman doth protest too much. If Japhet does not walk free from the court this day, if it takes every penny of my fortune, I shall spend it willingly to prove that you have lied, Mrs Yorke. Can you prove that you did not steal those jewels? If not you will find yourself in the dock and feel the hangman's rope tightened around your neck.'

Without a backward glance she swept past the entourage which had gathered around the actress. Gwendolyn was certain that she had been right in her judgement of Celestine and she was determined to act upon it if Japhet was judged guilty this day.

Chapter Four

When Edward returned to Trevowan he was near to exhaustion. His chest hurt and he could feel the heat of fever burning in his blood. He dismounted from his gelding Rex and was assailed by such a rush of dizziness he was forced to hold on to the saddle for support.

The stonework of Trevowan House was pale in the sunlight; its three gables and tall chimneys outlined in perfect symmetry against a cloudless blue sky. As the weather was mild, several of the mullioned windows were open to air the rooms.

The bow-legged figure of Jasper Fraddon, the head groom, came out of the stables to lead Edward's horse away. His wrinkled face looked worried.

'Be you feeling unwell, sir? Shall I summon Dr Chegwidden?'

'I am well enough.' Edward had no wish to cause concern. Too much fuss had been made over his health in recent months. 'There is good news, Fraddon. Master Adam has returned.'

'For that I praise the Good Lord.'

As Edward walked from the stables he absently rubbed the dull ache in his chest. There were puddles in the stable yard from last night's rain. The door to the coach house stood open and another puddle visible within showed where the roof had leaked. Normally some of the carpenters from the shipyard would have been sent to do the work, but a fire last winter on the brigantine they had nearly completed had meant no men could be spared. Work at the yard had to come first for no payment would be received on the brigantine until it was launched.

His critical eye travelled over the jumble of outbuildings, housing ploughshares and tackle for the horses. The stables were half-empty and eerily quiet. Several of the horses had been sold as a result of the economies he had been forced to instigate as the family faced one financial crisis after another. The carriage and plough horses had been sold, and also his own hunter and two of his sister's mares. At ploughing times he had used the shire horses from the shipyard.

There was the clatter of hooves behind him and Edward turned to see his sister Elspeth and St John's young daughter Rowena riding into the yard. A brown and white crossbreed spaniel that was covered in mud accompanied them. The dog belonged to Amelia's son Richard who was currently serving in the navy as a midshipman. The lad had been away at sea for over a year and a half and she fretted over his absence. Amelia had never wanted Richard to go into the navy but he had been influenced by the Loveday tradition of serving at sea. She blamed Edward for the fact that her boy now faced the dangers of life afloat rather than safely adopting his own father's profession of lawyer.

'Grandpapa! We have been on the moor.' Rowena held out her arms for Edward to lift her to the ground. At six she was as fair as a cherub. 'But my Shetland pony is too slow and small. Before Papa left he said he would buy me a bigger one. That was so long ago.'

'Your pony is not too small or too slow, young lady.' Edward smiled at her affectionately.

'She is! She is!' Rowena wriggled to be released, her mouth turning down. 'If Papa were here he would not be so mean. He promised me a bigger pony. When is Papa coming home?'

'Not for some time, you know that very well, Rowena,' Elspeth returned, her usually strident voice mellowed by compassion for this child who was missing her parents. Elspeth dismounted and drew down her walking cane from where it was secured to her saddle. 'And you are ungrateful. I was eight before I had my second pony.'

Rowena stamped her foot, her blonde curls dancing in the breeze. Her eyes were bright with tears. 'But that is years and years away. You *are* mean. Why did Papa have to go away? It's not fair.'

'Go into the house, Rowena.' Edward was annoyed at her

rudeness. 'You will gain nothing by this show of temper.'

Her lower lip jutted and she was about to defy him when she thought better of it. She sniffed and wiped a tear from her eye and put her head on one side. Her smile was winsome. 'If I cannot have a pony, can I have a puppy?'

'You have Faith to play with.' Edward frowned at the spaniel, covered in mud. 'Amelia does not like too many dogs in the house.'

'But Faith is Richard's dog. It's not fair he has a dog when he's not even here. Papa would buy me a puppy. *You* sent Papa away.' Her pout was mutinous.

'You demand too much.' Elspeth struck the flagstones hard with her walking cane. 'You are too like your mother. She was endless in her demands.'

Tears replaced the petulance in the child's eyes. 'Mama went away too. I want my papa and mama! Why did they leave me?'

A tart reprimand withered on Elspeth's lips and she looked helplessly at her brother. 'Your papa will return soon, my dear.'

'Must it be a puppy? One of the cats at the yard has just had a litter, would you like a kitten?' Edward offered. It was difficult to refuse the child. She had been callously abandoned by her mother, who had run off with a wealthy lover, and with St John in America, Rowena missed her parents and often cried herself to sleep.

'Can it sleep in my room?'

'If Amelia agrees. Now run along with you, young lady.'

Rowena flashed him a broad smile and bobbed a pert curtsy. 'You are wonderful, Grandpapa.' She ran into the house.

'You spoil the child, Edward.'

Elspeth tapped her riding whip lightly against his shoulder. She was leaning on her cane with the other hand, her thin face flushed from her ride. She had injured her hip a decade ago in a riding accident but no amount of pain could keep her from horseback. Horses were her passion, replacing the children she had never borne.

Wincing with pain, she shifted her weight from one leg to the other as she regarded her brother. Her figure was slender and wiry from hours spent in the saddle. Her hair was now completely grey, swept back from her face and secured by a black snood under a military-style riding hat. A forthright and practical woman, Elspeth had no inclination to powder her hair or suffer the discomfort of a wig. She was wearing her favourite dark blue habit that was faded and showing wear at the elbows. She kept her best one for attending the hunts arranged by her friends.

'You are looking out of sorts, Edward.' She frowned and took his arm as they walked to the house. 'Is that wife of yours still sucking lemons and turning your world sour? You would think that with a new baby, she would be more forgiving.'

'Nothing I say makes any difference,' he confided. 'Amelia will accept things in time.'

'She's unhappy and she's hurting. But it is all self-inflicted. I thought better of her. She used to have uncommon sound sense. She makes too much of the gossip our family attracts.'

'Do you think I was wrong to allow Tamasine to stay with Senara?'

'Did you have another choice? You could not send her back to that disgraceful school where they were treated like servants and sold in marriage to aging lechers.' They were close to the laundry at the back of the house. Two of the tenant farmers' wives who helped with the weekly wash were chatting as they worked over the wooden tub and the door to the laundry stood open. Elspeth lowered her voice lest the women should overhear. 'I was shocked when the young minx arrived here without a by your leave. But if Lady Eleanour Keyne was the girl's mother, it would be wrong to condemn her to a life of drudgery. And I could not imagine a girl with Tamasine's spirit accepting the role of governess.' She shuddered. 'I couldn't have stood such a life myself. You spared me that. I may not say it very often but you have never failed me or any member of our family, Edward.'

'A compliment, Elspeth?' he teased. 'I am honoured. Usually your words contain more aloes than honey.'

'I speak as I find, brother. As for that minx you fathered, you can hardly lock her away until a suitable spouse is found for her. Since the county thinks Tamasine is your ward, Amelia should accept the situation with good grace. I have told her so many times.'

Edward hid a smile. His sister was nothing if not forthright and

41

her tongue could be sharper than a whiplash when she chose. But he owed her a great deal for during the twenty years he had been a widower, Elspeth had managed the smooth running of his house and helped raise the twins.

'You have always been a great support to me, Elspeth, even though we do not often see eye to eye. I could not have managed without you when the boys were young.'

She eyed him impassively, turning aside his compliments as foolish sentiment for which she prided herself on having no time. She returned to practicalities. 'Tamasine will be sixteen in a few months. It's time you found a suitable husband for her – for the good of your own marriage. Your first loyalty must be to Amelia.'

'I have been too busy to think of finding a husband for Tamasine.' Irritation broke through. 'Because of the scandal of St John's trial and now Japhet's arrest, Amelia refuses to accept invitations from our neighbours. How am I expected to find a suitable husband for the girl? At any social gathering it would naturally be expected that my ward should also be present. How otherwise can I enable Tamasine to meet the right people? I have too many other concerns at the moment to devise other ways of finding her a husband.' Edward was breathing heavily and the lines of worry that scored his brow were deeply etched.

Elspeth regretted broaching the matter. 'Perhaps I could take Tamasine with me when I visit our neighbours if they have company? Though Amelia will resent my action.' At the tightening of her brother's jaw, she added, 'But I will do my duty by you, if it will ease your load.'

'When Tamasine is sixteen I will deal with finding her a suitor, but in the meantime I appreciate your offer.'

'It was foolish of me to mention it. It is more important that you take care of yourself, brother. You gave us all a scare when we thought you would die from your wound.'

'It will be easier for me now. Adam docked at the yard this morning. He is half-starved from his ordeal but otherwise well. He will visit tomorrow.'

'Blessed be! That is one less worry for you. Perhaps it is time that St John also returned. For Rowena's sake, if not yours.'

'All in good time,' Edward sighed. 'And you must stop fretting over my health. I keep telling you that I am well enough.'

Even as he spoke he inwardly winced at the pain stabbing his chest. He told himself that Elspeth was right. He needed to do less for a week or so and give himself a chance to regain his strength. Despite the sunshine there was a cold bite in the wind and during his ride it had chiselled deep into his wound. Though he made light of it to his family, Edward was worried that it was so slow to heal. He was often weak and tired these days when he needed to be strong. Until the shooting he had never suffered from ill health, but he had no intention of giving in to his malady at such a crucial time when the shipyard was struggling to survive.

On her visit to London last year, a magistrate friend of her family had taken Gwendolyn on a tour of the Old Bailey and she remembered its layout. She darted down a side corridor. Coming upon a door, she opened it without knocking, to find herself face to face with Judge Cornelius Bathurst, who would pronounce sentence upon Japhet later that day.

'Madam, what do you do here?' The judge was attired in his scarlet gown and long white wig, and sipping a glass of Madeira as he waited to be called for the trial. He had small eyes encased in heavy folds of flesh and a broad puce nose which sprouted a nest of ginger hairs in each nostril.

'I am Gwendolyn Loveday, formerly Gwendolyn Druce of Traherne Hall in Cornwall. My mother is the Lady Anne Druce and my sister is married to Sir Henry Traherne. Please, your honour, you must listen to what I have to say.'

'Your family connections are of no interest to me … though you must also be related to the knave Loveday who appears before me this day?'

'I am his wife, your honour.'

'Then I cannot discuss his trial with you. Leave at once. It is most improper for you to be here.' His copious jowls wobbled above the Geneva bands at his neck and his thin lips puckered into a prim line.

'But my husband is innocent!'

'Your husband may be many things but he is no innocent, madam.'

Gwendolyn stared into the judge's florid face. 'My husband is the son of a parson who is greatly respected within our community. He is related to a family of eminent shipbuilders and friend to many of the noblemen of Cornwall.'

Bathurst waved one hand to silence her. 'All this was previously brought to my attention by character witnesses for your husband. He has been accused of highway robbery, a most serious felony. It is only matters pertaining to this crime that are relevant to the court.'

Gwendolyn would not be silenced. 'A woman of low and ill repute has accused my husband of these crimes: one with no morals who has amassed her considerable fortune as mistress to countless men of wealth and position.'

'Silence, madam! You do your husband no service by your conduct.' He pulled a bell-cord on the wall. 'You will leave now or I shall have you forcibly removed.'

The court bailiff entered the room and Judge Bathurst snapped, 'Take this woman away or I will have her clapped in irons for seeking to pervert the course of justice.'

Her arm was gripped in a bruising hold and Gwendolyn was dragged towards the door. 'Please, your honour, I beg your clemency. Celestine Yorke will do and say anything to regain her popularity on the stage. She is a vindictive woman. Do not heed her lies rather than the testaments given by men of position who have spoken eloquently of my husband's true character.'

When Gwendolyn emerged from the judge's room, a worried-looking Thomas Mercer was pacing the corridor. His back was to her and he was running his long slender fingers through his short blond hair. Japhet's cousin Thomas was a leading London banker and dressed in the height of fashion in a black-and-gold-striped waistcoat, and navy cut-away coat and breeches. A profusion of ruffles adorned his neck and wrists. Though a fop, he had a sharp business mind and was also making a reputation for himself as a playwright.

He swivelled round at the sound of her footsteps and his eyes flashed with anger as he saw the way she had been apprehended. 'Unhand my cousin!'

The court bailiff gave her a rough shove, his tone belligerent.

'She's lucky the judge didn't 'ave 'er arrested, breaking in on 'im like she did. If she's with you, better keep 'er under control. Any more nonsense from 'er and 'is 'onour will 'ave 'er bound over in prison.'

Thomas looked non-plussed. 'Good Lord, Gwen! What have you been about?'

She shook her head. 'I tried to reason with him. It was to no avail. I fear I have but made matters worse for Japhet. I am so frightened, Thomas. What if he is sentenced to hang?'

'Half the nobles of Cornwall have vouched for Japhet's character. They will not hang a man with such influential friends. But he *did* confess the truth to me about Lord Sefton's jewels, and the Yorke woman *did* find the necklace in his possession … He was a fool not to learn who had been robbed that night and return the jewels while he had the chance. The Yorke woman has ensured that some powerful men have accused Japhet of the theft of other articles.'

'But it is only their suspicion that he took Sir Marcus Grundy's stock pin. Sir Pettigrew Osgood would say anything to condemn Japhet.' Gwendolyn wrung her hands. The air in the corridor was close and her rising panic made her feel as if she was being smothered.

'It is best to be prepared, Gwen,' Thomas advised gently. 'If Japhet escapes hanging, it could still be that he is transported to Botany Bay.'

Gwendolyn put her hands over her face; the consequences of his being found guilty were too terrible to contemplate.

Thomas put her arm on his and pressed a handkerchief into her palm. 'Dry your eyes. Chin up, shoulders back. Do not let Japhet see you upset. He has been summoned to the dock and Judge Bathurst has just taken his place on the bench.'

'I do not know if I can bear to hear the verdict,' she groaned.

'It will give Japhet strength if you are there, my dear.'

She nodded and took several deep breaths before she walked into the court on legs that trembled so much they threatened to give way beneath her. Thomas squeezed her hand in encouragement, his head tilted proudly as he called out a greeting to an acquaintance.

This brought a frown from Peter Loveday, seated on the end of the settle where his family had positioned themselves. He moved along to make room for Gwendolyn and Thomas. Peter was several years younger than his brother Japhet but with the same handsome dark looks though there was an air of asceticism about him, his frame over-slender from days of fasting. He had become a preacher like his father, but lacked Joshua's more worldly compassion and understanding of human frailties.

'May the Good Lord guide the jury into a wise and just decision,' Peter said piously by way of greeting.

Gwendolyn scarcely noted him; her gaze was on Japhet who was being led into the dock. His hazel eyes were dark with remorse as they settled upon his wife. He managed a crooked smile and winked at her.

Gwendolyn returned his smile. Three months in prison had stripped the healthy colour from his face and accentuated the lean lines of his handsome features. Nevertheless his tall figure was straight-backed and his head held high. He was clean-shaven and his long black hair neatly tied back with a ribbon. Gwendolyn had sent to the prison the clothes he had worn on their wedding day so he could appear to best advantage in court. He looked elegant and poised, every inch the gentleman. Her heart swelled with love, her need for him stark in her eyes. Despite the seriousness of his situation, Japhet appeared relaxed and nodded to those of his friends who had come to support him.

From the public gallery a heavily rouged woman in a bright auburn wig called out, 'Gentleman James, you can hold me up any night! I bain't got no jewels but I got other riches to make a man feel like a king, me 'andsome.' She gave a lecherous cackle.

Japhet turned to the gallery and bowed to the woman. 'Generous as your offer is, madam, I beg you to spare the blushes of my dear wife.'

'You didn't spare 'er blushes or 'er shame when you were the lover of Celestine Yorke,' an ageing man with a powdered face and numerous patches jeered. 'I'd rob a few coaches myself to pay to get into the Darling of London's bed.'

Celestine Yorke rose from among the spectators and majestically blew the man a kiss amidst a chorus of catcalls.

Another ageing roué in an elaborately curled and powdered wig guffawed: 'Then, my friend, you'd be the one being robbed. The Darling is past her prime.'

John Bathurst rapped his gavel loudly. 'I will have order. Has the jury reached its verdict?'

An expectant hush descended on the court.

Gwendolyn held her breath. She was having difficulty swallowing, her throat dry with fear. Beside her Peter mumbled a fervent prayer.

'We have, your honour,' the spokesman announced. 'We find the prisoner guilty.'

Gwendolyn's heart plummeted and she put one hand to her mouth, her gaze frantically locking on to her husband. Japhet masked his expression; his full lips were clamped grimly shut and his hazel eyes hooded. Close to swooning, Gwendolyn clutched Thomas's hand, willing herself to be strong.

Uproar broke out in court, the babble of voices drowning the judge's command for silence. His gavel was rapped impatiently and slowly the voices quietened.

'Hang 'im! Hang the rogue!' a man demanded.

'Spare 'im! That man ain't Gentleman James,' a pretty young actress pleaded. 'Everyone in the theatre knows Mrs Yorke invented the story about being attacked to bring back her dwindling audiences.'

Sir Pettigrew Osgood stood up. 'I was robbed by that felon! Japhet Loveday *is* Gentleman James.'

Others in the court began to bay for Japhet's blood, which sent shivers of fear and panic through Gwendolyn. She was close to swooning but for Japhet's sake she needed to be strong. She breathed deeply, plastered a confident smile on her lips and steadfastly fixed her gaze upon her husband.

Japhet stood proud and unflinching as the nightmare was enacted around him.

Cecily sobbed, 'Dear Lord, spare my son! Let him not be hanged!'

Gwendolyn silently echoed her mother-in-law's words as the judge threatened to clear the court if silence did not prevail.

Next to her Peter was at his most pious as he pronounced

stiffly, 'The wages of sin …' His words were cut off by a grunt as Georganna, sitting on the other side of him, stamped down on his foot with her heel.

The judge waited until the hubbub in the court subsided then sat forward to peer at the prisoner through his eyeglasses. He rapped hard with his gavel, silencing the last of the chatter. The abruptness of the silence was menacing, as oppressive as the quiet of the tomb.

'Japhet Edward George Loveday, this court has found you guilty,' Judge Bathurst pronounced. 'The punishment for such a crime is to be taken from this place to spend your last days in the condemned hold until you are taken to the scaffold to be hanged by the neck until you are dead.'

The cries of protest from Japhet's friends were deafening. Judge Bathurst was puce-faced with outrage as he banged the gavel again, demanding silence. At the sentence Cecily had swooned and Margaret was waving smelling salts under her nose, gesturing to Thomas to tend to Gwendolyn. Her knees buckled and only Thomas's supporting arm around her waist stopped her from falling. The judge's words thundered in her head. Japhet was to be hanged. He was to be taken from her. How could she live without him?

The judge had regained order in the court and was speaking again. Gwendolyn could no longer make out her husband's figure through the rush of her tears.

'Listen, Gwen, take heart,' Thomas urged.

She struggled to regain her senses as Judge Bathurst proclaimed, 'Crimes of this nature will not be tolerated, but many men of repute have spoken for the prisoner. And it has been brought to my attention that the evidence presented by the plaintiffs may not be without some malice aforethought. The laws of England will not be mocked and in these extenuating circumstances I transmute the prisoner's sentence.'

The judge paused to sip from a goblet before him and Gwendolyn's nerves were stretched to breaking point. A glance at Japhet showed her that his expression remained a frozen mask.

'Japhet Edward George Loveday, I therefore pronounce that you will be taken from this place to be incarcerated until such time as you will serve a period of fourteen years' transportation to land across the seas.'

Gwendolyn hid her face against Thomas's chest. Japhet would not be hanged but had been condemned to a living death on the other side of the world in the new penal colony of Botany Bay.

'May God have mercy on him,' Thomas declared, his face ashen. 'Gwen, they are taking him from the court.'

With a scream she broke from his arms and ran to the dock.

Japhet saw her approach and spoke to the guard who had taken his arm to lead him away. 'A moment, if you would be so kind, sir. My wife ...' His voice broke. 'There will be a guinea in it for you.' He was well aware that every privilege, even to the food and drink he received in Newgate, could be acquired through paying 'garnish', as the turnkeys called their bribes.

The guard hesitated, which gave Gwen time to arrive under the dock. 'Japhet, I will never forsake you! I will do everything in my power to get this judgement set aside. I will petition the King himself.'

His eyes were stark with torment. 'You should go back to Cornwall and forget me. Annul our marriage and find happiness for yourself.'

'I will never forsake you. I love you, Japhet.'

'And never doubt my love for you. But I am unworthy of you. I never meant to bring this shame upon you ...'

The guard nudged him forward. 'Get a move on. Yer wife can visit you in Newgate. You'll be there for some weeks, if not months, afore a convict ship is ready to sail.'

Gwendolyn held out one hand to touch him, but Japhet was out of reach and her hand fell to her side. She ached with emptiness. Her world had no reason or substance without Japhet. Nausea gripped her and she doubled over and took a deep breath to control the urge to vomit. She had been sick every morning for the last month. At first she had thought it was from fear of what would happen to Japhet. Yesterday she had fainted and his Aunt Margaret had summoned a physician to tend her. He had told her she was expecting a child – one her husband knew nothing about. Gwendolyn placed a hand on her flat stomach.

'Little one, you will not grow up without a father. I will see that his name is cleared.'

Chapter Five

Two weeks after Japhet's trial Pious Peter brought the news of his brother's sentence to Trevowan. Accompanying him on the journey by post-chaise was a sullen Lisette, who had not wanted to leave London. She had been recuperating at Margaret and Thomas Mercer's house in the Strand after her course of treatment in Dr Claver's asylum for the insane. The treatment had been drastic but the family had seen no other choice when her behaviour had become increasing wanton. After years of tantrums and ungovernable rages Lisette was now more docile but her moods remained sullen and stubborn. With all the publicity surrounding Japhet's trial, the spiteful side of her nature had again surfaced. She delighted in constantly taunting them, saying that Japhet would be hanged and the reputation of the businesses ruined.

With the fears of the family all for Japhet they had again lost patience with her. They had refused to allow her to attend the trial and decided that it was time for Lisette to return to Cornwall to await the arrival of her husband William with the British Fleet.

Throughout the journey Lisette's mood had been mutinous. The long hours when she had refused to speak to Peter were as unnatural as her rages of the past. During the silences he had however been grateful to be free from her usual demands for attention. This new demure side to Lisette did not deceive him. He was ill at ease in her company, nursing painful memories of the infatuation he once had with his volatile French cousin, a connection of the family's through Edward's first marriage. His feelings then had led to the shame of allowing her to seduce him. His humiliation had been complete when, after he had declared his love for her and intention of marrying her to save her reputation, Lisette had laughed at his naivety, and then brazenly declared she intended to marry his uncle, William Loveday.

Peter was long past his infatuation and now despised her as a wanton. She was selfish and spoilt, her tantrums brought on by having the least desire thwarted. Throughout the journey he had kept a watchful eye on her. Although Lisette ignored him, she flirted outrageously with the other male passengers who joined them for various stages of the journey. When they stayed over-night at a coaching inn, Peter lectured her on the sins of the flesh then locked her into her room to ensure she spent a chaste night in her own bed.

She had mocked him on the last night of their journey when he escorted her to her room. Lisette leaned her petite figure against the doorframe, back arched and breasts thrust out so that they rose above the low-cut neckline of her gown. Her dark hair was elegantly curled into a Grecian style on top of her head, and her carmined lips pouted.

'But, Peter, your lusts are no less than mine. At least I am not afraid of my passions.' She grabbed his hand and held it against her breast, her eyes smouldering with mischief.

He had snatched it away. The constant jolting of the post-chaise had given him a headache and it had been insufferably hot inside the vehicle. The inn was dirty and smelt rancid. The supper they had just eaten had been a glutinous soup of indistinct origin accompanied by a pie of gristly, tough meat. He was tired, in pain, and feeling distinctly nauseous from the foul air and food.

'Jezebel!' he had raged. 'Devil's handmaiden! You are without shame and you are evil. You will burn in hellfire if you do not mend your ways. I will pray for the redemption of your undeserving soul.' With that he opened the Bible that he always carried with him.

She merely laughed and knocked the Bible aside, winding her arms around his neck and kissing him fervently, her whole body moving sinuously against his.

Disgusted, he wrenched her arms away and stood back. 'You shame yourself and your husband. Repent of your sins, it is not too late. The Good Lord will ...'

She slapped his face. 'I will not listen to your sermons. You are a hypocrite, hiding your lechery behind false piety.' She entered her room and slammed the door in his face.

The next day they continued the journey without speaking to each other. When they reached Liskeard, Peter hired two hacks for the final part of the way to Trevowan.

'I do not want to go there.' Lisette stubbornly refused to mount her mare. 'I shall stay here tonight and tomorrow return to Plymouth and take rooms until my husband returns.'

'You will do nothing of the kind, Uncle Edward will not stand for it. Uncle William placed you in his charge. You are to live at Trevowan.'

'I refuse,' she shrilled, stamping her foot. She folded her arms and glared at him.

Peter was growing angry. He loathed any public display of this sort. The coaching inn was busy and they were attracting curious glances. He was dressed in the garb of a preacher, a black suit and Geneva bands, and ever aware of his position, wanted to avoid any ridicule from the onlookers.

'Young parson's got himself a handful there,' an ostler sniggered.

Peter glared at the man and finally lost patience with Lisette. 'You will ride to Trevowan, or I shall have you locked up in the Bridewell for immoral and indecent behaviour.'

'You would not dare! Uncle Edward wants no further scandal attached to the family name.'

He leaned closer, his voice low but laced with menace. 'I will say you are mad, and a threat to public morals and safety. You can rot there until Uncle William returns and decides what to do with his wanton wife. I suspect he will be happy to leave you there.'

The defiance faded from Lisette's eyes. Her recent incarceration in the asylum was too fresh in her mind for the threat not to terrify her. She mounted her mare without further protest and they eventually arrived at Trevowan an hour before dusk.

Edward, Amelia and Elspeth were in the winter parlour, which caught the evening sun. The pale yellow Chinese wallpaper with its pattern of peacocks, and the blue window hangings streaked grey by the intensity of the sun, created an impression of faded elegance and homely comfort. It was the hour when the children left the nursery to join the family. Elspeth was reading a story to Rowena who sat on a footstool by her chair. Amelia had baby Joan on her lap and Edward entertained two-year-old Rafe by lining up painted wooden soldiers on a table.

The maid, Jenna Biddick, entered and bobbed a curtsey as she announced Peter and Lisette.

Edward strode over to Peter and shook his hand. 'Welcome to you both. Lisette, you look well. And Peter, you must stay here unless your parents have returned with you?'

'They remain in London, sir.'

Edward's smile of greeting faded. 'Then the news of Japhet is not good. Has he stood trial?'

'Yes, and I regret to say that the judge found him guilty. He has been sentenced to fourteen years' transportation.'

Both Amelia and Elspeth cried out in dismay. Peter was quick to reassure them, 'Gwen is determined that the sentence will be set aside. She has a cousin at Court and her godfather is the Earl of Craigsmoor. She also intends to seek an audience with the King, though that will take months. We must all pray that she will be successful.'

'But Japhet has been found guilty,' Amelia groaned. 'Poor Cecily and Gwen – they must be devastated. And this is a further shame we must all bear.'

She broke off at an angry glare from Edward and rang a bell to summon the maid. When Jenna reappeared she was told to take the children back to the nursery. Rowena protested and began to cry.

Elspeth tutted, but could refuse the child little. 'Tears will avail you nothing, young lady. I shall come to you later and finish the story. Go on up to bed and I will bring the kitten that Grandpapa gave you.'

Rowena's tears dried immediately and she skipped out of the room.

'Japhet has reaped what he has sown,' Peter began.

'Have you no compassion for your brother?' Elspeth rounded on him. 'You call yourself a preacher, yet where is your tolerance for those less fortunate than yourself?'

'If he were to repent then ...'

'Repent!' she exclaimed. 'We are talking of his life. No one condones the crimes he committed.'

'How strong was the evidence against him, Peter?' Edward cut across his sister's indignation.

Peter outlined the details of the trial. As he began Lisette yawned openly. 'I am tired, I will go to my room. I weary of this continual talk of Japhet. The family has spoken of nothing else for months.'

'Because we care for him,' Elspeth rapped out. 'Some of us think of the well-being of others and not just our own.'

Amelia sighed, unwilling to endure the strain of further dissent. She did not know how she could cope with this new scandal, having expected Japhet to be freed. To still her unrest, she made an attempt to mediate. 'Let us not quarrel. Lisette too has had a trying few months. How are you now, my dear? You look well.'

Lisette sighed wearily. 'Life was dull in London with all the fuss over Japhet's trial. We were invited to no entertainments. I hope life is less onerous here.'

'We have lived quietly since his arrest,' Amelia informed her. 'As is fitting in the circumstances. Though some news may hearten you: Adam has returned. He escaped from prison in La Rochelle and when he landed your brother was with him. Etienne is still in Cornwall, I believe, but was not welcome here after the way he treated you and your mother.'

'Etienne in England!' Lisette became animated. She clapped her hands then hugged them to her heart. 'You talk of family loyalty and then do not accept him in your home. He is my brother! All I have left of my French family. I must write to him ... you cannot stop me seeing him!'

'If you wish to see him a meeting can be arranged,' Edward replied. 'He has taken rooms in Fowey.'

'I want to see him tomorrow,' Lisette demanded.

'We will discuss it in the morning,' he declared, wary of the hysteria Lisette could display when her wishes were thwarted.

For a moment her eyes blazed with a feral light then her lids lowered, veiling her expression. Her voice was deceptively sweet. 'You cannot be so cruel as to stop me seeing my brother? Etienne took Maman and me to a convent for our protection. He did not abandon us.'

'Arrangements will be made for you to meet your brother, if that is your wish.' Edward hid his own misgivings that Etienne's reappearance in Lisette's life could have disastrous consequences. She had clearly chosen to forget her brother's former callous treatment of her.

Lisette swept regally from the room and Edward turned to Peter. 'How has she been since her release from the asylum?'

'She has been on her best behaviour according to Aunt Margaret, but I do not trust her. She is wilful and wanton, greatly resenting the curtailment to her social life in London. The sooner Uncle William returns the better. I pray daily that she will see the error of her ways.'

Edward sat down and put one hand to his chest, the wound aching. He was tired to the bone and longed for a semblance of order and peace to return to his life.

'You have not been well yourself, Uncle,' Peter observed. 'I trust your wound no longer troubles you?'

'You all fuss too much.' He shrugged off the enquiry. 'Now that Adam is home I can relinquish some of the responsibilities of the yard into his capable hands.'

'Will he not continue his merchant enterprises? It is an ungodly life ...'

'There is nothing ungodly about the calling of a merchant captain, Peter. I want no sermons on the matter. Adam will live his life as he chooses. But he has no immediate intention to return to sea and has been talking of hiring a captain for *Pegasus*'s next trip to America. He won us tobacco contracts there. Unfortunately, because the French took the last cargo, we have to reimburse the plantation owners for their loss. Money we do not have at present.'

Peter had been frowning. He suddenly brightened and took a document from inside his jacket. 'This should relieve some of your financial problems. Cousin Thomas asked me to give you this letter and banker's draft. He said it covered the remainder of the money that was lost in bad investments by his father. He apologises that it has taken so long to repay you.'

'Thomas was under no obligation to repay our losses. His own father paid with his life when those investments failed.' Edward stared at the amount of the bank draft with relief. 'This could not have come at a more opportune time. It will clear the loan raised to build the dry-dock, and the debts we owe to the chandler and timber merchant. It will also ensure that Adam can compensate the plantation owners for the lost cargo. There should even be enough to enable us to improve the herd here at Trevowan.'

Edward smiled across at Amelia. 'Thomas also writes that the loans his father had raised on the property left in trust for Richard and yourself in your first husband's estate have all been cleared. You will once again be receiving an income from those properties. For the first time in years the yard and estate are free from debt.'

'That is wonderful news, Edward.' Some of the tension left Amelia's face. 'I did not worry about the money for myself but feared for Richard's future. And, of course, now there is Rafe and a dowry for Joan to provide for. I will rest easier knowing that the future of my children is secure. If it were not for the dreadful fate which could await Japhet, this would indeed be a day of celebration.'

Edward felt the burden of the years of financial crisis lift from his shoulders. Even so, he was not so optimistic that all their problems were behind them.

One member at least of the Loveday family now found her days to be carefree, each bringing her a greater contentment. After years of feeling unwanted, unloved and living a miserable existence at Mrs Moxon's ladies' academy, Tamasine was blissfully happy in her new life.

She would often break into song as she helped Senara with chores in the house. Most of all she loved the freedom of their rides to the ruined manor of Boscabel which Adam and his wife one day hoped to make their home. At the academy there had been no outings, other than to walk in single file and silence to church twice every Sunday, to listen to long dreary sermons that condemned all sinners to hell or years in purgatory. Tamasine had no fear of hell. Her years at the academy, being treated no better

57

than a servant, half-starved, beaten or severely punished on the slightest whim of the headmistress, and never once hearing a kind word, had been a living hell for her.

Tamasine had an inquisitive mind; she wanted to know about every aspect of the shipbuilding business and delighted in her afternoon visits to Edward there when he would spend an hour with her. She would also bombard Senara with questions about the herbs they gathered, and the poultices and remedies Senara made for the patients who visited her when they were sick. Never having mixed with infants before, she adored the twins and Nathan, pleading to help with their feeds or keep them amused if they cried.

Her previous life had been constricted and sheltered from the ways of the world; Tamasine was fascinated by Senara's time with the gypsies before she met Adam, and she would encourage Senara's mother, Leah, to talk of her own adventures in a diverse and active life. But her greatest hunger was for knowledge of her new family.

To be part of a family was exciting, but to be part of such a family, one whose ancestors had been wild adventurers on the high seas as well as on land, enthralled her. She could not hear enough about the buccaneers, smugglers, fortune-speculators and pioneers who spiced the Loveday family tree. Most of all she loved to hear of their marriages and great romances.

Adam had accepted her without any show of prejudice or resentment, and until Sir Gregory had left yesterday to attend to matters on his estate, he too had treated her as a lady of position and importance. It had reassured her that she would one day find her place within society, and be accepted.

This morning Tamasine and Senara's sister Bridie had delivered a herbal remedy to a farmer's wife whose property was a mile from Trewenna. Tamasine had remained outside in the lane while Bridie delivered the package. She was aware of the curiosity of their neighbours and felt uncomfortable when they questioned her about where she had lived before and about her family. It was easier to avoid such encounters unless her father, Senara or Adam accompanied her.

Tamasine was relieved when Bridie returned quickly, for three of the farm's milkmaids had seen her and were nudging each other and whispering. Tamasine urged her mare to a fast trot, causing Bridie to call out, 'Hapless bain't as fast as Hera. Slow down!'

Tamasine waited for her to catch up and frowned as she stared at the other girl's donkey. Bridie was a few months older than herself. Her elfin face was animated; long brown hair under a close-fitting bonnet hung to her waist, concealing the twist in her spine. 'it does not seem right that I ride Senara's mare and you are on Hapless. As Senara's sister you are as much a part of Adam Loveday's family as I am. More so, as he has known you longer.'

Bridie eyed Hera warily. 'I prefer Hapless. Horses terrify me. You never know if they will bolt and throw you. Hapless shambles along at his own pace and nothing could induce him to break into a trot. He is far too lazy.'

'But don't you mind being seen on a donkey?'

'Why should I mind?' Bridie shrugged. 'Hapless is an old friend. We had him long before Senara met Adam. I have no desire to ape the great ladies. Hapless gets me where I need to go. And if riding a donkey is slow, it is faster and less tiring than walking – and I've done my share of that in the past.' She stroked the donkey's tufted mane with affection.

'I do not desire to be a great lady either,' Tamasine corrected her, 'but Hera runs like the wind. Sometimes when I gallop on the moor I feel that I am flying.'

'Now flying would be an improvement on walking,' Bridie agreed.

They approached the crossroads leading down to the shipyard in one direction and Penruan in the other.

'Let's not return to the yard immediately,' Tamasine declared. 'Senara has no other tasks for us this morning. She told us to enjoy our ride. Shall we take the Penruan road and cross to the moor?'

Bridie did not like to disappoint her friend but her back and leg were aching. The curve in her upper spine made it difficult for her to sit upright in the saddle for long, and also set the nerves in her shortened leg afire. She suggested, 'Could we not sit in the shade of the chestnut tree by the stream for a while?'

Tamasine was about to protest until she noticed how pale her friend looked. She cursed her own thoughtlessness at not remembering Bridie's disability. It was easy to forget, for the young woman never complained and would push herself to the limit of her endurance to comply with another's wishes.

'Are there trout in that stream?' asked Tamasine. 'Show me how you tickle them and flip them out of the water without using a fishing line.'

'There are no trout but we could search for lampreys. I'll take them home for Ma and me to cook tonight.'

Tamasine dismounted and sat by the edge of the fast-running stream. She stretched her hand into the cool water and let it trickle through her fingers. She giggled. 'If that old crow Mrs Moxon could see me now she would have an apoplexy! We weren't even allowed to walk on the grass at school.'

'It sounds a dreadful place. I was lucky to have my schooling at the shipyard. Mrs Loveday had the school built there.' Bridie lay on her stomach, peering into the water looking for lampreys. Her voice was strained. 'It was the first time I was accepted by other children. I was always ridiculed before because of my limp. Some would call me Crookback and throw stones. But at Trevowan Hard school, the children did not mock me. Though they would have had to answer to Adam if they had.'

'The world can be a cruel and intolerant place, but you are now accepted by the villagers.' Tamasine's eyes lost their sparkle and her mood became sombre. She sat up and began to gather wild flowers that grew within her reach. 'How long will it take for them to accept me? And where is my place? I bear the blood of two ancient families of high standing, yet an accident of birth bars me from entrance to that society. Even the ordinary folk would despise me if they learned that I was a bastard.'

'Your father seeks to protect you from that. You will have a dowry to assure you of a place in society one day.'

'And surely Adam will provide a dowry for you? You will marry well, Bridie,' Tamasine stated.

Bridie shook back her hair and squinted against the sun as she regarded her friend. 'Marriage is not for me. I do not expect to find love. To live with dignity would be enough.'

Tamasine was not convinced. 'We all have our dreams. Who would be your ideal lover?'

'Not a gypsy, that's for sure – I dislike the travelling. Or a rich man. I would never be at ease as Senara is in the company of Adam's friends. I'd be no use to a farmer either, for I have not the strength for the work. A man of intellect in a respectable profession would suit me. That is, if he was also kind and considerate.' She went back to studying the water. 'But that would not be very exciting and it would take me away from the countryside which I love. I would hate to live in a large village or town. So I am content as I am.'

'But the world is such a wonderful and exciting place. Do you not want to experience all it has to offer?' As she spoke Tamasine concentrated on weaving the flowers into a wreath for her hair.

'My needs are simple. I loved attending school … had waited so long to be able to say my letters and read. And Adam was so kind! He lent me his own books so that I could improve my knowledge of the world and its history. I find I would rather read about great moments in history than be part of them.'

'The school at the yard has been closed for a month now.' Tamasine remained thoughtful as she threaded the last flowers into the wreath. 'Did not the teacher marry and take a more lucrative post at a grammar school in Truro?'

Bridie sighed. 'The children need their learning but Mr Loveday has been too busy to interview a new teacher.'

'Why do you not take on the role?' Tamasine suggested. 'You have the knowledge.'

'But I have no training for such work.'

'You have the knowledge and the patience. Is that not enough? The children of the shipwrights and local farmers have no great interest in learning. They are content to know their letters and numbers and be able to write their name. You could teach them that.'

'I would love to be a teacher.' Bridie rolled on her back and put her hands to her face, embarrassed that she had revealed so much. 'That would be something special. To be able to read and write gives a person a better chance in life. Most people are illiterate. And to teach would be something that I could give to others – it

61

would be something special from me.'

'But like Senara you have knowledge of healing herbs and how to help the sick.'

'I acquired that because I respect and admire my sister's achievements. But healing is work that touches her heart, not mine. Now teaching ...' She sighed. 'It is a foolish dream.'

'No, it is not! You would be good at it,' Tamasine encouraged her. 'Though I confess I would be bored to death at the prospect. That was why I ran away from school. I was either going to be farmed out to a dreadful family with spoiled children as their governess or married off to a festering old lecher.'

Bridie sat back on her heels, her eyes round with shock. 'You exaggerate.'

'No. Those were the prospects for most of the girls there.'

'But Mr Loveday would never have allowed that to happen to you.'

'Why would he not? He did not know me then. At that time I was an encumbrance he did not care to acknowledge. My arrival at Trevowan proved that. I will never be accepted there.'

'That was his wife's doing. She will accept you in time.' Bridie picked a celandine and twirled it in her fingers. To ease the sadness that had crept into Tamasine's eyes, she teased her friend, 'So if you do not wish to be a governess, you must be hoping that Mr Loveday will see you married well. Will it be to the handsome young man of your dreams?'

Tamasine flopped back on to the grass, her arms spread wide, and giggled. 'He will be handsome. He will be dashing. He will be an adventurer – a man of property – a man of action! A bold dashing captain in the army or the navy who has become a hero in this war and whose renown is fêted by the entire country.'

'You do not mention wealth.' Bridie grinned. 'Young men in the services are often younger sons with no fortune of their own.'

'He will be immensely rich and ride a white charger!' Tamasine sat up and placed the flowers on her head. 'And can you truly say you have no such ideas about your own husband? Have you ever been in love, Bridie? I met no boys of my age at school.'

Bridie heaved herself to her feet. 'Love is for daydreams. I will be happy to be a school teacher.'

'But you must have had dreams of a handsome lover,' Tamasine urged. 'What would he be like?'

Bridie answered abruptly, 'No, really, you do not know me at all if you think that. There is no one.'

She mounted Hapless and turned him towards the shipyard but not before Tamasine had seen the scarlet flush rise to her cheeks.

'Senara will worry if we are late,' Bridie urged.

'There is someone. You are hiding something from me. You are already in love.' Tamasine clapped her hands.

Hapless halted and Bridie turned a furious gaze upon her friend. 'There was someone I once liked a great deal, but we are too different. I can see no point in nursing false expectations. What man would want my twisted body?'

'But you have great beauty,' Tamasine protested, 'and the most generous of spirits. Any man would be proud to call you wife.'

Bridie shook her head. 'I will be a school teacher. I will ask Mr Loveday this very day.'

Chapter Six

Etienne Rivière remained in Cornwall. He had taken temporary lodgings near the Assembly Rooms in Truro and had also changed his appearance, cutting his dark hair short so that it curled softly over his brow and the nape of his neck, and growing a goatee beard. He was wary of meeting any of his countrymen who might recognise him and reveal the part he had played in the early days of the revolution. Etienne regretted none of his actions. The old regime was corrupt. That he had married into the aristocracy to advance his own status in society he chose to forget. His wife's family had been amongst the victims sacrificed on the guillotine in the first year of the Terror. To save himself he had denounced them together with his wife whom he had never loved, and had come to despise.

Afterwards he had bought a commission in the army and served the new regime with zeal until, after the execution of the King and Queen, the wheel had begun to turn. Many in the new government had feared that Robespierre was too powerful and in the next wave of executions he had lost his head. Those who had had the blood of the aristocracy on their hands began to find it was now their own which fed Madame Guillotine.

These were dangerous and uncertain times in France and Etienne had made many enemies. It seemed it would be only a matter of time before he too was arrested. He had accrued a fortune in jewels plundered from the victims he had arrested in the early days of the revolution and had saved a chestful of money from bribes paid by families to free their relatives from prison. He had kept the money while the relatives died or else remained incarcerated. Even the money paid for the ransom of Adam and the crew of *Pegasus* was still in his possession. That was why he had fled La Rochelle. He had needed Adam and his crew to sail *Pegasus* to England or else he would have left them to moulder in the French prison.

Even so, Etienne was not at peace in England. Too many people knew he had betrayed their trust. That was why he avoided London and the larger cities. But life in the country bored him. He had a plan to start a new life under an assumed identity in America or Canada. He wanted to put his French nationality behind him; too many of his countrymen had fled the country with no possessions and those with money were subsequently looked on with suspicion.

To truly prosper and be accepted in the new life he planned for himself he needed an accomplice and Etienne intended to use his sister. He had been furious to learn that she had married William Loveday. That rage intensified on hearing that the Lovedays had shut her away in an asylum. Lisette had always been volatile but he knew how to handle her. His sister adored him. He would not let this marriage to William Loveday stand in his way, as he had not let Lisette's betrothal to Adam Loveday prevent his plans to marry the lovely girl to a nobleman. Lisette had not been so averse to that marriage as she had later proclaimed. She was as ambitious as himself to have unlimited wealth and enjoy all the pleasures it could offer.

Lisette was a beautiful and accomplished woman with the skills and morals of a courtesan. Such beauty and attributes were assets he intended to use again. He had learned that she was back in Cornwall. It was time to seek her out.

Japhet Loveday refused to show the world how great a fall his pride had suffered, or how the shame and humiliation of prison life had altered a previously stalwart disposition. It took all his fortitude to endure incarceration in Newgate, but outwardly he made the best of it. Amongst the hierarchy established within the criminal underworld, highwaymen were regarded as the elite, and their notoriety made them popular in prisons. That Japhet was also a gentleman by birth made him something of a romantic hero. Providing that a prisoner had money to pay the turnkeys the garnish they demanded, life could be relatively comfortable for prison inmates.

It troubled Japhet that Gwendolyn had ensured he had the best of everything. She paid lavishly for him to occupy a single cell that overlooked the Press Yard; clean sheets were provided for his bed and meals sent in from a reputable inn. He had money to pass the time gambling in the Association Room when he chose to mix with other prisoners.

He did not feel he deserved such generosity. He had destroyed her good name by their marriage, and his sordid affair with Celestine Yorke, which had been the cause of his downfall, must have caused Gwen a great deal of unnecessary pain.

Japhet lay on his pallet and shifted his limbs to ease the weight of his fetters which had rubbed the skin from his ankles. This discomfort was slight compared to that suffered by the majority of criminals. Most such unfortunates had neither money nor friends. They lived without hope of reprieve, close to starvation, locked into overcrowded cells that were stinking cesspits of humanity, overrun with cockroaches and vermin. Even the mouldy bread and thin gruel they were given for sustenance had to be paid for. Without money you either fought and stole food off your companions or you starved. Some in desperation resorted to catching rats and mice to stay alive.

Even Japhet's strong stomach shuddered at the thought of such deprivation and squalor. In those cells it was survival of the most brutal and strong; new prisoners fell prey to threats and demands for money from their fellows. If they had no money, they were beaten and stripped of all their possessions, even their clothes. Prostitution was rife – women would sell their bodies for food, and the hope that they could plead their belly. If sentenced to hang it would then be delayed until after the birth of the child.

In his three months of incarceration Japhet had become used to the stench that pervaded every corridor and room of the prison: nothing, even brandy, could get the taste of that foul ordure from the back of his throat.

He knew he was fortunate that Gwen could provide the money for his privileges, but even so his existence was bleak. To be shackled night and day, and his freedom so drastically curbed, was constant torture to him. His wild and restless nature could not abide being cooped up in a confined space. None of his inner anguish was apparent to those who met him, though, for he hid it well. With visitors and the other prisoners his wit was at its sharpest and his manner relaxed and carefree. But once the door to his solitary cell banged shut at night, the demons governing his fears were resurrected to taunt him. He would lie shaking and sweating from his terror of the fate that awaited him.

Since the early years of his manhood Japhet had flouted convention. He had never stayed in one place for long. Had travelled to race meetings across the country, entering and riding his mare Sheba in some of the top prize races. His winnings supported his gaming and gained him many friends amongst the gentry and nobles. They would invite him to their houses and he would enjoy the hunts and balls, dallying with the ladies and gaming with the men.

It had been an agreeable life. In recent years his contacts and knowledge of horseflesh had enabled him to act as an agent, visiting the horse sales and breeders' yards to procure thorough-bred horses for his patrons. It had long been his dream to establish a stud of his own and rear a horse that would win racing's greatest prize, the Derby. By his marriage to Gwendolyn he had come so close to achieving the first part of that goal. They had found an estate to buy. They would make it their home and he could extend the stables.

Yet fate had mocked him. To be arrested on his wedding day for a robbery he did not actually commit was a cruel irony. Not that Japhet was entirely innocent.

As he lay on his pallet bed in the darkness of his cell, he grimaced and ran one hand through his long hair. Though he had not physically held up Lord Sefton's coach and stolen jewels from him and his wife as he had been charged with, he had been on the heath that night and fully intending to hold up a passer-by, in a desperate attempt to pay his gaming debts and avoid being sent to a debtors' prison. His family had enough financial problems of their own, he could not expect them to settle his debts. He was too old to expect his Uncle Edward to save him from his own recklessness and stupidity either. Those

67

gaming debts, he realised now, had only become so vast because Celestine Yorke had frequently drugged his drink when he was gaming at her house. Until he had met Celestine he had made a good living at the gaming tables and had never wagered more than he could afford.

He cursed the arrogance and pride that had tempted him to take Celestine as his mistress in the first place. He had seen it as a challenge for she was known never to take a lover unless they showered her with jewels. In his vanity he had wanted to win her because she could not refuse his charms and had had no intention of ever buying her favours. He should have known that Celestine gave nothing without making a man pay highly. She was a spiteful and vengeful woman, intent only upon her own wealth and gratification. When Japhet refused to bend to her will, she saw to it that he became embroiled in debt, believing he would be forced to marry her as a way out.

Having refused, and under the threat of public dishonour and arrest for welching on his gaming debts, he had found himself on the heath intent on robbery. After four hours of shivering in the cold he had given up. As he had returned to London he had heard gunshots in the distance, which he guessed were coming from another robbery taking place. He had cursed his own lack of fortune and continued on his way.

A short time later a figure had stepped out from behind a gorse bush, pointing a pistol at him and demanding that he dismount and surrender his horse. Sheba was Japhet's most prized possession, he would not lose her without a fight. He had overcome the robber and during the scuffle Sheba's hooves had become entangled in his assailant's saddlebag. Japhet realised then that this was the highwayman who had just staged a robbery and that his own horse must have been shot.

Japhet had grabbed the saddlebag and galloped away, receiving a bullet wound in his side as the highwayman attempted to stop him. When Japhet had finally reached the safety of his rooms he had opened the saddlebag to discover that it was filled with jewellery from the robbery of Lord Sefton's coach that night. At last it seemed that Lady Luck had smiled on him. He had been jubilant before passing out from loss of blood.

But Lady Luck was the most fickle of women and she had only been toying with him.

The threat of the hangman's noose had for years haunted Japhet's dreams but he had been convinced of his own invincibility. Now, with bitter irony, at the moment he had sworn to reform and live a more honourable life, justice had prevailed. He may not have robbed Lord Sefton's coach but he had disposed of the proceeds of that robbery and some months earlier he had robbed another coach on the heath. That coach has belonged to Pettigrew Osgood and it had been the first time Japhet had encountered Celestine Yorke. The actress had instantly intrigued him, and part of her attraction for him was the dangerous quality she had. Celestine had fascinated him for a brief time, all that Gwendolyn was not. She was his salvation, Celestine his damnation.

Japhet smothered a groan at the recklessness that had drawn him deeper into Celestine's web of deceit and intrigue. She mercilessly used others out of sheer greed. No lover escaped her clutches without her exacting her dues. And the price was always high. She had never given her heart to any man other than her father who had died when she was a child. But she had fallen in love with Japhet.

He had not taken her declarations seriously for any aspiring lover presenting her with an expensive trinket had continued to be admitted to her bed. She was a wealthy woman from her years of attracting rich suitors; she surely did not need the mere pittance he could afford? That had been his first mistake.

His second had been to ignore her threats of blackmail after she had recognised him as the man who had held up Osgood's coach. She had demanded that they marry or else she would denounce him. By then her popularity as an actress was waning, with younger rivals winning the love of theatregoers. He refused to comply with her demands, realising that he had to end their relationship. As a parting gift he had given her an amethyst brooch, which had seemed to placate her, and he had believed that they had parted amicably.

'I should never have trusted her!' Japhet said now under his breath. 'I was an arrogant fool. How could I have believed she would not exact a high price for her favours? Had not honourable

69

men shot themselves after her greed brought them to ruin? I underestimated the pure evil of which she was capable.'

He rubbed his hands across his face. He had always known that Celestine Yorke was a dangerous woman; now he would pay the price for his own foolishness in underestimating the threat she posed. He was man enough to face the consequences of his actions. His greatest regret was that they had rebounded so severely upon Gwendolyn. It was a poor reward for her love and loyalty.

He took his hands from his eyes and swung his long legs over the side of the bed. A single candle cast a pale circle of light into the darkness of the cell. The moon was in its first quarter. Little of its feeble light penetrated the small barred window above his head. Somewhere in the city a clock struck the hour of two. Japhet paced his cell. His head was throbbing from the pint of brandy he had consumed during the day.

Sleep was impossible. The stench from the Press Yard with its open drains was oppressive. The clamour of voices in Newgate was never silent. Women and men screamed obscenities and profanity, fights and quarrels were constant, and those with money sought oblivion in drunken rambling and singing.

Japhet strode over to the door of his cell, meaning to return to the Association Room, and then thought better of it. He had left it an hour ago with prisoners sprawled in drunken sleep over the tables and benches, or openly copulating with the whores who had been brought in to ply their trade. The women were unwashed, riddled with lice and no doubt pox. They held no appeal for Japhet.

He returned to his bed and picked up the Bible his father had left for due contemplation upon his sins. He flicked it open and as quickly tossed it aside. There was no salvation in religion for him. Gwen had been his salvation and he had failed her abominably. If ever he escaped this living hell, he would never cause his wife another moment of pain or regret.

The next afternoon he was playing hazard in the Association Room and the dice had been kind to him. He sat in a corner away from the great hearth with its cooking pots over the fire. A clamour from the inmates made him hesitate. He looked up as he shook the dice in his hand. They toppled from his fingers on to the table with a clatter.

'Yer lose!' a companion chuckled.

Japhet did not respond, his hazel eyes narrowing as he studied the pair of masked visitors in fashionable clothes who had just entered the room. A bald-headed turnkey whose breath whistled through a slit nose escorted them. Japhet despised such visitors who paid to view the prisoners, regarding the inmates as being on the same level as a freak show.

''Bout time yer lost a throw, Loveday,' grunted the weasel-faced man opposite him who had been convicted of clipping coins. 'You've won a dozen or more on the trot. I were beginning to think the dice were loaded.'

Even the implied insult did not draw a response from him. He averted his gaze from the visitors and paid out his companions from his pile of winnings.

'That's Gentleman James over there,' a turnkey shouted above the din of the drinkers in the room. 'Loveday, yer got visitors.'

Japhet did not trouble to rise. He had recognised the couple and refused to be part of their entertainment. 'Send them my regrets. I am not at home to callers. Get them to leave a card. I'll call on them at my convenience.' His quip raised a guffaw around the room.

'Sir, you'd insult a lady?' A corpulent fop who looked to be in his forties with blood-shot eyes behind his mask minced towards the table. 'I should call you out for that.'

Japhet rose in one swift movement and the fop hastily stepped out of his reach. 'Were I a free man I would question your eyesight that you defend a lady and not one of London's most highly paid whores!' Japhet gave full voice to his contempt. 'Hey, gaoler, will you be my second if I meet this dotard in Lincoln's Inn Fields with pistols at dawn tomorrow?'

'You ain't goin' nowhere, Loveday.' The truculent turnkey had no sense of humour.

'Take back that insult or I will … I will …' The ageing roué raised his fist and shook it at Japhet. 'You insult the Darling of London? Our greatest actress, loved by all.'

'That's why he called her a whore, she's had more lovers than

I've 'ad lice.' The weasel-faced convict energetically scratched his head and armpit to emphasise his own attempt at humour.

Japhet surmised that Celestine had come to gloat over his downfall and wanted to witness the degradation she had brought him to. His usual courtesy towards all women deserted him. A man would have answered with his blood for such a treacherous betrayal.

'Oh, and I thought it was Celestine Yorke you defended.' His sarcasm was delivered with the harshness of a whip flaying the flesh from a man's back. 'They used to call her by such a name, but she has not worked on the stage for six months or more.'

'Mrs Yorke is playing at His Majesty's this very week,' the fop squeaked. Beneath the powder and patches on the lower part of his face, his neck had turned puce. 'She has played to packed houses. The audience adores her.'

Japhet turned a withering glare upon the actress. 'So my trial got you reinstated in the public's favour? You have reaped the full rewards of your treachery, madam.'

'So bitter, Japhet?' she scoffed. 'That is not like you. You were a fool to cross me.'

'I was a fool ever to get involved with you, madam. You put the Medusa to shame.'

'Do I indeed?' In her ignorance Celestine simpered and patted her hair. 'Who is this Medusa? Clearly a country actress! I know no such name.'

'She was one of the three Gorgons. They had snakes for hair, and any man who looked into their eyes was turned to stone.'

'You knave!' Behind the mask her eyes glittered with malice. Then she drew a deep breath. 'I would speak with Gentleman James, sirs. You may finish your game of hazard later.'

'Gentleman James is a figment of your imagination. Speak with him all you will but I have nothing to say to you, madam.' Japhet turned his head. 'It's your throw, Barker, or do you want someone else to take your place?'

'I am willing to forgive your rudeness, Japhet. I understand you are overset at your sentence, but I have information that could see you freed.' Celestine leaned across the table to whisper in his ear, her cloak parting to reveal large breasts exposed almost to the

72

nipple in a tight-fitting gown. The heavy musk of her perfume was overpowering. She smiled beguilingly. 'Is that not worth a few moments of your time?'

Japhet nodded to the other men to leave the table, but Celestine interrupted. 'In private.' She turned and flounced across the room to a chorus of catcalls and whistles. As she passed her champion, she ordered, 'Remain here, Sir Sidney.'

The fop scowled at Japhet, his carmined lips thinned by jealousy.

Tempted to consign Celestine Yorke to the devil, Japhet was at first too angry to follow her. Then common sense prevailed. He was intrigued that she had had the audacity to come here. What could she have to say to him?

The now obsequious turnkey escorted Celestine to Japhet's cell. She threw off her cloak and mask as she entered and crossed to the pallet, testing its softness with her hand. A curled blonde wig framed her fleshy features and cascaded around her shoulders; rice powder was thickly applied to her cheeks to disguise the cobweb of lines around her eyes and mouth.

'This is hardly the luxury you are used to,' she said with a sly grin. 'But it will be heaven compared to the hell that awaits you in Botany Bay.'

As she spoke she ran her hands over her hips and thighs and stepped closer towards him. 'Yet it need never come to that. Be my lover and I will persuade those fools to drop the charges against you. I have missed you so much ... I am quite prepared to forgive you for marrying that young miss to secure her fortune.'

Japhet sidestepped to avoid her touch but in the small cell there was little room for manoeuvre. He leaned against the wall, arms folded across his chest, his expression sardonic. 'Osgood dances to your tune but Lord Sefton has no reason to obey your commands. Why should they drop the charges?'

'You underestimate my powers of persuasion. But then, you always did.' She stood in front of him, her breasts pressed against his arms, lips parted in brazen invitation. She tipped back her head and ran her hands along his shoulders to cup his face. 'Sefton would not like his wife to know of the wild orgies he used to attend at my house before his marriage. He depends on the good graces of his father-in-law, the Earl of Pagham, for his place at Court.'

Her eyes were half-closed. She ran the tip of her tongue over her lower lip. 'Such a lover you were ... I miss you. I was hurt that you discarded me to wed another. But I realise now that it was only her wealth that attracted you.'

'I did not marry Gwen for her money but because I love her.'

The flaring of her nostrils and the pain in her eyes showed how much his words hurt Celestine. Perhaps in her own selfish and possessive way she did indeed believe that she loved him – but there was only one person she truly loved and that was herself.

'You were never meant to be faithful to one woman. You delude yourself, Japhet. There is no such man as a reformed rakehell,' she laughed, and slid her hands behind his neck.

He had heard enough. Her company nauseated him. 'Your offer is generous, Celestine, but I will not dishonour my wife.' He withdrew her hands and held her at arm's length.

Her face lost any remnant of its beauty as it twisted with spite. 'Is that prissy little wife of yours worth fourteen years' hard labour on the other side of the world?'

'If that is what it takes to redeem some semblance of my family honour, then that is the price I must pay.'

'Then rot here for the lovelorn fool that you are! Enjoy England while you can for you will never see these shores again once you are transported.'

She flung her cloak around her shoulders and, yelling loudly for Sir Sidney to accompany her, left the gaol.

Japhet slumped down on his bed. Confronting Celestine's evil had renewed his anger against himself. Through it, her words echoed with the unpleasant ring of truth. An icy finger of fear slid down his spine. Disease, floggings, humiliation and an early grave awaited him in Botany Bay. But he would not be broken. Somehow he would survive those fourteen years of hell and return to the land of his birth.

Chapter Seven

Lisette smarted at the reluctance of the Lovedays to allow her to meet Etienne. In defiance of their wishes she finally escaped the vigilant supervision of Amelia and Elspeth and rode to Fowey. She had called at every inn there, growing more agitated with each failure to locate her brother.

When she finally found where he had been lodging, it was to be told that Etienne had left for Truro. She had returned to Trevowan in a fury, her mare whipped mercilessly until her sides bled. Lisette stormed straight into Edward's study.

'You deliberately stopped me from seeing my brother and now he has gone,' she railed. 'I hate you!'

Edward, who had been writing a letter, looked displeased at this interruption. Lisette did not care and continued to rant. 'You treat me as though I am a child. How dare you stop me seeing my brother?' She stamped her foot. 'I hate you. And I hate this family.'

Edward returned his quill to the inkpot on his desk and folded his hands. The ingratitude of the woman, when his family had taken her in and cared for her, made it difficult for him to control his temper. He did so with difficulty, resenting this added turmoil she had created.

'I heard yesterday from Squire Penwithick that Etienne intended to visit Truro and Falmouth. I was not aware he had already left,' Edward informed her. 'And have you learned nothing as to how a gentlewoman should conduct herself? No lady enters an inn unescorted by a servant, even if it is to see her brother.'

'You should have told me Etienne had gone.' Her pretty face was stained crimson with rage. Her curled and powdered hair was dishevelled and the wide feathered hat she wore on top of it had fallen drunkenly over one ear, showing the frantic pace of her ride. Her ruby-coloured riding habit was splashed with mud and the lace of her petticoat trailed on the floor behind her where she had ripped it on a gorse bush.

'You have locked yourself in your room and refused to dine with the family most evenings and do not rise until noon – long after I have left for the shipyard. While you treat us with such lack of respect you will receive no further favours from our family.'

'I want no favours from you,' she fumed. 'I shall now live with my brother.'

'That is not what your husband would wish.'

'I did not marry William to be shut away like an anchorite.' She threw her arms up in the air, her whole body bristling with outrage. 'He was to buy me a house where I could entertain my friends.'

'And I am sure that he will provide such a home for you once he returns with the fleet. Until then he has placed you in my care.'

Edward spoke slowly as though to a child, which incensed her further. Anger had given her a headache. Edward too was visibly irritated and Lisette felt tears prick her eyes. A whirlpool of frustration churned in her stomach. She could not abide having her wishes thwarted. It made her feel as though she was slowly being smothered. Her hands clenched as she bit back the tirade she wanted to hurl at him. Life was so unfair. She did not want to live at Trevowan and the Lovedays did not want her here. Why would they not set her free? She had been a fool to marry William. She had thought he was the means to gain her freedom, but she had been wrong.

It took all her willpower to restrain the words of hatred threatening to erupt. The months in the asylum had frightened her. If she lost control of her temper they would send her back, then she would never be free. She battled to draw a calming breath, aware that Edward was watching her through narrowed eyes.

Before she could speak there was a cry of outrage from the entrance hall. Elspeth limped into the study and snatched the riding whip from Lisette's hand. Then pain flared across Lisette's shoulders and she screamed.

'Good God, Elspeth!' Edward wrenched the whip from his sister's grip. 'What devil rides you that you attack her so?'

'That evil creature has whipped her mare again. She has drawn blood in several places. The poor beast is sweating and distressed, and is kicking out at the groom. She was the sweetest of creatures when she was bought. I warned Lisette that if she took a whip to a horse again then I would take one to her. She is ruining a fine animal.'

Edward snapped the riding whip in two across his knee. 'Elspeth, you go too far. I will deal with this.'

'I will not tolerate the ill treatment of a horse. It is cruel and barbaric.' She rounded on Lisette who backed away from the older woman.

Edward stepped between them, confronting Lisette. 'Your conduct is disgraceful. You have disappointed me bitterly with your behaviour today.'

'You cannot stop me seeing Etienne.' Lisette showed no remorse for her behaviour and remained arrogantly defiant.

'When he returns to Fowey you will visit him suitably accompanied by one of the family.' Edward was white with anger and his command was cut short by a coughing fit.

Lisette escaped the room as he slumped into a chair and his sister fussed over him.

'Where is your tincture?'

He waved in the direction of the desk drawer and buried his head in a large handkerchief as he continued to cough. There was blood on the linen, which he hurriedly hid from his sister.

'You must calm yourself, Edward. That minx is not worth risking a return of your fever for. Shall I send for Dr Chegwidden?' She held out the bottle of tincture.

He sipped it and shook his head. Gradually the coughing abated but the attack left him weak and shaken.

'Get yourself to your bed, brother. I will tell Amelia you are resting.'

He took hold of her arm to prevent her. 'Say nothing to my wife. She worries too much. I have some accounts to go over here this evening.'

'I will say nothing to Amelia, providing that you go to your bed.' Elspeth stood over him, her expression set and determined.

He sighed and walked with her to the door of his study. 'You fuss too much.'

Elspeth stood at the foot of the curved staircase watching her brother as he mounted the stairs. His steps were leaden and his shoulders bowed. He took too much upon himself. Elspeth decided that she would be more vigilant over watching Lisette and would ensure that she caused no further distress. It would mean that she must forego some of her own days hunting, but she would put duty to her brother first. Lisette was capable of causing great mischief and Elspeth would not allow it to make Edward ill.

The following days at Trevowan were interminable for Lisette. She could go nowhere without a servant or member of the family accompanying her. She became bored and rebellious, hating life in the country. She could not set foot outside her room without Elspeth watching her and she was not allowed near the stables. This new constraint added to her resolve to escape from the family she had come to hate.

The Lovedays wished only to spoil her fun. They forgot that she was young, beautiful and possessed of her own fortune. Unfortunately, since her marriage the money was now under the control of her husband. She craved amusement and admiration. Each day she regretted her marriage more. When William was first home from sea, he had been so kind to her and was so like her loving papa. She had flirted with him to relieve the tedium, wanting to win him as an ally. As a widow she was expected to live a demure and respectable life, and she hated the constraints placed on her freedom.

Lisette had no time for convention. In the past her lovers had been numerous and she had used them for her own ends. She had deliberately seduced William, determined to marry him so that he would buy her a house and she would be free from the spying of his family. William had believed her to be innocent and blamed himself for taking advantage of her. He had proposed in order to save her reputation. But he had not been as gullible as she had thought. William refused to marry her immediately. He had his duties as a naval captain and England was at war with France. He had been recalled to join the fleet at Plymouth.

Undaunted, she had run away from Trevowan to Plymouth, further compromising herself. Horrified at the scandal which could follow her actions, William had been forced to marry her. It had been a disaster. He had refused to buy her a house before he sailed. She had been furious and in her rage had used the foul and obscene language of a whore – language her depraved first husband had taught her. William had been so shocked and disgusted that he had left the marriage bed and slept on his ship until he sailed, and Lisette had been taken back to Trevowan.

Her eyes narrowed with cunning. She hated her life. She was bored. Etienne would set her free. She chose to forget that he had used her for his own advancement in the past. He was her brother. She would forgive him if he took her away from the dreariness of her life in Cornwall.

To Gwendolyn's frustration it seemed that Celestine Yorke had covered her tracks well. As yet the men Gwendolyn had paid to find evidence against the actress had been unable to implicate her in any plot against Japhet. Every afternoon Gwendolyn would take a walk along the Strand accompanied by her maid and the men would seek her there if they had any information. Neither Thomas nor Joshua approved of her consorting with such ruffians and Margaret Mercer had forbidden such men to come to her house. While Gwendolyn was living as a guest there she had to respect the wishes of Japhet's aunt. Today one of them accosted Gwendolyn at the top of an alleyway next to a milliner's shop.

'The Yorke woman is more cunning than a vixen and just as difficult to corner,' Joe Grey informed her. He was an acquaintance of Japhet's and had contacts in the underworld fraternity with their own methods of gaining evidence. He was short in stature with an acute squint. He always wore a slouch hat over his thin greasy hair, the brim shading his eyes. He smelled permanently of cabbage soup, and two fingers were missing from his left hand where he had lost them in a knife fight. Despite his appearance Japhet had told Gwendolyn that Joe Grey could be trusted. Now he sniffed and rubbed his nose on his sleeve before continuing, 'Lord Sefton is 'er lover, so he ain't about to inform on 'er. I reckon she's got some kind of hold over 'er paramours. I ain't yet found a one of 'em to speak agin 'er.'

Her maid was absorbed in looking into the milliner's window. Gwendolyn held a nosegay to her face, partly to conceal her features from curious passers-by but also to mask the smell coming from this man so that it did not overpower her.

'Japhet said that she tried to blackmail him when he wanted to end their relationship. She said that she would denounce him as Gentleman James who'd held up Osgood's coach. Most of her lovers are married men and her demands on them for jewellery are extortionate, he says. Her lovers are nobles and influential men in the City. Many would not want their wives and family to learn of their liaison with such a woman.'

Grey tugged at the brim of his slouch hat. 'Lord Sefton is notorious for 'is affairs with actresses, and 'is wife 'as 'er own lovers. It ain't gonna cause no trouble in 'is marriage if Lady Sefton learns that Celestine Yorke was 'er husband's whore. Sefton must be right smitten with the doxy to believe 'er lies about the necklace.'

Gwendolyn frowned. She had not known Lady Sefton took as many lovers as her husband. Was Joe Grey trying to dupe her by saying this? It made her uneasy. 'I have tried to call upon Sefton, but according to his servants he is never at home when I visit. Yet I saw him enter the house as I approached on the last occasion. I have even tried to speak to Lady Sefton but she has returned to their estate in Northumberland, awaiting the birth of her seventh child.'

'None of Yorke's lovers lasts long,' Grey observed. ''Appen Sefton will tire of 'er greed soon. 'E ain't been at the playhouse the last three times she 'as performed.'

'Then somehow I must get to speak with him. Thank you for that information.'

Grey tugged his forelock. 'Costs me plenty to find out these things.' He held out a grubby hand. 'I'll be needing another ten guineas.'

'That is a great deal of money.' Gwendolyn was shocked. She had already given him fifty which he had said he needed for bribes.

He shrugged. 'Ain't yer 'usband's life worth it? Ten guineas ain't nothing to you. Ain't nothing to me whether Loveday swings or not.'

Gwendolyn counted out the coins from her purse and paid him but had the uncomfortable feeling that he was exploiting her. 'There will be no more money until you give me some positive information that will free my husband.'

Grey scowled, his face darkening with menace. 'That sounds like a threat. I don't like threats.' A dagger appeared in his hand and he pressed it to her throat.

Before Gwendolyn could scream, he had cut the strings of her purse and shoved her to the ground with such force her head slammed against the cobbles, knocking the wind from her lungs. Grey ran off down the alley.

The hysterical screams of her maid brought a flock of people around Gwendolyn and a gentleman helped her to her feet.

'What happened?' he asked. 'Shall I take you into that shop to sit awhile and recover?'

'She was attacked. I told her this was dangerous …' the maid began.

Gwendolyn cut in before her woman became indiscreet. 'A man pushed me over and stole my purse.' Her head throbbed and she was trembling but she did not want to go into the shop and rest, she wanted to get back to the Mercers' house as soon as possible. 'I am not hurt.'

'It is not safe to walk the streets,' a portly woman complained. 'These thieves should all be hung. They have no respect for decent folk.'

The gentleman shook his head sorrowfully. 'The villain will be long gone. There's no chance of recovering your purse.'

'It is not important. Thank you for your assistance, sir. I am quite recovered.'

Gwendolyn forced herself to walk away steadily, concerned that the fall might have harmed the baby. She felt no pain or twinges and prayed that all would be well. Before she entered the Mercers' house she swore the maid to silence.

But the incident had badly shaken her. She had given no thought to her own safety in her eagerness to help Japhet. Her

81

unborn child had also been placed in danger. Fear and desolation washed through her. How was she going to find the evidence she needed now?

The month following Adam's return was filled with duties. A detailed letter to the family from Gwendolyn, telling them of Japhet's trial and sentence and her belief that Celestine Yorke had fabricated the charges again him out of a lust for vengeance, prompted Adam to write to Long Tom asking for his help. His friend had replied that he would leave immediately for London. If anyone could find the evidence to save Japhet it would be him.

His duty to Japhet done, Adam familiarised himself with the current schedule of work at the yard, and many hours were spent in discussion with his father on how to attract new customers.

'Your designs for *Pegasus* and the revenue cutter prove the quality of the ships we can build,' Edward commented. 'Yet merchants are reluctant to finance new ships while we are at war.'

'The risks may be great but so are the rewards,' Adam protested. 'Overseas trade cannot grind to a standstill. *Pegasus* is fast. Even heavily laden she can outrun an enemy ship. I will sail her to Bristol. Once the merchants there see how well she fared, orders will surely increase. It should also end the rumours spread by Thadeous Lanyon before he was murdered that our vessels are unseaworthy.'

It still angered Adam that the ship the Lovedays had built for Lanyon had been shipwrecked by the man's own greed and incompetence. In his need for greater speed to outrun the excise cutters, Lanyon had paid another shipyard to fit an extended bowsprit and extra sail, which had made the ship unstable.

'You have been absent long enough from your family,' Edward commented with a frown.

'I shall only be away ten days. Just long enough to visit several old and valued customers and hopefully some new ones.'

Reluctantly, Edward had agreed and when Adam returned, although he had no definite new orders, it was with the news that two customers were considering expanding their fleet. They had promised that they would inspect the yard in the next three months before making their final decision. Lanyon's malicious rumours had done a great deal of damage to the yard's reputation and the customers had been reticent in their manner. The shadow of St John's arrest and trial for Lanyon's murder continued to have far-reaching repercussions, also Japhet's trial had been reported in the *Sherborne Mercury*. The Loveday name was now regarded with double suspicion.

Since Edward had received the money from his nephew Thomas, repaying the sum lost by his father in a bad business venture, Adam had been able to refund the loss on the tobacco cargo stolen by the French. He still needed money to rebuild Boscabel and for that he must find a new cargo for *Pegasus*. Again, the Loveday name went against him. Whilst in Bristol he had called on a dozen past clients and, although courteously received, the conversation inevitably turned to Japhet's trial, and excuses were made as to why no cargo was available for Adam to transport.

He vented his frustration by working long hours in the yard. Today Senara had insisted that he needed a break from work and in the morning they rode to Boscabel. He had found the time for only one brief visit since his return and it was necessary to consider how much further work he could afford to pay for in the next few months. As they rode through the arch in the high wall that formed one side of the entrance courtyard, he was delighted to see how far the renovations had progressed.

The grey-stone house had been built in the last years of the reign of Good Queen Bess. It had been empty and neglected for a score of years. At its centre stood a vaulted hall and solar.

The iron gates to the courtyard, which had been rusty and broken on their hinges, had been repaired in the shipyard's forge, painted and rehung. That was not the only difference. The gaping hole in the roof had been repaired and new rafters and shingles fitted. Also the tall brick chimneys had been repointed and the rotten wood had been replaced in the entrance porch; the fretwork of ivy was stripped from the walls, and new glass had been fitted where panes in the lattice windows had been broken.

A dolphin fountain, dry of water and covered in golden lichen, stood in the centre of the courtyard. The tangle of weeds and brambles beneath had been cleared, revealing flagstones.

Adam nodded in satisfaction.

'Now that the house is no longer assailed by the weather, work can begin inside. It looks almost as though we could live in it now.'

'It is far from ready,' Senara replied. 'The plaster is falling off the walls in the solar, great hall, and three of the bedrooms. But then, I have slept in less hospitable places during my time on the road with the gypsies. Your father has kindly said that when it is time we can make use of any of the old furniture that is stored in the attic of Trevowan.'

'Most of it dates from my great-grandfather's time and is not as elegant as the furniture produced by Sheraton and Chippendale. I would give you the best.'

'I am happy with what is practical since we cannot afford anything new. Why spend your money when it would be put to better use buying livestock for the estate?'

'Since I will never have Trevowan, Boscabel must be the best ...' Adam broke off, his handsome features lit by the passion of his desire. He gave a harsh laugh. 'You are right to be practical. It will cost a fortune to furnish the place and I fear it will be another nine months at least until we can inhabit even a few of the rooms.'

They walked through the musty-smelling empty house and Adam described his plans for it. 'These rooms have all been cleared of debris and swept while I have been away. You have worked hard,' he praised his wife.

'The stonemason who repointed the chimneys said the walls are all sound. But even using the furniture from Trevowan, this is a large house; we will need extra servants and workers for the estate. It is a huge expense. I am content at Mariner's House until we have the money to plant the land and buy the livestock that will provide an income from the estate. And you have your work in the yard, Adam. There is little time to spare to turn Boscabel into a home this year.'

'You are right. But the waiting is not easy. The yard will be in trouble if we cannot find new customers in the next few months. Also a cargo must be found for *Pegasus* and a captain employed to sail her.'

Senara slid her arm through her husband's as they entered the kitchen at the back of the house. A fire was alight in the large inglenook fireplace with a kettle hanging on a hook over the flames. A huge oak table had been scrubbed clean and a skinned rabbit had been put on to a spike to be cooked on the spit.

'A cooking range must be installed,' Adam observed. 'You must also make a list of what is needed in the laundry room and buttery.'

A man shuffled in from the laundry room where he had a truckle bed and tipped his forelock to Adam. He had been away from the estate attending a funeral during Adam's first visit here after his voyage.

'This is Eli Rudge,' Senara introduced him. 'He has done all the work of clearing the land and outbuildings and acts as general steward and gamekeeper.'

'You have done well, Rudge, my wife speaks highly of you. I trust there have been no further incidences of smugglers using the cave by the waterfall?'

'They've stayed away, sir. Enough mischief were done by their antics.'

Adam led Senara back to the horses. 'Is Rudge to be trusted? I want no smugglers using our land to store their contraband. Men like that can easily be bribed.'

'Rudge knows he will lose his job if so. He would not risk that.'

Adam entered an outbuilding where the roof and door had been mended and the interior cleared of broken farm tools. A plough and harrow had been cleaned of their coating of rust, and the wheels of a haywain had been replaced. But Adam's mind was not on the improvements.

'Senara, was Harry Sawle responsible for the contraband being hidden in that cave?'

'Yes. But he has not been near since.'

'Then he is responsible for my father being shot?'

The anger on his face frightened Senara. 'Adam, do not pursue the matter. What is done is done. Your father needed money from Sawle to pay your ransom, and St John was once Sawle's partner in smuggling.'

'Sawle broke his word to my father, that cannot go unpunished. And he has more to answer for. St John stood trial for the murder

85

of Thadeous Lanyon, yet it was Harry Sawle who had taken Lanyon's wife as his mistress and she carried his child. Sawle wanted Lanyon dead so that he could marry Hester and gain Lanyon's fortune. Sawle killed Lanyon and our family took the blame.'

'Let the matter rest, Adam. Have the Sawles not caused enough harm to your family? Harry held a shotgun to St John's head, forcing a marriage to his sister Meriel when he learned she was carrying St John's child. Your twin became involved in Harry's smuggling because of her, he must share some of the blame for the ills that have beset your family.'

'And now St John is lording it in Virginia while Father makes himself ill trying to run the estate.' Adam's brow wrinkled with a frown. 'He should be here. Why was word not sent him to return when Father was shot?'

'Edward is proud. He will not admit that he is weak from his wound. Before you and St John came of age he ran both the yard and estate, and thinks he is still able to do so.' Senara had tried to shield Adam from the seriousness of his father's bouts of fever but it was true: Edward needed both his elder sons to help him if he was to recover fully. 'Is it not time for St John to return now, though? He will inherit Trevowan. He should be at your father's side, sharing the responsibilities of the estate.'

Adam scrutinised his wife closely before asking, 'Father makes light of his wound. Is his condition more serious than he has told the family?'

'He will not rest. The wound festers. Each bout of fever leaves him weaker. If he does not recover his strength before winter ...' her eyes filled with tears '... he may not live to enjoy another summer.'

The colour drained from Adam's face. 'Then I will write to my brother immediately. He must return without delay.'

Chapter Eight

Senara and Tamasine approached the old cottage in the clearing of the wood that used to be Senara's home. Time had galloped past in the month since Adam's return. Senara had been kept so busy with the twins and discussing with Adam the plans for the renovation of Boscabel, she had found little time to visit her mother and sister. Today she had escaped her duties and taken Tamasine with her.

Hapless the donkey was tethered in the grass at the end of the stream. A dozen chickens pecked at the grain thrown on the ground, and a family of six geese squabbled with the dozen ducks kept by the household as they paraded along the riverbank. One gander eyed Senara suspiciously and began to honk loudly. They were better than a dog for warning the occupants of the cottage that someone approached.

From inside the small barn, Senara could hear her sister singing.

'Bridie! Ma!' she called as she dismounted from her mare Hera and tied her to the fence protecting the vegetable bed where onions, turnips and cabbages thrived. The wild honeysuckle, which grew over the doorway of the cottage, was in bloom, filling the yard with its sweet scent.

There was an excited yelp from the other side of the stream and Charity, Bridie's liver and white crossbreed spaniel, bounded into the water, scattering protesting ducks and geese. Adam's dog Scamp who had accompanied them crouched low, considering whether to chase the geese. He had hesitated, remembering the painful peck on the nose he had been given by the gander on his last attempt. Now he bounded towards Charity and the two dogs,

87

which came from the same litter, ran round in circles chasing each other. Chickens, geese and ducks clucked and honked, their feathers flying as they scattered before the playful dogs.

'Charity, behave!' Bridie ordered as she appeared carrying a pail of milk and leading Bramble the cow on a rope halter. A calf in a wooden-railed paddock called to its mother. Bridie loosed Bramble into the paddock before adding, 'Those dogs cause mayhem. The chickens won't lay for a week now.' She laughed as the two dogs ran into the streambed and sped along it down to the seashore.

The limp caused by her shortened left leg was barely perceptible. In the last year Bridie had changed from a shy girl to a beautiful woman. She had grown another three inches and was now almost as tall as Senara. Her figure was trim in a russet skirt and bodice, though still slender as a reed; her hair, several shades lighter than Senara's earthy brown, was hidden by a neat linen cap.

'I was about to take Bramble and Hapless to the edge of the moor to graze,' Bridie said by way of greeting. 'You nearly missed me, Senara. Good day to you, Tamasine.' She smiled at her sister and her friend. 'The animals can wait. Since the birth of the twins you do not often get a chance to visit us, Senara. Your family keep you busy. Are the children and Adam well?'

'Yes, thank you. I've brought two rabbits for Ma to cook. I was given five last week by grateful patients I'd tended. We shall never eat them all.'

Leah appeared at the open doorway wiping her hands, which were floury from bread-making, on her apron. 'You be abroad early this morning, daughter.'

'Adam has sailed to Dartmouth and then on to Plymouth to try and win some contracts for new ships to be built. He will be away for four days.'

While Bridie and Tamasine wandered off to look at the calf, Senara followed her mother into the cottage. She stared around the room, which served both as kitchen and living space in the two-roomed cottage. Dried herbs hung from the rafters. The kettle was steaming on the tripod over the fire in the hearth; the cauldron with its potage of chicken and vegetables kept warm by the side of the flames. Leah's rocking chair stood by the hearth, two wooden chairs by the table, and a rag rug brightened the hard earth floor.

'And Adam, does his health improve?' Leah continued. 'He looked so gaunt on his return.'

Senara smiled. 'He was half-starved in that French prison. He is thriving now, and has taken on the responsibility of running the yard to help Edward. But his father cannot stay away. They worry that no new orders have been received.'

Leah sighed. 'Things bain't too peaceful for Mr Loveday at home, so I hear. Mayhap he enjoys the company he finds at the yard. It be time that wife of his came to her senses. I thought better of her. She were never such a prissy madam when first they be wed.'

Senara glanced towards the door to ensure that Tamasine did not overhear her. 'Amelia still refuses to accept Tamasine. She will not even have her name mentioned. Edward dotes on his daughter.'

'And who would not once they got to know her?' Leah commented. 'Tamasine be like a fresh breeze. She be without guile or malice, yet there be a fierce determination in her when she sets her mind to something. She'll make her mark in the world, and I doubt she'll accept second best.'

'Tamasine is a true Loveday.' Senara lowered her voice as she continued, 'Amelia's attitude serves only to draw attention to the situation. Now Adam is back in England we have received several invitations, together with the family at Trevowan, to dine with neighbours. They are curious about the new member of our family and often mention Tamasine in conversation. At least until she is sixteen they will not expect her to be present at such gatherings.'

From outside the cottage there was a peal of laughter from the two friends. Leah's eyes misted with emotion. 'Tamasine has made a difference to Bridie's life. She has never had a close friend before, the circumstances of her birth and her deformities always set her apart. I used to fear for her future. I bain't getting no younger and would like to see her settled with a good husband.'

'She is pretty and has a loving nature,' Senara replied. 'She will make a good wife.'

'But she bain't strong. And she be a by-blow with no dowry.'

'Bridie will never be alone.' Senara was vehement. 'There will always be a place for her at Boscabel. If she chooses to marry, Adam has promised he will provide her with a dowry. Her connection with the Loveday family will attract a suitor.'

'Mayhap you be right. She do have her reading and writing and was the best pupil at the school at Trevowan Hard. There be farmers and fishermen aplenty who can't write their own name. Did you know she had got it into her head to teach at the school there? She took herself off to Trevowan to talk with Mrs Loveday and she has agreed to a trial period until Christmas. Bridie starts next week.'

'That is wonderful. But she said nothing to me. Adam could have arranged it.'

'She wanted to do it for herself,' Leah said with a proud smile. 'He has enough to do without worrying about Bridie. This way she feels she has earned the place. She told Mrs Loveday straight that she wanted the post because of her ability, not because she was family. Since she had told no one of her desire, she reckoned no one would be angered or offended if Mrs Loveday disapproved.'

'That was very brave of her. Bridie used to be very timid about drawing attention to herself. I am proud of her. To be a schoolmistress is not an easy task, some of the children at the yard are very unruly. I must congratulate her.'

Senara hurried outside to sweep her sister into her arms. 'So my little sister is to be a school teacher? You do us all proud, Bridie. Ma told me how you sought out Mrs Loveday on your own. That took some courage.'

Bridie's elfin features were radiant with joy. 'She was very kind and asked me lots of questions. I was with her for nearly two hours before she agreed. But it is only a trial until Christmas.'

'You will be successful, but if any of the older boys do become troublesome, you must tell Adam.'

Bridie pulled back her shoulders, saying firmly, 'If I cannot control the children I am no good as a teacher. I must do this alone to prove to myself that I am right for the job.'

'And you will succeed.' Senara hugged her sister again before returning to the cottage.

Leah had finished shaping the dough and was putting the bread into the brick oven built at the side of the hearth. Senara looked back through the open door to where the two friends stood leaning against the fence. Their heads were together and they were laughing.

'How quickly Bridie has grown up! She and Tamasine will both be sixteen this year: an age when girls dream of marriage. I was fortunate that I found a good man who loved me enough to forget my lowly birth. I pray they will find the same happiness.'

Leah shrugged, her smile warm upon her eldest daughter. 'You were blessed in loving a man who be honourable and who loved you enough to disregard convention. But it caused discord within your husband's family.'

Senara became uneasy at the reminder. 'Amelia did not approve of me and his father threatened to disown Adam. But family loyalty is important to Edward Loveday. He forgave Adam.'

'He needed Adam's expertise to save the shipyard,' Leah snorted, and returned to kneading the bread dough. 'Edward was not best pleased to be presented with a grandson of gypsy blood. That cost your husband any hope of one day being Master of Trevowan – the home he loved. Mr Loveday will have no child of a gypsy as master there. If St John dies without a male heir, the estate goes to their half-brother Rafe, not to Adam.'

'St John as the eldest twin will naturally inherit Trevowan. Adam gets the yard – that was always Edward Loveday's intention.' Senara had always been troubled by how much their marriage had cost her husband. She was the most blessed of women to have the love of such an exceptional man, she knew. Her love for him was deep and abiding.

Leah wiped the flour from the kitchen table and sighed. 'St John and Adam have been rivals since childhood over who would inherit Trevowan. Adam loves his old home, while his twin sees it merely as a means of providing the income to support his dissolute lifestyle.'

Senara glanced at her mother. There was defiance and pain in her voice as she replied, 'Adam is content with Boscabel. He loves me and dotes on the children. Why have you brought all this up?'

Leah shook her head. 'I can't help but worry about our Bridie.

91

Adam sacrificed much for you, and you will never want for a roof over your head or food aplenty for your children. But what future has Bridie got, even with her Loveday connections? Life can be hard and precarious for a woman.'

She lifted the kettle from the tripod and put it on the table then took down a wooden tea caddy from a shelf. She fumbled with the lid, the joints of her fingers swollen and painful with arthritis. It was rare that Leah complained or voiced her fears. Her whole life had been hard. She had run away from her brutal father the day her mother was buried, and had taken up with a handsome gypsy and borne him two children.

Senara rarely saw her older brother Caleph who still lived with the gypsies. When she was a child her father had been hanged as a horse thief, and on her way home after the trial Leah had been raped. Bridie was the result of that assault, but there was no sign of her father's, or grandfather's, brutality in the gentle girl. Bridie was sweet-natured and resilient and bore her deformities with uncomplaining dignity. If she had a fault it was perhaps that she was sometimes too eager to please, but as a child she had been tormented and mocked by others. Those experiences had made her shy and slow to trust.

'There is more to this than you are telling me.' Senara had a nagging feeling in her stomach that made her uneasy. Her intuition rarely failed her.

'Peter Loveday is back at Trewenna. He be preaching the sermons while his father remains in London for Japhet's sake. I had hoped that while Peter was in London Bridie would get over her feelings for him, but she blushes every time she sets eyes on the young preacher. And he takes a singular interest in her welfare.'

'Peter would never encourage her, and Bridie may be infatuated with him but she would never compromise her reputation. She has told me that she will remain chaste until she has a wedding band upon her finger.'

'She said much the same to me.' Leah looked unconvinced. 'But when a woman falls in love, the heart too often rules the head. Peter Loveday be a handsome man and I've seen the way he looks at her. He bain't as holy as he makes out. He be as tempted to sin as much as the next man. His brother was a womaniser for years before he married Gwendolyn Druce. And look where Japhet's wild ways got him ...'

Leah carefully spooned tea into a pot. Though Adam ensured that Senara's family could now afford the luxury of tea, Leah had spent too many years watching every penny to be wasteful. 'Bridie has taken to cleaning the church at Trewenna and regularly attending services. Now Peter will take over from his father, she will see more of him.'

'Bridie is sensible enough to realise that nothing can come of such an infatuation,' Senara reasoned.

Leah lifted one eyebrow at her daughter. 'History has a way of repeating itself. You were with child by Adam afore he wed you. And though I wed your father in the gypsy way, it were never recognised by the church.'

'Ma, I am sure you are worrying without cause.'

Even so Senara was concerned for her sister. If Bridie had fallen in love with Peter it was bound to bring her unhappiness in the end. They were too different in their ways.

She continued to reason, as much to convince herself as her mother, 'Peter seeks to convert all lost souls who were not brought up in his church. He is diligent in the service of God. He is a bigot at times, and sanctimonious, but I do not believe he is a hypocrite. He has condemned Japhet for a womaniser too often to force his own attentions on Bridie.'

'But she is vulnerable, and Peter has shown her kindness in the past. She has few friends.'

'And that is all it is – kindness. You are making too much of this.'

Leah pushed a cup of tea towards Senara, her eyes bright with her memories. 'I were innocent when I fell for your father. One look from his dark, brooding eyes and I were lost. I would have followed him to the ends of the earth. It were the same with you and Adam. Why should our Bridie be different?'

Before Senara could answer Leah sat back in her rocking chair, her lips compressed for a moment. 'Human nature being what it is, temptation can make a mockery of good intentions,' she said. 'And Peter be still a Loveday. That wildness in their nature be their undoing. Who'd ever have thought Edward Loveday would have a love-child?'

'He loved Tamasine's mother and would have wed her had she been free.' Senara respected Adam's father and was quick to defend him.

'I'd not judge his morals ...' Her mother shrugged. 'But until his new wife saw fit to judge him, Edward Loveday suffered no hardship on account of his affair. Not so his paramour. From what you told me, the Lady Eleanour Keyne, for all her riches and place in society, led a miserable life after Tamasine was born. Her husband shut her away from her friends. It always be the woman who suffers.'

Senara drained her teacup and stood up. 'It is not like you to be so fanciful. You are not ill, are you?'

Leah laughed. 'I be getting old, daughter. I've my share of aches and pains and shortness of breath, but who does not who has lived hand to mouth for decades? I worry about Bridie, but I know you'll always look out for her.'

Senara squeezed her mother's hand but Leah shifted and pulled away, uncomfortable at any show of emotion. Senara's gaze moved to the empty rug near the hearth. She swallowed against a lump in her throat and felt it was time to turn the conversation. 'It is strange not seeing Angel lying there.'

'You be soft in the head, my girl? Angel were but a dog. A good guard dog, but the ugliest beast I ever set eyes on with his scars and just one eye. After you rescued him from the bull-baiting he had a good life and a long one until his heart gave out last month.'

'I miss him. He protected me when I travelled alone before I was married.'

'A pity Bridie has no such guardian,' Leah returned. 'Charity is more intent upon chasing rabbits than ensuring her mistress is safe.'

'Bridie now has the protection of the Loveday name,' Senara reminded her mother.

Leah rose stiffly to her feet, the tight line of her mouth showing that she was still far from convinced. 'But will that save her from one of their own?' Her glance was pained as it rested on the two friends in the yard. 'Young girls will fill their heads with thoughts

94

of love and romance, but where will life lead those two?'

Senara followed her mother's gaze and a tingling sensation down her spine made her shiver inadvertently. She sensed an overwhelming feeling of heartache and a turbulent battle ahead before the two friends found the happiness they desired. It saddened her for it was rare such premonitions were wrong. She had inherited the gift from her gypsy grandmother of sensing what the future would hold for another.

An air of gloom weighted the hearts of the family in the Mercers' house in the Strand. It was six weeks since Japhet had received his sentence. Cecily cried for hours, her eyes reddened and her face puffy. Margaret, usually so stalwart, trailed from room to room, refusing to be at home to visitors. Joshua and Thomas spent long hours closeted together in the study, and always the conversation turned to Japhet and his punishment.

'We can but pray that my son does not face the full wrath of the law,' Joshua would insist. 'Thomas and I are petitioning church and government for a pardon. We must have faith.'

The family had returned from worship on a dreary wet Sunday when the drizzle outside echoed the greyness of their mood. They were gathered in the grand salon on the first floor of the house, awaiting the major-domo's summons to luncheon.

Gwen stood by the window, staring at the distant spires over the rooftops. She still held the hat with the thick veil which she always wore now when she ventured out of the house. Too many people recognised her from Japhet's trial. There had also been another spate of lampoons and pamphlets about his life. Even a ballad was being sung in the streets and taverns, declaring the treachery of a woman had brought the noble and gallant Gentleman James so low. Gwendolyn suspected that as it made Japhet into a hero, Thomas's friend the poet Lucien Greene had written it.

But the trial had brought many difficulties for the family, not least the fact everyone they met made their own judgement upon Japhet. Gwendolyn could not bear the censure or commiseration of friends, and the jeers of ridicule from others were even worse. If anyone slighted her husband she became angry and defensive.

Thomas's wife Georganna came to her side and eased the hat

from Gwendolyn's fingers. 'You should rest. Nothing can be done today.'

'I should go to my godfather. I heard that he had returned from the country.'

'You have left your card on several occasions. The Earl of Craigsmoor refused to see you.'

'Mama must have written to him. She has publicly disowned me for my marriage. Craigsmoor is my father's cousin. He has the ear of the Lord Chief Justice and of the King. He must see me.'

'His lordship is a man of high principles and is most assiduous in his campaign to halt the crime which abounds in our cities. He is particularly set against highway robbery. His coach has been robbed three times on the heath.'

'But Japhet is innocent of the crime for which he was condemned. The law must uphold the rights of the innocent as well as persecute the guilty.'

Joshua said pointedly, 'Gwendolyn, Japhet is not without guilt.'

'He did not commit the crime of which he was accused. He did not hold up the Seftons' coach. He was the victim of Celestine Yorke's spite. The entire case was based on her lies and the rumours she spread.'

'That has not been proved,' her father-in-law observed. 'Thomas has hired a lawyer to investigate the allegations you have made against the actress but without success.'

'That is because the Yorke woman is protected by Osgood and his cronies. None of her lovers will admit that she duped them. They would lose face.' Gwendolyn strode to the chair where Thomas was seated. 'Employ another lawyer. However many it takes. I will give my entire fortune to free my husband.'

Thomas rose and took her hands. 'Everything is being done that can be done to search out the truth. The lawyer is diligent and not in awe of Osgood or his faction. You must be patient, my dear.'

She swung away from him and said in a voice cracked with anguish: 'How can I be patient? I am in torment. I cannot even visit Japhet because he does not want me to see him in Newgate.'

'And in that he is right,' Thomas replied firmly. 'Newgate is no place for a lady. It would unman Japhet for you to see him brought so low. He is very much the hero of the people. Celestine Yorke was booed when her new play opened last week. She has not won the popularity she sought.'

'She is the one who deserves to be in prison, not Japhet,' Gwendolyn returned.

Georganna fidgeted in her seat, seemingly unable to contain some excitement. 'You must tell Gwen your other news, Tom. It will hearten her.'

'It is early days. Nothing may come of it.'

'Thomas is writing a play – a comedy deriding an ageing actress for her greed and unscrupulous manipulation of her lovers. She even stages a robbery to resurrect her career. It is based on the Yorke woman and is the most scathing, satirical and witty play he has ever written. Lucien Greene has agreed to produce it now that he is manager at a playhouse. The play will turn the public against the Yorke woman and make people question the case brought against Japhet.'

'Thomas, this serves only to bring further disrepute on our family. And what of the reputation of Mercer and Lascalles Bank?' Joshua was outraged.

'If I do not write such a play, someone else will. It is to retrieve the family's reputation that I am writing it. It will of course not be put on under my own name,' Thomas defended himself.

'I think it is a good idea.' Gwendolyn looked less strained. 'But I will still petition my godfather.'

'Then I must accompany you,' Joshua insisted. 'My Geneva bands do at least serve to remind others that our family is one that serves God, however humbly.'

Chapter Nine

Bridie was apprehensive. It was Saturday afternoon and she was on her way to Trewenna church to clean it before the services on Sunday. It was a job she enjoyed and she did it willingly and without pay. It gave her a sense of satisfaction that in some small way she could serve the people of the parish. Having felt herself to be an outcast all her life, she needed that sense of belonging. It was also why she wanted to teach; it would lend purpose to her life.

Trewenna was a small village with a cluster of some fifteen thatched and slate-roofed houses spread around a village green and duck pond. The villagers worked on the surrounding farms or walked the two miles to the Traherne tin mine. Apart from the church it had a small kiddley, providing the villagers with ale, a meeting house and general provisions store. The church with its square tower topped by a spire was six hundred years old, and six broad yew trees guarded the walls of its cemetery.

Bridie spent an hour in the church, polishing the silver candlesticks and cross on the altar, and the huge brass eagle which served as a lectern on the carved stone pulpit. She had gathered a large bunch of wild flowers on the way from her cottage and these were now arranged in clay vases on the window by the font and roodscreen. Lastly she swept the floor and beat the dust from the needlepoint hassocks in the Loveday family pew.

She checked everything was in order. With the Reverend Mr Loveday in London, the Reverend Mr Snell from Penruan had been taking the services in his absence. She had heard that Peter had returned without his parents and would now stand in for his father, but had not seen him as yet. She had decided that this was the last time she would clean the church until his father returned from London. She did not want to find herself alone in Peter's company, her attraction to him making her ill at ease.

The sunlight slanted through the stained glass window, the red, blue and yellow from its depiction of the Resurrection tracing rainbow patterns on the flagstones.

She liked the sensation of peace and tranquillity she always felt in this church. Joshua Loveday was no hell-and-brimstone preacher, his sermons dwelt on the bounty of his God's goodness and love. Mr Snell was less forgiving and she had been unnerved by his sermons on the deadly sins and weakness of the flesh. He also spoke with an air of superiority and a patronising manner that Bridie disliked. He was a man who was very much aware of his own importance. Because of the persecution she had suffered in the past, she distrusted such people.

With her work finished she lingered and knelt to pray for all the people she loved, and especially for Japhet Loveday and his wife Gwen. When she left the church, she saw by the angle of the sun that she had spent longer than she had intended at her work. She called to Charity who was panting in the shade of a yew tree, then noticed to her dismay that Hapless had managed to slip his tether by the lych gate and had wandered off on to the village green.

'I am sure that I tied him securely,' Bridie groaned. Hapless had a habit of straying and sometimes it could take hours to catch him. As Bridie approached her donkey she noticed two village youths, until now hidden from view by the fronds of a willow tree, throwing stones at the ducks. A mallard drake had been hit on the head and was bleeding as it lay on the ground, and the bodies of two ducklings were floating on the water.

'Stop that at once!' Bridie shouted. 'That is cruel and wicked.'

'What you gonna do about stopping us?' sneered the biggest of the boys who had ragged brown hair and a face covered in pimples. 'You bain't nothing but a crookback! You bain't got no right to tell us what to do.'

'Happen she thinks of herself as a Loveday now since her gypsy sister bewitched Adam Loveday.' His companion was bandy-legged with rickets and his cheeks and hands were grey with ingrained dirt.

99

Both youths wore frayed and patched breeches that were too large for them. There were holes in their smocks and they were barefoot.

'It is wrong to kill wantonly,' Bridie persisted.

'We gotta eat, bain't we?' the pimply lad sniggered.

'But the ducks are rearing young. They will all die.'

The boys began to swear at Bridie and chant names. The names could not hurt her, she had heard them all before. But the pimply boy picked up a stone and threw it at her. 'Bugger off or you'll get the same treatment.'

A stone hit her shoulder and she bit her lip to stop herself from crying out in pain. Charity growled and snapped at the ankles of the youths to defend her mistress. They began yelling and kicking out at the dog and two women who had been drawing water from the village well lumbered across the green.

'Get that dog away from my son!' one hollered.

Beneath their broad-brimmed cotton bonnets one had hair the colour of a wet rat and the other was as grey as Hapless. Both had rough reddened cheeks and their figures were barrel-shaped. One picked up a large stick and struck Charity on the back. The dog yelped and jumped back several paces.

'You leave my dog alone, Mrs Hawth.' Bridie tipped back her head, her eyes blazing. 'Your son threw a stone at me. He's already killed some ducklings and a drake. If Reverend Mr Loveday were here they'd not attack the ducks on the pond. My dog was protecting me from your son's attack.'

'This be common land.' Mrs Hawth scowled, showing blackened teeth. 'Did you throw a stone at the Polglase wench, son?'

'Nah, Ma. The uppity bitch told us we had no right here.'

'Then happen she should learn her place.' Mrs Hawth glared at Bridie.

Her companion Mrs Fennell chuckled nastily. 'You tell her. She grew up with tinkers and gypsies, so who do she think she be to tell us what to do? Leah Polglase were a whore who run off with a gypsy. They bain't fit to mix with decent folk.'

Charity growled and bared her teeth, placing herself between Bridie and the women. Mrs Hawth brandished her stick menacingly. We don't want your sort round here.'

100

Bridie stood her ground, but her heart was thumping in her chest and her throat had dried with fear. The boys were laughing at her discomfiture. It was children like this that she would soon be teaching. She could not back down now or she would lose any chance of winning control in the classroom. 'You know this is not common land. It belongs to Squire Penwithick and he allows the villagers to graze on it. Killing the ducks could be considered poaching.'

'You mind your tongue, you little bastard.' Mrs Hawth glared at Bridie. 'Your grandfather were a no-good drunk and your mother a whore!'

'You attend church each Sunday. Reverend Loveday would be appalled to hear his parishioners talk with such malice.'

The threat in the other woman's voice had sent shivers down Bridie's back. She knew that she was not physically strong enough to overcome any attack upon her person. But she would not show her fear and instead summoned all her dignity to turn away. Hapless had ambled to the edge of the duck pond and was drinking the water. As Bridie walked away from further confrontation a sudden vicious pain shot through her arm, causing her to gasp. Mrs Hawth's meaty arm swung back in an arc a second time, the blow from her stick landing on the slight hump that distorted Bridie's shoulder this time. The pain was excruciating and the force of the blow knocked her off balance. She fell to the ground.

The two women stood over her and their sons sniggered.

'Go on, Ma! Give the uppity bitch a thrashing. That'll show the crookback her place!'

The stick came down a third time and Bridie managed to raise her arm to ward it off but still it struck her a glancing blow to her temple. Bright lights dazzled her eyes as pain exploded through her skull. She could hear Charity barking and growling but the sounds came from what seemed a great distance away.

'You stay away from our church.' Mrs Fennell hawked and spat on her. 'Decent folks don't want the likes of you in our village.'

Bridie tried to rise but her wits were still addled from the blow to her head and she fell back on the ground.

One of the boys scooped up a handful of Hapless's droppings

101

and flung it at Bridie. It splattered on her neck and cheek. 'Clear off, gypsy bitch!'

Just then a man's voice shouted in anger, 'What is the meaning of this? Shame on you.'

Peter Loveday grabbed the eldest boy and cuffed his ear. The bully burst into tears and ran off, pursued by his companion. Peter then rounded on the two women. 'The devil is in your hearts. Get back to your work and repent of your evil.'

Mrs Fennell made to protest and Peter silenced her with a glare. 'Consider yourselves fortunate I do not have you put in the stocks for a day.'

There was a scampering of feet as the women and children hurried away. Charity whined and licked the blood on Bridie's temple. The sound of a horse's hooves came to a halt nearby. Although relieved, Bridie was ashamed to be discovered in such a manner. She hated to be seen as weak or vulnerable. She levered herself up and stood on legs which shook so much they threatened to give way. A strong arm came around her waist to support her.

'Those evil women will pay for this outrage.' Peter Loveday shook his fist at the vanishing figures and raised his voice to call: 'I know who you are. Sinners! The Lord will smite you for your wickedness.'

Bridie pulled away from her rescuer. Her face was hot with embarrassment. Holding her back as straight as she could, she took pains to control her limp as she walked over to Hapless.

Peter followed her. 'You are in no fit state to travel. Come to the Rectory. You can wash that filth from your face and rest awhile before you return to your cottage.'

She kept her head lowered, knelt by the water's edge and plucked a tuft of grass to wipe the worst of the mess from her face and neck. Her hand was shaking so violently she dropped most of the grass. 'It would not be right for me to enter the Rectory and be alone with you. People will gossip.'

'I am a preacher, they cannot think that I would compromise your reputation?' He sounded indignant.

'Rather it is the reputation of my family that would compromise you. You heard them call me gypsy and bastard.' She did not look up at him but stared at her reflection in the water. Her bonnet had fallen back and her hair hung down around her elfin face. It made her look more childlike than womanly.

'You are in no fit condition to travel. Their words were cruel.' Peter knelt down beside her and pulled a kerchief from his pocket. He dipped it in the water and held it against the wound on her temple. 'Your sister should tend to that. It is a deep cut.'

Bridie flinched at his touch. Her flesh was burning with humiliation and she blinked away the tears that threatened to overwhelm her. His nearness made her flustered. She had hoped that she was over her infatuation. She risked a glance up at his face to find his handsome features so close that her heart skittered with an erratic beat. Their last meeting had thrown her into confusion when it had ended in a kiss. Peter's action that day had shocked her. He was a man of God, and yet he had kissed her in a manner a woman should only be kissed by her husband. It had kindled her blood and her indignation. He had treated her as a wanton. Bridie had vowed at an early age that she would give herself to no man other than a husband. If that meant that she would never know the passion of physical love, then so be it. She had honed a sense of self-worth from the years of prejudice she had faced. A woman had few rights in this world and a poor woman even fewer, but she would not be used and cast aside as so many others of her class had been.

Her resolution to remain immune to Peter made her manner cool. 'Thank you for sending the women away. I heard that you had returned but not your father. In the circumstances I will not be cleaning the church until he resumes his position here.' She tried to keep her voice light but it sounded strangely husky and breathless. 'I was sorry to hear of your brother's sentence.'

Pain flared in his eyes and was quickly shielded.

' "So shall you sow, so shall you reap".' His tone was angry but it held a note of resignation rather than the condemnation Peter usually meted out.

'The law is harsh.'

' "Thou shalt not steal" is God's law.' Peter abruptly stood up to tower over her. ' "Vengeance is mine, sayeth the Lord." That is what we are taught. But the vengeance of Japhet's trial came from

103

the whore he had spurned.' He held out a hand to assist her to rise. 'Come, if you will not rest at the Rectory then I shall accompany you home. And of course you will continue to clean the church, or has your faith fallen by the wayside?'

'It has not.' She did not want to talk of her real reasons for avoiding him. 'I am now the teacher at Trevowan Hard. I have much to prepare for the children.'

'How you have changed!' His eyes appraised her. 'I heard the cruel names those children called you. They are ignorant and wrong.'

Then, before Bridie realised what he was about, he lifted her on to his own horse, saying, 'I do not want you falling off Hapless.' He collected the donkey's reins and handed them to Bridie, then swung himself up in the saddle behind her.

She held herself stiffly upright to avoid contact with his body, but as they rode his arms cradled her against him and she could feel the heat of his chest against her back and the soft caress of his breath against her hair.

As they rode in silence, Peter was aware of the rigidity of her figure and cursed the impulse that had driven him to escort her home. He had been appalled upon returning to the Rectory to find two women attacking another. When he had realised that their prey was Bridie a fierce need to protect her had overtaken him.

He told himself that she was after all one of his parishioners and his cousin by marriage, but that did not explain the intensity of his emotion towards this woman. The heat of her body was becoming a torture. And to his further shame he remembered the kiss he had forced upon her. She had reacted so angrily and had slapped his cheek. It had been a salutary lesson. He had known that she was attracted to him, and had expected compliance. Her eyes had shown only horror at his actions before she had fled his presence.

It was not a moment that he was proud of, though it had been but a kiss and should have been easily dismissed from his mind. Yet the image of that moment was still imprinted in his brain. He bemoaned his Loveday blood. He had tried for years to suppress the passionate side of his nature with prayers and constant fasting, but on occasion he fell from grace.

How easily this woman had once again set his blood racing. One glance into her eyes was both mesmerising and captivating. Had she bewitched him as he had once believed Senara had bewitched Adam with her heathenish potions and spells?

He curbed the impulse to make the Sign of the Cross. His gaze followed the line of Bridie's slender figure, the curve of her breasts and swell of her hips. The smooth roundedness of her thighs was revealed through the fine wool of her gown. A stray tendril of hair curled at the nape of her neck, begging him to place his lips against the flesh beneath. The devil whispered lustful thoughts in his ear, his sudden desire for her threatening to draw him into damnation.

'Is London all they say it is?' she asked. 'Is it exciting and bustling and filled with strange wonders?'

Her question jolted him back to sanity and he saw with relief that they were almost at the clearing around the Polglase cottage. 'It is a place of corruption and evil.'

'You judge it harshly, but then that is often your way. London must have some good qualities.'

Her words stung him. 'Do I judge harshly?'

She presented her profile to him and her expression was thoughtful. 'Mayhap you expect too much from places and people. Is not only God perfect?'

He was about to upbraid her for her blasphemy when he saw Leah sitting outside the cottage on a stool, weaving a wicker basket. She frowned upon seeing them together and stood up.

'Mistress Polglase, Bridie was ...'

'Hapless unseated me and I fell on the road and was badly shaken. Mr Loveday insisted that he should escort me home,' Bridie interrupted his explanation.

Clearly she did not want her mother to know that she had been attacked. She slid from his horse before Peter could dismount and assist her.

Leah touched the wound on her temple and her mouth tightened as she saw the mess on her daughter's gown.

Bridie gripped her hands together and inclined her head to Peter. 'I am sure that you have many duties to attend to. I have taken up too much of your time.'

Her dismissal disconcerted him. 'I will see you in church tomorrow. I trust you will suffer no ill effects from your fall. Good day to you both.'

As he rode away he remained unsettled. His prayers had been in vain. Bridie held a fascination for him he could no longer deny.

It took a month of persistent calling before Gwendolyn was admitted to Craigsmoor House in a fashionable London square. The elegant buildings with their iron railings and porticoed entrance made little impression on her. A thick ivory gauze veil hid her features. She wore her best Lincoln green watered silk dress and a cream pelisse bordered in emerald velvet. Her heart was beating so rapidly she had difficulty in breathing and wished that her maid had not laced her so tightly into her corset that morning.

A footman in scarlet and gold livery showed her to a small reception room on the first floor.

'His lordship will be with you directly, madam.' The door was closed with an abrupt click.

Gwendolyn put her hand to her lips to calm a rush of nervousness. She was feeling queasy from her pregnancy, a symptom that had not abated although she was now past her fifth month. The child stirred and kicked as though sensing her agitation. Gwendolyn inhaled deeply and gazed around the room. A clock struck the quarter hour, followed by the chimes of others throughout the house.

In a drawing room above her Gwendolyn could hear the voices of several guests gossiping and laughing. She remembered painfully the last time she had laughed so light-heartedly. It was when she and Japhet had stolen away from their wedding guests to be alone together. An illicit hour of love and pleasure – the happiest hour of her life. How cruelly that happiness had been snatched from her. Those memories of a single hour of passion were all she had to sustain her through the empty void of the endless nights since her husband's arrest.

The reception room was barely larger than an anteroom. An inner door to one side of the marble fireplace led off it. A pair of

106

Louis XIV gilded and brocade-covered chairs were placed to either side of the fire screen, and a walnut library table stood on a Chinese rug in the centre of the room.

Too nervous to sit, she paced the room rehearsing the words she planned to say. It had been over a dozen years since she had last met the Earl of Craigsmoor and that had been at her father's funeral. He was a man of natural gravity and dignity and had terrified the shy and self-conscious young Gwendolyn. They had barely exchanged more than a dozen words. He had always been a remote figure to her, even when her father was alive and on a few occasions they had been invited to the Craigsmoor estate in Devon.

Lord Ranulph Druce, Earl of Craigsmoor, entered the room wearing a powdered wig and navy satin court dress. He took out his fob watch and studied it. 'I have a few minutes before I must attend to my duties for His Majesty.' He snapped the watch shut and fixed Gwendolyn with a fierce glare. 'So, goddaughter, you have been persistent to the point of presumptuousness in your request for an audience.'

He stood a hand's breadth less than six foot tall and was corpulent, with legs as sturdy as tree trunks. His face showed the high colour of apoplexy and his hooded eyes were rheumy and myopic. He was close to three score years, his manner autocratic.

'I appreciate that you have spared the time for this interview. I am desperate for your help. You have influence at Court. My husband ...'

'Your mama has written to me copiously upon the subject of your unsuitable marriage. She condemns your husband as a fortune hunter.'

She should have realised that the Lady Anne would vent her anger in her letters. Her mother wished to safeguard her own reputation with a man of influence and would sacrifice Gwendolyn's happiness without a second thought.

'Japhet loves me,' she protested. 'But it is true that he has no fortune of his own for his father is the parson at Trewenna. We have known each other since childhood. His family is one of the most eminent in Cornwall.'

'They indulge in trade, do they not?' His lordship's scorn was vitriolic. 'Your dowry and inheritance were substantial. It was your duty to marry well – to a peer of the realm at the very least, like your sister Roslyn.'

'The Lovedays are an honourable family. They do own a shipyard but also have a large estate at Trevowan.'

'They are connected to Mercer's Bank through marriage. Was there not a scandal over bad investments and a run on the bank a year or so past? Charles Mercer committed suicide.' He was scathing in his reply. 'Many of my friends lost vast amounts of money through their investments with Mercer's. Can that be described as honourable?'

'The bank recovered and merged with Lascalles,' Gwendolyn heatedly replied, but she was feeling increasingly alarmed. He had clearly seen her only to call her to account for her marriage, and had no intention of helping her husband. 'Japhet had nothing to do with the downfall of his uncle. Indeed, he and his family did all in their power to recoup the losses.'

'So it has been reported to me. I have made my own investigations into the social standing of your husband's family. They are not without merit – though scandal has surrounded them in the last year to an unconscionable degree. Most of the scandal surrounds your husband. He is considered to be the black sheep of the family. You wed unwisely, goddaughter.'

This was worse than she had feared and she could feel herself close to tears. She knew the Earl despised any show of weakness and battled to control her emotions. 'I married a man I love and respect. He regrets the wildness of his younger years, and now we are married is intent upon leading a respectable life. We have purchased an estate and will breed racehorses. Japhet is determined to raise a Derby winner.'

Craigsmoor gave a derisive laugh. 'Racing is hardly a respectable occupation. It encourages excess in gambling. Gaming is the curse of our young bloods. Fortunes, if not entire estates, have been lost …'

'It is also deemed the Sport of Kings,' Gwendolyn retaliated. 'We shall be breeding Arab horses. Horses any gentleman or nobleman would be proud to own. Like your own Perseus, my lord.'

108

Craigsmoor grunted and thrust his thumbs into the fob pocket of his embroidered waistcoat. 'You have a quicksilver tongue. You used to be such a mouse, completely overshadowed by your shrewish sister if I remember rightly. Your father was my friend. I thought him a fool to wed the Lady Anne, but she kept her acid tongue under control throughout their courtship. You have much of him in you.' Her godfather thrust out his bottom lip as he studied her.

His manner was intimidating but Gwendolyn refused to be browbeaten. 'I do not believe that my father would have opposed my marriage. Mama has never cared for my happiness and in the past chose several suitors for me who were dissolute and impoverished fortune hunters, although they were the younger sons of noblemen. There was not one that I could respect, let alone come to love.'

'Such a marriage would be considered advantageous by many families,' Craigsmoor reminded her.

'If one cannot feel respect for the man one marries, one should not marry at all!' Gwendolyn tossed back her chestnut curls. 'I have vowed to do everything in my power to win my husband's freedom. I shall not fail him. If you will not help me, I will ask for an audience with the King himself.'

He raised a brow in query and before he could answer Gwendolyn had blurted out the background to Japhet's trial and Celestine Yorke's involvement in it. She was both surprised and relieved when he listened without interruption until she had finished.

'I have no time for sycophants or for people who do not stand up for themselves.' He rubbed his fleshy chin as he regarded her. 'However, you plead an eloquent, if perhaps misguided, case. You seem to have your father's stubbornness and determination. For that reason I will help you.'

Gwendolyn felt her legs sag with relief. 'I will forever be indebted to you, my lord.'

'We cannot have this slur upon the family, and you say the charges were fabricated by a common actress? By Jove, that simply won't do at all! Sefton is a weakling and easily falls prey to the whims of pretty women. Osgood is no better. But if as you say the actress acquired the necklace by illegal means and kept it in her possession for some time, we need proof to bring a case against her. I can do nothing without that.'

'And we shall find it,' Gwendolyn assured him.

He spread his hands. 'The Yorke woman is practised in the art of deception. It will not be easy. If your husband is to be transported to the new penal colony in Australia, time could also be against us. Get me the information to prove he is innocent and I will present your case to the King myself. And if the Yorke woman is guilty of possession of stolen goods, she will face trial. I leave London tomorrow for my estate. I will not return for six weeks. Contact me there if you have the information, but innocence is often harder to prove than guilt in cases of this sort.'

Gwendolyn felt she had won a minor victory. But how in the world was she ever going to break through the web of deceit Celestine Yorke had woven, to bring the woman to justice and gain Japhet his freedom? It seemed an impossible task.

Chapter Ten

The streets of Fowey were narrow, steep and winding. It was unfortunate that the two women and their groom arrived on horseback at the port whilst a ship was being unloaded. Their passage through the town was frequently blocked by carts heaving their cargo up the incline. At each delay Lisette lost her temper and became loudly abusive in her native French.

'You will calm yourself at once!' Elspeth demanded, her own patience strained to its limit. 'Such language is unseemly. I should never have agreed to this visit. It is a privilege and you are abusing it. Clearly the past months have taught you nothing. You are an ungrateful and wilful woman.'

'These simple townsfolk do not understand my words.' Lisette scowled. She was flushed and agitated. In her impatience she was sawing on the reins and blood-flecked foam dribbled from her mare's mouth.

'You will treat your mount with consideration or we will return to Trevowan. And as for the carters or townspeople not understanding ... they understand only too well your bad manners and ill-tempered attitude. Fowey is a port and while such delays are irritating, they are inevitable.'

'We are nearly an hour late for our meeting with Etienne.'

'Your brother demanded this meeting, he will wait.' Elspeth resented her role of chaperon. 'One moment you profess to hate him for the way that he abandoned you, the next you conduct yourself in this undignified and excitable manner in your haste for a reunion.'

'He is my brother – the only one of my family left alive.' Lisette tossed back her head, her high-pitched voice drawing the curious glances of several pedestrians. 'Sometimes I hate him … sometimes I love him. Is that not how it always is between brother and sister?'

Elspeth sniffed. 'Such swings of emotion are unseemly and unstable.'

Lisette glared at Elspeth, her eyes glittering with malice. 'My brother has much to answer for.'

The moment the last cart had passed them she kicked her mare to a dangerously fast trot and set off to the inn where Etienne had taken a room on his return from Truro. Elspeth was compelled to follow her with more speed than dignity, determined that Lisette would have no time alone with her brother for she did not trust either of them. Etienne had proved himself to be a traitor to his family and to his country. If he now sought the company of the sister he had callously abandoned, he had only his own interests at heart.

Elspeth was several paces behind Lisette as they entered the small parlour of the inn where Etienne was waiting for them. Fortunately no other guests were in the room. The low ceiling with its thick beams was gloomy, and little light penetrated the small window overlooking the stable yard. Etienne had been seated by the window, idly rolling dice to pass the time, and rose to greet them. His smile was wide and ingratiating and he bowed in an exaggerated and sweeping gesture.

'Dear, dear Aunt Elspeth. *Ma belle soeur.*'

Elspeth kept her hands clasped together so that he did not attempt to kiss them. 'You wished to see your sister. Against the better judgement of the family your request has been granted. You have an hour.'

'And we are honoured to have your company, dear aunt.'

'Good day to you, brother.' Lisette's tone was cool and when he stooped to kiss her cheek, she turned her head aside. 'You look well. Many émigrés are pale and emaciated when they arrive in England.'

'I have been fortunate until recently when fate set herself against me. But it gives me great joy to see you looking so beautiful. Are you happy in your new life, Lisette?'

'It is better than being at the mercy of the *canaille*, or shut away

112

in a convent. How could you have abandoned me?' She slapped his cheek and a stream of invective in French was hurled at him.

Etienne retorted in the same language, his face flushed with anger.

'You will speak in English,' Elspeth commanded. 'Or you will not speak to each other at all.'

'Your pardon, dear aunt.' Etienne recovered his composure, resorting to charm. 'Can I send for some refreshments after your ride? I have ordered some cinnamon cakes for you, Aunt Elspeth. I remembered that they are your favourite.'

'Thank you, and a cordial would be pleasant.' Elspeth remained guarded.

'I do not need a chaperon to talk with my brother,' Lisette snapped.

'In normal circumstances indeed not,' Elspeth returned, 'but you have yet to show us that you can behave in a reasonable manner. Etienne is aware that your recent behaviour has been unacceptable.' She turned to the Frenchman. 'It pains me to say this, but her conduct has often been wanton, wilful and irrational. We did not lightly take the decision for Lisette to be treated by Dr Claver. Our family has always had her best interests at heart. Now that she is married to William, her future comfort and security are assured.'

The conversation between brother and sister was stilted with Etienne taking pains to be polite as they waited for the refreshments to arrive. Lisette was strangely subdued but her hands, fidgeting with the rings on her fingers, revealed her agitation.

'I regret that your life has not been easy, Lisette.' Etienne frowned. 'But at least you have your life – many aristocrats do not. You were not averse to marrying the Marquis de Gramont. You were the toast of Versailles then.'

Elspeth sniffed her disapproval. 'A marriage that disregarded the wishes of her father and shamed Adam when Lisette jilted him for another.'

'I loved Adam,' she protested, and glanced furtively under her lashes at Elspeth. 'You forced me to marry that monster, Etienne. For that I cannot forgive you.'

'And I bitterly regret my actions, little sister. I thought they

113

were for the best. I would not have us at odds. Are we not orphans ... with just each other?'

'I am married.'

'Happily, I trust?'

Lisette nodded.

The maid brought in the tray with cakes, cordial and a bottle of wine for Etienne. He dismissed her curtly, and with his back to the women took some moments to pour the drinks into the glasses.

He passed the cordial to Elspeth. 'I thought Lisette would prefer some wine.'

'It is early in the day.' Elspeth was disapproving. 'Just one glass then.'

She was impatient for this meeting to end and drank the cordial quickly. Lisette sipped her wine, her manner towards her brother cool. Their conversation was perfunctory as they spoke of better times in France. The room was stuffy and Elspeth found herself struggling to keep her eyes open.

'We should leave soon,' she commented drowsily, her head slowly nodding towards her chest.

Lisette kept a sharp eye on Elspeth and when her eyes closed, followed by a gentle snore, she leaped to her feet and threw herself into her brother's arms. 'How clever of you to put a sleeping powder in her drink.'

She kissed his mouth. 'I have missed you so much. They will not keep us apart. Have you plans?'

He hugged her tightly. 'I have plans, but it will take a little time to put them into effect. Be patient, little one.'

'We will go away together?' Lisette asked.

'But you are recently wed.' Etienne held her at arm's length and grinned.

'It seemed expedient at the time. I was a prisoner at Trevowan.' She distorted the truth to win his sympathy. 'William was the only one who was kind. He was supposed to buy me a lovely house so that I could entertain my friends while he was at sea.' Her pout was mutinous.

Etienne brushed her cheek with his hand. 'You are more beautiful than ever. I adore you.'

114

'When can we leave this place? I have waited so long to be free. I will wait no longer. You see how I am spied upon. When can we meet again?'

'Come to the cave in Trevowan Cove tomorrow evening when it is dark. We will talk then. Our vigilant aunt is stirring. We must be careful so that they suspect nothing.'

Lisette giggled, her eyes bright with a dangerous excitement that warned Etienne that her moods of hysteria had been curbed but not cured. To stop her laughter he kissed her with a crushing brutality. Lisette resisted with a token struggle and he whispered against her ear, 'Life will be good for us. But for now we must bide our time! Everything you ever dreamed of will be yours, sweet sister.'

When Elspeth snorted and began to stir from her drugged sleep, the couple moved apart. When she opened her eyes they were seated on opposite sides of the room.

If life in England for the Loveday family was beset with problems and worries, for St John Loveday in Virginia this was a time of ease and good living. He revelled in the freedom he had found on his cousin Garfield Penhaligan's tobacco plantation, Greenbanks. There he was free from the financial constraints imposed by his family and from the nagging demands of his wife.

He had never loved Meriel and had courted her only because he and Adam had been rivals for her affections. Her departure with her lover had been no loss. When St John arrived in Virginia he had declared that his wife was dead, and as a young, handsome man with a tidy sum of money from his ventures as a smuggler to gamble with and spend, was fêted among the Virginian families.

The summer heat was balmy as the family returned from a week of celebrations to mark the marriage of a neighbour. St John was seated in an open carriage beside Desiree Richmond. The pretty widow was Garfield Penhaligan's niece by marriage and had been widowed last year. She owned the plantation Broadacres some miles down river from Greenbanks. In the six months that St John had been in Virginia, Desiree had become his constant companion and he was aware that the widow was expecting an offer of marriage from him. St John cursed his wife for the hold she still had over him. Meriel, daughter of Reuben Sawle, the owner of the Dolphin Inn in Penruan and a renowned smuggler, had brought nothing to their marriage. Her brothers had forced St John into the ceremony when they discovered that she carried his child. Rowena had been the only decent thing to come out of that marriage and even the love he bore his daughter was now tainted. As her parting gift Meriel had told him that Rowena was in fact Adam's child, not his.

During the voyage to Virginia hatred for his twin had almost driven St John to kill Adam. They had fought and Adam had denied being Rowena's father. St John remained unconvinced but his own pride and his love for his six-year-old daughter had made him choose to accept Adam's story.

They pulled up at the steps that led to the wide veranda of the mansion. Orlando the head house slave bowed to St John and held out a letter on a silver salver. 'This arrived for you yesterday, sir. An English ship put in at the landing stage. She had sailed from Falmouth.'

St John frowned as he recognised his twin's handwriting.

Desiree linked her arm through his. 'Is it news from your home? They must miss you.'

St John put it into the pocket of his jacket. 'It will be nothing important.'

'But what if your father wishes you to return?' Her lovely face was shadowed with sadness. 'You have been with us such a short time.'

'I am to stay a year at least.'

Garfield Penhaligan approached them then. He had a vigorous step for a man in his sixties though good living had thickened his waist. He was dressed to dine in a blue brocade jacket and navy breeches, his silvery hair tied back with a black ribbon. A widower who had lost both his sons in the War of Independence, he had a fondness for his young guest. 'You look troubled, St John?'

'It is nothing, sir.'

'St John has received a letter from his family,' Desiree replied. 'I shall be devastated if they have summoned him to return.'

'Much could have happened in the nine months since you set sail from Cornwall,' Garfield observed. 'Is all well at home?'

Clearly there would be no peace for him until he opened the letter. They were rare, especially those containing news from abroad. He scanned the contents. 'It is from Adam. He writes that he was captured by the French on his return voyage and languished in a French prison for some months until he made his escape. He says that although the cargo of tobacco was taken, a sum of money in compensation has been placed in Lascalles and Mercer's Bank in London.'

'It is a mercy that he escaped harm but the loss of the cargo is serious,' Garfield said heavily. 'We cannot afford to let our agents in London go unsupplied. This war will have a serious effect on trade with the old country.'

'We must hope that it is of short duration,' Desiree observed.

'Adam also writes of my cousin Japhet's marriage to Gwendolyn Druce.' St John was relieved to change the subject. He chose not to inform them of Japhet's subsequent arrest and trial.

'That Japhet has finally chosen to marry and settle down must be a great relief to his mother,' Garfield's sister Susannah remarked. She was a year younger than her brother and had been widowed for many years after a childless marriage. Her manner was gracious and indolent, rarely finding any matter worth troubling herself over.

'You seem preoccupied, St John. Do you not approve of the wedding?' Garfield asked. 'Or was there more to your brother's ship being captured than you have told us?'

'Nothing like that,' St John was quick to reassure him. 'It is my father. He took a fever last winter and it still plagues him.' He paused, shocked to read that Edward had been shot by excise men and that the wound was the cause of the fever. He kept that news from Garfield.

'Then perhaps it would be wise for you to take the first available passage to England.'

St John did not want to leave Virginia, and did not believe that his father was as ill as Adam proclaimed. Edward was still comparatively young and had always been strong. He had never been seriously ill before. Adam could work in the shipyard and also help on the estate. Had not his father managed both until recent years?

'Adam makes light of Father's illness,' St John lied. 'He wrote chiefly to tell us of Japhet's wedding and to reassure the planters that they have suffered no financial loss and thank you for your hospitality while he was here. I have no intention of returning to England at this time, unless I have overstayed my welcome here?'

'That could never happen.' Desiree was breathless in her urgency to reassure him.

'You are welcome to stay as long as you wish,' Garfield insisted. He glanced significantly from St John to Desiree and smiled. 'Who knows? You may find that Virginia holds such an irresistible lure that you have no wish to return to your homeland, especially once your year of mourning for your wife is at an end.'

Desiree blushed and St John felt his heartbeat quicken. Since Adam had departed Garfield had made it clear to St John that he would welcome a marriage between him and his niece. Desiree was all that St John had ever wanted in a wife: beautiful, witty and immensely wealthy.

He had only to gaze into her lovely face, aglow with adoration as she returned his stare, to put all thoughts of returning to Trevowan from his mind. Here he was popular and respected and led a life of idle ease. In Cornwall within a month his hands would become callused from hard work on the estate and the cloud of his trial would still hang over him. He would also have to face ridicule over Meriel's desertion of him. St John did not relish wearing the cuckold's horns; to him his faithless wife was now as good as dead.

Since Adam Loveday had returned to Mariner's House Tamasine found herself with more time on her hands. Senara now rode with her husband to Boscabel on regular visits and, though she was often invited to accompany them, Tamasine sensed that the couple sought privacy as they planned the renovations of their future home.

For the first time in her life she felt lonely. Recently, she had seen little of Bridie; her friend was now proudly established as the new teacher of the school in the shipyard. Tamasine's duties at Mariner's House were minimal and if she ventured to help with the twins or little Nathan too often, she could feel the resentment of Carrie Jensen and the wet-nurse, who felt that she was usurping their positions. And with Adam home, Senara no longer needed Tamasine in her role of companion.

The day was bright and sunny as she walked through the woods behind the shipyard. The sound of hammers, saws and shouts from the shipwrights receded as she walked. The trees thinned as she neared the crossroads, pigeons softly cooed in the branches and the song of a skylark came from the meadow as she approached. The scent of wild honeysuckle and meadowsweet drifted from the hedgerows and the warmth of the sun caressed her face and bare arms. She wore a simple sprigged muslin gown and a peaked straw bonnet trimmed with pink rosebuds. Away from the shade of the trees the heat of the sun increased but a gentle breeze, which made the poppies and cornflowers dance amongst the grasses, brought a refreshing coolness.

Tamasine had walked further than she had intended. When she reached the top of the hill that overlooked the crossroads she halted and leaned against the stile. She could see for miles inland across the valley towards the distant moor, the fields bounded by a patchwork of dry-stone walls. The faint lowing of cattle or bleating of sheep now replaced the thuds and bangs from the shipyard. She turned to survey the landscape, the wind from the sea ruffling the long curls of her hair. The turquoise sea reflected the sunlight beyond the cliffs falling away from the coastline towards Trevowan Cove. The chimneys and part of the east wing of the house were visible on the next rise. The sight of it brought a pang of sadness. She was so close to their family yet still so far from being one of them.

She shivered in the breeze, aware of her solitude. It struck her forcibly how much of an outcast she remained from the Loveday family, and she drew the light summer shawl closer around her shoulders. For years she had craved freedom and solitude at the ladies' academy. There every minute of every day she had been watched over by other pupils or teachers. It had been irksome and restrictive to have her life governed by petty rules. It had taken some while for it to dawn on her that the price of her newfound freedom was to find herself trapped between the worlds of the gentry and that of the people who served them. As

Edward Loveday's ward she was viewed with suspicion by the wives of the shipwrights; they would show her deference but their conversations halted when she drew close. Likewise her youth and mysterious birth set her apart from the family's friends and neighbours. She was gregarious by nature and missed the constant companionship of the crowded school.

'Better this life than the old one,' she chided herself. 'Bridie has taught me that there can be dignity in solitude. I was always too fond of the sound of my own voice.' She laughed, realising that she was talking to herself. 'The day is glorious, almost magical with the sound of the sea and the birdsong.' She closed her eyes and savoured the moment. If solitude was the price of freedom then she would make the most of it. The magic she felt in the air prompted her to make a wish. 'I will be mistress of my own destiny. I will marry only for love and my husband will revere and adore me. He will be handsome, witty and wise.'

She laughed and surrendered to the magic of the moment. Lifting her arms as if to embrace the sun, she began to twirl slowly at first then faster and faster. It was so good to feel the warm air on her arms and face and excitement pulsing through her veins. With eyes half-closed she hugged close the secret pleasure of her dream of romantic love, courted by a handsome beau, finally to be free and fulfilled as a woman. Her body dipped and weaved with a sensuous fluidity. Her music was the birdsong and the echo of her heartbeat. The warm air swirled around her, light and caressing as a lover's embrace. The scent of the grass and wild violets crushed beneath her feet was seductive. Her body came alive and pulsated with the joy of the moment as she spun faster and faster.

A trill of laughter burst from her throat, her mind floated free, she was no longer alone but in a meadow filled with imaginary dancers performing a carefree pavane. Blood throbbed in her veins and laughter turned to song as she sang a haunting refrain of love. She threw back her head, arms wide, shawl billowing like the wings of a butterfly behind her. Her heart ached with yearning as she danced for an imaginary lover, the man who would love her unreservedly, adoring her for her free spirit. Her beauty would enslave him; he would disregard her birth and declare that she alone would be the woman that he married.

It was a dream conjured up from her deepest longing. She knew that it was unrealistic and her dance became a homage to that which could never be. It was a dream to be savoured and hugged close in the deepest, most secret recess of her heart. As she pirouetted, her face glowed with inner ecstasy. She was unaware that the fine muslin now clung damply to her lithe figure, revealing the provocative swell of her breasts and hips. Lost in the magic she had created, she spun faster, the hem of her gown lifting in the breeze to display trim ankles and calves. The flush of exhilaration tinged her cheeks as she allowed the rhythm to slow and finally sank to the grass in a reverent curtsy.

'Bravo!' A male voice startled her. 'Do I behold a woodland sprite?'

Tamasine gasped without looking up. She was mortified at having been watched. She hated being so disconcerted and a sense of outrage seared through her at what she now regarded as an invasion of her privacy.

'You are impertinent, sir!' she replied, tossing back her head in defiance.

The stranger was mounted on a grey gelding and silhouetted against the sun. She sidestepped, disliking the fact that he could see her while she could not regard him. Her throat was suddenly dry with apprehension. She was alone in the field, unprotected and vulnerable. Though his voice had been cultured, he could easily be some ne'er-do-well bent upon mischief. She would not let him see her fear and drew the shawl, which was hanging loose around her hips, more decorously around her slim figure.

When she met his amber stare from beneath the brim of a domed beaver hat, she saw that his eyes crinkled at the corners in amusement. Her heart skittered in chaotic fashion. This could be no earthly man: he was as handsome as a Greek god, his complexion dusted with a golden tan and his long corn-gold hair tied back with a black ribbon. His lashes and brows were darker than his hair, accentuating the sculpted perfection of his face. For a moment she wondered if she had spent too long in the sun and that her fanciful mind had conjured up the image of her dream lover.

121

'Who are you?' she asked, trying to gather her wits.

When he laughed, she knew he was no dream image.

'I am a man who finds himself staring into the face of an angel, or at the very least the Queen of the Fairies. You dance exquisitely.'

He rested one hand easily on his hip as he sat his horse. Though he looked no more than a few years older than herself, there was about him an air of natural authority and gentility. His green jacket was edged with gold thread and a large emerald pin glinted in the folds of his stock. Moleskin breeches were moulded to his muscular thighs with almost indecent closeness.

'I thought myself unobserved. It was discourteous of you not to announce your presence.' She no longer believed that he was a threat to her, but his noble bearing made her uneasy. Yet she was aware of him in a way that seemed to sharpen all her senses. The husky resonance of his voice and teasing interest in his eyes set her pulses fluttering.

'To deny myself such an unexpected pleasure would have been unthinkable. Your pardon, dear lady, if I offended you! Such a vision held me in its thrall.'

His self-assurance further disconcerted Tamasine. There was no arrogance in his tone but she detected the note of a man used to having his wishes obeyed. It was rare for her to be at a loss for words, but before that taunting smile she was strangely tongue-tied.

He frowned and scanned the meadow. 'Clearly you are no servant, but you are afoot and alone. Does no maid attend you?'

Tamasine had disregarded Senara's and Edward's instructions not to wander from the shipyard unescorted. Now not only was her own reputation at risk, she was also anxious not to discredit the name of her father.

'My maid twisted her ankle and is resting in the shade of the wood. I fear she must have dozed in the heat,' she improvised.

Aware of the impropriety of conversing with a stranger, Tamasine turned to retrace her steps. It took all her willpower, for she wanted nothing more than to remain in the company of this handsome, beguiling man whose nearness was making it strangely difficult for her to draw breath.

'Please do not go,' he called. 'Tell me your name.'

His horse had come level with her. It was a large hunter, deep-breasted, and the gelding snorted and tossed his head with impatience until expert hands quietened it. A heat ran up Tamasine's spine that was not caused by the sun. She felt her stomach quiver. Neither reaction came from fear of the powerful horse, but from the magnetism of its rider.

'My name is unimportant. We are unlikely to meet again, sir.'

For a long moment that simmered with tension and expectancy his amber eyes appraised her.

'I am new to the neighbourhood,' he said unexpectedly. 'I know few people. I would very much like to call upon you.'

There was a brief uncertainty in his eyes. This chink she had glimpsed in his self-assurance deeply moved her. His gaze was admiring in a way that brought a blush to her cheeks. There was a touching hesitancy about his suggestion. Clearly he was no philanderer. Again she needed to summon all her willpower to say. 'That would not be appropriate, sir. We have not been formally introduced, my guardian would not approve.'

'Who is your guardian that I may pay my respects to him?'

She shook her head but was impelled to be honest with him. 'I am not of an age to mix in society, sir. Nor because of my circumstances will I mix in the same social circles as yourself.'

His brows drew together. 'I will insist that you are invited.'

'You know nothing of my position.'

'And that is what I wish to remedy.'

'You are too bold, sir.' She increased her pace but the horse remained abreast of her. She was nearing the wood and, not wanting to be caught out in a lie when he discovered that no maid had accompanied her, she started to run into the trees where the undergrowth was thickest.

'I mean you no harm.'

To her relief he made no attempt to follow her. 'I am Rupert Carlton. Will you not at least tell me your name?'

The warmth and sincerity in his voice destroyed her resistance; she paused and looked back at him through the trees. What harm could come from telling him her name? 'I am called Tamasine.'

'Tamasine who?'

She did not answer and disappeared through the trees.

Rupert was tempted to follow her, but held back. The young woman intrigued him but at nineteen he had little experience of their ways. He had been brought up to follow the strict code of etiquette that governed society. Tamasine was right, they had not been introduced. It would be impossible to present himself to her guardian and not be met with suspicion. But there must be some way they could meet again. He had been totally captivated when he had encountered her dancing, and before it was over had fallen hopelessly in love with her.

She would not elude him. He would ride this way every day and he was certain they would meet again. Then he would find the means to pay court to her.

Chapter Eleven

'Sir Gregory Kilmarthen is here to see you, ma'am.' The maid bobbed a curtsy and stood back to allow Long Tom to enter the grand salon of the Mercers' house.

He was dressed in a suit of fine worsted cloth and a scarlet waistcoat, a tiny figure next to the life-sized portraits hanging on the walls.

'Sir Gregory, this is an unexpected surprise.' Gwendolyn smiled warmly. She had agreed the maid should admit him when usually she turned away all visitors. Pregnancy was taking its toll on her. She was sick throughout the day and had no patience with the people who called to garner what gossip they could about her husband's incarceration.

Gwendolyn was alone in the house; Thomas was at the bank and Margaret and Georganna had gone shopping in the Royal Exchange. 'Adam's letter to Thomas told of your escape from France. It is wonderful that you are in London. And you look well. I trust your ordeal in France was not too dreadful?'

'It is not the first time I have languished in a French prison. Fortunately, they did not recognise me as Long Tom, the English spy.' He bowed over her hand and raised it to his lips. 'I am here to offer you my services, and hope that in my own way I am able to help your husband.'

Tears glittered in Gwendolyn's eyes and her fingers curled around Sir Gregory's hand. 'That is most kind of you. You did much to prove St John's innocence. But he was clearly innocent and the evidence against him circumstantial. Two witnesses have testified that Japhet stole from them, though I find it suspicious that the recovered jewels belonging to Sir Marcus Grundy and

Lord Sefton had first been in Celestine Yorke's possession, for some months. Both men have been the actress's lover.'

She broke off, belatedly remembering her manners. 'Please be seated, Sir Gregory. May I offer you some tea, wine or biscuits?'

'Tea would be most pleasant,' he replied as he sat down opposite her. 'I have already visited Japhet and heard the evidence against him. He said you had asked your godfather Craigsmoor to help you, and that you had also enlisted the help of an informer – a Joe Grey. Tell me what they have so far discovered?'

'I do not trust Grey. I am afraid I was rather gullible and paid him a great deal of money. When I demanded positive evidence against Celestine Yorke, he attacked me and stole my purse. I have not told my family or Japhet of this. It would distress them too much. Fortunately, I was not hurt, just badly shaken.'

'Then I offer my services to you at an appropriate time. It is too dangerous for you to mix with such riff-raff. You were lucky you were not harmed.'

She looked away from Sir Gregory, her body trembling with the memory of the fear that Grey's attack had provoked. His image was reflected in the cut-glass Venetian mirror over the fireplace. Unaware that she was watching him, his expression was strained. She went on to tell him of her suspicions concerning Celestine Yorke.

He nodded as she spoke and listened without interruption. Her voice broke as she came to the end of the story. 'Dear God, how I hate that evil woman! I have never hated anyone in my life, but I could flay her alive without a qualm. Is that not a dreadful thing to say? She even tried to blackmail Japhet to ensure that he remained her lover.'

'Hell hath no fury like a woman scorned. The actress is a vengeful woman,' Sir Gregory said bleakly. 'Your pain and anger are understandable. She is more of a thief than Japhet ever was. Be assured I will not rest until I can bring her to justice. Now what of Craigsmoor? Has he agreed to help you and learned anything that is relevant?'

'His Lordship has agreed to present any evidence found to the king, providing that it irrefutably proves that Japhet is innocent.

He agrees that if there is evidence of theft, or even receiving stolen goods, against Celestine Yorke, then she should be brought to trial herself.'

Sir Gregory stood up. He did not wish to dash Gwendolyn's hopes but he had heard that Craigsmoor had fallen foul of the Prince of Wales's set and made many enemies at court. 'There is much to do and too many weeks have passed since Japhet's trial for any more time to be wasted. I will do everything I can.'

'Thank you, Sir Gregory. You saved St John with the evidence you uncovered. I know you will do the same for Japhet. For the first time in weeks I feel that he has a chance to be a free man.'

He raised a hand in warning. 'The evidence has to be there before I can find it. Do not build your hopes too high.'

Gwendolyn would not be discouraged. 'Gossip has it that Lord Sefton has been discarded by Mrs Yorke, and that in the wake of her new notoriety following Japhet's trial, she performs regularly on the stage and is now the mistress of a royal duke. She is lavished with gifts and attention while my dear husband suffers the indignities of Newgate. Where is the justice in that?'

'Do not upset yourself, my dear. Mrs Yorke will not escape justice, I promise you.'

Renewed determination restored Gwendolyn's vitality and she sat forward, her face animated with excitement. 'Lord Sefton may be more willing to listen to me if he is smarting at being cast aside by Mrs Yorke. The woman is puffed up with conceit that she has brought Japhet down. She thinks she is invincible. That will be *her* downfall.'

An hour after Sir Gregory Kilmarthen left Gwendolyn, Georganna returned from her shopping bursting with news.

'Gwen, you will guess who was in Royal Exchange! None but Kitty Jones. We got to talking, for she is a great admirer of Thomas's writing, and she is to attend the play tonight with Lord Sefton. I said that we had taken a box this evening, and she insisted that we join them at the interval. She is eager to meet Thomas. Of course, she wants him to write a play for her. But is it not the perfect excuse for you to talk with Lord Sefton?'

'That is splendid. And Sir Gregory Kilmarthen called this

afternoon. He has promised to do everything he can to clear Japhet's name.'

Georganna gave a whoop of delight. 'Kilmarthen is a genius!'

Throughout the first act of the play Gwendolyn fluttered her fan in agitation. Her heart was in her mouth as Thomas escorted her to Lord Sefton's box. Aunt Margaret and Georganna remained in their seats. Margaret had not been happy about visiting the playhouse.

'If Gwendolyn is upset by meeting Lord Sefton, we will leave at once,' she said. 'I worry about her. She must safeguard her health and that of the baby.' She peered anxiously across the tiered boxes of the playhouse to where Lord Sefton sat with his friends and saw Thomas and Gwendolyn enter the box.

'Let us hope that all goes well.' Georganna bit her lip in her anxiety.

Lord Sefton stood up on noticing a woman entering his box, but when he recognised Gwendolyn, from when he had attended Japhet's trial, declared, 'I do not entertain the wives of highwaymen in my box. Leave at once, Mrs Loveday.'

Kitty Jones protested, 'My lord, the playwright Thomas Mercer escorts this woman. I have longed to make his acquaintance. I met his wife this afternoon and invited him to join us.'

The actress looked half a dozen years younger than Gwendolyn and had made her debut on the London stage to much acclaim at the beginning of the year. The young Welshwoman wore her dark hair unpowdered. Her heart-shaped face was alight with pleasure to meet Thomas Mercer.

She giggled ingenuously as he raised her hand to his lips, her voice breathless with excitement. 'Mr Loveday, I adored your play *The Landlord's Revenge*. I saw it several times.'

Thomas bowed to her. 'And I have heard much of your reputation, dear lady. You would be exactly right for a new play I am writing.'

She patted the empty seat beside her. 'Do pray sit and tell me all about your play.'

'But, my dear ...' Lord Sefton began, and was cut off abruptly.

'You cannot deny me this opportunity to speak with so

acclaimed a playwright. It is every actress's dream to have a part written 'specially for her.'

Thomas launched into a volley of improvisation, his agile mind devising the part of an innocent young girl from the country and her amorous adventures in her quest to find fame and fortune in London. It was a story that had been used many times but he brought a unique slant to the plot to make it sound fresh and exciting.

With Kitty Jones enthralled by every word he uttered, Gwendolyn put a hand to her heart and pleaded with gentle persuasion, 'My lord, you are a man of great wisdom and perception. My husband was falsely accused.'

'He was given a fair trial. More than the blackguard deserved.' Beneath his curled wig, Lord Sefton's cheeks were sunken. He wore a patch at the side of his full mouth and another at his temple. His ageing face was dusted with powder and rouge; he clearly fancied himself as very much a dandy of the first order. He was eyeing Thomas's intricately folded stock with keen interest.

'Information was laid against him several months after the robbery took place. Did that not strike you as odd?' Gwendolyn had learned that Lord Sefton had been sent down from Cambridge after his first year in some disgrace and was frequently mocked by his peers for being slow-witted. It would pay to explain this slowly. 'In all that time Mrs Yorke made no attempt to return the necklace to your wife.'

Lord Sefton frowned. 'Japhet Loveday had escaped justice for too long, by all accounts. If Celestine Yorke had not taken to her bed a heartbroken woman at the way the blackguard had tricked her, she would have realised sooner that the necklace he gave her was the famous Sefton diamonds.' His lips twisted into a sneer. 'You have my sympathies that you, an heiress, fell for his deceit. Your husband is a fortune hunter as well as a highwayman.'

'You malign him, Lord Sefton! My husband is neither a fortune hunter nor a highwayman.' Gwendolyn bristled with outrage. 'I have known Japhet all my life. He has never lied to me. He did not rob your coach that night, and he has no idea how Celestine Yorke came by your necklace.'

'Your loyalty is misguided, madam. I saw the man who held up my coach,' Sefton was insisting.

'Did you see him clearly?'

'Of course not, the blackguard was masked.'

'Then how can you be so certain that it was my husband?'

'The man was of the same build and spoke like a gentleman. Gentleman James held up my coach and Gentleman James is your husband.'

Gwendolyn struggled to cool her rising temper at his arrogance. 'With respect, your lordship, Gentleman James is a figment of Celestine Yorke's imagination. It is no secret that she was my husband's mistress for some months after she was robbed whilst travelling in Sir Pettigrew Osgood's coach. Why did she not recognise him before?'

'He is a wily rogue. He tricked her.'

'My husband is taller than the average man and has a distinctive husky voice. Did you recognise that voice?'

'The knave could have disguised it. And I was not previously acquainted with your husband so I would not recognise his voice during the robbery.'

'Then what of the highwayman's horse?' Gwendolyn persisted.

'It was dark,' he snapped. 'When you find yourself looking down the barrel of two pistols, you do not take note of the nag the blackguard is riding.'

'Was it a nag or an Arab mare?'

'A hired nag. I remember that the horse was blown and wheezing fit to drop. My coachman had a clear shot at it as the knave rode off. Must have winged it.'

'My husband prides himself on his knowledge of horseflesh. That is how he makes his living, by procuring horses for patrons such as yourself. His mare is an Arab and has won many races.'

'The nag was blown. He would not risk a valuable mare in a robbery.'

'Would not a highwayman need a fast mount to ensure his escape? If my husband had robbed you that night – which I assure you he did not – he would not have been so foolish as to ride a blown horse and risk arrest. No true horseman would.'

Lord Sefton frowned, but the set of his jaw remained stubborn.

130

'Celestine insisted that your husband gave her the necklace as a gift. Obviously he held up my coach and he will now face the consequences. The blackguard is lucky he will not hang.'

'Unless Celestine Yorke was lying. She wanted to bring my husband low because he had rejected her love. She wanted to disgrace him. The woman invented the highwayman Gentleman James in order to regain her popularity with the public. She will say or do anything to cling on to her fading career. Her lovers are legion – any one of them could have acquired the necklace and given it to her.' She spoke rapidly, giving Lord Sefton no chance to interrupt. 'Celestine Yorke did not return the necklace to you until she learned that Japhet and I were to wed. It was known throughout London that you had been robbed. Why did she not return it to you earlier if she had not intended to keep it?'

'She said it was a gift. She had thought the setting similar to one she had seen on a noblewoman in the audience but it was only later, when someone described my wife's necklace to her in detail, that she became suspicious they were the same.' His tone was haughty and dismissive. He was glaring at Thomas and Kitty Jones, still talking of the play.

Gwendolyn had heard all she needed. She smoothed the triumph from her voice to say with gentle concern, 'My lord, you said earlier that Celestine Yorke had not returned the necklace to you because she had taken to her sickbed. Now you tell a different story. Clearly she was not consistent in her fabrications.'

Momentarily his mouth gaped open, his expression perplexed. 'Madam, you misunderstood me.' He looked relieved as three men entered the box and greeted them effusively.

His companions eyed Gwendolyn with interest and one said, 'Do you not intend to introduce us to this lovely creature, Sefton?'

'The lady and her companion are just leaving.'

Gwendolyn knew it was pointless to pursue Japhet's case further at this stage. She curtsied to Lord Sefton and as she rose leaned forward to whisper in his ear, 'I would hate to think that the Yorke woman played upon your lordship's generous nature. She is known for her greed and would not easily have relinquished such a treasure. If it is proven that she came by the necklace by other means, it would distress me if your own reputation became

131

sullied through your previous connection to her.'

'Do you malign my reputation, madam?'

She was quick to reassure him and took a crumpled pamphlet from her reticule as she went on, 'The court case brought Mrs Yorke once again into the public attention and for the moment her theatrical career thrives. Has she not recently won the attentions of a royal duke? Consequently she no longer gives her favours to Sir Pettigrew Osgood. He is lampooned in the streets, an object of ridicule that she callously used to her own ends. Your lordship does not deserve to be treated in the same fashion.' She pressed the paper into his hands. It was the lampoon against Osgood which she hoped would make him reassess Celestine's story. It was particularly witty and scathing, cleverly written and privately circulated by Thomas's friend Lucien Greene.

Sefton's lower lip trembled and he dabbed at his mouth with a lace-edged handkerchief. He swallowed hard before replying, 'You have given me much to ponder upon. Good evening, Mrs Loveday.'

Thomas escorted her through the crowds, returning them to their seats as the bell was rung announcing the start of the second act. 'Do you wish to see the remainder of the play?' he asked.

'No. Take me home, Thomas.' Her legs were shaking after her confrontation with Lord Sefton and she was feeling queasy. Throughout the evening she had been subjected to curious glances as she was recognised by those who had attended Japhet's trial. The men eyed her with lecherous speculation and the women regarded her derisively from over the top of their fluttering fans. Many saw her as the dupe of an unscrupulous fortune hunter. In their eyes an heiress tricked out of her dowry by a handsome rogue was a creature fit only for ridicule. She held her head high and stared straight ahead as they walked into the foyer.

'I heard most of your conversation,' Thomas said. 'You did well, Gwen. Sefton certainly looked taken aback when you had finished.'

'Let us hope that Lucien's lampoon makes him realise how ruthlessly Celestine Yorke used him and that his wounded pride will make him question her story.'

'Lucien could pen another piece bringing this information to the attention of the public,' Thomas suggested. 'Japhet is after all a gentleman, the Yorke woman but a common actress and known for her greed. If we can find the evidence we need, society will believe Japhet over an actress. Celestine Yorke was a fool to discard Osgood and Sefton as her lovers. Neither will tolerate ridicule. She has brought much danger upon herself by her own greed and spite. She could be the one imprisoned if she is found guilty of receiving stolen goods.'

'It would serve her right, but my principal aim is to clear Japhet's name.' Gwendolyn drew her velvet cloak around her as they waited for their carriage to be summoned from the queue lining the road. The foyer of the theatre was brightly lit and ladies of the night paraded along the street outside, touting for business.

'It is time the Yorke woman received her comeuppance. Her greed has wrecked the lives of several families,' Thomas commented as he idly surveyed the street. He gave a low whistle. 'Speaking of comeuppance, is that woman huddled in a doorway not Meriel, St John's wife?'

Gwendolyn was jolted out of her fear for Japhet. Looking over to where Thomas had gestured she saw a white frightened face watching them. Then the woman lurched out of the doorway and darted down a side alley.

'It was Meriel,' a shocked Gwendolyn agreed.

'I should follow her, but I would not leave you unattended.'

'It could not have been Meriel.' Gwendolyn frowned. 'Not amongst streetwalkers? That woman was wearing a filthy gown and her hair was unkempt.'

'Perhaps she has ended up in the gutter where she belongs,' Thomas returned unfeelingly. 'Here is our carriage. Wait inside and I will go and investigate.'

He ran across the road and Gwendolyn sank back into the darkness of the coach, waiting for his return. She was soon thinking of her husband again. She prayed that he was surviving his prison ordeal and that justice would prevail and he would be pardoned.

It was several minutes before Thomas returned, his expression grim. 'There was no sign of her and none of the other women admitted knowing who she was, even when I offered them a guinea.'

'We must have been mistaken.' Gwendolyn had now convinced herself that this was so. 'Meriel is another opportunist like Celestine Yorke, but she would never sell her body on the streets.'

Chapter Twelve

Meriel did not stop running until she reached her tiny room in a rundown boarding house, on the edge of a labyrinth of hovels inhabited by criminals and prostitutes. She threw herself, sobbing, on to the crumpled bedding, the straw palliasse rank and infested with bed bugs. A single candle, the last she possessed, kept the darkness and demons at bay. A piece of ragged threadbare sheet hung at the cracked window and the floorboards were bare. How could she have fallen so low in less than a year?

Why could she not have been satisfied with the life she had won for herself as the wife of St John Loveday? In Cornwall she was fêted as a beauty, but in London many women were beautiful, and men of a philandering nature could pick and choose at their will.

A year ago she had lived in the Dower House at Trevowan surrounded by beautiful furniture and ornaments. Her allowance may have been smaller than she had wished, but she dressed in silks and velvets. And there had been the extra money when she encouraged her husband to join her brother, Harry Sawle, in his smuggling runs. In truth St John had provided well for her but she had not been content. Born the daughter of a tavern-keeper, she had always sought to use her beauty to marry well. She had accomplished that part of her scheme when St John became her lover, and her brothers had forced him to wed her.

She drew a stained coverlet that smelled of mildew closer to her body and hugged it to gain some semblance of comfort as her tears flowed unchecked. A year ago she had been expecting her second child. Disaster had struck when she had been attacked in Truro by Thadeous Lanyon, and left for dead. Lanyon, a rival smuggler, had once wanted to marry her but she

135

had escaped his unwelcome offer by taking St John as her lover. Lanyon had sworn vengeance upon the Lovedays and herself. He was a dangerous man to cross and she had been a fool to think that she could outwit him. But the years had passed uneventfully and the Lovedays were a powerful family. She had thought herself safe. She should have realised that a man such as Lanyon had no respect for wealth or position. Truro was a day's ride from Penruan and during a visit with her husband Meriel had wanted a new hat and gown. St John had fallen into a drunken sleep after a night of gaming and, too impatient to wait until he awoke, she had gone shopping alone. She had almost paid for that gown with her life.

Unknown to Meriel, Lanyon was in Truro on business that day. He had waylaid her and dragged her into an alleyway in broad daylight where he had beaten and kicked her despite the fact that she was heavily pregnant. He had then tried to strangle her. A shout from a passer-by who had seen the attack made him run off. Lord Wycham had been her rescuer. He had undoubtedly saved her life, but she had lost her child – a son.

The horrific memory of that day made her scream out again in pain and terror.

Her neighbour, a pickpocket, loudly banged on the wall and threatened, 'Shut that bloody row. Raving madwoman! Quit yer screaming or I'll come in there and bloody well shut yer up.'

Meriel ignored the threat. Her screams were a nightly occurrence when nightmares took hold of her and she awoke sweating with fear for her future. Lanyon may be dead but he haunted her from his grave. He had been murdered, she suspected by her brother Harry although it had been St John who had stood trial for the murder. Her nights were filled with terror as she relived his attack. Her nerves were paper-thin, and she saw assailants in every shadow or behind any sudden noise.

At first she had recovered well from her ordeal. She was young and had always been strong from her work in the tavern. Beautiful and wilful, she had also been confident of her ability to forge her own destiny. But even before the attack, she had known she was losing her hold over her husband and that he no longer loved her. It had heightened her discontent. The money problems the

Lovedays had faced added to her growing resentment against St John.

After rescuing her, Lord Wycham had become a constant caller at the Dower House. Within two months he had become her lover. During St John's trial they had kept their affair secret. When her husband was acquitted and it was decided by his family that it would be wise for him to spend a year in Virginia until the scandal died down, Meriel had had no intention of exiling herself to a foreign country. She had always dreamed of living in London where a beautiful woman could use her wiles to win the favours of the highest in the land. She had begged Lord Wycham to take her to London and he had agreed.

From the outset she had realised that Wycham could not be manipulated as she had controlled her husband. He had not set her up in a house as she had presumed he would but had merely rented a room for her in a respectable boarding house. He would visit her there twice a week and within a month she learned that he kept other mistresses. That was when the nightmares began. She had no money, no security. Her emotions became volatile and her moods unstable. Lord Wycham soon discarded her.

At first it had been easy to attract other men who were friends and acquaintances of Lord Wycham's, but they never lasted long as her lovers. Even though they paid her highly for her favours, the life of a courtesan was not the future she had envisaged. Then, as her night terrors robbed her of sleep, she became weak and her beauty faded. She lost track of the number of men she had slept with and inevitably one of them had infected her with the pox. The weight fell from her. The luscious curves that had attracted lovers were now gone and she was angular and bony. The violent manner in which she had miscarried had given her other health problems and she was in constant pain. She had tried to get work in a tavern or inn but the landlords told her she was too scrawny and weak. With no wealthy lover to support her, she had no choice but to take to the streets.

Meriel loathed the life and earned a pittance. She could not afford the medicine she needed and was becoming daily weaker.

It had been a shock to encounter Thomas Mercer and Gwendolyn Druce outside the theatre. She knew that Thomas

137

was a playwright as well as a partner in Mercer and Lascalles Bank and that he frequently attended the play, but she had thought that with the scandal following Japhet's trial the family would live in seclusion. Pride had made her flee when she had seen the shock of recognition of Thomas's face. She could not bear that St John's family should learn she had fallen so low.

'I was a fool to run,' she sobbed now. 'What good is pride when I am starving and sick? Thomas would have given me money. I am still a Loveday.'

Her confidence ebbed. The Lovedays were fiercely loyal but only towards their own family. She had betrayed them, and they had never approved of her marriage to St John.

'But I'll show them! I will get well. St John will help me. He will pay me to stay away from Trevowan. I shall still live in style ...'

The candle spluttered and burned low, casting grotesque shadows high on the walls which were running with cockroaches. The shadows formed figures with long arms reaching out for her. Meriel's screams could not be controlled until eventually she fell into an exhausted sleep.

Bridie rang the hand bell to summon her pupils to class and greeted each one individually as they filed past her into the schoolroom to stand behind their desks. There were ten children from the schoolyard, and another eight from Trewenna and the surrounding farms who only attended sporadically. They were often needed at home to help with the chores or run errands. Few of them attended class more than twice a week. She walked to the front of the classroom and waited until they had finished fidgeting.

'Good morning, children.'

'Good morning, Miss Polglase.'

Several of her pupils were missing today. It was the middle of September and they were needed to help with the harvest. Many of the wives of the shipwrights would earn extra money too by working in the fields. Education was a luxury; the first priority of the poor was to ensure they had enough money to provide food and warmth through the winter.

This was the end of Bridie's first week as a teacher and she had enjoyed it immensely. Her lessons concentrated on the children mastering their letters, learning writing and numbers.

Bridie started each day by reading them a story but this morning she was interrupted by the arrival of Peter Loveday. He strode into the room and waited at the back until she had finished speaking. She had not seen him since their encounter at Trewenna. That meeting still disturbed her dreams. The sight of him was enough to set her heart racing, and she cursed her own foolishness. He was dressed in black clothes and a wide-brimmed hat that he removed and held in his hand. His black hair was trimmed to the shoulders and hung loose. His expression was austere and she wondered how she could have displeased him. Surprisingly, the thought upset her. Yet Peter was nothing to her, why should it matter if he was displeased?

She reminded herself that this was her classroom and he was the intruder. She would not be intimidated by his presence. He found much to criticise in others. They had nothing in common and he was altogether too judgemental of those less pious than himself.

'Children, you may have a short break in the yard, but no going near the river or troubling the shipwrights.'

There was a banging of desks and thundering of feet as the children ran outside.

To help her retain her composure Bridie clasped her hands together. 'How can I help you, Mr Loveday? The matter must be important if you see fit to interrupt the children's lessons.'

Her rebuke brought a faint flush of colour to his cheeks. He may criticise others but did not like any judgement passed upon his own actions.

'Miss Polglase, I have twice been in the yard at the start of school and have noticed that you do not begin with a prayer or a hymn of praise to Our Lord.'

'This is a schoolhouse not a church, Mr Loveday.' Her reply was sharp with indignation.

'Children can too easily be led astray. It is your duty to instil a proper sense of fear and reverence for God in them. When you read to them it should be from the Book of Common Prayer. You were reading *Gulliver's Travels* – an ungodly parable of a man's descent into hell.'

'It is an adventure story about imaginary worlds,' she was stung to reply. 'The book was given to me by Adam who suggested that the children would enjoy it.'

'Adam is little better than the heathen he married!'

'Sir, you insult my sister!'

'I say nothing that I have not said to my cousin's face. Your sister rarely attends church, and of late you also have been absent from your devotions. A school teacher must be above reproach in all things.'

'I think you should leave, Mr Loveday.' Bridie's face flamed with the heat of anger and her eyes were dangerously bright. 'Mr Edward Loveday approves of my teaching methods. You have no right to come here and address me with such disrespect.'

'I come in the name of the Lord.' Peter closed the space between them. He was breathing heavily.

Bridie stood her ground. His closeness was unnerving and her whole body tingled with the memory of his kiss. She stamped the memory down, allowing her anger to take control. 'Please leave. This is my classroom and I will not be lectured by a pompous, arrogant ...' She paused. She hated confrontation and dissension of any kind, she had endured too much of it as a child. 'Just go away. It is not your place to lecture me.'

She braced herself for another verbal attack. It did not come. 'I did not come here to quarrel. Few of these children attend the scripture classes and it is obvious that they pay no heed to the sermons in church. I meant no disrespect.'

Bridie continued to regard him with scepticism.

'I ask your pardon. I have been clumsy with my words.' He thrust his fingers through his hair in agitation. 'I meant no disrespect to your good self.'

His manner changed, all his arrogance slipped away. It made him look younger. Bridie sensed that he was feeling wary and uncertain. This was a side of Peter Loveday she had not seen before. She realised with a start that he was ill at ease in her company. Peter's character had always been vastly different from his brother's and cousin's; he did not have the same self-assurance around women.

'I did not mean to criticise but rather to suggest that the school

140

day should open with a prayer and that a parable from the New Testament be read to the children as an example of a godly way of life.'

She considered his proposal. It was not unreasonable and she enjoyed Bible stories. 'I am not qualified to answer any questions asked by the children on religious subjects.'

'Would it be presumptuous of me to suggest that I take such a class for one hour a week?'

She hesitated before replying, 'That is most generous, Mr Loveday. I know your time is taken up with many good works and the service of the Lord. But I would not subject the children to lectures or sermons – the proper place for that is the church, not a schoolroom. Would you be prepared to tell them stories from the Bible without subjecting them to a sermon afterwards?'

He looked affronted. 'Sometimes they are necessary.'

'I do not entirely agree. The priority of this school is to teach the children to read and write. They struggle with basic addition and subtraction. Have you spoken to Mr Edward Loveday or his wife? Mrs Loveday set up this school. It is for her to say what is taught in it.'

'My uncle was happy with my suggestion but said that it should be your decision.'

The weight of such a responsibility was something Bridie had never had to deal with before. She wanted to do what was right, but she did not agree with many of the high-minded principles Peter Loveday embraced.

'I would rather not make so important a decision without considering it properly first,' she said.

'But the moral welfare of the children is as important to them as learning their letters.' He clearly had not expected her to delay a decision.

'That is why I would not make this decision without proper deliberation.' She tilted back her head to hold his gaze, her hands clenched tight together.

His figure tensed. 'It has been some weeks since you attended church. If your own faith is in question, are you suitable to teach at all?'

The accusation spurred her to anger. How dare he condemn

her in so pompous a manner? 'How dare you judge me, sir! What of your conduct? Where were your high principles and morals when you took advantage of me in the church? I will attend services when your father returns.'

'I was driven by the devil,' he blustered.

'You are a man and supposedly raised to be a gentleman. Do not blame the devil for your own base lust.'

'You are a beautiful woman.' He looked suddenly haggard. 'You are constantly in my thoughts.'

'Then it would not be appropriate for you to take a class at this school.' She picked up the hand bell and rang it for the children to return to class. 'Good day, Mr Loveday. We have nothing more to say to each other.'

'You misunderstand ...'

She had no intention of allowing him to pontificate further and cut across his speech. 'Are your intentions towards me strictly honourable then, Mr Loveday? I doubt it. You are a parson without a parish or income. I am the sister of a woman you judge to be a heathen. You believe in a God of fire and brimstone, and I believe in a more tolerant divinity who does not condemn his children but offers love, compassion and tolerance towards all men. The parables told by Jesus speak of love – not judgment and persecution.' She was breathing heavily and her face was flushed, her heart racing wildly.

'The church dictates ...'

The children were returning to the classroom, their expressions curious. Once again she interrupted him. 'The church is not my master. I would use my own mind to decide the way I lead my life. Our views are too different for us to have anything in common. Please leave, sir.'

The chatter of the children made it impossible for him to reply and Bridie felt herself close to tears. She bowed her head to hide them, and to regain her composure busied herself tidying her desk. When she looked up he had gone. A feeling of desolation knifed through her. She could no longer deny it: she was in love with Peter Loveday, but they had no future together. Even if their backgrounds were not so different, he could not afford a wife and she would be no man's paramour.

142

The health of her baby Joan was a constant worry to Amelia. During the first months of her life she had taken little milk despite the adequate supply from a buxom wet-nurse. The baby was small and cried throughout the day and night. Dr Chegwidden insisted that she was tightly wrapped in swaddling bands despite the heat and humidity of the summer. On his instructions the windows in the nursery were kept shut and the curtain drawn to prevent any light entering the room. Amelia had never approved of Senara with her gypsy background and had refused to allow Adam's wife to attend upon her daughter. Elspeth and Edward remonstrated with her; both of them had benefited from Senara's remedies. Finally when Joan had vomited throughout the night after being given one of Dr Chegwidden's potions and lay in her crib too weak to cry, Amelia agreed that Senara might tend to her.

She had stripped off the baby's swaddling bands and bathed her in tepid water, finding her skin was raw from the urine and excrement she had been lying in. Then Senara had dressed her in a thin muslin gown and moved her crib into the sunlight by an open window.

'This is against everything that Dr Chegwidden advised. Joan will take a fever and die!' Amelia wailed in alarm. She was thin and haggard, her auburn hair woven through with streaks of grey. Her shoulders were stooped and she carried herself as though she was burdened with the troubles of the world. She wrung her hands, her face bitter and condemning. 'Edward should be here. He spends too much time at the yard, fussing over that young ward of his when he should spare more time for our daughter.'

Senara had no intention of fuelling Amelia's anger over Tamasine. She tried to deflect the older woman's fears. 'Country babies are not smothered and cosseted in such a ridiculous fashion as the gentry think necessary. Fresh air, provided that it is not tainted by foul odours, can cause no harm.' She was adamant. 'Have the wet-nurse fan her so that she does not get too hot in the sunlight. The fresh air and light will raise and renew her spirits. Add a little honey to her milk and just one drop of this tincture.'

The wet-nurse was also antagonistic. 'I bain't never heard of such goings on. Raise and renew the spirit, what talk is that? Bain't right. Bain't decent. Lady Traherne had Dr Chegwidden tend her children regularly. They be a strong healthy brood.'

The wet-nurse had suckled Lady Traherne's last child eighteen months ago and never ceased to remind the family of her important connections. It was one of the reasons that Amelia had chosen her from two other women in the district who had recently given birth.

Senara defended her treatment in a firm voice. 'Mrs Loveday was not young when Joan was born. It can affect a child and make them sickly. Joan needs greater sustenance.'

'You will kill the child,' the wet-nurse declared. 'A baby should be suckled and given nothing else for six months at least!'

Senara noted the woman's appearance. Her hands were clean but her body was rank and unwashed. The neck of her gown was still unfastened from when she had been feeding Joan. The blue-veined breasts were caked in dried milk, and the skin grey from lack of washing. Senara stepped closer and smelled the sourness of the woman's breath.

'The wet-nurse should take more care that her breasts are washed before each feed,' she advised.

'I've never heard such nonsense!' the woman snorted.

'She must also eat no rich sauces on her food and must abstain from all alcohol.'

'I never touch a drop,' the nurse protested. 'I always dined on whatever was served at Lady Traherne's table. There bain't never been nothing wrong with my milk. This be the seventh child I've suckled along with seven of my own. Not one of them was sickly.'

'Clearly something you are eating disagrees with Joan,' Senara declared. 'And a mother's milk when it seeps from the nipples can become rancid as any cow's in this hot weather.'

'In all my born days I've never heard such talk. It bain't decent what she says.' The wet nurse turned her back on Senara. 'With respect, Mrs Loveday, Dr Chegwidden be the one you should pay heed to.'

'It shall be as Senara says,' Amelia replied after a momentary pause. 'Dr Chegwidden has done nothing to improve Joan's health.'

144

Within a day the child had stopped vomiting and after a week she was suckling better and her flesh was filling out. Even so, Senara feared that she would never be a robust child.

And Joan was not the only member of the Loveday family whose health she was concerned about. Edward too had lost weight and his cheeks were often tinged with unhealthy colour. He took a physic every day that Senara prepared for him, but refused to rest or allow her to examine the wound in his chest.

With the improvement of Joan's health some of the tension eased between Edward and his wife, but Amelia refused to allow him into her bed until Tamasine had been sent away. The couple were still barely civil with each other. Edward stayed away from the house, working longer hours at the yard when he should have been resting.

Chapter Thirteen

At the beginning of September, when Tamasine had been at Trevowan for almost a year and Edward was pushing himself to the limit of his strength as the last of the harvest was brought in, he was given a reprieve from Amelia's melancholy and bitter moods. Her son, Richard Allbright, now aged twelve and a midshipman in the navy, returned to England.

Amelia busied herself arranging a grand dinner for the family to celebrate her son's return. Richard had grown taller and his fair hair was bleached almost white from the sun. He had been away for two years, sailing to the new colony of Australia with settlers and convicts on board.

On his second day at home Richard had been eager to accompany Edward to the yard. His mother had forbidden this without any explanation. Two years at sea had matured Richard beyond his years, training him when to use his initiative as well as when to follow orders without question. Now he challenged his mother. 'I have always visited the yard. I want to see the new brigantine Adam designed.'

'I forbid it.' Amelia sucked in her lower lip, looking fierce. She was in the walled rose garden cutting flowers for the house. She dropped two pink roses into the basket her son was carrying for her.

'But why, Mama?'

'I do not need to give you my reasons. Suffice to say there are unsuitable people at the yard with whom I prefer you do not consort.'

'Mama, I have mixed with the roughest of common seamen. The shipwrights and their families are decent ...'

'Has your time in the navy taught you to question your betters?' Amelia snapped.

Richard blushed, shocked by the virulence of her outburst. 'I do not understand why you forbid me to go to the shipyard?'

'Some things are better left unexplained. I will not discuss the matter further. And it seems to me that the navy has taught you to be insolent.'

'My pardon, Mama, that was not my intent.'

Seeing how upset his mother appeared, Richard did not pursue the subject but his curiosity was itching to be satisfied. Later that day he sought out Edward who was in the cow byre tending a sick heifer.

'Mama has forbidden me to go to the shipyard and will not tell me why. She used to like me to take an interest in your work, sir. Is she cross with Adam, believing it was his stories of the sea that made me decide to make the navy my life instead of being a lawyer as Mama would have wished? She is not herself and seems very much out of sorts. Has she been ill?'

Edward continued administering a physic to the heifer, then stood back and wiped his hands on a piece of rag. He walked across the churned-up yard to lean his arms on a stone wall, and for some moments studied the cattle. 'The new stock will improve the herd. That will please St John. He has long complained that too much of the income from the estate has been used to pay the debts of the shipyard. The harvest has also been a good one this year.'

'These last years without the help of your sons cannot have been easy for you, sir.'

'An estate as large as this will always have its problems. Some years you weather them better than others.'

Richard regarded his stepfather in puzzlement. 'You did not answer my question, sir. Is Mama unwell?'

Edward had not deliberately avoided answering Richard's question. He had stalled for time, hoping to find the right words, but there were none to explain Amelia's discontent.

'Your mother is in good health. My ward is staying at Mariner's House and Amelia find her presence difficult to tolerate,' he replied heavily. 'Tamasine is not just my ward – I will be honest

147

with you because the family knows the truth – she is also my daughter. Her mother died last year. I did not know that I had a daughter until then. She is sixteen.'

Richard studied the cattle in silence, the flush creeping up his cheeks showing his embarrassment.

'Tamasine is known to our neighbours as the orphaned daughter of a distant cousin. Her stay at Mariner's House was to be temporary, but circumstances proved otherwise. Any mention of Tamasine upsets your dear mother. That is why she does not wish you to visit the yard.'

'But then I cannot visit Bridie. We are friends and Adam spends all his time at the yard. Am I not to see him?'

'Adam and Senara will be at the dinner tonight. If you wish to see Bridie some arrangements can be made.'

Richard regarded him with eyes darkened by anger. He was too respectful and well-bred to voice his true feelings, but responded with a diplomacy learned from his years at sea. 'If it upsets my mother, then out of respect for her, I will have no contact with this Tamasine. But I do not consider her presence to be a good reason why I cannot visit the others at the yard.'

'Then speak to your mother. I will not intercede in this.'

Edward did not intend to pursue the subject and walked through a field of recently cut hay back to the house. Richard kept pace with him without speaking for several moments; he cleared his throat several times, clearly finding it difficult to say what was on his mind. Life on a transportation ship filled with convicts and prostitutes bound for a penal colony would have opened his eyes to the rougher elements of life.

Finally he said, 'I thank you for your plain speaking, sir. If Mother permits I would still very much like to visit the yard.'

'Speak to Adam at dinner tonight. Tamasine will not approach you unless you address her.'

They parted company as Edward summoned Isaac Nance, the bailiff, to his study to discuss hiring extra labour for the harvest.

Richard entered the house and was halfway up the curved staircase when Lisette came running down. She was dressed for riding. He pressed himself against the wall to allow her to pass. She stopped on a level with him, eyes fixed admiringly upon his tall figure.

'Our handsome midshipman has returned. Too bad I was sick of the headache last evening and missed dining with you.' She leaned so close that her breasts pushed against his chest.

Richard blushed. Lisette was wearing powder and rouge and her lips were reddened with carmine. He had seen doxies as heavily painted in the ports where his ship had docked. She giggled at his obvious discomfiture.

'You have grown so handsome.' She ran her fingers over his smooth cheek. 'Did you become a man on your voyage?'

Profoundly shocked by her innuendo and the way she ran her tongue seductively over her lips, he swallowed painfully. 'Madam, I congratulate you on your marriage to Uncle William.'

'So prim and proper. Your mama must be proud of her little boy,' she scoffed. 'My marriage to your uncle was one of convenience. He ran off to sea, leaving me to find my entertainment where I will.'

Again she pressed close to him, her eyes bold and appraising as she whispered, 'Come to my room once the family has retired and I will show you how a Frenchwoman turns a boy into a man.'

'You are my uncle's wife! Shame on you, madam!' He was shocked by her invitation.

She laughed. 'I tease you. You English do not know how to flirt. Will you not ride with me? There is much that I could teach you about the language of love. It will be diverting.'

'I must decline. I have to attend upon Mama,' he answered stiffly, unsure what to make of her brazenness. He must have misunderstood her. Lisette had always been somewhat strange in her manner and behaviour. Before he had gone to sea he had been too young to be of interest to her, though the beautiful, volatile Frenchwoman had always fascinated him.

'It would not do to keep your mama waiting.' Her laugh had a brittle edge to it as she ran on down the stairs. She lifted a hand and waved to him when she turned the corner of the stairs and saw him watching her with a frown. 'I think your thoughts will be with Lisette not your staid old mama.' She blew him a kiss.

Elspeth hobbled out of the winter parlour to join her. 'You have kept me waiting for half an hour, young lady. I ride with you every day as a special favour, yet you show your usual disregard for the feelings of others.'

'I have very strong feelings about you, Elspeth,' Lisette remarked. 'Discretion prevents me from informing you of them.' She ran out of the house leaving Elspeth to hobble after her.

Richard hurried to join his mother. He felt foolish after the encounter with Lisette and was determined to put the incident to the back of his mind. She had always caused trouble and he had yet to come to terms with the news that Edward had told him.

He found his mother in the nursery with Rafe and Joan. Amelia was in a chair, rocking Joan in her arms and singing a lullaby. She stopped when Richard entered.

'Please continue,' he said. 'I remember you singing that song to me.'

Rafe was seated on the floor playing with some wooden soldiers. He held one out to Richard who squatted on his haunches to play with his half-brother. He turned to discover his mother watching him, her eyes filled with tears.

'Mama, what ails you?'

'You are so grown up. Soon you will be a man.' She dabbed at the corners of her eyes. 'I am being foolish, but I have been so worried all the time you were at sea.'

'Rafe is your little one now,' he laughed, but was concerned by her pallor and tense manner nevertheless. 'He is a fine lad. He has your hair and eyes.'

She gave a small shiver. 'I pray daily that he has none of the Lovedays' wild blood. I pray that he will be like you. Apart from joining the navy you have never given me any worry, and naval officer is a respectable profession. Your father would have been proud of you. I am proud of you.'

Tears brightened her eyes again and she blinked them away, staring down into Joan's serene face. Richard was sorry to see his mother clearly agitated and disturbed. He had thought that her marriage to Edward Loveday had brought her happiness. But she was far from content and he guessed that a great part of her problem was the knowledge that her husband had fathered an illegitimate child.

The information had shocked Richard but nevertheless he

admired his stepfather who had always treated him as a son. He knew Edward had been a widower for twenty years and, not knowing the full story, was loath to judge the man too harshly. His time in the navy had shown him much of the baser side of life and he accepted that these things happened.

Seeing his mother so distraught made it hard for him to broach the subject of visiting the yard, but he had also learned that once a decision was made it should be acted upon without delay.

'Mama, I have spoken with your husband and he explained the situation at the shipyard which you find so upsetting. While I respect your feelings in this matter, it would pain me not to be able to visit Adam. I will have no dealings with Mr Loveday's ward.'

'I forbid it! You cannot know the depth of my shame.'

'There is no shame attached to your name, dearest Mama.' He knelt at her side and took her hand. 'I give you my word I will have nothing to do with this child Tamasine.'

Amelia stared into Richard's eyes and he felt helpless before such distress. He wanted to protect her but had no experience of such matters. This was something that must be settled between his mother and her husband. She gripped his hand tightly.

'You do not know this creature,' she warned him. 'She is a minx, artful and wilful. She captivates Edward. She is beautiful, witty and charming, and she is no child but a young woman. Her mother, for all her loose morals, was of noble birth.'

'Then I shall not go to the yard, though I will miss my visits to Adam. He has always been like a true and beloved brother to me. But will it not cause more talk if I stay away? Before I joined the navy I spent much of my time there.'

She dropped her gaze from his while she considered his words, and then gave a small nod. 'You are a good son, and wise. There has been gossip enough. And I know how close you are to Adam, I would not spoil your leave. The navy will take you from me all too soon.'

'Thank you, Mama.' Richard rose. 'I will do nothing to cause you further pain. You have done so much to welcome me home. The house is filled with the delicious aroma of meats and pastries. After ship's rations I shall take pleasure in our meal tonight, and

Adam and Senara will be here, will they not?'

'They will.' Amelia returned the sleeping Joan to her crib. 'There is much to be done to ensure all is in readiness. I must speak with Winnie Fraddon. She has prepared your favourite dishes.'

As the evening lengthened and the sky was lit by the golden glow of the sun lying low in the sky, laughter echoed in the dining room of Trevowan for the first time in months. The only moment that threatened to darken the mood was when Richard asked after Adam's cousins and aunt and uncle.

'They are usually at all family gatherings,' he concluded.

Edward saw Amelia tense and did not want the evening to be clouded by talk of Japhet. 'After Japhet's wedding, Joshua and Cecily are visiting my sister Margaret in London. Peter is at Trewenna taking a church service tonight, and his sister Hannah and her husband are busy harvesting their crops. We will visit them the day after the harvest is in.'

To keep the mood light, Adam followed his father's example and spoke of his voyage to Virginia and his experiences there.

'I heard in Plymouth that you had been captured by the French,' Richard said. 'How did *Pegasus* fare in battle?'

'Please let there be no talk of fighting tonight,' Amelia said firmly. 'The navy will soon recall you to duty, Richard. And now we are at war, I fear for your safety.'

Lisette had drunk several glasses of wine and had been unsuccessfully flirting with Adam and Richard during the meal. Adam parried her comments and turned the conversation to family matters; Richard, who sat next to her, squirmed with embarrassment when she put her hand on his knee and stroked his thigh. His face was flushed and twice his mother had asked him if he was feeling unwell.

'The food is richer than I have become used to,' he answered, and pushed Lisette's hand away, but it was impossible to move his leg out of her reach.

'Perhaps our young officer should take some fresh air. I will show him the rose garden,' Lisette offered.

'I am quite well,' Richard said. 'I would not miss this conversation with the family. There is much news to catch up on.'

152

She yawned.

'Lisette, if you are bored by our conversation you may go to your room,' Elspeth retorted. 'We are interested in the welfare of our family even if you are not. But if you wish me to accompany you to Fowey to visit your brother again, you will behave yourself. Richard has been away for a long time. We are celebrating his return.'

'Richard knows that I would make him most welcome in his home.' Lisette raised her wine glass to him. 'To the most handsome man in the room. Does he not look *magnifique* in his naval uniform?'

Richard blushed and choked on his food. Lisette was once again stroking his thigh.

Amelia put her fingers to her brow. 'I will not have you spoiling Richard's homecoming. If you cannot behave, go to your room, Lisette.'

She pouted and drank another glass of wine, her manner now sullen. The conversation was changed to more trivial matters and by the time the port was brought in Amelia was looking pale and tired. She led Senara and Elspeth from the room to leave the men to their drink and cigars. Lisette sauntered behind them and paused by the door.

'Gentleman, this evening has been most diverting. I go now to my bed. You know where I am if you have need of me.' She giggled and gave a hiccup as she proceeded rather unsteadily up the stairs.

When Richard rose to follow the women as he had in the past, Edward put up a hand to stop him. 'You have served your country in the navy, you are a man now.' He poured a small glass of port for Richard.

Adam watched the women as they crossed the hallway; Senara was chatting with Elspeth and made his staid aunt laugh. He was delighted that she had now found her place within his family. To see the easy manner in which his wife now mixed with gentle-women, it would be impossible to guess that Senara was of gypsy blood. She had a natural grace and elegance, and had learned the manners and etiquette demanded from her role as his wife. He was proud of her and his love for her deepened.

As he followed the women's progress across the hall to the winter parlour, Amelia turned to speak to Senara. His stepmother had been the most virulent member of the family in her disapproval of Adam's marriage and it had caused dissension between him and his father. That was now in the past, but it had not been without its consequences.

He swallowed against an ache of yearning as his gaze swept over the panelled dining room with its central chandelier and walls hung with portraits and paintings. This was the home he loved. Trevowan was not the grandest house in the district by a long way, but to Adam there was no other place on earth that could stir his heart. He had always known that as the elder twin his brother would inherit Trevowan. It had not stopped Adam dreaming, however, that his father would change his will in favour of him, or that if St John died without a male heir, Adam or his sons would inherit. But Edward had been adamant that no child of gypsy blood would inherit Trevowan, and that if St John died without male issue the estate and home Adam cherished above all others would pass to his young half-brother, Rafe. Adam had bought Boscabel intending to restore it into a house and estate to rival Trevowan but it would never be the same.

He cast aside the regret that threatened to darken his mood. He had a wife and children he adored, and knew that he should count his blessings. One day Boscabel would rise from its ruin and neglect to be a home he would be proud of, a home fashioned from his own work and the fortune he had accrued. He loved Senara as he loved life itself. To sacrifice Trevowan for the happiness he had found with her was a lesser sacrifice than losing the woman he loved.

'How do you find life as a midshipman, Richard?' he asked.

'Harder than I had realised, and you were right when you warned me of the petty rivalries amongst the midshipmen and younger officers. Whenever I am forced to watch a man given twenty or even fifty lashes it turns my stomach. Fortunately, I soon found my sea legs and did not dishonour myself the first time I had to go aloft, although I have no great head for heights.'

'It can be a harsh existence. Much depends on the captain and how he maintains discipline. Some are unnecessarily brutal,' Adam replied.

'Discipline was strict on the transport ship. It had to be with thieves and prostitutes on board. There were many trouble-makers. Two of the convicts jumped overboard, fearing the life they would find in Australia.'

'How did you find the penal colony?' asked Edward. 'You hear stories of its brutality. I've even heard the climate is hotter than hell.'

Richard shook his head. 'It is everything you have heard and worse. I would not want to serve again on a transport ship. The convicts are battened down in the hold for most of the day and the conditions down there are horrendously foul.'

'What of the country? Is Botany Bay the hell they say it is?'

'The penal colony has moved from Botany Bay, where the land proved unsuitable, to Paramatta. The settlement is now established. The military have their barracks and a church is being built.' Richard paused to sip his port, but there was no enthusiasm for the new land in his voice. 'The country is beautiful but the heat and flies sap a man of energy, and the convicts are forced to work like slaves. We treat our cattle better. The soldiers guarding them resent being posted to the far end of the earth without any home comforts which makes them vicious towards their charges. The convicts are whipped for any insub-ordination, half-starved, and chained into closely packed cells at night. Many die from the heat and fever.'

Seeing the horror on the faces of his companions, Richard gulped down his port and added, 'The settlers fare little better. They have to rely on the convicts to clear the land, and their homes are mere wooden shacks. Food is always short and as yet little livestock has survived the voyage to allow them to breed more. Some of the settlers scrape by if they have a trade as, say, blacksmith or carpenter, they are much in demand, but the farmers struggle to raise their crops when the convicts are so disinclined to work.'

Richard fell silent, sensing by the stillness of the other men that it was more than morbid fascination that had caused his step-father and brother to question him.

155

Edward's face was grave as he refilled Richard's glass and regarded him steadily. 'Japhet has been tried and found guilty of highway robbery. He is at present in Newgate awaiting transportation. That is why Joshua and Cecily are in London with Gwendolyn.'

Richard blanched. 'Then God have mercy on him! Though it is the case that once a sentence is served the convicts are given land. And Japhet is strong. As the settlement grows conditions are improving.' He tried to throw the best light he could on Japhet's prospects but the damage was done.

'Whilst we are at war with France, the navy needs all her ships.' Edward replenished his own port and sipped it reflectively. 'Few prisoners are being transported. That could work in Japhet's favour. Many prisoners have now been moved to prison hulks. So far, because he is a gentleman, he has been spared that further indignity. We yet hope that this sentence will be repealed. Gwendolyn has written that she has found evidence that false charges were laid against him.'

The three men fell silent, each focussed upon the horrors that fate could yet mete out to Japhet. Edward recovered first, determined to keep the mood of the evening light. 'Let us rejoin the ladies. We have left them alone too long. Adam and Senara refused to stay the night and will wish to be home before dark.'

Edward strode off, but Richard waylaid Adam. 'I wish to visit the yard tomorrow but have promised Mama that I will have no consort with your father's ward. I want to hear all about your escape from the French prison.'

As Edward approached the green salon where the women were gathered, he heard Amelia's voice rise sharply, laced with venom that froze his blood.

'I will never accept that baggage into my home. Senara, how can you even consider it could be possible? If she sets foot in Trevowan I will walk out. It is time the bastard was wed and sent far away from my home. Edward has Joan now. It is an insult to me that he considers that by-blow's welfare before my feelings. If it were not for the scandal rife in London over Japhet's trial, I would have taken up residence in my house there.'

'You make too much of this.' Elspeth was equally sharp.

'Edward adores you. Your attitude is unworthy of him. He has responsibilities ...'

'His responsibilities are to his wife, not to his whore's child. The sooner that baggage is sent packing, the sooner this family can return to normal ... though what passes for normal to the Lovedays is usually unconventional and hard to tolerate.'

Edward stood inside the door, his expression glacial. 'So at last we learn the truth of your feelings towards our family. Senara, Elspeth, would you leave us?'

Senara hurried out of the room, appalled by Amelia's outburst. Elspeth eyed her brother's wife with contempt. 'You are a foolish woman with more pride than sense.' As she limped past Edward she put one hand gently on his arm but he was oblivious to her gesture of compassion, his eyes steely as he regarded his wife.

Adam gestured to Richard, who was looking pale and shaken, to follow him into the orangery and leave Edward and Amelia alone.

'Wife, this puritanical and unforgiving attitude of yours pains me deeply. I no longer know or understand you. I will move into the west wing and take my meals at the yard. You may remove yourself to London if you wish, but the children will remain here.'

He turned on his heel and marched from the room.

'Edward, I did not mean ...' Her cry of dismay was lost to him as anger overcame him.

When Edward did not return, Amelia burned with resentment fuelled by shame. Her love for her husband was smothered by her own outraged emotions. She did not regret her outburst, she told herself. She had spoken the truth as she saw it. If Edward could not see the error of his ways, then he could live in the west wing of the house.

She angrily wiped away a tear that ran down her nose. The pain of her love for Edward was excruciating. He had failed her, subjecting her to the ultimate disloyalty. She had never thought he would so dishonour her. If at any time in the last year he had banished his by-blow from his land, she would have forgiven him. But he had made it very plain where his loyalty lay, and Amelia did not feel it was with her. Wounded pride made her dig in her heels. To cover her hurt, she longed to escape to London but could not abandon Rafe and Joan.

If Edward loved her, he would understand why she was so upset – why the situation was unbearable for her. Until he apologised and his bastard child had been sent packing, they would lead separate lives.

Edward slept that night in the west wing in a room where there had been no time to properly air the mattress. As it was summer he refused to have the fire lit. The west wing overlooked the sea and was cold and often damp. When he woke in the morning he was aching in every joint and his chest was stabbed by a deeper pain and feeling of tightness.

He was still angry with Amelia and left the house early to ride to the yard even though the morning mist was thick.

When he reached the crossroads his hair and jacket were moist from the mist, and as he entered the office he began to cough. He gave Ben Mumford his orders and, knowing that Adam would be spending most of the day with Richard, he opened the ledgers to tot up the monthly figures. By mid-morning his head and chest ached abominably and although the day remained overcast he was sweating profusely. A physic from Senara would soon put him to rights but as he rose to call upon her he swayed, the office walls spinning like a top around him.

He reached out to the table to steady his balance, missed and fell to the floor, hitting his chest on the side of the table. The wound burst open, oozing blood and pus which spread across his shirtfront and soaked his jacket.

The men outside continued their hammering and sawing and sang a sea shanty as they worked. Edward was burning with fever when his senses returned. He tried to rise but fell back, weak and exhausted. No one heard his cry for help.

He lay lapsing in and out of consciousness for an hour before Adam entered the office. By then his father was barely breathing.

He was taken immediately to Mariner's House but after a brief examination Senara advised Adam to send for the physician.

'He is beyond my caring. An abscess has burst from inside his wound and the blood is poisoned. The wound is close to his heart. There is little time. Send for Amelia at once.' Her voice broke and she struggled to say through her tears, 'You must prepare yourself for the worst. Edward is close to death.'

Chapter Fourteen

The sudden shouting and disturbance outside in the shipyard distracted the schoolchildren. Two of the older boys ran over to the window to peer out.

'Jamie and Charlie, go back to your places,' Bridie ordered.

'But, miss, they be carrying Mr Loveday on a board to Master Adam's house. Is he dead, miss?'

'Come away from the window, it is rude to stare.' Bridie pulled the boys away and looked out of the window herself to see a group of men gathering outside Mariner's House.

There was now silence in the yard, all the men having stopped work. Clearly something was wrong. She was worried that an accident had indeed befallen Mr Loveday.

'What be happening, miss?' several of the children chorused. 'The men bain't working. We can't hear no hammering. Is Mr Loveday hurt?'

'I do not know. Now, children, you will get on with your work.' Bridie hid her own fears. If Edward Loveday had been taken ill, they would not want noisy children running round the shipyard.

She found it hard to concentrate and her glance kept going to the window. The men outside Mariner's House gradually dispersed but did not resume their work.

The children remained distracted and kept whispering to each other, or craning their necks to look out of the window. Bridie finished the writing lesson and to restore order to the classroom began to read them a story. There was a knock on the schoolroom door and Peter Loveday entered.

'Miss Polglase, may I speak with you?'

'Children, you will continue to copy down the passage from the blackboard.' Bridie walked to the door of the schoolroom. 'We will talk outside. The children are already unsettled by recent events. Have you news?'

Peter frowned. 'I have no idea what you are talking about.'

'Your uncle. Two of the children saw him taken into Mariner's House on a board. There must have been an accident. The men still have not gone back to work.

Peter surveyed the yard and glanced towards Mariner's House. 'I thought it was unnaturally quiet. I had no idea there had been an accident. I should call on Adam to see if aught is amiss, but I came to the yard to speak with you.'

Bridie did not want another lecture and said pointedly, 'I hope that Mr Loveday is not seriously hurt or ill. I will not keep you from enquiring after your uncle's health.' She stepped back.

Peter hesitated. 'Yes, I must go, but first I wanted to apologise to you for my conduct the last time we met. This is your schoolroom and I presumed to teach you how it should be run. Please accept this in heartfelt apology.' He pressed a book into her hands. 'I must now see how my uncle is.'

He strode away, leaving her dumbfounded by his apology. She turned the book over in her hands and was surprised to see that it was a copy of John Donne's poems. A blush heated her cheeks. She had read some of Donne's work; his poems could be sensuous as well as religious. He was not a writer Bridie had thought that Peter would appreciate. And for him to apologise when he always thought himself to be in the right was also unusual. Had she misjudged him?

Adam met Peter in the hallway and informed him of his uncle's condition. 'I've sent word to Dr Chegwidden and to Trevowan. There is nothing you can do, Peter, but you are welcome to stay in the parlour.'

'I will pray for Uncle Edward.'

Adam nodded. 'He has need of your prayers.'

He returned to the room upstairs. Senara had cleaned the wound and applied half a dozen leeches to Edward's chest. She spoke over her shoulder to Tamasine as she worked.

'The abscess must have been forming for weeks. He refused to

161

allow Dr Chegwidden or myself to examine him. Leeches may be able to stem the poison.'

'What can I do to help?' Tamasine rolled back the sleeves of her gown.

'Keep applying cool cloths to his brow. That will help keep the fever down. I must prepare a poultice also to help draw out the infection. Adam, try and get him to drink some brandy. It will strengthen him.'

Tamasine wrung out a cloth and flinched as she felt the heat of Edward's brow. His complexion was grey and his breathing shallow; she took his hand, willing him to live.

'You cannot die, sir. We have barely begun to know each other. Your family needs you.' She continued to talk to him although he was unconscious. 'You are strong. You will recover.'

The windows were open. Adam had ordered a stop to the shipyard's work to aid Edward's peaceful recovery. The sound of horses outside drew him to the window.

'Amelia and Elspeth are here.' He gently took hold of Tamasine's arm. 'I must ask you to slip out of the house through the kitchen. Go to the Ship kiddley and stay there until Amelia leaves. This is not the time for her to see you.'

'But he is my father! May I not stay?'

'We will keep you informed. We must consider her feelings at this tragic time.'

Tamasine nodded, but her heart was breaking. She had been happy at Mariner's House and had enjoyed her afternoon talks with Edward. It did not trouble her that she had been banished from Trevowan. Here she had had a special and important part of her father's life. She had never seen Amelia as a threat or a rival for Edward's affection, and she had certainly never intended that her arrival should cause a rift between him and his wife. That had all been Amelia's doing. Now, as fear for his life gripped her, Tamasine resented being banished from his sick room.

Her gaze lingered upon the bed and she had a terrible feeling that she would not see her father alive again. She ran out of the house sobbing, missing the arrival of Amelia by seconds. Senara had told her that Amelia and Edward had quarrelled last night over her presence at the yard. In that moment Tamasine hated

Amelia for keeping her away from her father. But she was powerless to act against her. It was so difficult to accept that her birth would always set her apart from the family she had hoped to join all the years she was imprisoned at the academy.

Elspeth, who was always so stalwart, broke down when she saw Edward. Adam brought her a chair to sit on by the window. Amelia looked drawn and haggard as she sat by the bedside.

'How did this happen?' she demanded. 'Edward has been so much stronger.'

'He had never lost his cough.' Elspeth struggled to speak through her tears. 'I warned him he should rest. The strain on him the last few months has been immense, taking charge of everything and sorting out every problem.'

Dr Chegwidden arrived and ordered everyone from the room. Adam ushered out the women but refused to leave himself. The doctor's manner was abrupt. He had come to Penruan four years ago to take over his father's practice. Before that he had served as a surgeon in the navy. Simon Chegwidden was tall and thin-faced with bushy side-whiskers. He was also arrogant and too aware of his own self-importance. He had married Annie Moyle, daughter of the chandler at Penruan, but refused to tend the local fishermen who could not afford his exorbitant costs.

Dr Chegwidden threw back the bedclothes and glanced briefly at Edward. The leeches Senara had applied were bloated and ready to be removed but he made no attempt to do so. 'I see your wife has seen fit to inflict her limited skills upon the patient. The wound is suppurating and from the smell it has become gangrenous. I should have been summoned to attend upon him weeks ago. Your wife's herbs and potions may ease trivial aches and pains but her inexperience here ...'

'My father collapsed in his office. My wife tended him only whilst we awaited you, Dr Chegwidden. The wound had been festering for weeks if not months, and during that time he has supposedly been under your care.'

'I should have been called long before this.' He remained obdurate. 'I fear that you must prepare your family for the worst. There is nothing I can do for him now. If he appears to be in pain, give him this.' He handed a phial to Adam. 'Your father brought this upon himself. He needed another operation to cut out the infected flesh and refused to heed my advice.'

'Did you not operate on him to remove the bullet when he was shot? Sir Henry Traherne said you almost butchered him. And you attended throughout the winter while he was recovering at Trevowan. The wound must have been infected even then.'

Chegwidden paled at Adam's accusation and picked up his bag. 'I have other patients to attend. If your father had heeded my advice this would never have come to pass.'

'Do you not intend to operate on him now, if the wound is so infected?'

'In his weakened condition he would die under the knife – my butcher's knife as you referred to it.'

Adam swallowed his anger. 'For that I ask your pardon, Dr Chegwidden. My fear for my father made me speak out of turn. You must operate. It is his only chance.'

'There is nothing to be done for gangrene, not when it is close to the heart. You must prepare yourself, it is just a question of time. The medication will ease his pain. I can do nothing.' He left the room.

When the women returned, Adam hid his worry. He could not believe that Edward was so close to death. 'Father needs rest and quiet. It would be better if some of us remained downstairs.'

'I shall stay at my husband's side,' Amelia informed him. 'Though I would rather he was at Trevowan.'

'It could kill him to move him,' Senara began, but was abruptly cut short by Amelia.

'I am aware of that. What did Chegwidden have to say?'

'He fears that nothing can be done. But Father is strong, he may rally.'

Senara slipped from the room. Arrangements had to be made concerning Tamasine and a room prepared for Amelia and Elspeth. Adam followed her.

'Chegwidden is a fool,' Senara said heatedly. 'He is too scared to tend to your father in case Edward dies in his charge. A skilful hand could operate and cut out the infected tissue, but Edward probably would not survive that butcher's knife a second time.

Chegwidden never even suggested a second operation. He is evading his own responsibilities.'

'Then it is for you to get Father to pull through. You saved my life when Chegwidden's father had given up on me.'

His faith in her was touching but in this case unrealistic. She shook her head. 'I will not lie to you, my love. Edward is dying. If the poison from the abscess does not kill him, then gangrene from the infected wound certainly will.'

Amelia and Elspeth had been too distraught at the news of Edward's collapse to give a thought to the vigilance they usually maintained over Lisette. She gave a cry of delight as the older women rode from Trevowan, and ordered her own mare saddled.

'Orders are you bain't to ride on your own.' Jasper Fraddon folded his arms over his chest and jutted his jaw when he confronted her.

'Fool! I was delayed. The others would not wait for me. I ride to Mariner's House. My uncle is ill. How dare you insinuate that I should not be at his bedside at this time?'

Fraddon believed her; both Amelia and Elspeth had been equally agitated when they had left.

'A groom will attend you.' Fraddon was determined to conform to propriety as he led her mare to the mounting block.

Lisette scrambled up, too impatient to await his help. 'I will catch up with the others. The grooms have more important work to do. Get out of my way!'

'Hoity-toity baggage!' Fraddon cursed her beneath his breath. He had never liked Lisette who had caused the family too much upset for him to respect her. The other grooms had been sent to the fields with the plough horses. His old joints ached and he was in no mood to go chasing across the countryside on a wild goose chase. No harm would come to the Frenchwoman, she would catch up with the others soon enough.

Lisette set off at a furious gallop and Jasper Fraddon removed his cap and scratched his bald pate as he watched the clods of earth fly up from her mare's hooves. When he saw her bring her whip down hard on the mare's flank, he shook his fist at her. 'That baggage be mad as a March hare. She'll ruin that plucky horse.

Hope she do take a tumble in a hedge. It would serve her right.'

He went into the stable to finish mucking out the stalls, his thoughts troubled. He muttered his fears as he worked. 'Don't seem right Mr Loveday be taken again with the fever. Nasty business all round. If that no-good wastrel St John hadn't got himself caught up with the smugglers, the master would never have been shot. That St John's got a great deal to answer for, if you ask me. And heaven save us and Trevowan when that young whippersnapper inherits!'

During her wild gallop Lisette gave no thought to Edward's condition. If he was confined to his sickbed she would be able to get away from Trevowan more easily. The prospect excited her. She resented being unable to meet Etienne alone. Even though they frequently slipped a sleeping draught into Elspeth's drink, they could never be certain she did not overhear their plans or when she would awake.

Lisette did not spare her mare as she galloped to Fowey. Her fears now were that Etienne would not be at his lodgings.

She cantered through the narrow winding streets at a reckless pace, forcing a barrow boy to leap out of her way. His handcart full of flour sacks was knocked over, the contents spilling and breaking open on the pavement. Etienne's lodgings overlooked the river. She tied her mare to a ring on the garden wall, disregarding the animal's mouth that was flecked with foam and blood. Lisette pushed past the gaunt, grey-haired landlady who had answered her knock on the door and lifted her skirts high as she ran up the stairs.

'Your brother is not at home,' the landlady called after her.

Lisette had reached his room and snarled in frustration to find it empty. Her eyes were wild and her cheeks flushed as she confronted the landlady on the stairs. 'Where is he? It is urgent that I see him at once.'

'Sir Percy Fetherington called. They will be drinking in one of the taverns.'

'But I must see my brother now,' Lisette raged. 'Which tavern?'

The landlady was a kindly matron with four daughters of her own. 'I will send a servant to look for him. You may wait in my

166

parlour. I will bring you some tea.'

'I will wait in my brother's room.' Lisette flounced back up the stairs. 'Tell your servant to be quick.'

The landlady sucked in her cheeks at such rudeness. 'How that dear Monsieur Rivière could have such a shrew for a sister is beyond me,' she muttered under her breath. Etienne had charmed her, and she secretly hoped that he would take an interest in her eldest who was of marriageable age. She had been encouraged by the way the Frenchman flirted with her daughter.

Lisette had been pacing Etienne's room for half an hour when her brother arrived, angry at being called away from a meeting with the dissolute new friends he had made.

Lisette threw herself into his arms. 'At last I have you to myself! I have been so upset waiting ... but you are here now.'

'I was at an important meeting. What is so urgent that you called me away?'

'I escaped my guards,' she laughed. 'We can be alone – truly alone.' She began to unbutton her riding habit. 'Is that not what you wish?'

'*Ma chérie*, but of course it is my most fervent wish. It is an unexpected surprise, that is all. Unfortunately it was not convenient for me to leave the contacts I am making.'

'Not convenient?' she screeched. 'I have not seen you for two weeks. If it were not for the fact that Edward has been taken ill, I could not have got away undetected. Do you want that Elspeth is always with me?' Her jacket was thrown on the floor followed by her skirt, and she ripped her stock in her haste to be rid of all her clothing.

Etienne had been watching her through narrowed eyes. He assisted her to loosen the laces of her corset, then pulled her close and kissed her savagely to calm her mounting hysteria. When they broke apart he said, 'You mentioned that Edward is ill. How bad is he?'

'He collapsed at the yard. He has been ill for months and keeps it from the family.' Lisette pulled off her chemise and stood naked in the centre of the floor. She ran her hands over her breasts and hips, her head thrown back and her eyes narrowed with passion as she laughed and added, 'While the family is concerned over Uncle

Edward we can go away together before my fool of a husband returns. Life will be wonderful again.'

Etienne appraised her porcelain-white figure that was still as slender as the first time he had taken her when Lisette was fourteen. It was the day he had learned that their father planned for her to marry Adam Loveday. Etienne had been against the marriage. He had seen the way men of wealth and position gazed at his sister with open desire. Only the richest and most noble would have her. A man who could further Etienne's own schemes and fortunes. Lisette had always adored her brother, but he had feared that she was falling in love with Adam. And if Lisette fell in love, Etienne would lose his influence over her.

So he had seduced her and taught her to enjoy passion without inhibition. Lisette had been the most apt and willing of pupils. If Edward were severely ill, Etienne realised he would now be able to regain control of Lisette's money and the jewels that she had smuggled out of France. Events were happening faster and more easily than he expected. But he had learned caution during the reign of terror in France. Lisette was too impatient. She must be controlled. He needed more time to put his plans of escape to the New World into action.

Etienne could see that his sister was close to losing control. He needed her to be at his side in the new life he had planned. From a young woman there had only been one way to tame her. Even while their father was alive Etienne had nightly gone to her bed. The meeting with Fetherington and his friends could wait. He needed to regain his sister's love and trust in the only way that she could understand.

His own clothes were carefully folded and laid aside before he joined her on the bed.

'Tell me you love me,' Lisette demanded. 'Tell me how beautiful I am. That I am the only woman you love and adore. Tell me how much you have missed me.'

'*Ma chérie*, I have told you all this a thousand times.' He kissed her into silence. He had seldom found a more imaginative mistress. Her body was exquisite and she was sexually insatiable; but her need to be constantly praised and adored irritated him. She was vain and shallow, but cunning as a vixen and as

168

dangerous as she was captivating.

'Only you understand me,' she sighed as she rolled on top of him, her hands rousing him to a fever of passion. Then she bit his shoulder, drawing blood. 'That is for abandoning me in France. Now love me – prove I am still your adored Lisette. Tell me you love me. Only me.'

He slapped her hard across the buttocks and her eyes were dark as she moaned with pleasure.

Etienne drew his lips back in a satyr's leer. 'My little one forgets who is her master.'

The family stayed at Edward's bedside throughout the night as he slipped in and out of consciousness. Amelia sat in a frozen silence at his side, a sodden handkerchief pressed against her cheek. With each hour she looked more shrunken and haggard. Elspeth sat in the shadows, her tears silent and unchecked. Adam took a chair at the foot of the bed, his head held in his hands. Throughout the vigil Senara kept a check on Edward's fever, which had risen alarmingly high, drenching the covers with his sweat. As darkness fell she slipped out of the house to ensure that Tamasine had a bed at the kiddley for the night and to inform her of her father's deterioration.

Peter had ridden to the Rabsons' farm to inform his sister Hannah of their uncle's collapse. She had insisted on returning with him to Mariner's House. No one slept throughout a night of prayers at his bedside.

The morning sun was rising above the treetops when Edward regained consciousness and swallowed a few draughts of restorative physic. He fell back exhausted and slipped in and out of consciousness throughout the day. Amelia was by now anxious about the children at Trevowan. Hannah put her arm around her.

'There is nothing I can do here for Uncle Edward. Let me take Rowena, Rafe and Joan to the farm, if that will ease your mind over them?'

'You have enough to cope with,' Amelia replied. 'Oswald is not well and you have the mares Japhet purchased to tend to as well as your work on the farm.'

'I can manage.' Hannah was tall and slim, face and arms

169

browned from the hours she spent working out of doors, her capable hands reddened. Despite bearing four children she had not lost her striking looks and could be as formidable as Elspeth when necessary. 'Rowena loves the farm and she will be unsettled at Trevowan with all of you away. The nursery maid can come too, there is enough room.'

Amelia nodded. 'That would ease my mind, but are you sure you can cope with the extra work?'

'It is no trouble. This way I will feel that I am doing something for Uncle Edward.'

As Hannah left, Adam accompanied her to the door and she suggested, 'Would it be easier if Tamasine also came to the farm? It must be awkward for her here.'

'She will not leave the yard. She needs to be close to our father, even if Amelia will not allow her into the house.'

Hannah sighed. 'This is a difficult time for us all. I adore Uncle Edward. I wish I could do more.' She kissed Adam's cheek and fought back her tears. 'May God answer our prayers and allow him to recover.'

For five days Edward battled against a raging fever, the family vigilant at his bedside. On the fifth morning he opened his eyes and his gaze sought Amelia. His voice was so weak it was hard to hear.

'Forgive me, my love.'

'You will be strong again, dearest. Rest and save your strength.'

'See how he rallies.' Elspeth burst into fresh weeping, this time from joy. 'He is stronger. That fool doctor was wrong.'

Edward raised a finger to beckon Adam closer. Each word was more difficult for him to form and his voice was fading. Adam knelt and leaned closer to hear him clearly. 'Look after Amelia and the little ones ... Do not forsake Tamasine ... You know my wishes ... See they are carried out ...'

'You have my word, sir.' He took his father's hand and felt his fingers twitch feebly as their gazes held. Then the light faded from Edward's eyes, the flame of his life extinguished.

Adam bowed his head and reverently closed his father's eyes.

'Edward!' Amelia sobbed.

'But he cannot be dead,' Elspeth sobbed. 'He was conscious.'

170

Senara went to console her. 'It happens that way sometimes. I am sorry, Elspeth, but Edward is dead.'

Amelia sank to the floor beside him, weeping uncontrollably. Adam put one hand on his stepmother's shoulder as she threw herself across Edward's body. Death had smoothed away the lines of pain etched into his handsome features and Adam bowed his head to say a prayer for his father's soul.

Chapter Fifteen

Because of the heat Edward's funeral was two days later. There was no time for the family still in London to attend. The coffin was driven from Trevowan on an open wagon. Behind it walked the family and the other mourners. Elspeth leaned heavily on Adam's arm, refusing to ride to the church. Amelia clung to Richard, her steps those of an old woman. Both Amelia and Elspeth wore long veils over their faces to hide their grief.

It was a solemn, silent procession across the windswept cliff top and down to the village church that had been built opposite Penruan harbour.

The family took their place in their pew at the front of the church. Adam, Peter, Richard, Sir Henry Traherne, Oswald Rabson and, after much dissension within the family, Etienne as Edward's nephew were the pallbearers. The number of mourners was so great that they overflowed into the graveyard. Villagers from Penruan, many of them tenants in fishermen's cottages owned by Edward; workers from the estate and from Trevowan Hard; friends and neighbours too; all came to pay their last respects. The Reverend Mr Snell performed the service and Peter read the committal at the family vault as Edward's coffin was placed beside that of his first wife and his ancestors.

To Tamasine the mile-long walk had taken an eternity, every step deepening her misery. From the moment she had learned of her father's death, she had been inconsolable. Edward's body had been taken from Mariner's House to Trevowan under the close supervision of Amelia, and Tamasine had been forbidden to see it. She had also been forbidden by Amelia to attend the funeral.

It was a vindictive and cruel act. Fortunately for Tamasine,

Senara had been outraged to think that the young girl should be refused permission to pay her last respects to her father. She had sneaked her into Trevowan House in the middle of the night when Amelia and Elspeth were asleep. Edward had been laid out in his open coffin on a table in the centre of the hall, tall candles burning at the corners. Adam had spent the hours since midnight in vigil beside the coffin, and Peter would take his place from four until the family came down to breakfast.

Adam had been Senara's accomplice when she had brought Tamasine into the house at one in the morning and allowed Edward's daughter to remain for an hour. They had stolen away like thieves in the night afterwards, which made Senara more ashamed of Amelia's actions. But at least it had brought some comfort to Tamasine although showing her the prejudice she must now face from some of the family.

'Mrs Loveday must hate me so much, but what have I done to her?' the girl had sobbed on their journey back to Mariner's House.

'Amelia disliked me when Adam took me as his wife, but she finally came to accept me. Her feelings are not important. Adam will never desert you. You are his sister and he will provide for you as his father would have wished.'

'Mrs Loveday shall not stop me from attending my father's funeral! Besides, would people not think it odd that his ward was so disrespectful as not to attend?'

'I have tried to put that argument to her, but she is adamant. The suddenness of Edward's death has thrown her into turmoil. She is too upset to be rational.'

Moonlight revealed the tears sparkling on Tamasine's cheeks. 'Have I not as much right as Richard to be at Mr Loveday's funeral? Her judgement is cruel and unfair. Whatever she feels, I am still Mr Loveday's daughter and his legal ward.'

'There will be many mourners,' Senara had consoled her. 'Edward was a popular man. If you pull the hood of your cloak over your face and keep away from Amelia, she will not know you are there. Attend with Bridie and Leah. Once the family has left you can remain at the vault to pay your private respects.'

Tamasine had found it deeply humiliating to play such an

insignificant role in the funeral. She made a vow to visit Edward's grave every week. Amelia could not prevent her from showing her grief and respect in that manner.

She had stayed in the middle of the crowd with Bridie and Leah as instructed. She too had believed that Amelia would be too distraught with grief to pay heed to the other mourners. But the summer's heat was stifling and the hood of Tamasine's cloak slipped back from her face as the family walked away from the vault. With an uncanny gesture, as though sensing hidden danger, Amelia threw back the veil which covered her face and her gaze seared into Tamasine. She recoiled from the hatred in Amelia's eyes. Clearly, her father's wife saw Tamasine as her enemy. Amelia would never allow her to be acknowledged as Edward's daughter or be recognised as part of his family. It was a cruel twist of fate to have found the family she had yearned to be a part of only to have all her dreams so quickly dashed to nothing.

'Even at the moment of his death, his fears were for his bastard!' Amelia paced Edward's study where the family had been summoned for the reading of his will. The guests who had returned to Trevowan for the funeral supper had left. The taffeta skirt of her widow's weeds rustled like the wind through leaves before a gathering storm. 'Where was the respect and honour due to me, or his legitimate children? I want that upstart minx sent away.'

'That was not my father's intention,' insisted Adam. 'Tamasine deserves better from us.'

'She deserves ...' Amelia would not back down in any confrontation but her words were cut short by a loud cough from Mr Dawkins, the lawyer.

'The hour grows late. If the family would please take their seats, I will read the Last Will and Testament of Mr Edward Loveday.' He unfolded the parchment and smoothed it out on the desk.

The will held few surprises for the family for Edward had made his intentions clear long before his death. St John as eldest inherited Trevowan while Adam inherited the shipyard. Amelia would live at the Dower House at Trevowan and receive an income from the estate throughout her lifetime. Rafe and Joan were to receive an allowance of one hundred pounds a year until the age of twenty-five and on their marriages would inherit a tenant farm each on the boundaries of the Trevowan estate. Provisions were also made to provide an allowance of seventy-five pounds a year to supplement Joshua's meagre living from the Parish of Trewenna. Elspeth, who was dependent on Edward, was to be provided with a home at Trevowan until her death and an allowance of two hundred pounds a year. William Loveday, Japhet, Hannah and Peter each received the sum of five hundred pounds. All grandchildren living at the time of Edward Loveday's death would each receive a bequest of one thousand pounds to be placed in trust until they married or reached the age of twenty-five. Tamasine was provided with a dowry of one thousand pounds, and her marriage was to be at the expense of the estate.

Amelia sucked in a sharp breath of disapproval at this last bequest. 'Can the estate afford to honour these provisions?' she demanded. 'Until recently the house was mortgaged and the estate heavily in debt.'

'Some years ago a trust was set up by Edward Loveday and money for these bequests set aside. Interest has accrued on this,' Mr Dawkins replied, then unfolded another sheet of parchment. He cleared his throat before adding: 'This codicil was affixed last month on Mr Loveday's instructions. If St John dies without male issue, the estate of Trevowan will pass to Edward Loveday's youngest son Rafe on proviso that he has spent at least six months of every year at Trevowan. If this proviso is not observed, the estate will pass to Adam and his heirs. If Rafe inherits before he is twenty-one, Adam is appointed guardian and executor of the estate trust until Rafe is of age.'

'And what if I decide to return to my former life in London?' Amelia demanded. 'How then can Rafe be expected to spend six months a year at Trevowan while he is under age? He must also attend school.'

'The proviso is meant to ensure that Rafe learns to work and manage the land he or his sons may one day inherit.'

'It is unacceptable,' Amelia fumed.

'Then I am afraid your son will sacrifice his chance of inheriting,' Mr Dawkins replied. 'Mr Loveday was aware of his son Adam's love for Trevowan. He regretted disinheriting him from any right of succession. If Rafe is not to be reared on the estate, Edward was adamant that Adam, or his sons, should then inherit.'

Adam was overwhelmed with emotion and struggled to keep his composure. He was no dreamer and knew that it was still highly unlikely that his sons would inherit Trevowan. The stipulations of the original trust set up for the estate by Edward's grandfather had ruled that no woman could inherit, so Rowena as St John's only extant child was barred, but that did not rule out the prospect that St John might one day remarry and have sons. It pleased Adam nevertheless that Edward had no longer barred his younger son's descendants from the possibility of inheriting Trevowan because of their gypsy blood. That meant everything to Adam. Clearly his father had forgiven him for marrying the woman he loved against Edward's wishes.

'And what is supposed to happen to my husband's ward meanwhile?' Amelia demanded in an icy tone. 'I will not tolerate her presence at Trevowan.'

'Tamasine will stay with us until her future is decided,' Adam replied.

'Even as I mourn my husband's untimely death, you would cause me to suffer further shame?' Amelia stood up, bristling with outrage.

'I but honour my father's wishes,' responded Adam.

'Then I will not receive you.'

'Your grief is making you irrational, Amelia.' Elspeth eyed her with impatience. 'Until St John returns from Virginia, Adam must attend to estate business. Or would you prefer it to be neglected? My brother's ward seems content enough at Mariner's House. Is that not so, Adam?'

He nodded.

'There is no need for all this to do, Amelia,' she continued. 'Is it not time to forgive Edward for an indiscretion that happened years before he met you? The girl is a Loveday. We do not turn our back on our own.'

Amelia gasped. 'Yet you disregard *my* wishes. Where is your loyalty to me?'

'You make too much of this.' Elspeth glared over the top of her pince-nez at Edward's widow. 'It is only right that my brother's wishes are respected.'

'I will never accept that creature.' Amelia put one hand to her temple, her eyes awash with tears. 'I will move to the Dower House. Any further conversations or dealings between Adam and myself will in future be conducted through the servants.'

Long Tom enjoyed his disguise of a bearded beggar. He wore a long black matted wig and bushy beard, his gingery eyebrows and lashes darkened by the end of a burnt cork, and was swathed in a patched and tattered cloak, a slouch hat with a wide brim pulled low over his face. He had been following Celestine Yorke for three weeks and had learned that she entertained several lovers. Her affair with the royal duke had lasted only a few meetings; he had been seen leaving her house, disgruntled at having lost a thousand guineas at cards there.

Anonymity appealed to Long Tom. He could observe people without their being aware that they were being watched, and by so doing learn a great deal. Celestine Yorke was devious but shallow, sly but not quick-witted. She was predictable, her scheming driven by greed and her lust for fame.

When not in disguise Long Tom assumed his real persona and as Sir Gregory Kilmarthen attended many of the haunts visited by Lord Sefton. His wit soon won him a place amongst Sefton's circle of friends.

Tonight he had joined them at White's and sat at his ease in the gentlemen's club, enjoying fine wines and brandy. They had been drinking steadily for four hours and those in their cups were becoming indiscreet. Lord Sefton was no exception.

'Kilmarthen, it surprises me that you have not spent more time in London,' he queried. 'The country can be so dull.'

'I have spent much of the last twelve years travelling the Continent. But the unrest in France has caused unease amongst the nobility of Europe, especially so now that this country is at war. It was time to return home and enjoy the pleasures my own land has to offer.'

'And what pleasures would they be?' Lord Sefton winked. 'There's no woman so fair as an English lass, wouldn't you say?'

'Every country has its beauties,' Long Tom replied. 'There's many a bonny wench in Scotland, and does not Wales abound with dark Celtic nymphs? And none more exotic than the lovely Miss Kitty Jones. You are a fortunate man, Sefton, to have won such a prize. But then, you have a reputation for discernment. Was not the luscious Celestine Yorke once your mistress?'

The peer's face lost its amicable expression. 'She has a heart of stone.'

'But did she not discover that a lover of hers had given her a necklace that had been stolen from your wife? It was most generous of her to return it.'

'Sometimes I wonder, though certainly my wife was delighted to have her necklace returned. It had been in her family for two hundred years.' Sefton remained sombre and brooding. 'But the Yorke baggage ensured that she was handsomely rewarded with other jewels that came to more than the value of the necklace. She is a succubus, would bleed a man dry of both wealth and his sanity.'

'I have found her company most pleasing.'

'Has she granted you her favours?' Lord Sefton looked displeased.

'We have met only once, but she was not averse to my calling upon her.'

'Then you had better go bearing diamonds. She'll give no man the time of day without an expensive trinket for her trouble, and she takes to her bed only those prepared to be lavish in their appreciation. You would be wise to stay away from her evil lair, Kilmarthen.'

'She invited me to an evening of cards.'

'Then your purse had better be deep, my friend. You'll lose a fortune at her tables. She's brought more than one man to ruin.'

'Is she then an expert at cards? You have quite a reputation yourself, Sefton.'

'I never came away from her table with more money than I started with. The woman is trouble. I would advise you to stay out of her clutches.'

'You make her sound quite fascinating! She seems to me most remarkable. Has she not resurrected her career on the stage when

178

other young women had begun to eclipse her popularity?'

'The trial of the highwayman did that. You heard of the scandal, I suppose?' Lord Sefton had been drinking heavily and leaned closer to Long Tom in confidential manner as they sat smoking together. 'Gentleman James was her lover but she brought him to his knees. Though the knave deserves to hang, right enough. He robbed my coach on the heath.'

'I heard that she was in love with Gentleman James but that he ended their affair when he married. From what was said at the trial, did he not deny robbing your coach? He said he too had lost all his money at her gaming tables, yet he made his living by gaming and horse dealing, I believe?'

Lord Sefton regarded him blearily. 'You know a lot about the knave.'

'After all you have said I wonder that you are not more sympathetic to his plight. What if he is innocent? You make it sound as if Celestine Yorke does nothing without a motive. Hell hath no fury like a woman scorned, as they say. Are you so certain this Gentleman James was guilty? From what you tell me, it sounds as though Celestine Yorke wanted him ruined out of spite.'

'She would be capable of it. The harlot tried to blackmail me when I had finished with her. She demanded a thousand pounds or threatened she would tell my wife of our liaison. I told her to tell and be damned. Lady Sefton leads her own life now that the children are grown.'

Long Tom shook his head. 'Celestine Yorke sounds a most disagreeable woman. I thank you most sincerely, Sefton. I could have become embroiled in her evil schemes. Makes you wonder, though, about that highwayman, does it not? I'd wager a hundred guineas the man is innocent. It doesn't seem right that the Yorke woman could do that – a gentleman, was he not, from a good family? She could have come by your wife's necklace by any manner of means if she was determined to use it to ruin her lover.'

Lord Sefton frowned into his claret. 'She has no scruples or morals. Not to be trusted at all.' His mood was maudlin and after a long pause he added cynically, 'You're not the first person to suggest Celestine may be as guilty as the highwayman. I thought it strange when she also discovered the emerald stock pin belonging to Sir Marcus Grundy some months after he had lost it – and he always swore he had last been wearing it when he visited her. She said she had found it in the possession of her lover, or Gentleman James ... as she preferred to call him. Japhet Loveday had not struck me as a thief on the two occasions I met him, but who can say in this day and age?'

'This is all most interesting. It bears closer consideration, does it not? You would not want to discover that the Yorke woman had used you and Grundy as her pawns, merely to gain revenge upon a lover who had discarded her. Especially as that man may now pay with his life and his family must bear the shame. And the Yorke woman is more popular than ever after the trial when before her star was waning. Justice is strange, is it not, Lord Sefton?'

The peer was frowning and his lips twisted into a bitter line. 'If I thought that trollop had duped me ... made a fool of me in public ... I would bring her to justice myself.'

Long Tom was satisfied that he had gained the information he needed and an accomplice who would be prepared to bring Celestine Yorke to trial. He still needed more proof against the actress, but the more he could defame her character, the more her evidence against Japhet would be discredited and he would win his pardon.

Chapter Sixteen

'It has been almost a year since you came to Virginia, St John.' Desiree Richmond fluttered her fan, eyes bold and inviting. She stared up at him, spreading her skirts and settling herself on the seat of a gazebo overlooking the river at Greenbanks. She twirled her parasol as she spoke, her manner coquettish. The sunlight brightened her blonde hair and her loveliness caused his pulses to quicken. 'How quickly time passes! Your period of mourning for your wife must soon be over. I have not seen you for some days. You were often in my thoughts.'

The pointedness of her remark made St John uneasy. He hesitated before answering, eyes narrowed against the sun as he studied the riverbank. On the river a merchant sloop tacked in the wind. The leaves turning russet, yellow and red, were already beginning to fall and carpet the ground. He would soon begin to outstay his welcome on his cousin's plantation, though Garfield had been adamant that Greenbanks was his home for as long as he wished.

His cousin was a generous man who lived in great luxury in his grand house with its sweeping veranda and Grecian columns. His tobacco plantation was so vast that it made Trevowan look like a peasant's holding. Tobacco swallowed up vast tracts of land and depleted the soil in a few seasons, so new land was constantly being cleared. Garfield owned forty slaves to work on the land and in the house, their wooden quarters shielded from view by a copse. Trevowan had four tied cottages from which farmhands numbering no more than ten adults worked on the land and five servants ran the house and stables.

This afternoon St John had collected Desiree in the carriage from her own plantation, Broadacres, where she had been staying for the last ten days. It was the longest she had been away from Greenbanks in the year since he had arrived. Although she allowed her overseer to run the plantation, she had weekly meetings with him and drove to her home every fortnight to inspect work in the fields and house. She tolerated no lack of discipline or laziness from her slaves. St John was impressed with her diligence. Desiree knew every aspect of the efficient running of a plantation, the work to be demanded from the slaves and the yield of tobacco she could expect from every field.

St John was to be her escort tomorrow when they would attend a ball at a neighbouring plantation to celebrate a son's coming of age. They had arrived back at Greenbanks an hour before lunch and Desiree had expressed a wish to sit by the river.

'Your company is always missed at Greenbanks,' St John finally answered her. 'And it has been a year of surprises. I did not expect to find such pleasant diversion in Virginia, but I have missed my family, especially my daughter.'

'Children grow up so fast. It is a great sorrow I was not blessed during my short marriage. A man should not live alone for long, do you not agree? And your daughter has need of a mother to guide her.'

'Rowena is surrounded by women. My aunt Elspeth did much towards the raising of Adam and myself, and there is also my stepmother Amelia who adores Rowena.'

In the distance the voices of the slaves working in the fields were raised in song and the occasional sharp order from the overseer was heard. Since Adam had left Greenbanks, St John had relaxed and enjoyed his stay in Virginia. His eligibility as a supposed widower ensured that he was popular among families with daughters of marriageable age. Garfield Penhaligan delighted in entertaining and social engagements were frequent. Musical evenings, picnics, balls, hunting and gaming parties were weekly events. It was a life without responsibility and it suited St John. The hard work on the estate at Trevowan expected of him by his father was a distant memory, as now were the horrors of his trial. That could not be said for Meriel's betrayal. He would still wake in the middle of the night, sweating and his heart racing, when in

182

his dreams she followed him to Virginia and his lies were discovered.

Even in the warmth of the autumn sun the memory of the humiliation that Meriel had brought upon him caused his stomach to clench and a shiver to pass through his body. He hated his scheming, greedy wife and was well rid of her. It was only a pity that she was not really dead, for then he would be truly free.

'St John, you look as if you have seen a ghost, are you unwell?' Desiree, who was always so considerate of his well-being, was frowning.

'I had thought I had put my grief behind me. Speaking of Rowena brought it back.'

'How thoughtless I am!' She pouted prettily. 'We have all tried so hard to help you recover from your bereavement. Your dear wife must have been deeply loved. Do you still miss her?'

'You have been my greatest comfort.' He smiled and bowed over her hand. 'But yes, her death was a shock. She was so young.'

'You have never said how she died?'

'A tragic accident.' He broke off and turned his face away from her as though overcome. In fact he needed to hide the flush of anger that the memory of Meriel aroused.

Desiree rose to her feet and gently laid a hand on his arm. 'I know how bitterly you suffer. Garfield introduced a dozen or more worthy suitors to my attention. They only served to remind me of all that I had lost. I vowed I would never remarry without love.'

'You have been very courageous.' He smiled into her eyes. 'You have made this year bearable for me.'

'It pleases me to hear you say so. Then perhaps you did miss me just a little while I was at Broadacres?'

'How can you doubt that?'

'But you did not visit?'

The possessive note in her voice put him on his guard. Desiree had always acted like a lady but there was boldness in her eyes whenever they were alone. She was no wanton but did not hide her attraction to him.

'You are cruel and unfeeling,' she sighed, drawing away from him on the seat.

He laughed softly and raised her hand to his lips. When she did not pull it away, he tipped up her chin with a forefinger. 'You know I have missed you.' He kissed her, and when she responded slid his hand down her neck to caress her breast. He could feel the frantic beating of her heart. She wanted him and his arousal was instant; but he released her with a sigh. On previous occasions when his ardour had got the better of him, Desiree had made it plain that she would permit no man other than her husband any further liberties.

'You drive me to distraction at times,' he said breathlessly. 'Will you not take pity on me? I adore you.'

Her eyes flashed with anger. 'What sort of a woman do you take me for? I am mortified that you think so little of me, sir.'

'I hold you in the highest esteem, Desiree.'

'Then do not treat me as though I am a wanton. Morals may be viewed differently in Cornwall, but here in Virginia a woman's reputation is everything.' She paused and when he did not respond, his gaze again distracted as he studied the sloop that had drawn closer, her tone became impatient. 'You are soon to return to England.'

He deserved her set down. Reason counselled him to curb his desire for the beautiful Virginian, but she captivated him. Desiree was everything he admired and wanted in a wife: beautiful, vivacious, caring, a woman of good breeding and most import- antly wealth. Broadacres was as large as Greenbanks and equally profitable. Desiree was everything that Meriel was not. Had he been free he would have offered for her hand and counted himself the luckiest of men. Again he cursed Meriel, condemning her to rot in the gutter – the fate she deserved.

St John held back from professing his devotion. How could he declare his feelings for Desiree while Meriel still lived? He knew that Garfield was awaiting an announcement from him that he had requested Desiree's hand in marriage. His cousin had hinted as much on several occasions.

Desiree was looking at him now with anticipation. If he did not declare himself soon, he would lose her; and that would be

184

unbearable. He lived in hope that word would come from England that Meriel was dead, but knew it was only a dream.

Her tone became impatient. 'You are soon to return to England, are you not?'

'I cannot outstay my welcome here.'

The sloop he had seen earlier had let down its single sail and pulled into Greenbanks' dock. A thickset sailor disembarked and walked towards the house set back half a mile from the river. He pulled a short brown jacket over his shirt as he walked and pressed a wide-brimmed slouch hat on to his head.

'We have a visitor,' St John said to Desiree.

Greenbanks always gave hospitality to any respectable traveller and, as no servant had appeared to approach the man, St John hailed him.

'We have letters from England for Mr Loveday and Mr Penhaligan,' the sailor announced. 'They came over on a merchantman from Plymouth to Washington and I offered to deliver them on my way home.'

'Will you come up to the house and take some refreshment?' St John offered. 'I am Mr Loveday from England. Mr Penhaligan is my cousin.'

The sailor handed over the letters and shook his head. 'Thank you kindly for the invitation, but I've been away from home a month and it's another three hours' sail. I wish to be home before nightfall. Give my regards to Mr Penhaligan. Tupping is my name.'

'Are you sure I cannot persuade you to come up to the house? Mr Penhaligan will be sorry to have missed you.'

'I don't want to miss the tide.'

The man tipped his hat to Desiree and departed in haste, pulling his jacket off in the heat and tossing it over his shoulder.

St John stared thoughtfully at the letters, recognising his father's handwriting on both of them. He dreaded opening his. The letter could be a summons for St John to return to Trevowan. That was the last thing that he wanted. He was enjoying himself here.

He returned to Desiree. When she saw him holding the letters, she walked to the pony trap that St John had used to drive them to

185

the river. 'You will wish to read your letter in peace. Let us return to the house. I hope that all is well with your family?'

St John went to his room to read his letter before lunch. He scanned it quickly and saw no reference to his returning to England. It was dated two months earlier. Edward informed him of news of the family and estate and mentioned nothing about his own health. St John breathed a sigh of relief assuming that his father had recovered from his fever and stretched out on his wide four-poster bed to read the letter properly.

He was saddened to read Japhet remained in prison, proud to learn that Rowena was doing well with her schooling and riding, but when Edward mentioned Adam's children, his anger flared. He resented his twin having two sons while he had yet to produce an heir for Trevowan.

'Dammit! I need a son to inherit after me. Why should I slave on the land for the future benefit of Rafe?' he groaned. In his years shackled to Meriel she could at least have proved her worth as a wife and given him a son. Desiree would give him fine sons, he mused, and his temper became savage.

It calmed as he read on. It was obvious that his father was burdened with more than his share of troubles and hard work. He read a paragraph through again, hearing his father's voice as he did so. 'Japhet's trial has overshadowed the gossip surrounding your arrest and trial. I have sadly missed my two sons this last year.'

If that was a reprimand at his absence, St John ignored it. A twinge of conscience told him that his father must be working long hours.

St John tossed the letter on the coverlet and folded his hands behind his neck. He had no intention as yet of finding a passage to England.

He joined the Penhaligan family and Desiree as they entered the panelled dining room for the evening meal. He sensed an aloofness about Desiree but could not see her face clearly as the shutters were partly closed to keep out the glare of the setting sun.

Garfield did not mention Edward's letters until the women had retired from the table and the men had lit their cigars.

'It has been a difficult few years for Edward,' Garfield stated.

186

'Do you intend to return to England? Though you are most welcome to stay, of course.'

St John smothered a stab of conscience. 'In my letter from Father, he said he did not wish me to return. My trial, even though I was proved innocent, has adversely affected orders for the shipyard. I would not jeopardise his endeavours to regain the trust of our customers.'

'It is ludicrous that people pay such mind to gossip.' Garfield waved his cigar in the air like a banner. 'But Edward is a proud man. As you know I have no son of my own. You have taken a keen interest in the plantation here and I am considering making you my heir, though as you have responsibilities at Trevowan I think it time for you to consider remarriage and the raising of sons. Though of course your daughter Rowena could inherit Greenbanks, providing that she weds a man who knows how to raise tobacco, naturally enough I would prefer a son to continue the line of our ancestors.'

St John was startled by the proposal. 'I am honoured, sir. This is unexpected.'

Garfield smiled. 'I am but sixty. God willing, it will not be for some years yet. And you must learn more about tobacco planting. For that you will need to spend further time in Virginia. But if your father has need of you, then you must of course return to England.'

St John was torn by indecision. He wanted to stay in Virginia but he also felt that he was being tested by his cousin. Garfield was generous but he was also a good businessman who valued integrity and loyalty.

'I would be a poor son if I failed my father. Much as I would prefer to stay and learn everything I can at your side, sir, I should return to England to resume my duties at Trevowan. I will make enquiries about the next ship to sail.' He expected Garfield to protest.

'I respect your decision.' Garfield nodded. 'It proves I was right in deciding to make you my heir. Family loyalty is important.'

Though St John inwardly cursed his cousin's compliance, he presented a brave face to the Virginian.

Three nights later a hurricane struck Virginia and the river flooded. The force of the winds alarmed St John. Unlike Adam he was no stalwart sailor and the thought of traversing the Atlantic at the mercy of such storms filled him with dread. He made excuses and delayed his departure.

Garfield did not seem displeased and when they rode alone the next morning, talked much of the future of Greenbanks. He finished by saying, 'The plantation is prosperous, but we need more land or the crops will fail. Consider remarrying, St John. Your time for mourning is past. Desiree would make a fine wife, and the union would please me and unite both plantations.'

St John swallowed against a lump of fear that had lodged in his throat. 'I hold your niece in the highest esteem, but in light of the uncertain future that my father's yard faces in England it would be inexpedient of me to marry without his consent. Especially as it would mean I would spend many months in Virginia. I have the future of Trevowan to consider.'

'So wed and raise a brood of sons,' Garfield advised. 'You are right to respect your father, but Desiree is a beautiful woman and wealthy. A dozen men would be eager for her hand if she gave them the slightest encouragement. You would be a fool to lose her.'

St John did not need this warning. He fully intended to acquire both Desiree and the riches Garfield had promised him.

Chapter Seventeen

After the reading of the will Adam needed some time to himself. His father's death had shaken him profoundly. Edward had been the strength, the foundation, and the guiding force through any crisis, holding the family together.

Adam walked through the gardens of Trevowan to the meadows beyond where the new herd of cattle grazed. He leaned on a dry-stone wall and stared across the fields of harvested wheat and corn that waited to be ploughed. Pheasants had escaped from the gamekeeper's rearing pens and strutted amongst the stalks, pecking at the fallen seed heads. Now that the harvest was in, the heifers and bullocks would be sent to market, and trees needed to be felled and wood chopped to provide them with heat through the winter.

He turned to gaze back at the house. Pewter and gold-coloured clouds were reflected in its mullioned windows, the tall chimneys silhouetted against the darkening sky. The house was in partial shadow as rain clouds blew in from the sea obscuring the evening sun. Swallows and house martens swooped across the sky in a graceful aerial dance and three swans flew along the coast to the river.

There was an unnatural silence pervading the estate. The usual cries of the children and labourers living in the tied cottages had been muffled out of respect for the family's grief. Trevowan would not be the same without his father to run it. Adam's hands gripped the rough stones of the wall so tightly that blood ran between his fingers but he was unaware of any pain. Edward Loveday had died too young – twenty years at least before his time – and now St John was the new Master of Trevowan.

189

Rivalry and resentment towards his twin scalded through Adam's veins. To numb the pain of his grief he had drunk several tots of brandy but it had served only to fire his anger and make his grief even keener. His brother did not deserve Trevowan. Edward would still be alive if St John had not allowed his greed to get him mixed up with the local smugglers. No doubt his scheming wife Meriel had encouraged him too.

So many of the ills that had struck the Lovedays in recent years had been caused by the intervention of the Sawle family. When hard times had almost brought the family to ruin, Meriel had continued to demand to be clothed in fine silks and lavished with jewels. She had married St John for his money and from a desire to be Mistress of Trevowan, accepted by the gentry. High ambitions for a tavern-keeper's daughter. Then, the Sawles always did see themselves as a cut above the other villagers. Meriel's brother Harry was leader of the smugglers in this area and at Meriel's encouragement had hidden contraband in the cave at Boscabel. When Edward had learned of this he had gone to investigate. That was when he had been shot. The Sawles' greed had caused his father's death. In his drink-befuddled state Adam wanted Harry Sawle to pay for the anguish he had brought to the Loveday family.

The pain of his raw grief fuelled Adam's anger. His father's death could not go unavenged. If St John had been here Adam would have picked a fight with his brother. Throughout their childhood and youth their rivalry had always ended in fights.

The lusty cries of Joel came from the open window of the nursery at Trevowan, a reminder that Edward had forgiven Adam for his unsuitable marriage. In his need to find some inner peace he walked to the cliff overlooking Trevowan cove. There was a heavy swell to the waves, and as they crashed on to the granite rocks milky spume splashed high as fountains. Normally the movement of the sea in the cove calmed him but not this evening. His emotions were in turmoil and he could find no peace.

His steps took him along the headland to where the track led down to Penruan. When he neared the village he saw several fishermen were on their sloops preparing to sail with the rising tide. It was a sharp reminder that life went on. The fishermen had missed the morning tide to attend his father's funeral; they could not afford to miss another catch tonight.

The number of villagers who had turned out to pay their final respects to Edward today had shown how greatly respected his father was. Adam had stood beside the Reverend Mr Snell and Peter as the villagers filed past the coffin and offered their condolences. Even Reuban Sawle, Harry's and Meriel's father, had been carried to the funeral on the back of his eldest son Clem. Reuban had lost his legs when Thadeous Lanyon's carriage had run him down. Reuban had been a man with a vicious temper and a reputation for violence until his accident. Now he was old and wizened and his wits were addled by drink. His wife Sal had once been a match for Reuban, and had been the driving force behind the efficient running of the Dolphin Inn. Yet at the funeral she could not meet Adam's gaze as she had muttered her condolences. She was a broken woman since Meriel had deserted her husband, and rumours were rife that her daughter was now a courtesan in London.

'Mr Loveday were a good man,' Sal had observed. 'A saint compared to my brood. He never took against us at the way our Meriel shamed you all. He were a proper gentleman and no mistake.'

All the villagers echoed her sentiments. Yet one prominent resident of Penruan had not shown his face. Harry Sawle had been absent. At the time Adam had been grateful for he itched to fight Sawle for his part in Edward's shooting. Now anger blotted out everything but the need to teach Sawle a lesson.

With determined tread he strode down to the quay but there was no sign of Harry's fishing smack. But then he rarely fished these days, the only catch he was interested in bringing ashore was contraband brandy and tea from France. Adam cursed as he recognised Clem Sawle sailing past the harbour arm and out to sea. Just then a slender woman came out of the general store and lifted up one of the wicker baskets displaying goods, taking it back into the shop. She reappeared and, seeing Adam, came over to him. Hester Lanyon had slipped away from the funeral without speaking with the family.

'I be sorry about your father's death, Mr Loveday. I had to leave the church ... my daughter was teething and fractious. No one wants a screaming baby at such a solemn occasion. I meant no disrespect to your father.'

Apart from the funeral this was the first time he had seen Hester since his return. During her marriage to Thadeous Lanyon, she had lost her pretty looks and sparkle. Adam was glad to see that the widow had regained her former vivacity and beauty.

'And I must congratulate you on the birth of your daughter. How are you managing, Hester?' He frowned as he glanced towards the shop. Hester was only a few years younger than himself and as a child he had mixed freely with the villagers. He had liked her then because she had been saucy and audacious. She was one of the daughters of the village chandler and Adam had been surprised when she had later chosen Thadeous Lanyon as her husband. She had been courting Harry Sawle for years. 'I thought all Lanyon's property went to his first wife? I was sorry to hear he had tricked you and that your marriage was not legal. That must have been a terrible shock.'

She gave a harsh laugh and for a moment Adam wondered if she had not lost her wits. He had heard that her father had turned her from his door when he learned it was Harry Sawle's child she carried and not her husband's. 'Do you work for the new owner of the store? That must be hard for you.'

'You *have* been away a long time.' Hester seemed amused when he would have expected her to be offended. 'Much has happened. I be in partnership now with Goldie who was Lanyon's first wife. She took me in when the baby was due. She has no reading and writing and could not make head nor tail of the ledgers. My father taught me to keep his books so I was able to help out. It shocked the village that we made friends. It certainly put that knave Harry Sawle's nose out of joint.'

Adam cocked his head to one side. 'I thought you two were close?'

There was a bitter tinge to her laughter and she rested her hands on her hips, speaking boldly and forcefully. 'He wanted to wed Lanyon's widow to prove he was a better man. Hah! They were both scum – both the dregs of the gutter. When he learned

192

I'd get nothing, he abandoned me. I were well rid of the rat. He wanted me run out of the village but Goldie showed me I still had a place here and could hold my head high.'

'That must have taken courage, Hester. Harry can be difficult when crossed. And what of your family?'

'I was born here and will not be run out so Harry Sawle can rest easier. I be a constant reminder of all he's lost. As for my family,' her voice dropped and her self-assurance slipped, 'Father has nothing to do with me. And since my sister Annie wed Simon Chegwidden she thinks herself better than the common folk of this village. But we were never close. It sticks in her craw too that I continue to live in Penruan, but Goldie says I bain't got nothing to be ashamed of. Lanyon deserved all he got and one day Harry Sawle will get his comeuppance too.'

'This Goldie sounds a remarkable woman.' Adam had only a hazy memory of Lanyon's first wife who had appeared at St John's trial, her evidence helping to clear his twin's name.

'Come in and meet her,' Hester offered. Adam hesitated. He had come to Penruan to seek out Sawle, not make social calls. At that moment a woman with bright gold hair appeared in the shop doorway. A parrot sat on her shoulder and bobbed his head up and down as he regarded Adam with a wary eye.

'Best whoreshop in town,' the parrot announced to Adam's amazement. 'Goldie's a winner.'

'Best *shop* in town,' she scolded the bird. 'Don't you learn nothing?' She was middle-aged, her face scored and hardened, showing that her life had been far from easy. She shrugged as she noticed Adam. 'The bird was given to me by a sailor to pay his rent. He bain't used to living in a respectable neighbourhood. You be Adam Loveday. I remember you from your brother's trial.'

'And I should thank you for your evidence, Mrs Lanyon. You saved his life,' Adam replied.

'Didn't do it for him. I did it to get back at Lanyon – the evil cur I married. He'd destroyed too many lives by his cruelty and greed.' She chuckled. 'I see Hester has told you about our arrangement. It caused quite a stir, I can tell you. And it's just plain Goldie. Haven't used Lanyon's name since he sold me to a brothel when I was his wife. He married me for my money and cast me aside when he had squandered it.'

Adam did not know what to make of her directness. She was obviously a survivor and must have a kind heart or she would never have taken Hester as her partner.

'We will not keep you, Mr Loveday,' Hester said. 'It must be something important that brings you to Penruan again today.'

'It is. Is Harry Sawle still living at the Dolphin? His fishing smack is not in the harbour.'

Hester blanched at his words and said warningly, 'You want to stay away from him. He bain't no better than Lanyon. Thinks himself a law unto himself now.'

She narrowed her eyes. 'Still, if you have a score to settle with Harry, I reckon you won't let it rest. He bain't in Penruan. He spends most of his time in Truro. His henchman Guy Mabbley is at the Dolphin most nights. They'd begun losing trade when Goldie took over the Gun Inn and we gave the villagers better service. But Harry let it be known that if any fisherman wanted work as tub men when he landed a cargo, they had better do their drinking at the Dolphin or go without the money from landing a cargo.'

'Is the Gun still open?'

'No point in running a public house if there be no more than a handful of customers,' Goldie replied. 'But then, Sawle did us a favour. There be enough work running this shop. The Gun were a rambling place with all its outbuildings. There be plenty of them émigrés looking for work and a roof over their heads so I turned the place into three cottages, got in some looms and now employ three families of weavers. That were Hester's idea. She has a good head for business. Some of the émigrés are teaching the fisher-men's wives to weave. I buy anything they can make and sell it in Bodmin.'

'You have made your mark in Penruan, Goldie.' Adam was impressed. 'The extra money the women can earn will help feed their families when the pilchard and herring catches are small.'

He left the two women who had formed such a strange bond out of adversity, still resolved to seek out Harry Sawle. Half a dozen men were drinking as he entered the Dolphin. Reuban

Sawle was drunkenly regaling the men with his exploits escaping the excise men in younger days. The men laughed uneasily. They had heard the stories a hundred times but even now it didn't do to cross Reuban; many of them were in debt to Harry Sawle who was now also a moneylender, and they needed to keep the right side of the family.

The inn stank of rancid fish stew, stale ale and the vomit on the floor close to Reuben's chair. Adam squinted round in the poor light. The tiny windows were so encrusted with dirt he could not see out, and the once whitewashed walls were brown from the smoke of the fire and the fishermen's clay pipes. Reuben sat in a rickety chair by the bar, his cadaverous face malevolent as a gnome's, a blanket disguising the missing legs. He clutched a battered pewter tankard of ale to his chest. The wispy grey beard that covered his upper chest was matted and greasy from vomit and the slopped fish stew he had eaten for his supper.

'Where's Harry, Reuban?'

'What you be wanting with my boy?' Reuban peered blearily over the top of his tankard.

'He and I have some unfinished business.'

Sal shuffled into the taproom from the kitchen. 'That be no way to be talking to Mr Loveday, Reuban.' She looked embarrassed and haggard. Her clothes hung loose on her frame and beneath a grimy mobcap her grey hair looked straggly and unkempt. She looked as if life had defeated her and she had shrunk not only in size but also in stature in the last year.

Reuban ignored her and scowled at Adam. 'He bain't here. And a Sawle don't come running when a Loveday snaps his fingers. I 'spose you reckon you be Lord of the Manor now your father be in his grave?'

Adam ignored the taunt. 'When you see Harry, tell him I'm looking for him.'

A figure reared up like a bear and detached himself from the group of drinkers, lumbering towards Adam. The man jutted out a thick neck and his tone of voice was menacing. 'What business you got with Mr Sawle?'

'That is between Harry and myself. If you're his lackey, give him my message. There's a reckoning due between us.'

'Now look here, no one gives Mr Sawle orders.' Guy Mabbley drew his dagger to threaten Adam.

Reuben cackled and Sal cried out in alarm, 'I want no violence here!'

Adam had spent too many years in rough seaports to be intimidated. He had not worn his sword to the funeral, but out of habit kept a dagger at his waist. He had seen Mabbley's movement and his own dagger was in his hand and pressed against the henchman's throat before the man could react. Mabbley was a dullard used to using his brawn and not his brain.

'You may think you can throw your weight around in Penruan and bully a few men into thinking you are cock of the roost but it will not work with me.' Adam hated bullies and, being denied the chance to challenge Harry Sawle, was tempted to teach this lackey a lesson. But that would make him no better than Sawle. Adam swallowed his anger, but his voice remained antagonistic. 'A gentleman would not normally sully his weapon with blood from the likes of you but I could make an exception … Just tell Sawle I want to see him.'

'I'll tell him, but that won't be for some time. He's got business in Truro and Bristol. Don't reckon he'll be around for some weeks.'

Adam returned to Trevowan on foot. Sawle had escaped facing him this time, but he could not stay away from Penruan for long. He had murdered Lanyon and been prepared to let St John stand trial for his misdeeds. Now he was responsible for Edward's death. It was time Harry Sawle paid his dues.

With Edward buried and Adam busy managing the estate and shipyard, Etienne decided it was time to insist he should see more of Lisette. A week after the funeral he called at Trevowan and asked for his sister. Jenna Biddick, who had answered his ring on the doorbell, was flustered by his request.

'I will inform Miss Elspeth that you are here, sir. Mrs Loveday is indisposed and is not receiving guests.' She led him to the winter parlour.

'It is my sister I have called upon, not my aunt,' Etienne ground out in his abrasive manner.

'Mrs William Loveday does not receive visitors unless another member of the family is present,' Jenna informed him.

'Enough of your insolence! Summon my sister. Now that my uncle is dead, I am head of my sister's family and responsible for her well-being while her husband is at sea.'

Jenna knew from past experience that Etienne Rivière had a nasty temper and did not want to run foul of it. She hurried to seek out Elspeth who was answering letters of condolence in the morning room. 'Mr Rivière is here, Miss Elspeth. He is demanding to see Mrs William Loveday. With respect, I think he means to cause trouble.'

'I will deal with this.' Elspeth picked up her walking stick. Despite the pain in her hip her stride was resolute as she entered the winter parlour.

'Good day to you, Aunt.' Etienne gave her a cursory bow but his mouth was thinned with displeasure. 'Delightful as it is to have your company, it is Lisette I have called upon. We will go riding together.'

'Edward forbade you to see Lisette unless I accompanied her. You are not welcome at Trevowan.'

'My uncle is no longer here to prevent me from calling upon my sister.' Etienne narrowed his eyes and his lips twisted into that unpleasant smile. 'You cannot hold her here against her will. In her husband's absence it is more fitting that I, as her brother, see to her welfare than a family in bereavement.'

'It is not fitting that Lisette goes gadding about the countryside whilst we are in mourning. Have you no sense of propriety?'

'I have witnessed too many deaths in recent years in France to mourn another overlong. Lisette has spent months shut away in an asylum. Her health is my primary concern.'

'You are disrespectful to your uncle's memory. You will not flout Edward's wishes. As William's wife, Lisette's duty is to our family now.'

'Is that Etienne?' a voice called and Lisette's light footsteps came rapidly down the stairs. 'Etienne … how wonderful!' She threw herself into his arms.

'I came to take you riding.' He smiled at her. 'But Elspeth forbids it.'

'She has no authority over me! Of course I shall ride with you. I will change while my mare is saddled.' His sister laughed and ran from the room.

Elspeth glowered at him. 'You are encouraging her in her wildness.'

'Do not the horses need exercising?' Etienne returned, making an effort to be more pleasant. 'A gentle ride cannot be frowned upon, surely? And it will keep Lisette tranquil. I do have her welfare at heart. When she is cooped up too long she can be difficult, as I am sure you have learned.'

'Amelia will find it upsetting. And Adam will not approve of the fact that you have come to Trevowan against his father's wishes.' Elspeth sniffed to convey her own disapproval also. She considered calling Isaac Nance to have Etienne forcibly removed from the estate, but such a scene would be distasteful to her. She sucked in her cheeks and considered him balefully. 'Do you intend to take a house and for Lisette to live with you? William would disapprove of that. He was most emphatic that she should remain at Trevowan until his return.'

Etienne heaved a dramatic sigh. 'Dear Aunt Elspeth, why is it that your family considers me such an ogre? Lisette's place is with her husband – when he returns.'

'You forced her to marry a libertine then later abandoned her and your mother in a convent,' Elspeth accused. 'Why should we trust you now?'

'How callous you make it sound. Both of them were ill. Maman had been struck with palsy and Lisette had begun to show signs of the affliction which later compelled you to commit her to an asylum. And I did not force her into any marriage. She wanted to marry the Marquis de Gramont. It gave her entry to Versailles and a life of luxury.'

'Lisette says otherwise.'

Etienne spread his hands. 'If I had treated her so badly, would she now be avid for my company? Lisette simply told you what she thought you wanted to hear. She was scarcely rational after that ordeal in the château when her husband was murdered by the rabble.' He placed one hand over his heart, his expression contrite. 'You cannot imagine how horrendous it was to live

198

through the years of the Terror. Even now fear governs people's lives. No one is safe from Madame Guillotine. She is hungry for traitors against the new regime and no one is safe.'

'You have turned your coat when it suited you, Etienne.' Elspeth had no sympathy for him. He had committed an unforgivable sin in her eyes by abandoning his family and seeking his own glory with the revolutionaries of France.

His eyes flashed with anger. 'You do not know the circumstances or how it feels to live in constant fear. Your life has been pampered, sheltered and protected.'

'For that I was daily grateful to my dear brother. He knew the value of family loyalty. Unlike you. Your dear father must be turning in his grave at your actions in recent years. He was an honourable man.' Her stare swept over him in scathing condemnation. 'I do not trust you to give Lisette the care she needs.'

His face turned puce and he looked as though he could throttle her. Elspeth pulled herself up straighter.

Etienne bit back a tart retort. The old lady was a termagant, stalwart and indomitable. A battle of wills would only make her more stubborn and she could yet call the male servants to have him thrown ignominiously from the house. Then he would be unable to see Lisette. He forced an ingratiating smile. 'I understand how you might distrust me – not knowing the full story of my life these last years in France. But sometimes a man must put his country before his family. That too can be the act of an honourable man.'

She did not answer and continued to look unimpressed, so that he hurried on. 'Was not the convent the best place for my mother and sister at the time? I could not protect them as I would wish, I was in danger myself.'

He made it all sound very plausible, but Etienne had always been sly. Elspeth did not trust him. But what was she to do? Was it even right to prevent Lisette from seeing her brother? It would be a relief to be free from her for an hour or so. Lisette's moods remained unstable and erratic. The family needed peace while it mourned Edward, not the constant disruptions her wilfulness caused.

Elspeth did not like disregarding Edward's wishes, but Etienne had exercised control over his sister when they were younger. 'You must assure me that while she is in your company Lisette will do nothing to bring disrepute upon her husband, or break the mourning of our family?'

'I ask only that I accompany her on a ride two or three times a week. Is that so disrespectful?'

'Each ride will last no longer than two hours,' Elspeth reluctantly conceded. 'You might as well know now that Lisette's money is held in her husband's account. She receives a small allowance each month for her needs. Now that Edward is no longer Lisette's guardian, only William has access to her money.'

'I call upon my sister out of duty and love, not for her money.' He did not flinch from her piercing regard, although anger flared within him at the information. Lisette had not mentioned she was no longer in control of her own money.

'So long as we understand each other, Etienne.'

'I am ready,' his sister called, standing in the doorway.

'Two hours – no more – or the rides will not be permitted,' Elspeth declared. She then ordered Bracken saddled and rode to Trevowan Hard to discuss Etienne's visit with her nephew.

Lisette was in high spirits as they trotted away from the house. 'Where shall we ride? You should have brought a carriage and then we could have spent the night in Bodmin or Truro and attended the Assembly Rooms.'

'You are too well known for that to be possible. Society would not condone your being seen in public so soon after Edward's death.'

'I do not care what society thinks. Can we not go to London? You could make your fortune there.'

'All in good time, my sweet. You also have family in London. I have no wish to cross swords with Thomas Mercer if he learned you were in London.'

'They are too involved in Japhet's appeal to care what I do.' She remained defiant, and her high colour warned Etienne she would not be easy to persuade to his bidding. She was still wary of him. He needed her more completely under his control and willing to obey his every wish without question.

'You underestimate your cousins. I do not.' He winked, intimating a conspiracy. 'The time is not yet right for us to make a life of our own.'

'But if we do not leave Cornwall soon, William will return. Then I shall be trapped.'

He laughed. '*Ma chérie*, we are more than a match for that old man. In the meantime we have each other. We will ride to the moor. It is a glorious day and there we will find a secluded place where we can make love.'

Adam was appalled to realise how much was involved in running the estate and the yard, and amazed that his father had managed both for so long on his own. Now he would have no choice but to hire a sea captain for *Pegasus*'s next voyage, and for that he must travel to Falmouth. Once there he would also find a ship bound for Virginia to deliver a letter to St John who must now return to take up his duties in Cornwall.

First, he had to ensure that a schedule of works for the yard and estate was drawn up. There were also the necessary renovations to be completed on the house at Boscabel. The old rivalry with his twin was returning. If St John was Master of Trevowan then Adam wanted his own house and estate habitable as soon as possible.

He ground his teeth in frustration. He did not relish the prospect of his twin's return. It would stick in his throat to see St John lording it at Trevowan.

He was in the office surrounded by paperwork when Elspeth strode in.

'Etienne has taken Lisette riding,' she burst out without a greeting. 'The young coxcomb ignored Edward's orders to stay away from Trevowan. Perhaps I should have had him thrown out, but it would have put Lisette in a taking. Amelia is overset enough as it is. This morning she threatened to have Lisette locked in her room when the girl threw a tantrum at breakfast.'

'Amelia has enough to contend with.' Adam suppressed his own unease at Etienne's actions. He was not entirely surprised for Etienne and Lisette had been whispering together throughout the funeral supper. 'I have enough to deal with without taking on the role of guardian to Lisette. She may behave better if she spends time with her brother. Though I do not like the notion, nor do I trust him.'

'I've told him Lisette's money is in William's charge. I thought I would put him straight on that at least. And I've insisted that he sees Lisette for no more than two hours.'

'As long as she remains at Trevowan that is the best we can do for William. She is housed and fed. I am not the keeper of her morals. Etienne is her brother after all. At least if he keeps her amused life will be more peaceful for you at home. When the fleet returns Uncle William can decide what is best for his wife. St John will not want her at Trevowan. He has no patience with her hysterics and moods.'

'Your father took such responsibilities more seriously.'

'I am not my father.' Adam groaned and sank his head into his hands, then rubbed them over the back of his neck. 'I miss Papa. Dear God, I wish he was here.'

Elspeth's stern visage crumpled and she put a hand on her nephew's shoulder in a rare show of emotion. 'I know. We all miss him. But your shoulders are broad and strong. If any son can stand in his father's shoes, it is you, Adam.'

Chapter Eighteen

Following Edward's death Tamasine was inconsolable. Her fire and vivacity left her and she became quiet and reclusive.

Senara sat on the side of her bed where Tamasine lay staring bleakly up at the ceiling. She had been crying all morning. 'You have a place with Adam and me for as long as you need it. Adam will never turn his back on you,' Senara promised her.

'But I am one more onerous responsibility for him and he has enough to deal with. You were telling him only last night that he will make himself ill if he continues to drive himself so hard.'

'That has nothing to do with you. You are not a burden. We enjoy your company. You help so much with the children that I could not continue to tend the sick without you.'

'I do not mean to be ungrateful but you are very busy, and Bridie has her teaching now. I feel so useless. That did not seem to matter when Mr Loveday was alive.' Tamasine raised her arm to cover her eyes. 'Just knowing I had a father, and that he was near and delighted in my company for an hour a day, made some sense of my life.'

Senara took Tamasine's hand from her face. 'That is your grief talking. It is only natural you feel such a loss. But we are still your family.'

'Yet my presence has caused a rift between Adam and Amelia. She refuses to see him when he visits Trevowan.' Silent tears streamed down Tamasine's cheeks. 'She will not forgive him. She did not forgive her own husband for allowing me to stay here.'

'That is Amelia's short-sightedness. Adam does his duty by the estate and Isaac Nance is a competent bailiff. Adam is more concerned about finishing the brigantine on time and his need to visit Falmouth.'

Tamasine did not respond, neither would she meet Senara's gaze. 'There are no school lessons until the end of the harvesting,' Senara added. 'Why do you not walk over to visit Bridie? You could help her with her work at Trewenna church. Edward would not want you to mope in this manner. It is a glorious sunny day, you should be out in the sunshine. And you could pick me some wildflowers for the parlour.'

To Senara's relief Tamasine swung her legs from the bed. 'I will visit Bridie. She seemed uneasy at going to Trewenna now Peter Loveday lives there without his parents which is strange. I thought she rather liked him.'

'Has Peter tried anything untoward with her?' Senara was alarmed.

'He is a preacher. How could you think that?' Tamasine's jaw dropped in astonishment.

'He is a man, and has shown an uncommon interest in her. A young innocent woman is vulnerable to unwanted attentions from men. It is something you should always be aware of.'

Her fears for Bridie remained, but Senara hoped that her sister's reluctance to go to Trewenna was because she was no longer captivated by Peter. She desperately hoped this was the case. He was too serious for her and too much of a religious zealot to accept that Bridie was less fervent in her own beliefs.

Even so, Senara could not convince herself that Peter did not nurse an undue fondness for Bridie. Her sister had told her that he had apologised to her after they had quarrelled, and that he had given her the gift of a book of poetry. That disturbed Senara; poetry was something to be pondered upon and savoured. It showed the sensual side of Peter, a side he usually suppressed. Senara knew that to repress one's true nature could often lead to dangerous fixations and obsessions.

Tamasine looked troubled. 'Are all young men not to be trusted? There must be some good men. Like Adam.'

Senara smiled. 'Adam was very persistent in his courtship, but I was aware of the social division between us. I was his mistress before we married. And before you go getting any romanticised ideas, a relationship like ours is rare. Any girl who gives herself to a man out of wedlock is more likely to end up with a child, abandoned and left to make her living on the streets.'

'I will never give myself to a man until our wedding night. I know what it means to be an unwanted child.'

'Do you think of your life in those terms? You were wanted. Your mother loved you, and if she had not been so proud and had told Edward of your existence, he would have brought you to Trevowan, I am sure of that. You were a child born in love – not lust.' Aware of the moral responsibilities she had towards the girl, and the trust that Edward had placed in her, Senara added, 'Edward wanted you married, secure and happy. A man is weak in his lust, it is for the woman to be strong. Save yourself for marriage, Tamasine. It is what he would expect from you.'

'It is the least I can do. I have taken the Loveday name and will not shame it.'

Senara prayed that after all the rejections that Tamasine had faced in her life, she would fall in love with a man who would treat her with respect and honour.

As she followed the girl out of the room, and saw her pull back her shoulders in a bid to shake off her misery, a shiver passed down Senara's spine and the hairs on her neck prickled. She gasped, her heart clenching with fear. Let the sensation not be a premonition that Tamasine would be treated badly by a lover. Too often such premonitions of Senara's had been proved right.

When Tamasine joined Bridie and they rode to Trewenna church, she made an effort to shake off her misery but conversation was sparse. Neither of the young women displayed their usual high spirits. Bridie, who normally chatted incessantly, had lapsed into silence, preoccupied with her own thoughts. Yet it was not an uneasy silence, for as in all strong friendships the other's presence was comforting.

The past week had been exceptionally hot. There was not a cloud in the sky and no breeze to cool the relentless heat of the sun. The light muslin of Tamasine's gown stuck damply to her shoulders and the straw bonnet afforded her little respite from the heat. The earth was baked hard and cracked, the grass brown, wildflowers drooping from lack of rain. They rode in the shade of the trees and tethered Hera, who Tamasine had borrowed from Senara, and Hapless the donkey in the shade of the lychgate at Trewenna church. Sun radiated off the tilted gravestones patched with golden lichen.

'It will be cool in the church and I have little work to do,' Bridie said. She looked towards the Rectory, her body tense. Out of duty to Joshua Loveday she had continued to clean the church. She both dreaded and longed for sight of Peter while she worked, and cursed her own foolishness.

'Is aught amiss between you and Peter?' Tamasine asked.

Bridie shook her head. 'There is nothing between Mr Peter Loveday and myself, so how can aught be amiss?'

'You were friends. I thought you liked him.'

'We have never been friends,' Bridie replied firmly.

She was saved from explaining further when two figures sauntered out of the church. One was Peter Loveday, the other a young man Bridie had not seen before.

Tamasine reacted strangely. 'Oh, my, there is Mr Carlton. What can he be doing at Trewenna.'

'You know him?' Bridie whispered.

'I met him when I was out walking.'

Bridie saw the deepening blush on her friend's face and added wryly, 'He is very handsome.'

Rupert Carlton recognised Tamasine and tipped his hat to her.

'Do you two know each other?' Peter observed.

'We have not been formally introduced, but we met on the road one pleasant afternoon,' Rupert replied.

'May I present my late uncle's ward, Miss Tamasine Loveday, and the sister of my cousin Adam's wife, Miss Bridie Polglase.'

Rupert bowed to both women, but the smile in his eyes was for Tamasine. 'This is indeed an unexpected pleasure. I am interested in church carvings and Trewenna has some particularly good ones. Mr Loveday was telling me some of their history. The tomb of Sir Harold Penhaligan is most impressive, though his family no longer live in the district, I hear.'

'My great-grandmother was a Penhaligan but the family died out and the estate was sold to Lord Fetherington,' Peter explained. 'He built his own chapel on his land and does not use Trewenna. There is a branch of the Penhaligan family in Virginia. My cousin St John is visiting them at this moment. I expect he will return soon, now that he is Master of Trevowan.'

'Most of my relatives settled in the colonies. It is my intention to visit them once this war with France is over.' Rupert still could not take his eyes from Tamasine.

His patent interest made Bridie uncomfortable. 'You must excuse us. We are to prepare the church for the service on Sunday.'

Tamasine reluctantly followed her inside. She took the besom from Bridie's hands and vigorously swept the leaves from the aisle while Bridie polished the brass lectern and silver candlesticks and altar cross. The work was done in half the usual time and she was flushed from her exertion.

'There, we are done. I wonder if Mr Carlton is still with Peter?' Tamasine said breathlessly.

Bridie bit her lip. 'It would not be seemly for us to be seen in their company.'

Tamasine paid her no heed, already hurrying out of the church. Bridie followed at a more sedate pace that concealed the worst of her limp. Peter and his visitor were standing by Rupert's horse, tethered in the shade by the Rectory.

When Bridie made to mount Hapless, Tamasine protested, 'Please do not ride off so quickly.'

'You cannot be so forward, Tamasine. We cannot wait around hoping that Mr Carlton will speak with you. It is unseemly.'

'But they are coming over. Please, Bridie, would it not be impolite to ride away?'

Rupert Carlton smiled at the two friends. 'I am staying with Lord Fetherington as my family are currently in London and not expected to return to their estate for several weeks. Will you be attending the ball he is holding next week?'

'Our family is in mourning, sir,' Bridie informed him. 'And besides, I do not mix in such circles and neither does Tamasine.'

'How thoughtless of me not to have realised. A pity. It would be pleasant to become better acquainted.'

'If you are interested in woodcarvings, there are excellent ones at Boscabel,' Tamasine informed him. 'The house is Tudor. I am sure that Mr Adam Loveday would show you round. He has recently purchased the property which was in ruins and lives at Mariner's House at Trevowan Hard until the house is made habitable.'

'I will call upon Mr Loveday, though I would not intrude upon his mourning.' Rupert Carlton bowed to the women. 'Good day.'

Bridie had turned away to lead Hapless to the mounting block and was conscious that Peter had followed her. He held the donkey's bridle while she mounted.

'Have I offended you, Miss Bridie?' he asked.

'Why should you think that?'

He led Hapless behind the yew tree at the side of the lychgate, sheltering them from prying eyes. Alarmed, Bridie gazed back at Tamasine to see her deep in conversation with Rupert Carlton and the pair of them laughing.

'I feel you have been avoiding me.' Peter's manner was serious. 'I called at the cottage and your mother said you were not at home. And once at the shipyard I waved to catch your attention but you did not respond. Did you not like the book of poems?'

'They were beautiful, and I have not been avoiding you. It is merely that I do not feel it is right for us to see too much of each other.' She kept glancing round, aware now that they were out of sight of Tamasine or any of the villagers. She knew she should kick Hapless into a trot and escape Peter for she did not trust him not to try and kiss her again. It was what she feared and wanted most at the same time.

'You are angry that I kissed you.' His voice was now a soft caress. He took an apple from his jacket and fed it to Hapless, an action that would stop the donkey running off, however hard Bridie tried to persuade him. 'I ask your pardon, but I do not regret my action. It would never be repeated without your permission.'

Bridie briefly closed her eyes and swallowed hard before replying, 'How can you, a preacher, talk in such a manner? It is disrespectful.'

'But I mean you no disrespect. Miss Polglase, would you be offended if I asked Adam if I might call upon you at the cottage?'

Her heart pounded erratically. 'People will gossip. With my background I must protect my reputation. I could lose my job at the school if Mrs Loveday thought I had behaved in an improper manner.'

Peter smiled. 'There would be nothing improper if I were to call upon my fiancée. I have been offered the living of Polruggan church. The income is modest but it is sufficient and the Rectory is a fine home.' He knelt on one knee and took her hand. 'Miss Polglase, will you do me the honour of becoming my wife?'

Bridie almost swooned with shock. She could not have heard him aright. But he was still kneeling before her, his expression earnest. Her throat was too dry for her to speak.

He stood up, his manner abrupt. 'I see I have spoken out of turn. You are offended.'

'No, how could I be offended? But why would you wish to marry me? A parson needs a wife who upholds all his religious views. You know that mine are very different from your own.'

'You are a lost sheep I would return to the fold, but I would also cherish you to the end of my days. You do not have to answer me now. Please consider my proposal.'

Love overrode her nagging feeling that their differences were a major hindrance to true happiness. 'I will marry you, Peter, but can you accept that my views may remain different from yours?'

'I will talk to Adam and arrangements will be made after a decent period of mourning for my uncle. I take up my post at Polruggan in November. Now we must return to Miss Loveday and Mr Carlton, they have been too long unchaperoned. Adam would be angry if Miss Loveday's reputation were to be jeopardised.'

He clearly did not view Bridie's reputation as being in any danger when he had led her to a secluded spot. But his intentions had been honourable enough and she chose to forget that he had not directly answered her question.

Tamasine did not stop talking about how handsome and charming Rupert Carlton was throughout the journey home. Bridie rode in silence unable to stop a broad smile from settling on her face. Finally Tamasine stopped talking about Rupert Carlton to say, 'What is so amusing? And I noticed you and Peter managed to slip away to be alone. Why was that?'

'He asked me to marry him and I accepted. Of course we must have the permission of the Loveday family.'

Tamasine squealed in delight. 'How could you have let me ramble on so? You must be overjoyed.'

'I am, but the family may not feel the same.'

'You two love each other, that is enough.' Tamasine giggled. 'It is so romantic.'

'We must say nothing until Peter calls upon Adam, and he is away at present.' Bridie was visibly anxious. 'He may not approve. And Senara and my mother have little liking for Peter's religious zeal.'

The harvest had been brought in at Trevowan and Adam had returned from a four-day visit to Falmouth where he had engaged a captain and crew for *Pegasus*. He had also attended a meeting with his agents in the port, who had bought the next cargo of furniture and cloth to be transported to his customers in Virginia. The letter Adam had written to St John informing him of their father's death had been taken to Plymouth by a servant, but no ships were sailing to Virginia until after *Pegasus* was due to sail so her captain would take the letter. *Pegasus* would return with a cargo of tobacco and St John could also take passage on her return voyage. It would be winter before he arrived at Trevowan.

Adam was feeling the strain of dividing his time between overseeing work at Trevowan, Boscabel and the shipyard. Twice Peter had called at Mariner's House while he was away and Senara had said he would call again this morning, but Adam had more pressing matters to attend to than hearing lectures from his cousin. He had left the yard early in order to be at Trevowan to pay the farm workers and servants' wages. On Edward's death money earned from the estate and shipyard had to be kept separate. The bank manager in Bodmin was dealing with separating their finances into two separate new accounts in St John's and Adam's names. Fortunately, the repayment of the Loveday money that had been lost in the bad investments made by cousin Thomas's father had paid off the debts on the yard. There was a small mortgage left on the estate, which St John could choose to pay off from money received from this year's harvest. There would certainly be none left in the coffers to support his passion for gaming.

The finances of the shipyard now depended on the successful delivery of the brigantine due for completion next month. There were scant reserves in the shipyard's coffers either and as Adam intended to buy some livestock for Boscabel the winter ahead would be a time to tighten their belts a little, with no cash for anything other than bare essentials.

He was in his father's study. As Isaac Nance read out the name of each farm worker and the amount due to them, Adam counted out the coins and the worker made his mark in the ledger. When the wages were paid, Adam studied the accounts. Feed would be needed for the cattle and horses during the winter. He had to make decisions now as to what crops should be planted to be harvested in the spring, and what cattle and sheep were to be sent to market. He doubted that any decision he made would please his twin.

A commotion from the hall outside the study made Adam frown. Then to his astonishment Captain William Loveday, in wig and full naval uniform, strode into the room. He looked distraught.

'I hired a skiff to bring me from Plymouth to Penruan and have just learned from the Reverend Mr Snell of Edward's death. I cannot believe it is possible! Snell said Edward had been shot.'

Adam dismissed Isaac Nance and took a brandy decanter from a cupboard, pouring two glasses as he explained the full circumstances of Edward's death and recent events within the family. William took several minutes to regain his composure as Adam went on to tell him of his own capture by the French and Japhet's arrest. His uncle refilled his brandy glass.

'So many ills have afflicted the family. Your ordeal must have been terrible and Japhet's still continues. But this news of Edward has shocked me.' His eyes were glazed with pain. 'My brother took much upon his shoulders. My own indebtedness to him is immeasurable.'

They had been talking for some considerable time before Adam realised that William had not mentioned Lisette.

'You will be wishing to see your wife? Unfortunately she is not here at the moment,' he said. 'Etienne is in England. That is another long story we can talk of later. He takes her riding two or three times a week. They seem to have resolved their differences.'

'Has she caused any trouble? My marriage must have been a shock to Edward. I had no choice but to sail two days later with the fleet. I had not realised Lisette could be so headstrong. When she arrived so unexpectedly in Plymouth, I married her before I sailed to spare her reputation.' His voice was strained and Adam suspected that his uncle regretted his hasty marriage. 'I have several weeks' leave while my ship is repaired. I will relieve you of the responsibility of her. We shall take lodgings in Plymouth.'

'It was necessary for Lisette to receive some treatment in London,' Adam explained. 'She was greatly disturbed in the early months you were away. She spent several months under the care of Dr Claver in an asylum. I am sorry to be so brutal with the facts, but I know little of the circumstances as I was at sea at the time. But you must stay here. Father would have expected it. St John will not return from Virginia for some months.'

William nodded. 'I will use my leave to find accommodation for Lisette. She is not St John's or your responsibility. She can be difficult. Edward warned me that her moods could be unstable though I never saw it in her before we were wed. Lisette was always so sweet and gentle towards me, and seemed so desperate to be loved. But I glimpsed something of that instability in Plymouth.'

The weariness in his voice disturbed Adam and he wanted to reassure his uncle. 'She seems stable enough at the moment. Since Etienne's return she has been easier to manage, but as her closest family some of the responsibility for her welfare is now his. I hope we did right in allowing his visits?'

'I trust your judgement.' William pushed back his chair to rise. 'I should make my condolences to Amelia and speak with Elspeth.'

'Amelia has moved to the Dower House – another complicated story which you will learn of soon enough. Richard is also here on leave and is comforting her.' Adam sighed and rubbed his temples. 'Elspeth is currently visiting Hannah. Japhet had bought a couple of mares before his marriage and stabled them at the

212

farm. Both have foaled, and you know Elspeth and horses – she seems to prefer them to people.'

Adam poured them both another brandy and answered his uncle's questions about his young family. Then his own curiosity at his uncle's unexpected appearance prompted him to ask, 'How is it you have returned to Plymouth? The fleet was not expected back.'

'Two days of storms brought down the mizzenmast and it splintered most of the fo'castle. Three men were killed.' William made light of what must have been a dangerous time on board. 'During the same storm another ship caught fire when the galley fire had not been properly extinguished. The ship could not be saved and we brought back the men who had been badly injured. Some were so bad they did not survive the voyage.'

'Shortly after I returned in June there was news that Lord Howe had engaged the French fleet off Ushant. Were you involved in the battle?'

'We trounced the French that day, then sailed on to Gibraltar.' William rose to pace the room, staring out towards the sea and his voice became distracted as he went on, 'The storm hit before I could engage in further action.'

'I would hear more at another time. You must dine at Mariner's House.'

'I thought Amelia had accepted your marriage to Senara and that your wife was welcome here?'

'She has, but Amelia does not approve of my current actions concerning Father's ward.'

William raised a questioning brow. 'Which ward is this?'

'There is much family news for you to catch up on, I fear. This will come as another shock for you. I have a half-sister who will be sixteen in a few weeks, and I promised Father I would protect her until she marries. Amelia will not acknowledge her.'

William choked on his brandy. 'Edward has a daughter of sixteen! Did I hear you aright?'

'Yes.'

'I would never have thought it of him.' He shook his head. 'You never really know someone. But then, I have been at sea for most of the last thirty years.'

213

'The family has increased since you sailed.' Adam changed the subject to a happier one. 'Rafe has a sister, Joan. And I am now the father of twins. A boy and a girl.'

'Another generation of twins, that is good news and the birth of Joan, of course.' He turned his head towards the sound of high-pitched laughter accompanied by a man speaking French.

William stood up, his manner becoming stiff. Adam went into the hall to call to Lisette. Etienne had his arm around her waist and she was leaning against him and giggling, her face flushed and her hair in disarray.

'Lisette, William has returned,' Adam announced, surprised that his uncle had not followed him from the study.

Belatedly, William came to his side. The laughter faded and Lisette's head shot up. For a moment there was horror in her eyes as she regarded her husband. Then quickly it was replaced by a strained smile. 'William, my darling husband! Your Lisette has missed you so much.'

She ran and threw her arms around him. William had never been at ease with displays of emotion and recoiled from her touch; his voice was icy as he addressed her. 'Madam, I trust you are well. Such a display of emotion is unseemly. Have you learned no decorum?'

Adam was startled at his uncle's tone and, when he looked at Etienne, his cousin was glaring at William as though he would kill him.

Chapter Nineteen

'I must urge you to listen to reason, Peter.' Joshua Loveday regarded his son who was pacing the small parlour of Trewenna Rectory. 'Marriage is a difficult step for a parson. Your stipend will barely keep you, let alone a wife and the inevitable family.'

'Bridie will have a dowry, Adam told her so.'

'Perhaps that is true, but he now has the full responsibility of the yard on his shoulders. Is that yet free from debt? Unlike Edward, Adam has no income from an estate to help pay the yard's debts. How can he give Bridie a dowry at this time?' Joshua had returned from London last night and been shocked to hear of Peter's desire to marry, especially to so young a bride.

'Then he can defer the payment in some manner.' Peter remained stubborn.

Joshua sat back in his chair and tapped the ends of his fingers together. 'It would be wise to wait another year or so. And delightful as Bridie is, are you sure she is the right woman to take on the duties of a parson's wife? She is much like her sister in her beliefs, and they are far from orthodox.'

'That will change when we are wed.' Peter was confident that he would hold sway over Bridie in such matters. 'Because she is young, her mind can be moulded to fit her for her new role. And I am not averse to her using her skills with herbs when tending the sick of my parish.'

'But has she not recently become schoolmistress at Trevowan Hard? Though the income from her teaching will not go amiss. A parson is hard put to survive on his stipend.' Joshua could see many pitfalls ahead for the couple. Their natures were very different. Peter could be dour at times and Bridie was always so

215

carefree and full of laughter. But then, that could be what his son needed. And it was true that her caring nature would be of benefit to their parishioners. Peter would take his duties as parson too seriously, if he were not careful. Opposites often did attract ... but Joshua was still not convinced the union would be happy.

'Bridie will have new duties as my wife. I would prefer she did not teach, but she is determined upon it. For now, I have agreed.' Peter clasped his hands behind his back and stood rigid and unbending. 'I see no cause for delay. A parson should have a wife. Parochial duties are far-reaching. Could you have handled them without the help of Mama?'

'Your mama was some years older than Bridie when we wed, and she was a parson's daughter and knew exactly what those duties entailed. It is a hard and selfless life.' Joshua dabbed a kerchief across his temple.

Cecily had sat in the corner by the hearth, biting her lip so as to remain silent throughout the conversation. She was delighted that Peter had decided to settle down and marry. A wife would have a steadying influence on him, for though he had shown none of Japhet's interest in womanising and gambling, she had seen how young women eyed him. A man was but a man, and she guessed he had inherited the same passionate nature as his father and brother. It was better for him to be wed than for Peter to fall prey to his desires in an inappropriate manner. But Bridie! Was she the right choice of wife? She was diligent and content to serve others, as her work with Senara had shown, but in the last year Cecily had seen a change in the girl. She had become a confident young woman with a strong determined manner.

Joshua glanced across at her and raised one eyebrow, inviting her opinion. Cecily said, 'Your father is right. Bridie is young and you hardly know each other. If you care for each other there is time aplenty for marriage. And how can we rejoice at your wedding when such a terrible sentence hangs over your brother's head?'

Peter clipped back a tart retort concerning his brother's fate. His mother had been distraught when they had spoken of Japhet's ordeal. Cecily feared she would never see her eldest son alive again.

'Japhet is constantly in my prayers, but the wages of sin ...' He broke off abruptly at the fury glittering in his father's eyes, but his tone was accusing when he added, 'I would have thought you would be pleased that I wed so much younger than my brother. You urged him for years to take a bride.'

He turned to his father. 'Do I have your blessing, sir?'

Joshua's hesitation was brief. 'A parson should have a wife. Bridie is a good choice. You have my blessing, though I urge you to wait.'

Peter did not want to wait to make Bridie his wife. The sooner he could save her from her heathenish practices the better it would be.

Adam drove the shipyard wagon to market at Launceston, leaving the yard shortly after dawn. Earlier in the week he had selected the lambs and cattle that would be sent to market. To build up the Trevowan flock and herd, he kept the ewe lambs and heifers unless they were unfit for breeding. The rest would be sold for slaughter. Isaac Nance had been in charge of driving the stock with two other farmhands and they had left the previous morning. Adam would join Nance at the pens in Launceston market. It was a day he could ill afford to spend away from the yard. His customer was expecting the brigantine to be finished in a week and a crew would arrive to sail her to Falmouth. There were all the small details to be checked and her sea trials to be undertaken to ensure that the brigantine performed all her manoeuvres perfectly.

Adam arrived at the market after the sale of the sheep but before the cattle had been sold. He was hot and dusty from his ride, the sun beating down without compassion from a cloudless azure sky. Hordes of flies buzzed around the cattle pens and the smell of animal excrement was overpowering.

Isaac Nance handed over to Adam a pouch of money from the sale of the sheep. 'Unfortunately, we didn't get the best price. The market is full today. Let's hope we do better with the cattle.'

'How much did the sheep bring in?'

'Twenty pounds. We should get thirty for the cattle.'

'Perhaps we kept too many back?' Adam frowned. 'I doubt my

brother will be happy with so small an amount.'

'You've almost doubled the size of the sheep flock and those dozen extra dairy cows will bring Master St John a good profit in the coming year.' Nance whistled the words through the gap from his missing front teeth. 'He'll need to take on an extra dairymaid, though, but she can help out in the house too. There be extra work for the maids now that Mrs Loveday is in residence in the Dower House.'

Adam nodded. 'How long before you are finished here, Isaac?'

'Another hour, sir.'

'Meet me in the tavern and then I will pay the money into the bank. I've some business of my own to deal with first.'

He left the market square, walking through the flocks of geese that honked incessantly and tried to nip anyone incautious enough to get too close to them. A goatherd had a dozen kids tethered to a post and chickens in wooden cages were stacked in piles.

Although his finances were tight, Adam was determined to buy stock for Boscabel. Once the brigantine was finished, there was two months' work at the yard from two ships coming into the dry-dock for minor repairs and their keels overhauled. The keel for another brigantine was due to be laid down but he had not yet received the initial payment for work to begin. The owner lived in Looe and Adam would visit him before he returned to Trevowan Hard. With the lull in work at the yard, he had put some of the carpenters to work on the house at Boscabel, and other men had turned their hand to repairing the walls and roofs of the outbuild-ings. Six pig pens were now able to be used and the cow byre and one of the four tied cottages on the Boscabel estate was again fit for habitation.

Adam inspected the stock of beef heifers and purchased fifteen. Sir Henry Traherne had offered his bull to service them. He also selected twenty ewes and a ram, and six sows also to be served by Sir Henry's boar until Adam had his stock established. He also bought seed for two fields to be sown with corn. The blacksmith at the shipyard had repaired the broken plough at Boscabel and he would use the yard shire horses – which were normally used to move the timber logs – to plough his land.

He then went to the corner of the market where servants offered themselves for hire. A dozen men and women stood waiting forlornly. It was now late in the morning and the best of the workers had already found employment. One of the men looked familiar. It was not until Adam drew closer that he saw that the man's left arm ended in a metal hook where he had lost his hand.

'It is Billy Brown, isn't it?' he said. The man was in his early twenties with a close-cut beard, wiry body, wide shoulders and heavy thighs.

'Aye, Cap'n Loveday. I were cabin boy, serving on *HMS Goliath* when you were midshipman. I heard you'd made Lieutenant then got yourself cashiered for duelling. I also heard you had your own ship. This bain't the usual place a captain would look for a crew?'

Adam laughed. 'No, I get mine from the docks. I am looking for farm workers. I have recently purchased an estate. It was neglected for many years and there is much work to be done before the house can be lived in. It is time the land paid its way.'

'I may have lost me hand, but I can still work with animals. If you hire me, you won't regret it, Cap'n.' Billy's brown hair flopped over his brow and he brushed it impatiently out of his eye. 'I got a wife, Gilly, over there. She be hardworking.'

Adam turned to the woman who stood behind Billy. She was plump and sturdy-looking, also heavy with child. She gave him a nervous smile.

'How did you lose your hand, Billy?'

'Got it tangled in rigging in a storm. It were mashed to a pulp. I weren't no use to the navy after that, bin doing odd jobs ever since. Now I've got a kid on the way I need work and a house if possible. Even with one hand you know I be a hard worker, Cap'n. I'd not let you down.'

Adam considered for a moment. Eli Rudge had proved he could turn his hand to most work on the estate and Adam would appoint him overseer. The finished cottage was supposed to be for him to live in, instead of the room he had made for himself behind the kitchen of Boscabel House. Until a second cottage was fit for habitation in another month, Rudge would have to stay where he was. Adam needed workers who were versatile. He had liked Billy when they served on *HMS Goliath*. The cabin boy had often been bullied but he had taken his punishment bravely and without complaint.

'Apart from the livestock, can you manage plough horses?'

'I did some ploughing last year for Mrs Rabson, her husband were sick at the time. She were satisfied with my work. When her husband got stronger, she did not need me.'

'Mrs Rabson is my cousin. I will give you and your wife work, Billy. But it will be farm labouring for your wife. I do not yet live on the estate and have no need for servants in the house.'

Gilly bent her knee in an ungainly curtsy. 'I worked on a farm for five years as a dairymaid and in the fields. I bain't much of a housemaid. I'd rather help Billy with the livestock. We need a roof over our head desperately, sir. I bain't afraid of hard work.'

The navy made cripples of many of the men who served in her and most of them lived as beggars afterwards. It was a poor reward for their bravery and the hardship they had suffered. Adam had engaged another former sailor with whom he had served on the same ship. Seth Wakeley had lost his leg, but despite his peg leg as replacement had proved a valuable asset to the yard with his carpentry skills. A man who had a family to feed and who knew that few other men would employ him would be diligent in his service. Billy Brown would be honest and hardworking.

'I have a wagon you can ride in when I return to Boscabel, Mrs Brown. You will be sharing it with six sows. Billy, you can help the men I brought with me from Trevowan to drive the cows home. I now need to employ a shepherd for the new flock I have purchased. Wait for me at the market cross.'

Adam hired a middle-aged shepherd with his own dog. He would have to share the Browns' cottage or sleep over the stable block. He then went to the tavern to meet with Isaac Nance, and took the money to the bank to put into the account for Trevowan. As he left the bank his head pounded with plans for Boscabel. By this time next year the estate should be yielding an income. It would not amount to much but it would be enough to expand the stock and engage more farm workers. Once his fields were ploughed, the horses would be needed for work in the yard, and only then would they be available to plough the fields at

Trevowan. When St John returned he would have to buy his own plough horses for the future. Adam would not overwork his team.

He could ill afford the money he had spent on the stock and worried that they would be struggling to meet the wages through the winter unless more work was found for the yard. That would be his next priority. The yard no longer had the money from Trevowan estate to help it weather a lull. It would take years for Boscabel to be profitable. They would be lean years, but his dreams to make his own estate greater than Trevowan burned through Adam's blood.

It was four months since Japhet's trial and each day his incarceration became harder to endure. Too many of the prisoners who had been tried after him had been hanged, and several times the prison had been cleared of the criminals awaiting transportation who had been taken to the rotting prison hulks on the Thames. Japhet had been spared that indignity only because Gwendolyn continued to pay the high bribes demanded by his guards.

Thomas visited him regularly, bringing fresh clothes and word of the family. Japhet had taken the news of Edward's death hard. It added to his guilt for the shame his selfish and hedonistic lifestyle had brought on his family. His uncle, who he respected and admired, had struggled to run the estate and yard with Adam and St John away. If Japhet had not allowed his own pride to drive him from Cornwall and into the disastrous course of events that had led to his arrest, he could have done the decent thing and offered Edward Loveday his help. Edward had paid his debts in the past and provided him with a good education. He could not forgive himself for failing his uncle.

His father had visited last week on the eve of his parents' return to Cornwall. 'I have neglected my parishioners for too long. I will lose my stipend if I do not return. Our thoughts and prayers are always with you, my son. Sir Gregory Kilmarthen will prove your innocence, in that I trust.'

Japhet knew it was impractical for his parents to remain in London but his father's visits had been a great comfort to him. They had become closer than they had been in years and Joshua had never delivered any recriminations for his wild ways.

It would have been all too easy to spend every day in the Association Room drinking himself into a stupor to forget the horrors that could await him in the future. But Japhet had decided he would remain sober. Some of his old acquaintances might visit unexpectedly and Newgate had always been a source of entertainment for outsiders viewing the inmates. Japhet would not further shame Gwen or his family by appearing before them drunk.

He had stayed in his cell this morning and was wearing the clean shirt and suit of clothes that Thomas had brought in yesterday. He had shaved and tied his hair back. Thomas had told him that Gwen would visit him today and no one had been able to dissuade her. When Japhet had demanded that Thomas stop his wife from visiting the prison, his cousin had shaken his head.

'You must see her, Japhet. She has been working hard to prove your innocence and has even placed herself in danger. That was before Long Tom offered his services, but Gwendolyn is making herself ill with worry over you.'

'And seeing me shackled, and witnessing the deprivation and squalor of this hell-pit, will ease her mind?'

'I will bring her myself and leave you two alone together. She will be protected from the worst of the sights, I promise you.'

'I want to see her, but I could not bear her distress. She has suffered enough because of me.'

Thomas had nodded in sympathy but remained adamant. 'You must see her. She is stronger than you think and a very courageous lady. Our family has come to love her very much.'

The door to his cell stood open and Japhet sat on his bed, his nerves taut at the prospect of seeing Gwendolyn again. He had not believed it was possible to miss someone so much. The light tread of a woman's footsteps in the corridor brought him to his feet and he grimaced at the jangle of iron made by his shackles. No amount of bribery could persuade the turnkey to unlock his fetters.

The freshness of Gwen's lemon and rose perfume accompanied her entrance to his cell. She stood hesitantly in the doorway, her blue taffeta cloak billowing around her and the hood pulled low over her eyes. Beneath it she wore a black silk mask to conceal her identity. The scent of her perfume filled the cell and his throat dried with desire. With a sob she threw herself into his arms and returned his kiss passionately.

'Japhet, my darling! I have missed you so much.'

'I love you, Gwen. You are always in my thoughts and dreams.' He held her close, drinking in the sweetness of her scent and body. His own responded to her warmth with desire. He had not had a woman since their wedding. He would not use the whores within the prison. 'I've missed you more than I thought it possible to miss anyone. Yet you should not have come. I have failed you in the basest manner.'

She put one finger, covered in a black lace glove, to his lips. 'Never say that.'

He pulled her hard against him, their kisses wild and abandoned, and both were breathless when they broke apart. Japhet was conscious of the chains upon his wrists as his hands fell away from her. She was gazing into his eyes, her expression so filled with love that Japhet was almost unmanned. He blinked rapidly to dispel his own tears and, inwardly cursing the rattle of chains that accompanied his every movement, lifted back her hood and removed her mask.

'You are more beautiful each time I see you.' Even the dark circles beneath her eyes could not mar her loveliness for him. 'What a fool I've been, Gwen! If only I could have seen the riches in your love that were there for me in Cornwall.'

Thomas appeared briefly at the door. 'I will await Gwendolyn outside in the corridor. You have an hour together.' He pulled the door shut, giving the couple the first privacy they had had together since their wedding.

Japhet untied the fastening of Gwendolyn's cloak and threw it over the end of the bed. 'An hour of your company is more than I deserve, my sweet love.

Gwendolyn sank on to the bed but Japhet pulled back, gallantly declaring, 'I want you so much, but this is no place for us to make love. You deserve better.'

She shook her head. 'I do not care. This hour is precious.'

She kissed him with such thoroughness he could not refuse her and the passion of their lovemaking after months of deprivation left them replete and exhausted. Gwendolyn lay in his arms until, aware that most of the hour had passed, she rose reluctantly and adjusted her clothing. 'There is much we must speak of,' she said between kisses. 'Have you noticed anything different about me?'

'Have I not spent every minute since your arrival lavishing compliments on you?' he answered with a chuckle. 'There is no woman to hold a candle to you, Gwen.'

'I was not searching for compliments.' Her eyes danced with pleasure. 'Japhet, you are to become a father. Is that not wonderful? The child will be born in January. That was why I had to see you. I would not allow Thomas or Joshua to tell you the news only a wife should give to her husband.'

'The news delights me.' He kissed Gwen with renewed passion, but his pleasure was tinged with fear for her. If his innocence could not be proved and he obtained no pardon, the child would be brought up without knowing its father. And a child would make life so much harder for Gwen.

'You will be pardoned,' she said, as though she had guessed his thoughts. 'My godfather will put your case to the King once we have the evidence. Lord Sefton may yet be persuaded to speak out against Celestine Yorke. He is suspicious that she kept the necklace so long before it was returned. He feels she used him to get revenge upon you.'

She broke off as anger consumed her at the way Celestine Yorke had betrayed Japhet. Gwen had forgiven him long ago for the pain his affair with the actress had caused her, but she could not forgive the woman who had reduced him to this. She took a calming breath before continuing, 'Lord Sefton has become disenchanted by her greed. He has admitted that on reflection the man who robbed his coach was shorter in build than you, and the highwayman's mount was not Sheba but a winded nag. Sir Marcus Grundy will also give a statement that he has no proof the stock pin was ever in your possession. Mrs Yorke has angered him by her greed for more jewels. She tried to blackmail him and also Lord Sefton to extort more money.'

'But will their evidence be enough? I was also condemned on Osgood's evidence that I robbed his coach.'

The happiness faded from Gwendolyn's face. 'He hates you because Mrs Yorke gave you her favours freely whilst he paid out a fortune to keep her in his bed. He is still besotted with her, and though she flaunts her other lovers, he will not give her up. It is Mrs Yorke's own evidence that we must repudiate next. She must be put on trial for her crimes, and her evidence against you discounted.'

Japhet frowned. Gwendolyn sounded so full of anger and hatred for the actress when she was usually such a gentle and forgiving woman. 'You must not let the pain I caused you by my foolish liaison justify your bringing false evidence against her.'

'You would defend her lies!' Gwen stood up, her eyes filled with pain. 'You did love her?'

'That is nonsense and you know it. She is capable of great malice, but is my freedom worth another person being hanged? That does not sit comfortably with me.'

'But she is a thief and a liar, and has brought many men to ruin. She does not deserve to escape justice.'

'Every man who fell prey to her charms and her greed has only himself to blame. They chose to pursue her for their own ends. In that respect I was equally guilty. Mrs Yorke was a diversion that enabled me to salvage my wounded pride.'

The hurt in his wife's eyes made him reach for her and draw her close. 'I was a reckless and arrogant fool. Mrs Yorke was everything that you are not. She is the devil's handmaiden while you are an angel. Only by becoming entangled in her web of deceit did I realise how much I had lost by rendering myself unworthy of your love.'

'My mother is to blame for that. I will never forgive her for the cruel words she spoke to you.'

'The Lady Anne's assassination of my character wounded my pride but the wild and reckless manner in which I rebelled against her words only served to prove her judgement right. If I am pardoned, you will have my eternal devotion and will never again regret our marriage.'

'I do not regret it now.'

He wiped the tears from her cheeks with his kisses. 'I do love you, Gwen. You are the only woman I have ever loved.'

A rap on the door reminded them that their hour together was over.

'You will get your pardon, Japhet,' his wife declared. 'You will be a free man before your child is born.'

Her faith was reassuring, but Japhet had heard many stories in the prison from men who professed they were innocent, and all of them had awaited the hangman's noose or transportation. After Gwen had left he stared around the dank walls of his cell where one corner by the window was slimy with green moss. The feeble light penetrating the bars was depressing. Japhet could not rid himself of the feeling that Lady Luck had given him the greatest prize he had ever won in his marriage to Gwen, and then snatched it away in order to mock him.

Chapter Twenty

William despaired of his marriage and longed once again to escape to sea, but he could not expect Adam to take on the responsibility of Lisette. Etienne had been antagonistic, demanding that his sister live with him when William rejoined the fleet. If only he trusted Etienne it would have been a tempting offer. It was his brother-in-law's insistence that he should be in control of Lisette's money that made William uneasy.

It did not help that relations with his wife were strained. He had returned to Trevowan knowing that he must make the best of his marriage, but he could not forget the obscenity of Lisette's behaviour and language on their wedding night. Thomas had sent him a detailed report of her treatment by Dr Claver, and the only way that William could countenance her behaviour was to blame it on her illness, and pray that the treatment had been successful.

In his wife's favour, Lisette was at pains to please him, though he had glimpsed the darker side of her nature again when he refused her request to buy a house in a fashionable district of Truro. She had screamed insults at him and smashed two valuable Chinese vases.

Used to months at sea, William was an abstemious man and more puritanical in his morals than others of his family. Lisette often drank to excess and some of her antics in his bed appalled him. When he showed his distaste she ridiculed him.

He had left their bed this morning after another argument. Lisette's manner was sullen. 'You are a poor lover. Then, the English are so cold and unfeeling. You will never beat the French in this foolish war. You lack our passion in all things.'

He ignored her and went into his dressing room. She followed him, standing naked at the door. 'I do not wish to stay at Trevowan. If you will not buy me a house, I will live with Etienne.'

'Your brother is untrustworthy.'

'You do not understand him. Etienne loves me.'

'He abandoned you in France when you needed him most.' He kept his back to her while he shaved. The mirror's reflection showed her scowling face.

'*Mon Dieu!* How conveniently you forget that your precious Adam abandoned his vows to wed me. When Papa died Etienne wanted to protect me from the troubles that were brewing in Paris. He thought that marriage to the Marquis de Gramont would save me. I do not trust Adam or your family. They locked me up in an asylum. I suffered more at the hands of that fiendish doctor than I did when I was violated in France.'

'My brother did what he thought was best.' William rounded on her. 'Your behaviour had become unacceptable. It was not normal.'

She let forth a stream of invective and, disgusted, he retaliated, 'Such language makes me suspect you are far from cured. Rather than inflict your tantrums on everyone you should be locked away for another cure while I am at sea.'

'I hate you!' She flounced into the bedroom but returned within a few minutes wearing a dressing robe. Her manner was calmer. 'Forgive me, William. I do not mean to be nasty. You are a good man. I am bad because of things I have lived through. I will be a good wife. You are kind, like my papa. He adored me.' She burst into tears.

William could not stand to see a woman cry. Did he judge her too harshly? He had little experience of women. In many ways Lisette was as vulnerable as a child.

'I will rent a cottage for you in a good area of Plymouth if that is what you wish.'

Lisette nestled her head against his shoulder and her petite figure heaved with the force of her sobs. 'I will be a good wife, William. You will be so proud of me if I have my own house and can make new friends.'

He had to trust her, William did not see that he had a choice.

And he also had to trust that Etienne would protect his sister when her husband returned to the fleet.

'We will look at property next week.' He kissed her forehead. 'Now I have said I would visit Squire Penwithick this morning, would you care to accompany me? Mrs Penwithick will enjoy your company.'

'I doubt it. Oh, William, Dorothy Penwithick is so old! I have no young friends.'

'There is Lady Roslyn Traherne.'

'She is so dour, and did not like me when I was a Marquise and outranked her. She can be as critical as Elspeth. Besides, Roslyn and the Lady Anne Druce will have nothing to do with the Lovedays nowadays. They cut off their association with us because of Japhet's trial, and the Lady Anne has washed her hands of her daughter.'

'Then why do you not visit Cousin Hannah at the farm?'

'Hannah is very pleasant, but her children are noisy. I do not like children, and Hannah is always so busy with work on the farm. She turns herself into a peasant and forgets she is a gentlewoman.'

'Hannah is a good wife to Oswald.' He was angered by her snobbery and unkindness. 'They would have lost the farm long ago with him being so ill if Hannah had not worked to save it. Such qualities should not be derided. They are commendable in a wife.'

'One has servants for such work,' Lisette returned. 'And when I have my own house I will need a lady's maid, a cook and a maid of all work.'

'On a captain's pay I can afford but one servant. You must manage accordingly.'

'We can surely afford two servants? There are my jewels. In my château in France there were thirty servants, and another dozen tended the gardens and stables.'

'And you almost paid with your life for such an existence! You cannot squander your money away now. I will be as generous as I can afford. Some of your money can be used for a dress allowance, but it is time you learned to curb your extravagance.'

Lisette stamped her foot. 'You are mean and nasty! You used to be kinder. I thought you loved me, as Papa loved me. He would refuse me nothing.'

'Your father was a wealthy man, not a humble naval captain.'

'I was a fool to wed you.' Her voice started to rise with hysteria.

He turned from her, tired of her complaining. Lisette bit back a tirade of derision and abuse. William could not be wound around her finger as so many men had been in the past. He was a disappointment as a husband. But he could make it difficult for her to see Etienne if she gave in to her true nature. She assumed a false contrition.

'You are so wise, my William. I am but a foolish woman. Papa spoiled me. I am used to having everything I wish. I do try not to demand new clothes or pretty jewels, but it is not easy when they have always been lavished upon me. I like pretty things. Could I not have more of my jewels from the bank to wear? I do like to look pretty for you, William. It is such a waste that those beautiful necklaces and bracelets are hidden away. Do you not think I would look pretty in them?'

He sighed. 'You have been selling the jewellery, that is why it is locked away.'

She pouted and looked crestfallen. 'I sold but one necklace and a bracelet. I had debts to settle. One must honour one's debts, must one not?'

'They were gambling debts, and according to the family you sold several pieces of jewellery.'

'They are gaolers and spies! They lie. I hate them!'

William did not answer and continued to shave. The mirror reflected her rapidly changing expressions. 'Thank God I have Etienne to amuse me. He likes to make me happy. He feels guilty for all I suffered in France and believes he should have done more to ensure I was safe. He loves me. Is that so wrong?'

Her smile was enigmatic before she turned her back on him and flounced back to the bedchamber. His unease at her conduct deepened but he did not believe in regret. He was responsible for the future security of his wife and would no longer rely on his family. That meant he had to trust Etienne. He could see no other way.

After her husband had left to visit the squire, Lisette walked to

Trevowan Cove. The day was overcast and it looked as though it would rain. When the weather was good she would ride with Etienne to a secluded place on the moor where they would make love. On days like this he would not call at the house but they would meet at noon in the cave in Trevowan Cove. They had done so several times before. With William home, Elspeth had stopped spying on Lisette and no one paid much attention to her strolls on the beach.

She reached the cave to find her brother already there. He was angry that he had been kept waiting, but she pulled her dress over her head and was already naked beneath.

'I had to be careful to escape without being seen,' she giggled as she pulled at his clothes.

The danger of their illicit meetings excited Etienne. He was impatient to leave Cornwall but Lisette had not yet persuaded William to allow her access to his bank account. Etienne had been losing heavily at cards and his own resources were dwindling. He needed Lisette, for her money would fund the future they would build together in America.

Adam had spent most of the month away from the yard trying to interest customers in his designs for the brigantine or the cutter. New orders would ensure the stability of the yard. A few customers showed interest in his designs but were reluctant to commission a ship while the war with France continued.

It was now November and the shipyard could not lie empty. When an expected order was cancelled, Adam had taken the gamble of laying down a keel for a brigantine to keep the shipwrights working. It was an expense he could ill afford but if the yard remained idle it would give future customers a poor impression. Even so, he could not pay the men indefinitely. His other hope for income was the *Pegasus*. The ship had sailed for America and would return in three months with a cargo of tobacco. The captain had been told to avoid any engagement with French ships and Adam prayed that this time the voyage would be without mishap.

He was at the rear of the yard where the timber was stacked. Tree trunks were brought in by cart and left to season in the yard.

The supply was low but he could not afford to pay wages and buy fresh timber. There were large tracts of woodland at Boscabel.

A peal of feminine laughter carried to him as he left the timber stacks to enter the forge. Tamasine and Bridie were chatting outside the schoolroom. The children had just been dismissed for the day. Tamasine's ready laughter was infectious and he found himself grinning as he watched the two friends walk arm-in-arm towards Mariner's House. Leah had called earlier there and Bridie would return to the cottage with her mother before dark.

Bridie walked with a new assured air and her limp was barely perceptible. She had changed much in the last year and her duties as schoolmistress had given her a dignified confidence and grace. There was a proud tilt to her pointed chin. Her slender figure was dressed in a demure gown of dark blue with a wide lace collar. He had not realised how lovely she had grown. Her elfin face had an ethereal beauty and radiance.

Adam entered the forge to ensure that they had enough iron in stock to produce nails. Local farmers also used the forge to mend their ploughshares. After seeing the wrought-iron work the blacksmith had done to repair the gates at Boscabel, Sir Henry Traherne had commissioned a set to replace the wooden ones at the lodge house of his estate. Adam knew it was his friend's way of supporting the yard when orders were low, but he could not afford for the forge to be idle.

After a short conversation with the blacksmith Adam entered the carpentry sheds. Here at least the scene was busy. The windows were large to let in the maximum light. An apprentice was sweeping wood shavings into a pile in the corner of the room to be put into sacks. The off-cuts of wood were sold for kindling. Seth Wakeley was an accomplished carpenter and his carving of the figurehead of *Pegasus* had brought in many orders from owners for similar adornments.

Seth stopped his work on the figure of a woman holding a trident aloft and hobbled over to Adam on his wooden leg.

'How much work have you on the figureheads, Seth?'

'Another month, Cap'n.'

'No more of the captain, Seth. My days at sea are over. I am plain Mr Loveday now, shipbuilder.'

232

'You earned the right to be captain, and you steer this yard as skilfully as any ship in my book, sir. Any man here would agree with me.' Seth squinted up at him from under bushy brows.

Adam slapped him on the shoulder. 'It's a poor captain who cannot bring in orders which we badly need. If the excise office would commission another cutter, our future would be assured. But the government is diverting all its funds to building frigates for the navy who are using only the established naval shipyards for their orders. If an order does not come soon, I will have to lay some of the men off. That is not something I wish to do during winter. I can only afford to pay a skeleton workforce to begin work on the new brigantine and gamble that a customer will want her. But I would not see the men and their families homeless if they can get local work. Unfortunately, in winter such work is scarce.'

Seth shifted his weight on to his good leg and lowered his voice so that the three apprentices working under him would not hear. 'This maybe bain't my place to say, as Ben Mumford be the master shipwright here, but the men already speak of their concern for the winter. They will work for half-wages on the brig, as long as they have a roof over their heads and food enough for their families.'

'I could probably stretch to that.' Adam felt some of the weight of his responsibility towards the shipwrights lifting. They were experienced men and would be hard to replace if an order came in and they had taken work elsewhere. 'Call a meeting for tonight in the kiddley. I will talk to the men then.'

He had left the shed, still troubled by his lack of finances, when he heard female voices coming from the direction of Mariner's House. It was the first time that he could remember hearing Bridie, Senara or Tamasine raise their voices to each other. Something must be seriously amiss. He reasoned that women's matters were best settled amongst themselves and no doubt Senara would inform him of the disagreement later.

He frowned when he saw Bridie run out of the house.

'Adam, you have got to make them listen to reason,' she cried, clearly distressed. He could see that she had been crying.

Peter followed her out of the house, his face flushed with anger. Leah and Senara were not far behind him. Both women looked ill at ease. Bridie was in no state to be pacified and, to avoid a scene, Adam returned to his house. As he drew level with Bridie, he took her arm, saying, 'Calm yourself, it cannot be so bad.'

'They are being mean. I never thought Senara would not wish me to be happy.' Bridie struggled to overcome her tears.

Peter stepped back as he approached, causing Adam to challenge him. 'Have you said something to upset Bridie? When will you learn that your sermons can be harsh and upsetting for someone like her?'

'I am not always sermonising. This is a private matter. One of grave importance.'

Adam paled. 'Have you received bad news about Japhet? Has he been transported?'

'This is nothing to do with my wayward brother. As far as I know Sir Gregory is still working to prove him innocent. As I suspected, it is not proving an easy task.'

Even now Peter could not restrain himself from adding his own judgement on his brother. Adam was irritated at being dragged in to calm a domestic dispute, which no doubt had been stirred up by his cousin.

They gathered in the parlour. Tamasine was nowhere in sight so this obviously did not involve her which was a relief. Adam was aware that soon he would have to deal with his half-sister's future and effect some form of reconciliation between himself and Amelia.

He frowned upon seeing Leah's wrinkled face looking strained. He glanced at Senara who sat tight-lipped and held her fingers to her mouth, the gesture telling Adam that she was worried. She had spent all the previous evening voicing her concern for her sister, saying Bridie seemed preoccupied and secretive.

Peter burst out in a rush, 'I wish to ask your blessing for Bridie and me to wed. She had agreed to be my wife, but her mother and your wife do not approve.'

Adam was stunned at the news and could guess something of the reservations Senara and her mother might feel concerning this marriage. He glanced at his mother-in-law for a sign of her feelings on the matter. Her expression remained guarded. 'This is sudden, is it not, Peter? Do you not think that Bridie is too young?'

'I have my father's approval,' Peter curtly informed him. 'I have been given the living at Polruggan and take up my duties there at the end of the month. The Parsonage is a fine house. A village parson needs a wife at his side to help him serve the interests of his parishioners.'

'Bridie is your daughter, Leah. Do you agree to this union? It is for you to decide more than I.'

'Do I have no say in the matter?' Bridie protested. 'I wish to marry Peter.'

Leah sighed. 'We want what is best for you, my dear. For you to be the wife of Mr Loveday and have the responsibilities of his calling is more than I had envisaged for you.'

It was a guarded statement and Adam guessed that she had reservations about the union. He knew Bridie had been infatuated with Peter for some time, but their personalities were very different. Could she be happy with him? Was he being unduly prejudiced against his cousin because his piety had been such a dampener to many of their meetings in his youth? Peter was serious and conscientious. He would not become a drunkard or abuse Bridie in any fashion. Peter clearly saw the kindness of her spirit and did not allow her limp and her twisted back to detract from her beauty in his eyes. Senara had often voiced her concern that Bridie would never marry. Peter would provide for her, and though the wife of a parson would never be rich, at least she would never go hungry.

Adam regarded his wife. 'What are your feelings, my dear? You know your sister better than I. My cousin can offer her a good life.'

'That I do not dispute, but will he understand her, allow her the freedom she needs to be true to herself? He has a religious zeal that could stifle Bridie.'

Adam sighed. 'What is your answer to that, Peter?'

His cousin's eyes flashed with anger. 'I know you and Japhet have always mocked my piety but I am not inhuman. Bridie has taught me to see some matters in a more compassionate light, though I will still stamp out the evils of sin in my community.'

'But do you love her?' Adam interrupted before Peter could launch into a lecture on the sins of his parishioners.

'Indeed I do. I have spent months wrestling with my conscience. She has the kindest heart of any woman I have met. I would give her the full respect her virtue deserves.'

It was a strange declaration and did little to soothe the unease Adam felt at such a union. But though Bridie may appear fragile and vulnerable she could be a tough creature when she was up against the odds. He did not think that Peter would be able to smother her beliefs in what she believed to be right.

'Please, Adam.' Bridie gripped her hands over her chest. 'That is what I want.'

'Then I have no objections, if Leah agrees.' The joy lighting up Bridie's face was his reward and he suppressed his own reservations. Many people had said that he and Senara were too different to find lasting happiness and they had been proved wrong. He was more in love with his wife now than ever.

Leah kept her gaze steady upon Peter. 'If he loves Bridie, and he will never raise her background against her, then the match has my blessing. Though I do think she be too young.'

Adam held out his hand to Peter. 'I give my blessing to your betrothal, but I agree with my mother-in-law. Let the wedding be in a year.'

Peter turned to Leah, a muscle pulsing in his cheek the only sign of the anger he was keeping in check. 'How old were you when you ran off with your gypsy lover?'

'I were sixteen when I wed my husband by the rites of his people,' Leah responded. 'But I had no choice. My father were a brutal man. I only stayed at home because of Ma. When she were buried I left, refusing to accept my father's brutality any longer.'

'You led a precarious life with the gypsies whereas I offer Bridie stability. She will be respected within the community she serves. I will wait a few months but no longer. In that time my mother can advise Bridie on the work that will be expected of her.'

Leah nodded and Adam felt easier. 'Then so be it. I had always intended that Bridie should have a dowry when she married but this is a difficult time, Peter. I have little spare funds.'

Peter waved his hand. 'I do not marry Bridie for her dowry. Though my stipend is not large, it will provide for a wife. She is of a practical disposition.'

'She will have a dowry as soon as I have funds available,' Adam insisted. 'Once she is wed, will Bridie continue her duties at the school? The children have responded well to her teaching.'

'She does not wish to give up her duties here. There is a dogcart at Polruggan Parsonage for our use. I will teach Bridie to drive it. It is more fitting than her riding that donkey. If Amelia agrees, she will attend the school in the mornings only. The money she earns will not go amiss.'

'I am sure Amelia will be happy with that arrangement. The children are needed for their chores and often miss a full day of school. Her teaching has become important to Bridie. I am glad you would not curtail it.'

'It is a godly profession.'

'And what of Bridie's beliefs?' Leah challenged him. 'Your father preaches the doctrine of love and compassion and of finding God in hard work and diligence. You have been known to be more judgemental in your sermons. Bridie is a gentle creature. A god of fire and brimstone is not the saviour she worships.'

Peter's spine stiffened at this censure. 'I was over-zealous in my youth. I trust I have grown wiser and more considerate of the needs of my flock. The scriptures tell us how we must live. I would expect my wife to follow those beliefs. Bridie understands this.'

'I will trust you to remember those words, Peter.' Adam felt the need to confirm them. 'Bridie is a gentle creature. She sees kindness and beauty in people, not sin. Do not make her unhappy.'

Chapter Twenty-One

'The pettiness and self-importance of men never ceases to appal me.' Long Tom met Thomas Mercer and Lucien Greene in a coffee house in the late afternoon. 'Lord Sefton continues to have nothing said against Celestine Yorke. If he did he would have to admit that a common actress had gulled him.'

Although his height made people notice him, during his years as an English spy in France Long Tom had become adept at creating disguises. He never met anyone connected with Japhet without adopting such a disguise, wary that if his true identity were known, it would somehow get back to Lord Sefton or Sir Pettigrew Osgood and impede his investigations.

Today he was in a blond wig and beard, and a satin suit of bright yellow. He had entered the coffee house walking on his hands to pass round a leaflet proclaiming the entertainment extravaganza of a troupe of acrobats and travelling performers who had set up their pitch on an open space on the south bank of the river. Lucien Greene had recognised him immediately and, after Long Tom had passed the leaflets around several of the tables, had called out: 'Here is an interesting fellow dressed in yellow, a sight to stir our hearts so bold. Come hither, my good man. What spectacle do you ask us to behold?'

'A better entertainment than that poor rendition of a verse,' Long Tom had quipped. 'Lucien Greene is a poet of great repute, but after such words his reputation I would dispute.'

'The knave is a scoundrel. Throw him out.' One of Lucien's many acolytes had risen from his chair, clearly spoiling for a fight to win favour with Lucien.

'Leave our little champion be. He diverts me,' Lucien returned,

238

and gestured for Long Tom to join them. He glanced across at the acolyte who hovered by the table eager to be invited also. He was a fop of the first order, dressed in bright silks, his stock intricately folded and ruffles at his wrist. His blond hair was elaborately curled, his handsome face lightly powdered and patched. Lucien waved him away. 'I dislike violence of any kind. Be off with you, Johnnie, my dear fellow.'

The acolyte scowled but returned to his seat. Aware that too many eyes were watching them, for several minutes Long Tom and Lucien continued their repartee then gradually lowered their voices as the spectators returned to their own conversations.

The day was overcast and a sulphurous smog was beginning to form over the city. The interior of the coffee house was gloomy, the air heavy with tobacco smoke and the stench of guttering candles which threw sinister shadows around each table. The coffee houses were popular meeting places for the gentlemen of the city. Usually Long Tom would have mixed with his intellectual peers and the members of the Royal Society who would discuss their scientific experiments. Today he played the role of fairground entertainer and produced three balls to juggle as he reported his findings to Thomas Mercer in a low voice.

'If Lord Sefton decides not to give evidence against the Yorke woman, I doubt that Osgood will either.' Thomas was exasperated at how long it was taking to clear Japhet's name. Time must be running out for him. The prison hulks in the Thames were overflowing and the government would soon dispatch a transport fleet to Botany Bay. 'Osgood sees little of the Yorke woman of late. But he hates Japhet.'

'I came close to calling the blackguard out when he announced at the playhouse that Japhet should have been hanged.' Thomas allowed his frustration to show. For all his foppish dress he was an accomplished duellist.

'You were wise not to call him out. That would not help Japhet.' Long Tom frowned. 'Osgood has friends in high places. If he hates Japhet so much he will do everything he can to ensure he does not receive a pardon.'

'But we have Gwen's godfather to help us,' Thomas reminded him.

'Craigsmoor will do nothing without clear evidence. And so far that is what evades us.' Long Tom shook his head. 'For the time being we must forget trying to bring Celestine Yorke to justice. I have also been endeavouring to locate the highwayman who held up Sefton's coach. If we can get a confession from him then Japhet will go free.'

'But this man continues to elude you?' said Lucien. He took out a gold snuffbox and tipped some on the back of his wrist before raising it to his nostrils.

'The knave has gone to ground. I've been spending my nights in a tavern frequented by highwaymen, footpads and cutpurses, and I have my informants in other haunts. If the rogue shows his face in London, I will hear of it.'

'Then let us hope it is sooner rather than later,' Thomas stated. 'Japhet is taking his imprisonment hard. It has been seven months.'

'I agree.' Long Tom then told them a ribald joke and as his companions laughed loudly he juggled four empty tankards, raising his voice to encompass all in the coffee house. 'Come see the fattest woman in England and the tattooed man! Come see the tightrope walkers and jugglers at our fair! Come all and bring your whores, not your wives, for the Belle Madeleine will dance and she wears no drawers.' He then walked out of the establishment on his hands and several customers tossed coins at him, which he stopped to gather up before winking across at his friends.

'It does not look good for your cousin,' Lucien addressed Thomas.

'I have faith in Long Tom,' Thomas replied. 'He did wonders when he learned of the existence of Goldie Lanyon and saved St John's hide. If anyone can discover the identity of the highwayman and get him to confess it will be Long Tom.'

The last of the leaves had fallen from the trees when *Pegasus* docked at the landing stage of Greenbanks. Captain Matthews, who had been engaged by Adam, reported to the house and handed St John the letter from Adam.

He was uneasy upon recognising his twin's handwriting.

240

Captain Matthews bowed his head, his voice grave. 'I fear the news is not good. That is why your brother did not sail himself.'

Garfield Penhaligan held out a hand in welcome. 'You will join us to dine this evening, Captain Matthews? We would hear of news from England.'

'Thank you, sir. I have unloaded the cargo of furniture in Richmond, to be sold at auction by Mr Loveday's agent. The tobacco from the other plantations is already aboard. Tomorrow we will load your tobacco and set sail with the first tide. Mr Loveday wishes our speedy return to England.'

St John had broken the seal on his letter. He groaned and sank into a chair. 'My father is dead! I have to return.' His hand shook so violently he had trouble deciphering Adam's writing and had become deathly pale. 'The infection in his chest never healed. I cannot take this in ... forgive me.' He strode out of the house to walk down to the river and collect his thoughts.

He was badly shaken. He had thought that his father was invincible, that no wound could bring him low. He sank on to a stone seat by the river and dropped his head into his hands. He must return with Captain Matthews. There was much to be done and little time.

He wiped away the tears that ran freely down his cheeks. He had failed his father. He had thought only of himself by staying in Virginia. He should have returned when he received Edward's last letter. His father must have been gravely ill then but had been too proud to ask for his help. His grief was intense, the pain of his loss grinding and relentless. How long he remained by the river he did not know. It was not until the air grew cold and he saw the red streaks of the setting sun that he realised some hours had passed. His body felt stiff when he made to rise. It was then that he felt a hand on his shoulder.

'St John, my dear, how can I express my condolences? This must be a terrible shock to you.' Desiree sat beside him and reached for his hand. 'I am so sorry. You will have to return to England, will you not?'

'I have no choice. There is much to be settled. The estate ...' He broke off to battle against the pains of his emotions. 'I must pack. Captain Matthews will be sailing as soon as Garfield's tobacco is loaded.' He stared across to the landing stage, watching *Pegasus* bobbing up and down on the swell of the river.

'Will you return to Virginia?' Desiree asked uncertainly.

'Yes, that has always been my intention. But there will be many responsibilities at home for me to deal with.' He could not think straight. All he could feel was the void that had been created by the absence of his father.

'This is so sudden. I had hoped ...' she faltered. 'You are clearly not in the right frame of mind to consider such matters. But if you leave so soon ...' Again she broke off. 'I should not be so forward but I have no choice. It could be months, perhaps years, before you return. I believe Garfield has expressed a wish to make you his heir?'

He looked at her. Her lovely face was lit with a pink glow from the dying sun and tears sparkled on her lashes. 'And what of us, St John?'

He had difficulty following her words, his bemused mind filled with thoughts of his father. When he did not answer, she covered his hand with both of hers. 'I will say no more. Garfield wishes to speak with you. You will sail imminently. But you should know that I will miss you, more than it is proper for me to say.'

'I am aware of that. I will miss you too, Desiree. You are all a man could dream of and wish to make their own.' The words seem to come from outside himself, his raw emotions making him indiscreet, spoken from his heart not his head.

'St John, does that mean I dare hope that you care for me?'

He realised the error of his rash words. 'I care for you very deeply but this is not the time for such talk.' He stood up abruptly. 'I can think only that my father is dead. Forgive me, my dear.' He was impatient to speak to Garfield and make the final arrangements for his departure.

He was still deep in thought as he walked back to the house arm-in-arm with Desiree. To his relief she did not press him to speak further of his feelings for her.

Garfield had been watching their approach from his study and smiled to himself. There was much to be settled before St John sailed. This may not be the time to discuss such important matters when St John was suffering from shock and grief but he had no option, now that his young relative was to depart.

After ordering his packing to be done St John was on his second brandy as he sat opposite Garfield in the book-lined study. A fire had been lit in the hearth to take the chill from the evening.

'This is a very sad day,' Garfield said. 'Edward was a man I much respected.'

St John nodded. 'He was a fine man. I think I begin to realise only now how much I owe to him.'

'I felt much the same when my father died. But you must look to the future. You have many new responsibilities. I had thought we would have some years in which you could visit Greenbanks occasionally and learn more of the tobacco trade. But it is still my intention to make you my heir.'

'I am overwhelmed by your generosity, sir. But you do under-stand that for now I have Trevowan to consider and my family in England?'

'That is how it should be. But I do not want you to leave here without first making clear your intentions towards my niece Desiree.'

St John was brought up short. His lies had caught up with him. He wished now he had never said he was a widower. Clearly Garfield expected him to make a declaration to Desiree.

'I am currently mourning for my father.'

'No further prevarication,' Garfield said tersely. 'There is no time for shilly-shallying. Do you care for my niece? It would please me most highly if the two of you wed. You have been widowed for over a year.'

'I do care for Desiree, but to think of marriage now ...' He pressed his temple with his fingers. What Garfield asked was not unreasonable had he himself not told so many lies about Meriel.

'This is the very time to consider it, I would have thought. You have additional responsibilities now. A man needs a wife by his side. Your daughter needs a mother.'

'My family would be greatly shocked if I returned to England with a bride. Desiree is a young woman. She is but two and twenty. There will be mourning at Trevowan. I would bring a wife to my home at a time of celebration, not a time when we will not be entertaining.'

243

Garfield sucked in his breath and considered this with some displeasure. 'Have you been toying with her affections?'

'Certainly not, sir! I hold Desiree in the highest esteem.' Beneath his jacket St John began to sweat.

'Then I will speak plainly,' Garfield continued. 'Your father's untimely death changes matters. You will be needed at Trevowan. You also need sons. Marry Desiree and Greenbanks will be merged with Broadacres. You will be master of one of the largest plantations in Virginia, and she will give you fine sons.'

'It would not be fair on her to bring her to England at this time,' St John prevaricated with deepening fear at this turn in the conversation. 'I ask for your patience and understanding, sir. I will return next year once the harvest is in and stay until the spring.'

'You cannot expect her to keep waiting on hope alone.' Garfield was not a man to be swayed from his intentions and allowed anger to show at St John's prevarication. 'She is not without other beaux interested in making her their wife, though she has shown her preference for you. She is a beautiful as well as a wealthy woman. At least announce your engagement before you sail. Is that so unreasonable?'

St John wrestled with his conscience. Marriage to Desiree would fulfil all his dreams, but he still had a wife. One who was as good as dead to him, true, and unlikely to return to Cornwall, but Meriel was a scheming and dangerous woman to have as a dark secret in his past. While she lived, how could he remarry? Yet Garfield offered him so much. If he refused to become engaged to Desiree he might lose Greenbanks. Yet would not his lives in England and Virginia remain separate from each other? St John doubted that his brother would ever return to Virginia now that he was in charge of the shipyard, and no one else connected with him here knew the truth about Meriel. Dare he risk it? What if he denied himself this chance of happiness and then when he returned to England he learned that his wife was dead in reality? The life she had chosen was a precarious one. He could not envisage that Lord Wycham would tolerate her constant demands for clothes and jewels for long. A discarded mistress only had one other choice in life and that was to work as a whore. Few of them lived long in London.

He took a deep breath. 'I shall ask Desiree to marry me tonight. We will wed on my return to Virginia next year.'

Garfield stood up and grasped his hand to shake it enthusiastically. 'This is a union made in heaven. You have made the right choice.'

St John accepted his congratulations whilst smothering his own misgivings which continued to taunt him. He waited until after they had dined and Captain Matthews had retired before he asked Desiree to walk with him in the garden. The night was cool but she did not refuse and sent a maid to fetch a shawl for her. When St John proposed he was not surprised that she immediately accepted.

After they kissed she drew back in his arms, her voice bubbling with excitement. 'I have so little time to prepare myself to meet your family, but my maid can pack my trunks and they can follow me to England.'

Panic gripped him. 'But I do not wish you to return with me now. When my bride comes to Trevowan it should be to feasting and celebration. That is not possible with my father so recently dead. I have been away a year and there will be many legal matters to deal with and other duties. I will have little time to spend with you.'

'But it will be months before I see you again.' Her eyes filled with tears of disappointment. 'I do not need to be constantly entertained. If you love me ...'

'It is because I love and wish only for the best for you that I wish us to wait. It would also be disrespectful to my father's memory to wed in such haste. There will be no entertaining for at least six months after his death and any visits to our neighbours will be of a quiet nature. That is no way to introduce you to Society. I want you to be fêted in both Cornwall and London, but until matters are settled at Trevowan I cannot afford the time away in the city. I am no idle landowner. Now that the yard and estate no longer support each other, I have to work my land.'

'But you have field hands for that!' Her usually agreeable demeanour slipped and her shoulders stiffened with wounded pride. 'I fear you prevaricate, sir, and that your intentions are not

245

honourable. A wife would be a great comfort to a man at this time.'

'My dear, you are overwrought. Have I not just learned that my father is dead? I thought you more compassionate than to press such a matter at this time.' He could feel panic welling. Desiree had a stubborn set to her chin but he was too distraught to think clearly of the future. He drew a deep calming breath, wanting to placate her without making her suspicious. 'I cannot consider my personal happiness at this time. My family and other duties must come first. And as you know there are no slaves in England. Our labourers demand wages as well as the upkeep of their cottages, and in recent years we have accrued debts that must be repaid. My twin's ransom for one.'

'But when we wed my money will be at your disposal.'

How tempting that knowledge was, but the spectre of Meriel haunted Trevowan. He had to remain firm in his resolve. 'I see my future as lying in Virginia, not Cornwall.'

Her face lit up with pleasure. 'That pleases me, for I was born here and would miss my friends and dear Garfield and his sister. But I have always wanted to visit London.'

'And so you shall, my love. In time. We have our whole lives together. I need only the next few months free to manage my estate and finances. Then I will return to you, I promise.' He kissed her again to silence her protests.

She drew back, frowning in displeasure. 'If you have so many responsibilities in England, how will you find the time to return to Virginia?'

'I will inform my family that I am to wed here. Garfield wants our estates united, but I need to know more of the tobacco business first.' His mind was racing. He clearly saw the solution to his problem. He did love Desiree, and the lifestyle here in Virginia was more opulent than in Cornwall. 'My future lies here with you. There is no need for you to come to England unless you wish to meet my family later. It is here we will raise the children who will one day inherit one of the largest plantations in Virginia.'

'And who will run Trevowan?'

'My bailiff. Isaac Nance is an honest man and his son is the estate gamekeeper. Trevowan will be in safe hands. My brother

246

will not fail me and out of loyalty will manage the financial side of the estate.' He doubted Adam would be so obliging in fact but that would be a problem to solve in the future. He needed to appease Desiree for now.

St John's reasoning seemed to satisfy her. It was not until he had retired for the night that his thoughts returned to his father. He knew he was embarking on a deception that would have appalled Edward. Thank God his father would never discover the tangle he had created for himself. But if Desiree stayed in Virginia, why should he not live two separate lives between America and England?

How that would gall Adam! St John felt a rush of triumph that he was now Master of Trevowan. In comparison to Greenbanks and Broadacres it was a small farm, but to Adam Trevowan was the home he would give anything to possess. At last St John had won the greatest victory of all over his twin.

In the night he awoke sweating and gasping for breath. He was floundering in a sea of fire. Meriel's face loomed above him and she was laughing cruelly as he struggled to reach land. He wiped a shaking hand across his brow, panic gripping his heart. He had been a fool to propose to Desiree and believe he could make a new life for himself in Virginia. Garfield had described the match as made in heaven. With the demons of his conscience plaguing him, St John saw it as a commitment made in hell with the potential to destroy him. But it was too late now to retract his proposal. Garfield would disown him and then the riches of the New World would be lost to him. The secret of Meriel must be buried in the past and on no account must Desiree visit England. That was his only hope of keeping his two lives separate.

Elspeth had become a frequent visitor to Mariner's House on the days she was not out hunting. At first it was with the excuse that she wanted Senara to look at one of her mares, saying that the animal had some minor ailment. She always brought Rowena to play with Nathan and would usually stop for most of the morning or afternoon.

Senara found this awkward as it interfered with her treatment of the sick. Elspeth often joined her if she visited a patient, but the families were ill at ease in her company when usually they were friendly if respectful towards Senara.

It was obvious that Elspeth missed her brother, and she was worried about Amelia.

'I cannot persuade her to visit or to be at home to any of our neighbours if they call at Trevowan. This shutting herself away in her grief cannot be good for her. She no longer has Richard to comfort her now that he has reported for duty on his ship,' she confided one morning whilst Senara was playing with her two sons. Elspeth was holding Rhianne who was gurgling and smiling as she sat propped up in the older woman's lap.

'Amelia will be feeling her grief more acutely because she and Edward had not healed the rift between them,' Senara told her.

Joel had been crawling on the floor following Nathan as his older brother ran round the room with a carved hobbyhorse between his legs. Nathan was laughing and Joel screamed out in temper when he could not keep up with his brother. Rowena was bored with the antics of the younger children and had gone into the garden to play with Scamp. To distract Joel, Senara waved his wooden ship and he pulled himself up to tug at her skirts, demanding her attention. She gave him his ship to play with and he pushed it across the room, finally content.

'I hear Amelia crying for hours on end,' Elspeth continued. 'Only Rafe and Joan can give her any comfort. And the baby is sickly. Amelia frets over her.' These confidences from her husband's usually reserved aunt showed a softer side to her nature than Senara had seen before.

'Shall I prepare a tisane for Joan?'

'Amelia will not use it. She has that fool Chegwidden attending her. She has also summoned doctors from Fowey and even Bodmin to consult them. She fusses over the infant and will let no one else nurse her.' Elspeth handed Rhianne to Senara and then gripped the handle of her walking cane tight in her hands, her austere face revealing her worry. 'Amelia is not sleeping. I have seen her pacing the gardens of Trevowan at night or walking along the cliff top. It seems as though she is unable to lay a ghost.'

'When Amelia first came to Cornwall she was always the

248

peacemaker in the family. I know she did not approve of me at first, or of many things that happened to the family, but she was never so strident in her prejudices as she became in the last year. She has a fear of gossip which is almost irrational,' Senara observed.

Joel pulled himself up by the legs of a chair. He toppled over and fell on his ship. He gave an outraged scream and Senara put Rhianne on the floor to rescue him, but he would not be pacified and wriggled to be put down again. She called to Carrie Jensen to keep him occupied upstairs in the nursery and to take Nathan with her. This conversation with Elspeth was too important for her to be distracted by the children.

'I was shocked that Amelia was so unforgiving towards Edward over the matter of Tamasine.' Elspeth had regained some of her old fire. 'I told her she was a fool. Was not his affair with Lady Keyne over with years before he met Amelia? But she would not listen. I had thought better of her. She even quarrelled with Richard before he left and the boy used to be able to do no wrong in her eyes.'

'Amelia dotes on her son. This is so unlike her.' Senara was worried about her too. She needed help, but would she be prepared to accept it?

'Why did Amelia quarrel with Richard?' she asked.

Elspeth shrugged. 'She refused to speak of it. She had been upset at finding another posy of wild flowers by the family vault – she believes that Tamasine put them there. I think Richard told her that she was being unreasonable.'

'I cannot stop Tamasine laying flowers by her father's grave. She loved him very much. She has experienced little happiness in her life yet is always so bright and cheerful. She hides her pain deep.'

They lapsed into silence, Elspeth apparently absorbed in watching Rhianne who was contentedly playing with a rag doll. Senara asked, 'How are Lisette and William? Does he not rejoin the fleet soon? We have seen little of him though he has done much at Trevowan to help ease Adam's duties there.'

'They argue all the time. William does not seem happy. Etienne is at Trevowan too often by my way of thinking.' Elspeth was sharp in her disapproval. 'Though it's true he does have a calming influence on Lisette. They ride together for hours. William leaves for Plymouth in ten days. He has promised to rent a house there for her.'

'That should make Amelia happy. Lisette is disruptive to family life.'

Elspeth nodded. 'Her removal from Trevowan is one less problem for us to deal with. Amelia may be more settled once Lisette is gone. She has always found her mood swings and tantrums unnerving. Perhaps you could make up a remedy for me to give to Amelia that will help her to sleep?'

'I will get one for you.' Senara fetched a phial from her cupboard of medicines stored in the herb room at the side of the kitchen. 'I think Amelia needs not only the relief of sleep, she needs to talk. You are the closest to her. Try to get her to talk about Edward. It may ease her grief.'

'She will not talk to me. I have tried.' Elspeth struggled and abruptly changed the subject. 'How is your sister? I have not seen much of her since you announced her betrothal to Peter. She will make him a good wife.'

'Bridie is kept busy at the school and is spending her spare time with Cecily. She wants to learn the duties expected of her as a parson's wife.'

'As is right and proper. We all have our duties which cannot be shirked.' Elspeth became tense and her stare fierce. 'It is time St John returned. Adam is looking tired and doing too much. He takes his duties very seriously. He cannot be responsible for everything at Trevowan when he has the yard and Boscabel to run also.'

These words echoed Senara's feelings. She was cross with St John for idling his time away in Virginia while Adam was burdened with so many responsibilities. '*Pegasus* should have sailed by now. Though I am not sure how Adam will take to St John being Master of Trevowan. He is driving himself hard to make Boscabel habitable, though I feel that the money should be spent on the yard.'

Elspeth gave a caustic laugh. 'The rivalry between them has always been fierce.' She sagged back in her chair, looking suddenly weary. 'I shall move into the Dower House with Amelia when St John returns. I have rarely seen eye to eye with him and do not wish to witness him squandering all that Edward built up over the years.'

Chapter Twenty-Two

Amelia could find no escape from the agony of her grief. She could not shake off the guilty feeling that she had not supported her husband as she should have done after he had been shot. He had always been so strong that after his initial recovery she had not believed the wound would kill him. Yet she had never stopped loving him; and was tormented now because her stubbornness had caused a distance between them for so many months. But even if she had the chance to live those months again, she doubted she could have acted otherwise. The humiliation she had felt ran too deep.

She had slept only a few hours. Joan had been fractious most of the night. In the last month she had begun to take a little more food but showed no inclination to crawl when she was placed on the floor. She was now cutting another tooth, which always caused her to have a cold. Her breathing was laboured and Amelia had spent the night rubbing her wheezing chest with a concoction of herbs and goose grease that Senara had recommended when Rafe had been teething, and which seemed to bring some relief to her daughter.

When Joan's breathing eased as dawn lit the sky, her mother placed her in her cot. Amelia's head ached from lack of sleep and her body felt heavy but she was driven by an inability to sit or lie still. If she went to her bed, sleep would evade her. The dawn hours were always the worst for her. It was when she felt the absence of Edward the most. To escape her unhappy memories she left the house to walk the grounds. The maid sleeping in the nursery would tend the children if they woke.

The rising sun was obscured by cloud and a thin sea mist

drifted across the cliff top and grounds. Amelia wrapped her cloak tighter around her and pulled the hood over her hair. The great house of Trevowan loomed in the dark shadow; the only light visible was the candle burning in Rowena's room. Since her parents had left without her she would not sleep without a light.

To push aside the unhappy memories of her last months with Edward, Amelia's thoughts returned to Richard. Again they were coloured by feelings of guilt. How could she have lost her temper with him, when he was about to rejoin his ship? But he had been pressing her to end the rift with Adam. Richard had often visited the yard and though he had been careful not to mention Tamasine, she knew that he had seen her. His silence about the young woman somehow made her presence even more substantial. Amelia knew Richard thought she was being unreasonable. Their quarrel had been heated and he had been hurt by her manner.

'Mama, I do not know you these days,' he had cried out in his pain. 'It is as though you have closed your heart. You who were always so warm and loving.'

Amelia squeezed her eyes shut against her troubling memories. How could Richard know of the pain from the past that had come back to haunt her? How long can you keep on smiling for the outside world when inside your emotions are like splintered glass, the edges sharp and lacerating?

Those memories threatened to overwhelm her again and impatiently she thrust them aside. What good was there in reliving old pain? She had enough misery to bear in the present. Yet increasingly of late the past mocked her and would not lay its ghosts to rest.

She wandered aimlessly for an hour and it was not until she heard the shouts from the men in the fishing sloops that she realised she had walked to the headland that sheltered Penruan. The church clock struck six as she continued her walk down into the village and through the churchyard. The church itself brought her no peace for they rarely worshipped there though it contained the family pew. The family now worshipped at Trewenna. She continued on to the Loveday vault. A stone angel guarded the door of the long rectangular tomb and she sat by it on the stone

253

seat the family had erected. She closed her eyes and prayed, needing Edward's forgiveness.

A shiver passing through her chilled body returned her to the present and she was startled to hear the church clock strike eight. She rose and winced at the stiffness of her limbs. Glancing at the heavy pewter clouds, she hoped that the rain would hold off until she reached Trevowan.

A sharp gasp alerted Amelia that she was no longer alone and her heart thudded with alarm as she spun round. The cloaked figure of Tamasine was standing on the far side of Edward's grave. She clutched a posy of wild flowers to her chest. Her eyes widened with distress as she held Amelia's gaze.

'How dare you intrude upon my grief!' Amelia shook with the intensity of the anger that consumed her.

'I did not expect anyone to be here. I did not mean to intrude. Your pardon, Mrs Loveday. I will return when you have left.' Tamasine turned to walk away.

'I told Adam I did not want you laying flowers on Mr Loveday's grave.'

Tamasine whirled back, her cloak billowing around with the violence of her movement. 'You cannot stop me laying flowers on my father's grave! That is cruel. I loved him. I had barely come to know him and you would have denied us even that short time together. He was the only one to offer me hope that I was worthy of someone's love. All my life I faced rejection and in that dreadful school never heard a kind word. We were considered worthless because our parents had abandoned us, constantly reminded that we were their shame.'

Amelia was shocked into silence by the young woman's outburst. Tamasine was trembling and her mask of defiance dropped. She looked young, vulnerable and alone, clutching the flowers to her chest, her eyes pleading for understanding. 'I never took Mr Loveday's consideration for granted. At my school, when we were sixteen we were sold to the highest bidders as their wives. They were usually old, lecherous men with a brood of children the new wife would be expected to look after. It was a life little better than prostitution or slavery. I give thanks daily that Mr Loveday spared me that.'

Before Amelia could reply the girl burst into tears. 'I never meant to be a burden! I never meant to cause dissension between you and my father. He loved you so much. It was obvious in everything he did for you.'

'He expected me to take on his bastard. Where was the love in that?' Amelia's own pain surfaced sharply.

'Mr Loveday adored you. He never considered that I would be part of his family. When we returned to Trevowan, after he'd learned how dreadful my school truly was, you had already left for London. With respect, I think it angered him, and that was why he did not send me away. I was placed with Senara. Then Mr Loveday was too busy in the yard and estate to find the time to deal with my future. He was very lonely during those months.'

'He never told me that.' Grief tore through Amelia and her legs buckled. She sat down again on the stone seat with a jolt. 'I thought you were more important to him than my happiness.'

'He considered your feelings above all others. He was such an honourable man.'

'There was no honour in the way you were conceived. Your mother was an adulteress.'

'She was a desperately unhappy woman. I did not even know that she was my mother until Miss Elspeth let it slip when I came here. She was forbidden by her husband to acknowledge me as her child.' Tamasine brushed tears from her cheeks and tilted back her head as she fought to regain her composure. 'I will leave you to your grief now, but I beg of you, Mrs Loveday, do not stop me laying flowers on the grave.'

Amelia saw the pettiness of her own action. The past pressed down upon her. 'Lay your flowers. I ask only that you are discreet.'

Tamasine nodded. 'One day I hope that you will forgive me for the pain I caused you. I was young and thoughtless.'

'You are so like Edward,' Amelia said softly. 'You are strong and healthy whilst my little Joan is so weak, I fear she will not thrive. I wanted to give my husband a daughter he could be proud of. He was clearly proud of you. I failed him.'

'You never failed Mr Loveday.'

255

'Did my husband speak much of your mother?' Pain crackled in Amelia's voice.

'Very little. He said it would be disrespectful to you.' Tamasine was aware of Amelia's feelings and felt guilty that her own actions had caused her father's wife so much unhappiness. She attempted to ease Amelia's distress. 'You were blessed to have a husband who loved you so much.'

To Tamasine's horror, Amelia dropped her head into her hands and her shoulders shook with the force of her sobs. She put out a hand to the older woman, but knew her compassion would be rejected and withdrew it. 'I should never have come to Trevowan. I was wrong to ask your forgiveness. But if you could understand how desperately unhappy I was, you would know that everything Mr Loveday did for me was done out of duty. He loved you and was proud of Rafe and Joan. He never stopped marvelling at how like you his daughter was. He was an unusually caring man. You have much to be proud of in your children, Mrs Loveday. Mr Loveday was also very proud of your son Richard.'

'He kept your existence a secret. That was what hurt me so much.'

'It was done to protect you.' Tamasine was uncomfortable in her role of mediator, but knew she had to say something to ease this woman's pain. She prayed that she could find the right words. 'Mr Loveday came to visit me for the first time after my mother died. It was not long before St John's trial. He wanted to spare you further distress. I do not think he would have kept my existence a secret otherwise. He was not a man to live easily with deceit. Do not secrets have a way of rebounding and returning to haunt us? I heard Senara say that once.'

Amelia kept her face hidden with her hands until her tears dried. She had not expected such comfort and wisdom from the young woman she had viewed as a rival for Edward's affections. When she eventually looked up the graveyard was empty, but throughout the walk back to Trevowan Tamasine's words stayed with her. Secrets did indeed have a way of returning to haunt a person.

'I kept my secret from Edward,' she said to herself as she climbed the cliff path. 'Perhaps he would have understood my pain if I had told him the truth – that Richard was not my son.'

The need to speak of her pain was overwhelming. She entered the walled rose garden at Trevowan. It had been a favourite place for her and Edward to walk on a mild evening. It was easy to imagine him beside her now and she spoke softly, needing him to understand why she had acted so irrationally. 'My darling Edward, my first husband, Mr Allbright, was cold-hearted and given to bouts of temper when crossed. I have never liked dissension and it was easier to give in to his demands than face weeks of silence when we were alone together. Within a month of our wedding Mr Allbright showed his true character and I found his moods frightening.' She sighed and shook her head. 'My darling, you would find it strange that I was so formal in the way I addressed the first man I married. I performed my duties as his wife and was the perfect hostess in our home when we entertained, but from the moment the baby came into our house, I only ever referred to him as Mr Allbright. He became authoritative and domineering and was no longer the considerate man who had courted me. Mr Allbright had become a stranger to me.'

She circled the rose garden, stopping to smell the scent of some of the blooms. Gradually the tension was leaving her body. As she drew level with the central statue of Diana the huntress she felt a breeze lift her hair and caress the nape of her neck. She gasped. So often Edward had kissed her neck on that very spot. She turned her head expecting to see him standing behind her. The garden was empty, but she was moved to continue her confession.

'I was forced to accept Richard's existence when I had been wed but months. He was Mr Allbright's child, born of the housekeeper whom he'd dismissed before we married. Richard was born six months after our wedding and the housekeeper died. At my husband's insistence, we left London to live in Brighton for four months. When I was allowed to return to London, the child was installed in our house and I was told to present him to the world as my own. I did so to hide my shame. It is the secret that haunts me still.

'When Tamasine arrived at Trevowan it was the same humiliation for me to face over again. Yet you were not the tyrant Mr Allbright turned into, Edward, you were loyal and always loving.

257

Now you know why I feared scandal so much. I was afraid that somehow people would find out the truth about Richard. Even he does not know that I am not his natural mother.'

She clasped her hands over her heart. 'Oh, Edward, I was so foolish. If you were here now I would go down on my knees and ask your forgiveness.'

The wind rustled the leaves of a large chestnut tree that overhung the wall on the far side of the rose garden and provided shade for the garden in summer. Did she imagine it, or did she hear Edward's voice whisper 'There is nothing to forgive'?

Her tears flowed freely, blurring her vision, and she hugged her arms across her chest. But the pain in her heart had lessened. The tears were purifying and healing. Amelia knew that Margaret and Elspeth had condemned her for her lack of understanding towards their brother. Her secret mocked her for she had found it impossible to confide even in her husband. Edward had believed, as did all her friends in London, that she had led a sheltered life, cosseted and cared for by her first husband. The truth was the very opposite. From the day the baby was forced on her, she had been estranged from Mr Allbright. After she had suffered a miscarriage she had felt his sins had been visited upon her and had never permitted him into her bed again. He was content to bed the female servants and they took their meals in silence when they were alone, though when in the company of friends they had appeared to be a doting couple. Her first marriage had been a living lie. Yet she had come to love Richard. In her lonely marriage her maternal instincts had become centred on the child. That was not difficult for Richard adored her.

She shook her head to clear her thoughts, but they persisted. She had come close last week to destroying his affection when she had become unreasonably jealous that he had seen Tamasine at the yard against her wishes. And to her bitter regret now she had come close to destroying her marriage to Edward through her jealousy that Lady Keyne had born him a beautiful and vivacious daughter. Edward had never looked at another woman since they had first met. He was not a man to be unfaithful and had remained true to her to the end.

Tamasine had asked for her forgiveness but it was she who

needed forgiving by Edward. To honour her husband's memory she reasoned that she should put her injured pride aside and show more compassion towards his daughter. That was what he would have wanted.

For the first time since Edward's death Amelia could feel a glimmer of light entering her heart. She went straight to her room in the Dower House and slept for the rest of the day. The following week she stopped pacing the grounds in the dead of night. Some measure of peace had returned to her life.

Adam had spent a week visiting as many of the old customers of the shipyard as possible. His travels had been hampered by heavy rain and his patience was wearing thin. He was forced to hide his frustration as he showed the customers designs for the cutter and brigantine, and each of them used the well-worn excuse of the war with France for not placing an order. Even orders for fishing smacks, which had been the most lucrative work for the yard in the past, had dried up. There were many more small shipyards around the Cornish coast and most were struggling to bring in work. Disappointment at his own failure made him angry and increased his worry. He was inexperienced in selling ships, for that had always been his father's work. He suspected that many of the old customers were suspicious that he was too young and inexperienced to run the yard. His time in the navy and his recent voyages had given him more of a reputation as an adventurer than a businessman. He had to prove his ability to win their orders.

Adam had also spent an uncomfortable morning with his banker raising a loan on Boscabel. Again due to his inexperience they had been reluctant to advance him money, but he had bargained persuasively and a loan had finally been agreed. He now had enough funds to continue work on the brigantine, and as the shipwrights had agreed to a cut in their wages against a full settlement of the money when it was sold, Adam had managed to keep his workforce. The men would also do work at Boscabel, rebuilding the barn and outbuildings. A second tied cottage was to be refurbished, and if the estate was to pay its way Adam had decided to rent out another cottage and two fields to a tenant farmer.

He had spent the afternoon inspecting the work at Boscabel. Before he'd died his father had told Adam that he could use anything he needed from the attic at Trevowan. Since his grandfather's time an amazing amount of broken furniture that could easily have been repaired had been stored there.

Two dismantled four-poster beds were selected, and also a coffer filled with bed hangings and curtains which Meriel had discarded when she insisted that new hangings be brought for the Dower House. He had also found two tapestries that had been rolled up and stored and would look well in the old hall at Boscabel. Some heavily carved Jacobean benches and chairs would provide seating in the dining room, and Adam had remembered a large oak table that had been in one of the barns since his father's first marriage. He found the table badly scuffed, the wood dull and cracked on the surface. It could be planed down and restored with beeswax. In various coffers in the attic he had found an assortment of wooden and ironwork candlesticks and two mirrors whose frames had been damaged. Seth Wakeley had the skill to repair and regild these. The goods were taken to Boscabel in a wagon where they would be cleaned and repaired.

Adam was determined to move to Boscabel by the spring. He rode back to the shipyard, feeling the weight of so many responsibilities on his shoulders. He had entered the isolated lane leading from the estate when a rider pulled out of the trees.

'I heard you be looking for me,' Harry Sawle stated. His eyes were dark and menacing in a face scarred and blackened on one cheek where his shotgun had misfired when he had tried to frighten Senara into allowing him to store contraband on Boscabel land. 'I bain't hard to find. And I've a proposition for you.'

Anger blazed through Adam. He had not forgotten his rage at Sawle for using the cave and causing his father to be shot.

He leaped from his horse. 'I've a score to settle with you! My father would be alive if you had not used my land to store your cargo.' He launched himself at Sawle and dragged the stockier man out of the saddle, landing a punch on his jaw and sending Sawle careering back into his horse. The gelding neighed and shied away from the men. 'My brother was put on trial for murder because of his involvement with you.'

Sawle swung out, his fist crashing into Adam's eye and splitting his brow. 'I had a deal with your father, he were paid handsomely. And he came to me for a loan to pay your ransom.'

A blow to his stomach doubled him over. As Adam advanced closer to grab his throat. Sawle brought up his head and butted him under the chin with a loud crack. Adam's head exploded with pain and he fell to the ground. Reflex made him roll aside but when he tried to rise to his knees he was dazed and shook his head to clear it.

Sawle shouted, 'I bain't here to fight you, Loveday! St John *chose* to be my partner. Getting mixed up with Lanyon and then the trial resulted from that.'

The smuggler delivered another blow to Adam's gut that toppled him but he rolled several times and managed to rise, on shaking legs. Sawle charged at him with his arms outspread in a wrestling hold. Their bodies collided and they both slammed into the ground. Adam kicked and punched, his face contorted as he tried to push Sawle's heavier body off his own whilst blows were landing on his head and chest.

They were evenly matched, but Sawle fought with the savageness of a street fighter and Adam had to suppress his gentlemanly side. He managed to bend one knee and jerk it into Sawle's stomach. His assailant grunted and fell to one side, enabling Adam to spring to his feet, but Harry Sawle was no sluggard. He was notorious for his fights in Penruan after the fishermen had spent the night drinking. In the fading light Adam saw a dagger glinting in the smuggler's hand.

Knowing that his life depended upon it, Adam drew his own blade from the belt at the waist and the two men circled each other, both waiting for the other to let down his guard. Sawle slashed wildly and Adam sidestepped. The smuggler spun round, the dagger flashing, and fire seared down Adam's arm as it sliced through his jacket and into his flesh. He lunged forward. Sawle jumped back. They both hit out, making contact with vicious blows, and within moments were again grappling on the ground.

'You killed my father as surely as if you had shot him!' Adam spat.

'He knew what he was getting into,' Sawle grunted as Adam's fist connected with his ear.

Both men were breathing heavily. Adam had trouble seeing out of his cut eye and his punches were losing their force, his whole body aching from the bruising it had suffered. Harry Sawle's nose streamed blood and his lip was split. He was staggering and the lunges of his dagger were growing erratic. He staggered back from Adam.

'This proves nothing. Back off, Loveday. I were sorry to hear of your father's death. It were Lieutenant Beaumont who shot him. Beaumont wanted revenge on your family, and if he could not get at you or St John who'd made a fool of him then he wanted to ruin your father.'

Adam stood still, breathing hard while Harry continued to speak.

'Beaumont paid men to break into the yard and set fire to the ship being built there. He betrayed me. I paid him to keep his nose out of my affairs. He got greedy and would have suffered the fate of all the men who crossed me if he hadn't escaped at the last minute. He be running scared, but I'll see him dead yet.'

'I have not forgotten Beaumont's part in the shooting,' Adam ground out. 'He won't stay out of the district long. He'll do nothing to risk losing his inheritance from his grandfather, Admiral Beaumont. When he returns he too will pay for my father's death.'

'Beaumont resigned from the excise service and the Admiral has disowned him. He took off with his wife's money and she bain't seen him for months. He must have left the country or my men would have heard of him.'

'Then you and I still have a reckoning to make, Sawle.' Adam brought up his fist to swing at him, but the smuggler dodged it.

'Enough of this madness, Loveday! I bain't got no fight with you. You'd be wise to listen to my proposition.' Harry raised his hands and backed off.

'You will not use Boscabel for your contraband.' Adam swiped the blood from his eye with his cuff, still antagonistic.

'I've other places that do as well. What I want is a ship – a cutter like you built for Lanyon. The excise cutter *Challenger*, also built in your yard, is stopping my cargo from getting ashore. I need a ship to outrun her. How long will she take to build and what will she cost me?'

Adam's hand dropped to his side. He did not want Sawle as a customer, but the smuggler's order could save the yard. Yet how could he work with a man he held at least partly responsible for his father's death?

When he did not immediately reply, Sawle added, 'I need that ship, and you need the order. My agent in Guernsey is also interested in such a cutter to outrun the French warships. The Excise Office bain't commissioned any further cutters because *Challenger* does her work so well.'

Still Adam hesitated. Sawle was slippery as an eel and not to be trusted.

'So what is your price, Loveday?'

Adam told him and took satisfaction in seeing Harry wince. He did not like parting with his money. Still undecided as to whether he wanted it, Adam added, 'And I want half the payment before I lay down the keel. Another quarter when she's ready to be fitted out, and the rest before she's delivered. She'll take six months to build. If you want her before that, it will cost more. The men have to be paid for working longer hours and I will need to bring more workers into the yard.'

Harry Sawle scowled. 'I agree to the terms of payment but not the extra. I want her finished in four months.'

'That would not be possible at the lower price.'

'And if I persuaded my agent to commission a cutter, wouldn't it be worth your while to reduce the price of my ship then?'

Much as he resented dealing with Sawle, the two orders would save the yard and provide work until next summer. Adam owed it to his father to make the shipyard profitable. Edward was first a businessman; he would have accepted the order.

'Get confirmation from your agent with agreement for the cutter to be completed within a year and you can have yours at the lower price,' Adam bargained. 'The conditions of payment will be the same for your agent. Half up front.'

'You drive a hard bargain, Loveday. That cutter had better be capable of outrunning any excise ship!'

'She will be as fast as *Challenger*. To outrun her your crew will need to be more experienced.'

'Lanyon extended the bowsprit of his vessel and could take on an extra sail,' Sawle challenged.

'The work was not done in our yard and it made his cutter unstable. That is why she ran aground on the rocks and was lost in the storm. Lanyon would not pay for an experienced crew. You would be wise to learn from his mistakes.'

Sawle held out his hand. 'Then it's a deal. I'll pay the first instalment next week. My agent will contact you. And at those prices we're entitled to a penalty fee if the ships be delivered late.'

Adam agreed and they shook on the agreement. It had been a surprising encounter and had relieved him of the financial burdens that had been blighting his immediate future. 'The contracts will be drawn up by my lawyer and delivered to you for signature.'

'I don't hold with no lawyers. Are you saying my word bain't good enough, Loveday?'

'Lanyon had such an agreement with my father. Our transaction will be made legally or not at all.'

Sawle nodded though he did not look pleased. 'Those ships had better be delivered on time or you will find yourself with more trouble than you can handle, Loveday.'

'A deal would not be a deal for you, Harry, if you did not weight it with menace.' Now that Adam had accepted the order, Sawle's threats did not impress him.

Chapter Twenty-Three

For the first time since her betrothal, Bridie attended a sermon given by the new parson of Polruggan church. Cecily Loveday and Tamasine accompanied her. The three women had spent the last week cleaning the Parsonage and making it fit for Peter to inhabit. The last parson had died at the age of seventy-four, and for a decade had lived there with his widowed, crippled sister who was partly blind. They had died within two months of each other. The Parsonage had not been cleaned properly for years. Cobwebs garlanded the ceilings, cockroaches had colonised the kitchen and bedrooms, moths had invaded the linen chests and feasted on the hangings, and bed bugs had infested the mattresses.

The crockery was chipped and stained and the cookware encrusted with layers of burnt remains. Very little was usable. Even the sturdy Cornish range was covered with baked-on grease and grime it took Bridie two days of hard scrubbing to remove.

The women had stripped the house of its linen, hangings, coverlets and mattresses, and burned them on a bonfire in the garden. Then they tackled the accumulated grime on walls, windows and floors.

On the first day of their arrival in Polruggan several women had come out of their houses to study the newcomers with suspicion. They nodded politely to Cecily who had a reputation in the district for kindliness. She had told the two younger women to smile and bid the women good day in a pleasant manner.

Though Bridie smiled and held her head high she knew the villagers were wary of her, and some were old enough to remember that her grandfather had been a drunkard and a brutal man. One or two of them had called on Senara to tend the ills of their family, but her reputation was often viewed with suspicion. Such skills with herbs may be welcomed in times of crisis, but many villagers were superstitious and ignorant enough to fear that women with such knowledge were witches in league with the devil. That their new parson had betrothed himself to the sister of one of these women made the villagers suspicious and hostile. They also disapproved of the fact that the parson's wife had been born out of wedlock.

'They look so forbidding,' Bridie had whispered to Cecily as they rode up to the Parsonage. 'They resent me already.'

'You know well enough that villagers are always suspicious of newcomers,' Cecily had reminded her. 'You and Leah have kept yourselves very much to yourselves in recent years. But you have the protection of Adam Loveday and of Peter's name. The men in the village will be wanting casual labour on Adam's estate when it is available. They cannot afford to reject you.'

'They still do not appear very welcoming.' Bridie shivered at the realisation of how difficult her life as a parson's wife would be if the villagers did not accept her.

'You and Peter are both young. Happen some will resent that. And Peter has been known for the harshness of his sermons in the years past.' Cecily patted Bridie's hand, her smile encouraging. 'Joshua has counselled him to treat his flock less harshly. Peter's strict piety is not to everyone's taste or persuasion. Your tolerance and compassion will win the parishioners over. These things take time.'

The Parsonage although sparsely furnished was finally ready for habitation. Before Bridie married Peter she was to make some colourful rag rugs to brighten the dourness of the parlour and bedchamber. Polruggan was a small and impoverished parish. Peter's stipend was not enough to pay for a maidservant, and the churchwarden was a surly man who had informed the new parson he would abide no interference in the way he performed his duties. The villagers worked on the surrounding farms and Sir Henry Traherne's tin mine. Most of the men were also tub men used by Harry Sawle to land his cargo and disperse it inland.

The church bell was being rung to summon the parishioners to the service when the three women walked to the church. Every pew was filled. The villagers were curious about their new parson and how he would perform his duties. They watched as Bridie, Cecily and Tamasine took their places in the front pew. Bridie clutched her Bible close to her chest to calm her apprehension. The bell stopped its ringing and Peter appeared from the vestry and began the service.

Bridie was shaking with nerves and could feel the eyes of the congregation boring into her back throughout the opening hymn and Bible reading. She could not take her eyes off Peter who looked so tall and handsome. His dark hair had been trimmed so that it lapped over the back of his Geneva bands. His new black suit of worsted cloth was hidden under the pristine whiteness of his vestments. He gave no sign that he was nervous, his manner confident and assured, and her heart swelled with love and gratitude that this man had chosen her as his wife. The thought made her blush and she lowered her head to hide her reddened cheeks.

Cecily squeezed her hand. 'He does look handsome. Joshua is very proud of him.'

When Peter climbed the pulpit to preach his sermon, Bridie prayed that he had followed his father's advice and kept it to less than half an hour's duration. She found his words inspiring and the time he was speaking passed quickly for her but she was aware that there was much coughing and shifting of bodies behind her in the church, and at least two people were snoring.

At the end of the service Peter walked down the aisle to stand at the church door as his congregation filed past. Cecily stood up to follow her son and nudged Bridie to accompany her.

'Keep your head high and smile,' she advised.

Running the gauntlet could not have been worse. The congregation remained seated, waiting for the parson's family to pass. There were no smiles, no nods of greeting, only cold eyes fixed upon them, speculative and ruthlessly assessing. Bridie walked slowly to control her limp. Halfway down the aisle Tamasine who was at her side gave a sudden gasp.

'There's Rupert Carlton,' she whispered to Bridie, her voice breathless with excitement. 'How unexpected to encounter him here.'

Peter smiled at Bridie as she approached him. 'It was a fine sermon,' she said, suddenly overcome with shyness.

'You have done well this day, my son.' Cecily's round face was flushed with pleasure.

She took Bridie's arm. 'We will wait a short distance away. Peter will have a word to say to each of the congregation. Some of them may wish to make your acquaintance. Do not be nervous. Once they know you, they will come to respect and love you.'

Bridie braced herself for this ordeal. Apart from when teaching the children she had become adept at effacing herself. She had been bullied and ridiculed too often to be comfortable under close scrutiny from others.

A group of four women advanced upon them. They were the matrons of the village, their faces lined and eyes hardened from poverty and watching children die in infancy. They gave Bridie the barest nod of greeting and the nearest, a tall woman who was as wiry as a bramble and twice as prickly, addressed Cecily. 'Parson did not mince his words. We be simple folk. He be a mite young by our way of thinking to be preachifying as to how we should lead our lives. Old Parson Peasbody didn't go interferin' in what folk got up to weekdays, long as they attended church on Sunday. Reverend Mr Joshua Loveday be known as a good man and preacher. We but hope that Parson Loveday do be the same and follow his father's ways.'

'That is for my son to decide. Every parson runs his parish as he sees fit.' Cecily smiled but her voice remained cool. 'You are Mrs Wibbley, are you not? Your sister Dotty lives at Trewenna. May I remind you, Mrs Wibbley, that it is not for the parish to tell the parson – who is the moral guide to his flock – how he should conduct his duties, nor what he should preach in his sermons.'

The woman sniffed and eyed her coldly. 'Good day, Mrs Loveday. Miss Polglase, we hear you are to be congratulated that you be to wed our new parson?'

'That is correct, Mrs Wibbley,' Bridie responded with a nervous smile.

'We won't be appreciating any interfering in our ways from you either, young miss. Unless you be asked.'

Bridie hid her anger at their rudeness. She had learned at a young age to stand up for herself if people were antagonistic towards her, though by choice she avoided confrontation. 'I may be young but Mrs Loveday has given me instruction as to my duties. I will continue my work as school teacher at Trevowan Hard, but once I am married our door will always be open if the villagers have need of our services.'

'Happen she might do.' A shorter woman with a squint nodded to her companions.

'That be if she don't bring the evil eye on us.' Mrs Wibbley glared at Peter's mother, clearly angered that Cecily had put her in her place. 'Miss Polglase's sister bain't no better than a witch. God may turn from us if we let the sister of such a woman live among us.'

'You are talking superstitious nonsense!' Cecily was swift in her defence. 'May the Lord forgive you for the evilness of your tongue. And don't forget your sister Dotty was thankful to Senara Loveday when she saved her babbie's life when it was sick of the croup.'

The women left and mingled with others from the village. No one else approached Cecily or Bridie.

She sighed. 'They do not like me. How can they speak such evil of Senara? I do Peter a disservice by marrying him.'

'You must not believe that. They are fortunate to have such an intelligent, kindly soul as their parson's wife.' Cecily was as agitated as Bridie. 'Pay them no mind. Villagers don't like strangers in their midst. They will accept you in time.'

All the pleasure had drained from Bridie and she looked towards Peter, hoping for reassurance. Many of the men of the village had done no more than nod to him as they left the church, their faces taut and unwelcoming. Peter said to each as they passed, 'Go with God, my child.'

The comment often earned him a scowl from the parishioner. It was disheartening to witness the fact that the people of Polruggan were suspicious to the point of hostility towards their new parson and his future wife.

Tamasine paid no mind to the villagers, she had not been able to take her eyes from Rupert who had hung back until the congregation had filed from the church and was now talking with Peter.

269

'Tamasine, stop staring.' Bridie nudged her friend. 'People are watching you. You are too forward.'

'Will Mr Carlton talk with us?' Tamasine groaned. 'I have not seen him for some weeks. Peter said that he was visiting friends elsewhere in Cornwall.'

'You take a great deal of interest in this young man.' Cecily followed Tamasine's gaze. 'Bridie is right. It is not fitting for you to put yourself forward in this way.'

Tamasine blushed. 'But how will he know that I wish to speak with him, if I do not catch his eye?'

'It is for the gentleman to decide that he wishes to speak with you,' Cecily remonstrated. 'I think we should leave.'

'Please, Mrs Loveday, can we not wait just a little longer? Mr Carlton has glanced this way, but Peter is engrossed in their discussion.'

'We must leave,' Cecily said with firmness. 'I will not have your conduct cause speculation amongst the villagers, Tamasine. Your position is already a delicate one. You must not give any cause for further gossip to be attached to your name.'

At Tamasine's crestfallen expression, she said more gently, 'Who is this Mr Carlton? What do you know of his family?'

'He is visiting relatives, I know that much, and that he travels the countryside since his interest is in architecture.' Tamasine reluctantly related the few facts she had on the young man.

'He looks and acts like a gentleman,' Cecily said. 'Peter lunches with us most days. I shall ask him to invite Mr Carlton to join us. It would not be inappropriate if Bridie and you were attending the Rectory to help me with my duties and therefore joined us.' She laughed. 'I am becoming as scheming a matchmaker as Margaret Mercer!'

'Would you really do that so that I could meet Mr Carlton properly?' Tamasine could not contain her excitement.

'I know how you young women can build romantic notions which are entirely without foundation. Do not make too much of it, my dear.'

They had climbed into the pony trap that Bridie had driven to Polruggan when Peter and Rupert Carlton joined them.

Rupert tipped his hat to the ladies. He wore a fashionably cut grey frock coat with a black-and-silver-embroidered waistcoat and plain black breeches. Though his stock was folded in an intricate manner, his dress was elegant and not foppish.

'May I introduce Mr Carlton to you, Mama?' Peter said. 'You met my fiancée Miss Polglase, and my late uncle's ward Miss Loveday, when you recently visited Trewenna church, Mr Carlton.'

'Ladies.' Rupert bowed to them.

'Are you staying in the area, Mr Carlton?' asked Cecily.

'My family is still in London but at present I am staying with the Rashleighs in Fowey. I am also acquainted with Lord Fetherington and spent a week on his estate.'

At the mention of such eminent Cornish families, Cecily lost her reservations towards the stranger. 'I understand you are interested in architecture, Mr Carlton. My husband is something of an authority on the churches in our area, as I am sure Peter has informed you. It would please him if you took luncheon with us at the Rectory next Tuesday or Thursday, whichever is convenient to you. Peter will join us.'

'That would be most pleasant. May I suggest Tuesday?'

Cecily nodded. 'That is the day Miss Polglase and Miss Loveday help my work with the poor of the parish after the school has closed for the morning. They will also be lunching with us.'

'Then my pleasure will be all the greater,' Mr Carlton replied.

The arrangements made, Rupert Carlton bowed to the ladies, his smile broadening as it alighted upon Tamasine.

For the next two nights she could not sleep. She confided her excitement in Senara as they rode to Penruan to visit a patient and buy some goat's cheese from Keziah Sawle. 'Do you think Mr Carlton likes me? His smile is so wonderful.'

'The Rashleighs are an important family. If he is a friend of theirs, his family must be well-connected too. You still know nothing of them or his background. He may be married or betrothed. The Lovedays are shipwrights whose business is struggling to survive. His family may expect him to marry an heiress.'

'He is the first man I have met who I have truly liked. There is something about him I find so exciting, I cannot stop thinking of him.'

271

Senara laughed. 'That is a sure sign you are smitten.' Her expression sobered. 'The last thing we want is for you to be hurt, though.'

'I am sixteen next week. I am in no rush to wed for I am just beginning to know my family, but Amelia wishes me settled and no longer the responsibility of the family.'

'Your happiness is what is most important. Adam will not rush you into marriage.'

Tamasine blushed. They had reached the coastal path and she stared out at the turquoise sea where a tall-masted clipper was in full sail towards Plymouth. 'Mr Carlton is very handsome, is he not? Am I foolish to hope that a man such as he would think me a suitable wife? I could not abide to marry someone old, simply to have a home and be provided for.'

'Many women would be content with so little. Keep your dreams for as long as you can, Tamasine. Pray, though, do not pin your hopes on Mr Carlton. Not until we know more of his background and family.'

'But I think I am already in love with him,' Tamasine confided.

'Our first love is often an unwise one,' Senara counselled.

'It was not so with Bridie. She told me that she had loved Peter for a long time.'

'I still would not like to see you hurt,' Senara warned.

'Do you know these things? Bridie said you have the sight, that you sometimes know when something will go wrong.'

'She can be over-fanciful at times.' Senara could not bear to look into the girl's trusting face, so full of hope. Momentarily she had seen it shadowed by tears, her heart close to breaking. And as for Bridie, she already knew that her sister's happiness would not be so easily won.

The next morning Senara was in the kitchen sorting through freshly picked herbs when Tamasine ran in from the garden in a state of agitation. She placed a basket of eggs that she had been collecting on the table.

'Mrs Loveday has ridden into the yard with Miss Elspeth Loveday. Shall I go to the kiddley until she leaves? But in an hour I will need to change to ride to Trewenna. Peter is to collect Bridie and me in the pony cart.'

Senara frowned. She did not like the idea of Tamasine being forced out of her home because Amelia had chosen to visit. But it could mean that Edward's wife was prepared to end the rift between herself and Adam, which was too important to ignore.

'I dislike making you leave, but it would be for the best. Amelia will not stay long. If she is still here when you need to change, come in quietly and go to your room.'

Tamasine nodded. 'I'll leave by the garden once Mrs Loveday enters the front door. That way she will not see me.'

'It is too foolish for us to continue this way.' Senara had lost patience with Amelia.

'I do not mind.' Tamasine's eyes darkened with anxiety. 'I do not wish to cause Mrs Loveday any further distress.'

They heard footsteps on the wooden floor of the hall and Carrie Jensen hurried to meet the visitors and take the women into the parlour. Amelia spoke loudly enough for her voice to carry to the kitchen. 'Senara, I saw Tamasine run into the house, please do not send her away. It would please me if she joined us.'

Tamasine halted by the garden door, clearly flustered.

Senara raised her eyebrows and said softly, 'Tidy your hair, it had been ruffled by the wind, and take off that soiled apron. We will go into the parlour together. What has brought this about?'

'I met Mrs Loveday by accident in the graveyard of Penruan church,' Tamasine confessed. 'She was cross at first, but then accepted that I had a right to visit my father's grave.' Her hand went to her mouth in alarm. 'Do you think she was upset though? Perhaps she is going to insist that Adam sends me away.'

'He will not allow that to happen.' Senara removed her own apron and smoothed her hands over her hair, coiled in a chignon, to ensure that all the pins were in place.

Carrie appeared and Senara ordered her to bring in a tray of tea and the butter biscuits that they had baked that morning. 'Use the best china and the silver tea service.'

She entered the parlour. 'Elspeth, Amelia, this is a wonderful surprise. I trust both of you are well?'

'We are in fine health,' Elspeth replied.

Amelia had smiled wanly at their entrance though her face was pale and tense. She did not look at Tamasine.

Senara gestured for the girl to sit by the window and took a seat beside her. 'I trust Rafe and Joan are in good health?'

'Rafe thrives,' replied Amelia. 'Joan is taking more food but she is still sickly. The winters here can be so damp I fear that they will weaken her chest. Three physicians have examined her but their potions do nothing to help her. Would you look at her again? You have a different knowledge that may help her grow stronger.'

'I am not a physician. My remedies are but simple.'

Amelia twisted her hands together. 'I offended you by calling in Dr Chegwidden. My fears for Joan made me thoughtless.'

Senara shook her head. 'You did not offend me. You did what you thought was best for your daughter. Any mother who loves her child will go to the best physicians they can afford. If you wish, I will look at her. Sometimes a baby or child who will grow to be loving and caring of others responds to the mother in ways we do not understand. Joan was inside you for nine months – nine difficult months for you. Perhaps she needs only to be held, to feel that you are at peace, and then she will be at peace herself and take more food.'

'That is the most ridiculous notion I have ever heard!' Elspeth replied.

Senara did not take offence. She could not explain her intuition in these matters, but when such flashes of inspiration came to her, if acted upon, they usually worked.

'Are you saying I am to blame for Joan's poor health?' Amelia was aghast.

'No, I am not saying that. But your sadness and grief are like a cloak around your emotions. Allow us into your lives, Amelia. We love you and want to help you in this difficult time. You shut out Adam as you have shut out many of your friends because you feared their gossip about St John's and Japhet's trials. Edward always believed that the family should remain united for that was the Loveday strength.'

Amelia drew a shuddering breath. 'Edward was right. I failed him.'

'Do not think that,' Senara remonstrated. 'The last years have been difficult financially. You were Edward's rock, his comfort and his joy through many trials and tribulations.'

274

Tears sparkled in Amelia's eyes and she blinked them away. 'His death was a great shock to us all.' She turned to Tamasine and drew a heavy breath before adding, 'I have been wrong to isolate myself in my grief. Edward did believe in family unity, and to honour his memory I will abide by his wishes. Tamasine, I should have accepted with better grace that you were my husband's daughter, no matter what the circumstances of your birth.'

She paused, her throat working in her distress. She swallowed hard before continuing. 'Edward wanted you to marry well. I will be spending the winter months in London. The damp and cold of Cornwall will not be beneficial to Joan's health, and there would be too many memories of happier times for me at Trevowan if I spend Christmas there. I will take you with me to London.' It had been hard for her to broach the subject. Now, in her nervousness, the words tumbled out in a rush. 'Tamasine, you will have heard of Margaret Mercer's prowess as a match-maker? She will be delighted to launch you into Society. I cannot do so myself as it would be unseemly until my year of mourning is over, but we shall stay at my London house. We will also visit a dressmaker to have you suitably attired for the balls and plays you will attend.'

'That is most generous of you, Mrs Loveday.' Tamasine's voice shook and she found it difficult to meet Amelia's gaze. 'But I have no wish to inconvenience you. I love Cornwall.'

'It is no inconvenience. It is my duty to see you well provided for in the manner that Edward would approve.'

Tamasine felt her heart racing at this new dilemma. She did not want to offend Amelia Loveday who had swallowed her pride to offer this olive branch to her. Yet to leave Mariner's House at this time would mean she would not be able to become better acquainted with Rupert Carlton.

Senara smiled. 'Tamasine will be truly part of our family. It has always been her wish.'

Tamasine hid her misgivings. It was true that to be accepted by Amelia meant she was finally part of the family. Her interest in Mr Carlton was trivial in comparison. Yet a part of her remained downcast that she must be parted from him. 'I am most grateful to you, Mrs Loveday. I shall be pleased to accompany you to

London and meet others of the family.'

When Amelia had left the house Tamasine hurried to change into her best gown. She could hear Amelia outside talking to Peter who had just driven into the yard with Bridie. Tamasine was eager to look her best. This could be the last meeting she had with Rupert Carlton before she must leave for London.

Throughout the meal at the Rectory Tamasine found it hard to curb her natural vivacity. Joshua, Peter and Rupert spoke earnestly of their interest in church architecture and the churches built by Hawksmoor and Wren in the last century after the fire of London. During their visit to London Peter and Joshua had visited the churches, both to pray and for a few hours try to forget Japhet's plight.

The dinner plates were finally cleared and the maid brought in an apple and blackberry pie.

'You spoke earlier of your time at Oxford. Is that where you studied architecture?' Joshua asked their guest after the dessert had been served.

'It was, amongst other subjects.'

'Is that your profession?' he continued.

Rupert shook his head. 'It is an interest, that is all. Though it would be diverting to take on a commission if the subject were of particular merit.'

From his tone it was clear that Mr Carlton was financially independent.

'Does your family have an estate, Mr Carlton?' Cecily was inquisitive to learn more of the handsome young man for he had not spoken as yet of his home or family. Peter and Joshua would talk of church architecture all through the remainder of the meal if she did not change the subject.

'I do not, Mrs Loveday. My parents left me a town house in London and when I come into my full inheritance at twenty-five that is where I shall live.'

'Are both your parents dead?' she persisted.

'Two years ago they both died in a shipwreck off the Scottish coast. My father was an emissary from King George's Court sent to The Hague. Their ship was blown off course in a violent storm.'

'That was a tragic loss,' Cecily sympathised.

'Then we are both orphans,' observed Tamasine.

Rupert smiled at her across the dining table. 'Your parents died last year, did they not? That was when you became Mr Loveday's ward, I believe.'

Tamasine had finished her pie and sat with her hands in her lap. 'My mother died last year. My father ...' She stopped abruptly, horrified she had almost been indiscreet. She added sombrely, 'My father died some time ago.'

Rupert smiled tenderly at Tamasine and a slow blush crept up her cheeks. 'You are young to be an orphan.'

'And you are visiting friends while in Cornwall, Mr Carlton?' Cecily interrupted.

'Mama, is this inquisition necessary?' Peter said with impatience. He turned to Rupert who sat on his right. 'I thought we would walk to Polmasryn church as the weather has remained fine. It is a ruin but you will find ...'

'Peter, you cannot take Mr Carlton away from our other guests,' Joshua protested.

'I thought the ladies would like to join us. It is but a mile to Polmasryn.'

'I regret that I have another engagement this afternoon in Fowey,' Rupert declared. 'Another time I would enjoy walking to Polmasryn. I have enjoyed dining with you, but must leave soon or I shall be late for my appointment.'

'You should not rush off immediately after a meal.' Cecily's motherly instincts were roused. 'It is bad for the digestion and can cause an upset of the spleen, or so my dear mama always said. The afternoon is warm. A stroll to the stream would be most pleasant. There is a magnificent view across to the moor from there.'

'We must not detain Mr Carlton from his appointment.' Tamasine forced a smile to hide her disappointment. 'We are honoured that you could dine with us at such short notice. I will bid you farewell, sir. I leave for London on the morrow accompanying Mrs Amelia Loveday.'

Was that regret Tamasine thought she saw on Rupert Carlton's face? It seemed so unjust that she must leave Cornwall now.

'Are you to be in London for long, Miss Loveday?' he enquired.

'Some months, I believe.'

'Then I hope I will be permitted to call upon you there. I too will be returning to London at the end of the month.'

'My husband's sister, Mrs Margaret Mercer, would be delighted to receive you, Mr Carlton.' Cecily smiled. She had seen the interest in the young man's eyes as he regarded Tamasine. Margaret had always been the matchmaker of the family, but Cecily was proud that she had been the one to bring about a first formal meeting between Mr Carlton and Tamasine. It was not until the young man had left and Peter was driving Tamasine and Bridie back to their homes that Cecily recalled she had still not learned anything about Mr Carlton's family.

Chapter Twenty-Four

Trevowan was no longer the sanctuary William had always enjoyed whenever he was on leave from the navy. He spent much of his days helping on the estate and the evenings were fraught with tension as Lisette and Elspeth constantly bickered. Relations with his wife had deteriorated further. At night they slept in separate rooms. He had no patience with her tantrums and was relieved when Etienne appeared to take her riding. At least her brother was able to calm Lisette's moods.

Elspeth had left Trevowan this morning to spend three days at Fetherington Hall hunting with Lord Fetherington's pack. Amelia had left for London the previous day. William was expecting to receive orders to rejoin his ship any day now. The arrangements concerning Lisette must be settled before he sailed. Those arrangements had caused so many arguments and tantrums that this morning he did not want to face his wife who was still in her bedchamber and spoil an otherwise peaceful morning. He had gone into Edward's study to read the *Sherborne Mercury* before writing up the weekly accounts in the estate ledger. To his annoyance a maid announced Etienne Rivière.

He did not rise when the younger man entered. 'You are early, Etienne. Lisette is still abed.'

Etienne ignored William's gesture for him to be seated and glared down at him from across the desk. 'You will be returning to your ship soon and there are matters we need to discuss. The allowance you have agreed to pay Lisette each month is not enough. She is young and should enjoy the entertainments in Truro. She will need new gowns ...'

'The allowance is adequate,' William snapped. Etienne was trying to intimidate him by his posturing but it had no effect. 'Lisette must remember that I am but a humble captain in His Majesty's Navy. She has gowns aplenty and it is not seemly that she be seen too often in frivolous company now that she is married.'

'She is used to a different life from the dull one you would provide for her,' Etienne challenged.

'When she agreed to become my wife, she knew what was expected of her. I will not discuss this further.'

Etienne leaned over the desk, his manner menacing. 'She has a fortune in jewels. Some should be sold to provide her with a lifestyle that is more fitting.'

'I will not have her fortune squandered.' William stood up to face him, expression as resolute as when he had ordered a sailor caught stealing food to receive fifty lashes. 'It is time Lisette learned more decorum.'

'The jewels are her property.' Etienne jabbed a finger close to William's face. 'She should be allowed to use them for her own benefit.'

'They will be kept in the safekeeping of the bank.' William remained impassive, locking his hands together behind his back. His temper was rising and he was finding it hard to resist the urge to swing his fist into Etienne's arrogant face. Throughout his years of command, however, he had learned to control his temper. His hot-headedness as a midshipman had earned him many reprimands and twice had cost him his promotion to lieutenant. 'We have been through all this before. I have made my decision.'

Etienne's face darkened with fury. William stared him down. 'It is only with reluctance that I have agreed your sister may live with you. I do not trust you with her money. You have a reputation for reckless gambling.'

'You'll regret this,' Etienne spat.

'Do not threaten me. Perhaps it would be better if Lisette stayed at Trevowan.'

'She is unhappy here. Once you are at sea she will come to me.'

'Then she will come to you a pauper. I have yet to make

arrangements with my lawyer for her allowance to be paid. I could insist that it should only be so if my wife remains at Trevowan.'

'Damn you! You do not understand her,' Etienne raged. 'She is delicate – not like other women.'

William marched round the desk to stand inches from him. The Frenchman, seeing the fury in his eyes, took a step back. William announced, coldly, 'She has been spoilt all her days. It is time for her to realise that her life has changed.'

His brother-in-law continued to glare at him. William lost his patience and strode to the door of the study. Opening it, he blatantly dismissed Etienne. 'Do not provoke me further. I have right on my side. I have seen the worst examples of my wife's behaviour, and Dr Claver's report on her condition. If you give me reason to believe that you will worsen her instability, I will have her shut away for her own protection. Now I will bid you good day, sir.'

Etienne swore profanely in French and stormed from the study, shouting in a voice loud enough to reach his sister in her bedchamber: 'Lisette, I am here for our ride. I will await you in the stables. Do not be long.'

William returned to the desk and dropped his head into his hands. He could see no easy solution to the problem of his wife while he was at sea. He was not prepared to have his name tarnished by allowing her freedom to indulge in the wanton pursuit of pleasure.

He stayed in the study until he had heard Lisette and Etienne canter away from the house when he ordered Edward's gelding Rex saddled. While he was standing in the stable yard waiting a messenger rode in and handed William his orders to return to the fleet. He folded the document and placed it inside his jacket. He would leave Trevowan tomorrow and take his farewell from Adam this morning.

At Trevowan Hard he was disappointed to find that his nephew was at Boscabel and would not return for another hour. Senara was at home. Seeing William walking back to the stables, she invited him to join her.

'This has been a difficult leave for you, William. Especially as you must soon resume the war at sea.'

281

'It is what I have trained for all my life. I leave for Plymouth tomorrow. I have come to say goodbye to Adam.'

'We will miss you, and will remember you in our prayers.' Senara liked her husband's uncle though she sensed that he was ill at ease in the company of women. He was stockier than his brothers and his face rounder. Today his expression was shadowed by sadness. Senara felt her heart contract. The image of William before her wavered, becoming translucent and ghostly, then became a solid form again. Coldness gripped her. She could not shake off the feeling that this was the last time she would see the man who was about to sail away and face enemy fire at sea.

She summoned a strained smile, trying to dispel her fear. 'How is Lisette? It will be hard for you to leave your wife so soon.'

He did not reply but his face tightened. She cursed her own stupidity. It was obvious that he was not happy in his marriage.

He paced the parlour with his hands clasped behind his back. 'Adam has laid down a new keel for a cutter. At least that should ease the financial crisis the yard was facing.'

Senara noted that he had evaded answering her, but the subject of the keel was one she felt comfortable with. Even though the shipyard needed the business, she did not like Harry Sawle being their customer, and said so. The conversation faltered soon afterwards and Senara was at a loss as to how to continue. William seemed deeply troubled.

Tamasine appeared leading Nathan by the hand. The boy's dark hair was tousled and flopped forward over his brow. William smiled at him. 'He grows more like Adam each time I see him.'

Nathan held out his favourite toy. It was a wooden ship that had been carved by Edward for Adam when he was a child. There were tears in William's eyes as he lifted his great-nephew in his arms and inspected the ship with him. 'I recognise this. Do you like ships, Nathan?'

The boy nodded. 'Will build ships like Papa.'

William laughed. 'I am glad to hear it.'

Adam returned and, still holding Nathan, William walked with him out into the shipyard to inspect work on the new cutter that now rested in its cradle, the first of its ribs already in place. He did not stay long. When Adam re-entered the house, his expression was grave.

'Uncle William goes to sea a troubled man. This does not bode well,' he said heavily.

'He has much experience as a captain,' Senara reassured him, and moved into her husband's arms.

'Lisette will be leaving with Etienne,' Adam said with relief. 'That will make life easier at Trevowan.'

Senara was thoughtful. 'By the end of the week the house will be empty. It will be lonely for Elspeth. I am surprised she is not going to London to see Margaret.'

'And miss the hunting season!' Adam laughed. 'Elspeth hates London.'

'Do you think we should invite her to stay here and close both houses until St John returns?'

'She will not accept, but I will ask her. It cannot be long now before my brother arrives.' Adam frowned. 'I will miss Uncle William, though. This is the first time we have really become close. Everything has changed so much this year.'

'And there are more changes to come,' Senara said with a sigh. 'Let us pray they will be for the better.'

On leaving the shipyard William rode to Trewenna Rectory to say his farewells to Joshua and Cecily. His sister-in-law was tearful.

'You have been home so short a time! And now you go to fight in this war. You must take care of yourself, William. With Edward gone and Japhet in such dire ...' She broke off. 'I am being foolish.'

'Japhet will be freed,' William reassured her. 'It cannot be long now. And in a few weeks you will have your new grandchild to spoil.'

After an emotional farewell he headed for Trevowan. Lisette still had not returned from her ride with her brother. They had left four hours ago. She should by now be packing her clothes to leave. He would not burden his sister with Lisette any longer. She must be ready to leave Trevowan when he did tomorrow.

Most of William's possessions were already stowed in his sea chest. He ordered two maids to start on his wife's belongings. An hour later Lisette still had not returned and his anger deepened. To calm his mood he took a brisk walk along the cliff.

With Edward no longer at Trevowan an era had passed. The house no longer felt like home. Memories of his childhood filled William's mind. He had never felt for the land as Edward had done, but as he stared out to sea his heart stirred with fond memories. The cove had been the playground of his youth. He and Joshua had played pirates on the beach and learned how to sail a small dinghy in the sheltered bay.

Today the sea had a heavy swell, and he watched the breakers smashing on to the rocks near the cave. Seven fishing smacks sailed out from behind the headland at Penruan for the evening catch and he watched their sails pass out of sight around the next headland.

He climbed nimbly down the cliff to the beach and walked along the shoreline, still troubled by thoughts of how best to deal with Lisette. He was near the cave when he heard someone laughing and talking in a high-pitched voice. It was his wife, speaking rapidly and excitedly in French. During his voyages to many lands William had learned to converse in several languages. The words his wife was now crying out were shocking and shameful and he could not believe his ears.

The sand muffled his footsteps as he drew closer to the cave's entrance and peered inside. The sounds he heard now were unmistakably those of a couple in the throes of passion. Lisette had a lover! He felt no pain at her betrayal, only disgust. He moved closer to learn the identity of the man and, on recognising him, felt his stomach heave and vomit rise to his throat. Brother and sister, both naked, lay writhing together on the floor of the cave.

He staggered back, fury clouding his reasoning. He saw their horses tethered behind the outcrop of rock that formed the cave, where they would be hidden from anyone approaching from the house.

Driven by the sound of his own blood racing in his ears, William ran back along the beach. He climbed the cliff path and ran through the grounds and into the house. By the time he reached Edward's study he was breathing heavily but the strength of his outrage drove him on. His grandfather's duelling pistols were locked in a drawer of Edward's desk. The key was in an empty cigar box on a library shelf. He hurriedly opened the drawer and took out the pistol case. The weapons with their mother-of-pearl inlaid handles and engraved barrels had been prized by his brother. Edward had cleaned them every week, but not since their grandfather's day had they been used in anger.

It took only moments to prime and load each pistol. Then he took a third smaller pistol from the drawer, one that Edward had always carried on his person after being attacked one night riding home from the shipyard. This he loaded and tucked into the waistband of his breeches. With the case clutched under his arm, William returned to the cove. He was on the beach when Etienne and Lisette emerged from the cave, both dressed though in a dishevelled state.

William opened the pistol case and displayed the weapons. 'You will answer to me for this outrage, Rivière. You have sinned in the most heinous manner. A man who trespasses as you do does not deserve to live.'

Lisette threw her arms around her brother. 'You cannot kill him! Etienne is my life.'

'Stand aside, Lisette. Unless your brother chooses to hide behind a woman's skirts, he will answer to me for this base act. Choose your weapon, sir.'

Lisette's eyes were wide with terror. 'You cannot do this, William. Think of the scandal. The family will never live this down. You do not love me. Let Etienne and me go away together. We will leave England, you need never see us again.'

'*You* have brought this shame on me. How can I not challenge the man who has dishonoured my name and abused the trust of my entire family in this foul way?' He aimed a pistol at Etienne's heart. 'Do you take up the other weapon, sir? Or do I shoot you in cold blood?'

Etienne pushed Lisette aside and took the remaining pistol from the case, checking to see that it was loaded. When Lisette started to scream, he rounded on her. 'Be silent! Do you want to draw an audience to witness me killing your husband? I would surely hang then.'

She gulped back ragged sobs. Etienne nodded to William. 'We will take ten paces, turn and fire. Agreed?'

'Yes.'

There was a malicious glitter in Etienne's eyes. 'Have you fought any duels, Uncle William? I have fought many. And lived.'

William ignored the goading. At the moment, such was his shame, he did not care whether he survived or not. He was prepared to pay the ultimate price for his error in taking pity on Lisette and making her his wife.

He turned his back on Etienne and began to count ten paces. On the count of eight he heard a shot and pain seared his shoulder. He staggered. He should not have trusted Etienne. The cowardly blackguard had fired early to save his own miserable skin. William turned. He had been winged but the wound was not fatal. He raised his pistol to aim at Etienne's heart.

'No!' Lisette screamed, and hurled herself in front of her brother at the same moment that William fired. The bullet entered the side of her head, killing her instantly.

Etienne tossed aside his weapon and stared down at his sister's body lying in the sand. He snatched a dagger from a sheath in his belt and ran at William. He drew the second pistol and fired, the bullet entering Etienne's throat. The Frenchman fell to his knees, blood pouring from his neck, and then toppled sideways. He was not dead yet but would not survive for long.

William had not known why he had taken the third pistol from the study except that in his dazed state he had thought he might use it on himself. Now he had killed two people. Members of his own family. When their bodies were found, the scandal would be the talk of the county. He could not allow that to happen. Nor could he be arrested and face trial. The reason why he had killed his wife and her brother was too appalling to become the subject of gossip. He knew what had to be done.

He glanced up at the cliff but no one had appeared. The three shots must have been inaudible to the labourers working on the far side of the estate today, and even the stables had been empty, every able-bodied man needed to dig out a ditch before the winter rains flooded the far meadow.

The dinghy that Richard had borrowed from Adam on his last

286

leave was pulled up to the beach past the tide line. William took off his stock and tied it around Lisette's shattered skull. He carried her easily to the small boat then pushed it into the sea, water swirling around his calves.

Etienne was still battling for breath but too weak to resist when William picked up his legs and dragged him down the beach, hauling him over the side of the dinghy. William then returned to the beach to kick sand over the bloodstains, and with a handful of seaweed swept away the confusion of footprints that told their own story. He then gathered several large stones to weight the bodies and pushed the dinghy out further into the water. The light was beginning to fade, the sun setting over the headland on Penruan.

Until now he had barely noticed the pain from the wound in his shoulder, but as he pulled on the oars he had to bite down on his lip to keep himself from groaning at the agony searing through him. His strength was failing. In the distance he could just make out the sails of the fishing fleet catching the last of the light from the setting sun.

He pulled harder on the oars. No sound had come from Etienne for several minutes. His nephew was dead. William put the stones inside Lisette's and her brother's clothing before he pushed the bodies overboard. The weight of the stones should stop them being washed ashore.

The moon was rising in the sky as William rocked the dinghy, causing it to take on water. Gradually it began to sink lower into the sea. He wanted no evidence to remain of the last hour. The dinghy sank lower and with a final shudder began to sink beneath the waves. William kicked away from the boat and swam out to sea. He turned once to see a light shining from the Dower House at Trevowan. He prayed his family would never learn the truth of what had happened in the cove. Lisette had betrayed not only him, but the faith and trust of the whole family.

His arms grew weary and his body heavy, waves splashing into his face at every stroke. His final prayer as he began to sink beneath the water was that the disappearance of Lisette, Etienne and himself would remain a mystery.

Chapter Twenty-Five

Adam was selecting the next tree trunks to be cut into planks for the cutter from the pile stacked at the rear of the yard when Isaac Nance appeared on horseback and hailed him. The bailiff's face was grey with worry. He leaped from his horse, blurting out, 'Your uncle and his wife be missing from the house. Captain William bain't been seen since late-afternoon yesterday. Winnie Fraddon saw him walk down to the cove but he did not return from his walk for his supper. Mrs Loveday failed to return from her ride either. I went down to the cove last night and saw that the dinghy had gone. I thought it odd.'

'It is not like my uncle not to have left word with the servants.' Adam instantly became anxious too.

'Aye, that be so. So I went to the cove again this morning and found Mrs Loveday's and Mr Rivière's horses tethered, but no sign of them. I didn't see the horses last night, they were tethered out of sight of the path.'

'Could it be that Mrs Loveday and her brother took the dinghy? Lisette can be thoughtless. She may simply have omitted to inform the servants of their plans.'

Nance shook his head. 'It don't feel right somehow. Cap'n were to leave for Plymouth today, his sea chest packed and ready. He'd not have left without it.'

Adam agreed and his worry intensified. 'I will come to the house with you. Did anything untoward happen yesterday, Nance?'

'Winnie Fraddon said there'd been words. Mr Rivière were in a taking and quarrelled with Cap'n William in his study.'

'My uncle was here later in the day and mentioned nothing amiss.'

Adam did not want to worry Senara so merely sent word by an apprentice to tell her that he was needed at Trevowan. Once there he went straight to his uncle's room, finding his sea chest packed as Nance had described. Lisette's travelling chest was also packed. Jenna Biddick had been the last person to speak to William. Adam found her in the kitchen crying.

'Are you sure my uncle and his wife did not ride out and ask for their chests to be taken by a carter to Plymouth?'

'Captain Loveday told me to pack for his wife and that they would be leaving in the morning.' Jenna burst into fresh tears, which streaked her rosy cheeks.

Winnie Fraddon put a comforting hand on her shoulder, her large barrel-shaped figure dwarfing the maid's slender body. 'People don't just disappear. Happen there be a simple answer. That Frenchwoman could be a flibbertigibbet. She could have gone off somewhere and Captain Loveday went after her.'

Adam decided to search the cove and Isaac Nance followed him out of the house.

'The horses – had they been on the beach all night?' Adam asked him.

'It were their whinnying that took me to the cove. They were hungry and thirsty. Reckon they had been there all night.'

'You had better tend to your duties here. I will search the cove. There has to be a simple answer to this. As Winnie said, people do not just disappear.'

'Not unless they were caught by free traders when a cargo were being landed,' Isaac Nance said with a frown.

'Have there been signs of smugglers using Trevowan Cove?'

'I've had no reason to go there for some weeks. But after what happened to Mr Edward at Boscabel, I doubt any local smuggler would come so close.'

Anger burned through Adam at the possibility that Harry Sawle had landed another cargo on Loveday land. He had not thought the smuggler would be so foolish if he wanted his new cutter built.

'If any smuggler has been in the cove, they will regret it,' Adam vowed. He left Nance and climbed down to the beach. He was quick to notice that the dinghy had gone. Could William have taken it and rowed Lisette to Fowey for the evening as Nance had suggested? He had never done so before, and the sea at night could be treacherous in these parts. His uncle was too experienced to risk two lives on a whim. Then there was the matter of the horses. Etienne had been here. Why had he not ridden back to Fowey? Unless Uncle William had taken him with Lisette in the dinghy … Again it did not make sense.

Adam combed the edge of the tide line and was brought up short when he saw the heel of a shoe protruding from some seaweed. He picked it up, the silver buckle glinting in the sun. The dainty object belonged to Lisette. She would have gone nowhere wearing only one shoe. Alarm made his heart race. Something untoward had happened in the cove.

He scanned the beach thoroughly, searching for signs of a struggle. There were marks made by the dinghy being dragged down to the sea but the tide would have obliterated most of the footprints. Near the entrance to the cave he made another discovery: a pistol half-buried in the sand. He was shocked to recognise one of his great-grandfather's duelling pair. Only William could have brought that here. For what purpose? With whom would he fight a duel and why?

Lisette must be the reason behind this. Had she been with a lover in the cove? She had taken lovers in London, which had led to Amelia and Thomas deciding that she needed treatment from Dr Claver. If there had been a duel resulting in a death, where was the body? Or bodies?

Adam was drawn to the cave. Inside was an earring of Lisette's and a handkerchief with the initials ER. Etienne had then been here. Had *he* taken the pistol from the study and shot Lisette's lover? Etienne had fought many duels. He would not have hesitated to dispose of a body in the sea. Had he taken Lisette away afterwards, and had William discovered what had happened and followed them to bring Etienne to justice?

It all seemed so far-fetched but Adam could think of no other solution. Etienne was capable of killing to defend his sister's honour, while William would ensure that he was brought to justice. Adam was shocked by his own reasoning. Whatever had happened here was bound to bring new scandal on the Loveday name. He did not see how it could be avoided.

There was nothing he could do until he heard from his uncle. In the meantime he would tell the servants that William must have taken his wife out in the dinghy last night as the boat was missing.

During the journey to London Tamasine tried to constrain some of her natural exuberance, fearing that she might antagonise Mrs Loveday. Amelia was given to long silences, and Tamasine spent her time staring out of the window or singing rhymes to entertain young Rafe who was bored from the long hours of confinement. The coach lurched and swayed dangerously as its wheels ran into deep ruts caused by the autumn rains. Tamasine was bruised from the violent shaking but did not complain. Locked in her unhappiness, Amelia seemed oblivious to her surroundings.

Three days into the journey a heavy frost made the roads firmer but the inside of the coach was like ice. Heated bricks were placed under the women's feet as they drove away from each coaching inn, and hand warmers were slid inside their fur muffs. Each of them travelled in a cloak lined with fox fur, but they continued to shiver.

'It was foolish to engage upon this journey in winter,' Amelia said as the coach came to a sudden halt and the driver ordered the passengers to alight so that the horses could climb a steep hill.

Old sacks were placed on the frost-hardened road and blocks placed behind the wheels to stop them rolling back. It was a slow process for the four horses to pull the heavy coach to the top of the hill. Amelia slithered on the grass at the roadside and would have fallen if Tamasine had not caught her. The jolting woke the baby who whimpered fretfully. Tamasine also had hold of Rafe's hand to stop him running off. The women laughed in embarrassment at their predicament and Amelia kept her arm linked through Tamasine's until they reached the crest of the hill and could return to the carriage.

'Will you not be glad to meet with your old friends in London?' Tamasine enquired as they started out on the eighth day. She was nervous about meeting the rest of the Loveday family and they would arrive in London tomorrow. Forced to eat and spend the night in the same room together, Amelia had gradually thawed in her manner towards Tamasine and had told her much of the family history.

'Seeing my friends will be a mixed blessing. I do not wish to relive the gossip surrounding Japhet's trial. I had hoped he would have been pardoned by now. And my last visit to London was not a happy one.'

'I was to blame for that. I am sorry.'

'I brought my unhappiness upon myself. It all seems foolish and irrelevant now. I wasted a year of my time with Edward through false pride.'

'No one could have imagined that he would be taken from us so soon. I know it was an unhappy year for you, but it was one I shall never forget. In that short time I came to know and love the man who was my father. Had I stayed at school he would still have been shot by the excise men and I would not have known him or any of his family. My life would have been very different and without much prospect of happiness in the future. I am forever indebted to Edward Loveday. And now to you, for accepting me,' she was quick to add. 'I know it had not been easy for you. You are a very kind and generous woman, Mrs Loveday.'

'You are a daughter that Edward would be proud of.' Amelia held Joan close to her breast; the baby was now sleeping peacefully and appeared to be suffering no ill effects from the journey.

'Joan is a fighter,' Tamasine said, smiling at her. 'She is stronger than you think.'

Rafe demanded a story then and Tamasine put her arm around him and told him one until he fell asleep, lulled by the rocking of the coach. She looked up to find Amelia smiling at her, and knew that this journey had started to mend the antagonism between them.

When Tamasine finally visited the Mercers' house in the Strand after first spending the night in Amelia's town house, she was greeted enthusiastically by Margaret Mercer.

'Welcome to London, my dear. You are just what our family needs to shake us out of our melancholy. This will be a quiet Christmas. It would not be right to entertain too lavishly so soon after your father's death, but we will accept the invitations of close friends and you must be fitted out with a suitable wardrobe. Thomas has a play running in Drury Lane so it would not be inappropriate to attend the theatre to support him, or to see a play written by one of his friends. The occasional musical evening would also be in order providing that the gathering is small.'

'I had not expected so much. I trust that you will not change the way you would have conducted your time of mourning?' Tamasine was overwhelmed by her welcome.

'It is what Edward would have wanted.' Margaret was emphatic. 'I have a vast circle of friends, many of them with eligible sons. It would be most remiss of me if I did not do all in my power to ensure that you enjoyed your first season in London. And, of course, there is no better opportunity to meet a husband.'

Tamasine liked Margaret, though she was not so sure she wanted to be put on the marriage market. Her dreams were filled by images of Rupert Carlton. He was the perfect beau for her and had said that he would call on her when he came to London.

A week later Gwendolyn was brought to bed of a son. The baby was named Japhet Edward. Though overjoyed at the birth of a healthy son, she was fretful during her lying in.

'Japhet has been in prison for so long,' she said tearfully when Georganna called in to visit her, 'and still we are no nearer to clearing his name. Japhet Edward needs a father.'

'You must not overset yourself so,' Georganna reasoned. 'You will sour your milk, and you will not hear of a wet-nurse being engaged to feed your son.'

'Japhet Edward is so precious to me, I do not want anyone else caring for him.' She held the baby in her arms. He was sleeping soundly and contentedly, while Gwendolyn's eyes were sunken from her ordeal and her fears for her husband. 'Thomas visited Japhet to inform him of his son's birth but Japhet was insistent that I did not take the baby to the gaol to see him.' She sniffed back the tears which were threatening to spill on to her cheeks. 'How can he not want to see his own son?'

'Japhet fears the risk of infection for the baby. Newgate is rife with gaol fever, consumption and the bloody flux, to name but a few. You cannot wish to risk Japhet Edward's life?'

Gwendolyn kissed the baby's brow. 'Of course not! But what if Japhet is transported? What if he is taken suddenly and never gets to see his son? I've heard the transportation fleet will sail soon. A man has the right to hold his son in his arms.'

Georganna frowned. The family had agreed to keep that news from Gwendolyn until she had fully recovered from the birth. Georganna would not allow her friend to lapse into despondency. 'Japhet will be pardoned, you must trust in that. Is Sir Gregory not confident that he will prove Japhet's innocence?'

'But he has learned nothing of this other highwayman, the one who held up Lord Sefton's coach. The man has gone to ground. He would be a fool to return to London, he must have heard that Japhet was condemned for his crime.'

'That could make him careless,' remarked Georganna.

Gwendolyn shook her head. 'I fear it is too late. But I will not allow Japhet to serve his time in Australia alone. I will sail with the fleet and buy land there if necessary, and petition that he is bonded to me for the term of his punishment. That can be arranged, so I have heard.'

'Even if that were possible, it would be a dangerous life for you. I am sure that Japhet would not agree.'

'He will not know until I am in the colony. I am his wife. Where he goes, I go. I did not wait so many years to marry him only to abandon him now. Japhet was innocent. He did not hold up Lord Sefton's coach. I will stand by him.'

Georganna shuddered. Gwendolyn was stubborn enough to follow him to the ends of the earth if necessary.

'And they used to mock you for being timid as a mouse! You are the bravest woman I know, Gwendolyn. But I will still pray for Japhet's release. I have faith in Sir Gregory.'

'As do I,' Gwendolyn assured her. 'But I fear that time is fast running out for my husband.'

'I hear that the wife of that knave Gentleman James has been brought to bed of a son,' Celestine Yorke flung at Sir Pettigrew Osgood the moment he entered her bedchamber. She wore a pink diaphanous robe edged with ostrich feathers and nothing beneath it.

294

'Why do you still trouble yourself over the cur?' Sir Pettigrew was far from pleased at this reception. 'He will get little joy of the child, rotting beneath the sun of Botany Bay. The place is a living hell.'

'He has yet to sail,' Celestine reminded him, her eyes venomous with hatred. 'He is fêted within Newgate as a notorious highwayman, and that wife of his ensures he has every luxury. I thought you wanted him hanged for the robbery?'

Sir Pettigrew's eyes narrowed. 'It would have given me greater satisfaction to have shot the blackguard dead in a duel. But the ways of justice are sometimes harsher yet. Even with his wife paying the bribes at Newgate, incarceration for such a man as Japhet Loveday will be torture. Do you want his torment to end too quickly?'

'He played us for fools! Tricked us both. He has not suffered enough. Not yet.' Celestine paced the room which was strewn with discarded clothing.

Sir Pettigrew roughly pulled her into his arms, his fingers steely about the nape of her neck. 'For what would you have him pay: robbing my coach or discarding you to wed a younger woman? His wife is quite fetching and passionate in her love for him. She continues to petition for his pardon.'

'The woman has no pride. He has shamed her.' Celestine glared up at Sir Pettigrew. Candlelight was no longer enough to conceal time's ravages. Hatred and her lust for vengeance had hardened her features in the last year. The loss of her former popularity on stage had turned her seductively pouting lips to thin sour lines. She had not been in a play for several months and Sir Pettigrew was the only man of any influence or social standing who continued to visit her as a lover. And he had become niggardly with his gifts.

Her eyes darkened with cunning. 'And where is your pride, that you allow him to mock us from his prison?'

'Take care, madam. You forget to whom you speak. You still have more passion for this knave than you show to me. I did not visit you to talk of Japhet Loveday.' He pushed her from him and took up his gloves and hat which he had placed on the bedside table. 'I will go where my company is better appreciated.'

Fear spiralled through Celestine. Osgood had at least two other mistresses that he visited. One was married to an Italian count, and he had also been seen in the company of Kitty Jones who was no longer Lord Sefton's mistress. Celestine cursed her own anger at Japhet for making her careless. If she lost Osgood, she would be without a noble protector. She did not want to be the mistress of mere burghers or shopkeepers; they would not bring her public acclaim.

She ran to Sir Pettigrew and put her arms around him. 'You cannot leave, I shall be bereft. I have missed you. It has been several days since you last came to me.' She took his hand and drew him towards her bed. 'You are the only man I care for. How can you doubt that?' She began to remove his clothing. 'Loveday should pay for the way he tricked us. How often did he laugh at us behind our backs for not recognising him? He robbed your coach and then, playing his role of gentleman, sat at the same card table as you and many of your friends, and robbed you all blind at cards. He must have used sleight of hand. He has forgotten the meaning of honesty. But you will have the last laugh, Sir Pettigrew. You have your contacts. He would not be the first man to die in a prison brawl.'

'I have done many things in my life that I have not been proud of, but I have never paid for a man to be murdered. The depth of your evil astounds me, madam.'

He pulled back from her and adjusted his dishevelled clothing. He had long despised Celestine for her greed and spitefulness, but she was the most exciting bedfellow he had known. Yet even that had paled in recent months. She was too often tired when he visited, and this constant spite towards Loveday was wearing. The room stank of gin and he had noted that Celestine's stance was unstable. She had been drunk most nights since Loveday's trial, and the gin was fast ravaging what was left of her looks. Though she had always professed to love him, he knew that Loveday had held a far greater attraction for her. Sir Pettigrew was aware that women like Celestine used men like him purely to enhance their own fame and fortune. The few times he had visited Kitty Jones he had found her refreshing and unassuming. She made no demands and had been genuinely pleased to receive him.

'I will bid you good day, madam. I feel it is time to call an end to our association.'

'But you cannot desert me!' Celestine screamed.

'I can do exactly as I please.' He turned abruptly on his heel.

'Then while Japhet Loveday lives he continues to mock you,' she lashed out, angered that Sir Pettigrew also would desert her. 'Use your connections at Court. Was justice itself not ridiculed the day a highwayman was allowed to live?'

'His mockery is of you, madam, not myself,' Sir Pettigrew responded with equal venom. 'You were the whore he boasts he never paid a penny for the privilege of her favours. You were the one who made a fool of herself over a penniless vagabond. You recognised him long before you claimed and only denounced him after you discovered he was to marry. I went along with your schemes then because I wanted the blackguard brought to justice. That has been done.'

His anger was scathing and his expression harsh with contempt as he glared at her. 'Sefton knows you only returned his wife's necklace in order to implicate your lover. Sir Marcus Grundy believes you stole his stock pin and recalls that money often went missing from his purse when he visited you. They will not denounce you to the authorities because it would tarnish their own reputation, but no man of note will have anything more to do with you, madam. Your days as the Darling of London are long past. So are your days as an actress. Use your ill-gotten gains wisely, madam. You have gulled enough men to keep you from the poorhouse.'

He walked out of the house and her life, finding the air of London suddenly smelled sweeter.

Celestine collapsed on the floor. 'Good riddance!' she screamed at his departing figure, but his words echoed her darkest nightmare. She dreaded a life of obscurity. She could live comfortably from her income as a landlady, but where was the pleasure in that? No longer would she be fêted for her beauty, or be able to parade through London on the arm of a doting lord.

She reached for the gin bottle and sought solace in its contents.

Chapter Twenty-Six

A week after William disappeared there had still been no word from him. Adam was worried when he received an urgent summons from Elspeth. When he arrived at Trevowan his distressed aunt took him into the winter parlour and shut the door so that their conversation could not be overheard.

'There is a Captain Barton from the Admiralty here. He is waiting in Edward's study and refuses to leave until he has spoken to William, or learned why he has not reported for duty.' Elspeth was clearly agitated and wrung her hands. 'What happened to him while I was at Lord Fetherington's? The servants said that his belongings were still at the house but that the dinghy had gone from the cove. Lisette and he must have gone to spend a few days in Fowey. But her clothes? She would not leave without them, surely?'

'I do not know much more than the servants have told you. I did not want you worrying unnecessarily.'

'I am not some milksop of a woman who must be protected,' his aunt snapped. 'Tell me what you know?' She rubbed her hip as she hobbled to a chair and sat down.

Adam paced the room before speaking. 'It is possible a duel was fought in the cove. I found one of Great-grandfather's duelling pistols there. Or they could have been used to warn off smugglers, but I do not think that was the case. Somehow Etienne was involved for both Lisette's and his horse were found tethered in the cove. Etienne also has disappeared.'

'Why was I not told of this?' Elspeth regarded him fiercely. 'William is in danger. Something has happened to him. He would not fail to report for duty unless he was gravely ill. Could the duel have been between him and Etienne? The two of them have been arguing over Lisette's jewels lately. William had refused to hand them over to Etienne before he sailed with the fleet.'

'William would not fight a duel over that. It is possible, however, that Lisette used the cave to meet a lover and Etienne found them there together. He would be hot-headed enough to kill a man over Lisette.'

'I knew that baggage would bring trouble down on our heads!' Elspeth was incensed. 'She took lovers when she was in London so nothing she does surprises me. But William must be involved in this somehow.' She put one shaking hand to her heart.

'He would wish to save the family name from another scandal. It could be possible that he persuaded Etienne and Lisette to leave Cornwall together.'

'Without their possessions! I think not. And all this talk of a duel – would there not have to have been a body, or someone grievously injured, to make them run away?'

Adam agreed with her. 'I do not know the answers. I had better speak to Captain Barton.'

The interview was difficult. Barton was in his sixties, his face weathered and wrinkled, and spoke with a lisp, having lost most of his teeth. His rheumy eyes regarded Adam belligerently. He had been present during this young man's court-martial and did not view him favourably.

'Where is Captain Loveday? He is derelict in his duty and will be court-martialled if he does not return with me to Plymouth.'

Adam did not wish to disclose any of the events he believed could have taken place in the cove. They were only speculation. He announced simply that the dinghy had gone and his uncle and his wife had not been seen at Trevowan for several days. He concluded, 'My uncle has never failed in his duty or service to his country. I am certain he is on his way to his ship now.'

Captain Barton continued to cross-examine Adam, firing off questions as to the state of his uncle's health and mind. After more than an hour he concluded, 'Many a brave man has suddenly turned coward after a vicious encounter with the enemy.'

'My uncle is no coward, I can assure you, sir.'

299

'Then why the devil has he not reported for duty?'

Adam battled to control his anger. 'There is a simple answer, I am sure.'

There was a rap on the door then and Isaac Nance entered. 'Your pardon for this intrusion but I've news that couldn't wait, sir. News concerning Captain Loveday.' There was a haunted look in the bailiff's eyes. Nance swallowed hard and his voice shook as he announced, 'A body was found yesterday, washed up on the rocks some miles down the coast. The fishes and rocks made it difficult to identify, but the clothes were what Captain Loveday was wearing the last time he was seen, according to the description you gave the coastguard, sir.'

'Thank you, Nance. Where is the body?'

'In a coffin on a cart outside, sir. Reckon the funeral should be today.'

Adam turned away from Captain Barton to control his emotions and a wave of grief.

'Do you wish my assistance in identifying the body?' the naval man offered.

'If you please, and may we do so before I inform my aunt.' Adam led the way outside. It was not pleasant identifying a body that had been in the sea for a week, there was little flesh left on its face, but the clothes and build were unmistakable.

'My condolences, sir.' Captain Barton bowed stiffly to Adam. 'But an inquiry should be made as to how Captain Loveday drowned and whether it was an accident.'

'Are you insinuating that my uncle committed suicide?' Adam bristled with affront. 'That is a gross slur upon his honour. His wife is also missing. Clearly the dinghy capsized. Though my uncle was experienced in handling it, the currents hereabouts can be dangerous.'

When Barton had left, Adam sent word to everyone that William would be buried that afternoon in the family vault at Penruan. It was a simple ceremony, with a hurried funeral feast prepared by Winnie Fraddon. When the family had left for their homes, Adam found Elspeth standing by the open door of Edward's study, looking forlorn and lost.

'Do you wish to return with us to Mariner's House? Hannah

has taken Rowena back to the farm with her to spend a few days with the other children. I do not think you should be alone tonight.'

'Trevowan is my home. I will not leave it.' She sighed and turned to stare at the portraits that hung on the wall of the staircase.

The central chandelier had been lit, casting deep shadows over the walls and black and white marble floor. A picture of Edward and Amelia, painted shortly after the birth of Rafe who was depicted on Amelia's lap, hung at the lowest point over the stairs. Four generations were represented, though Adam and St John had last been painted as young boys, standing alongside their father and grandfather. There was no portrait of William, who had joined the navy as a midshipman at the age of eight and had never been home long enough for one to be painted.

Elspeth's pain-wracked body was stooped, all vitality stripped from her. 'The news will be a great shock to Margaret and Amelia. I will write to them.'

'Why do you not spend the winter in London with them?' Adam suggested.

'And miss my hunting!' Elspeth was indignant, a spark of her normal resilience returning. 'I have never cared for London. My mares need to be exercised.' She patted Adam's arm. 'Do not worry about me. I am spending Christmas with Cecily and Joshua. It will bring me much solace to attend the services at Trewenna church. Will you be joining us?'

Adam nodded. 'And afterwards you are welcome to stay at Mariner's House, if you reconsider.'

'I am in no mood for festivities. And I will not be alone in the house for long. St John should return soon. Mayhap then I shall move into the Dower House. The house will be full of his friends and I prefer to live quietly now.'

In his concern over the disappearance of his uncle, Adam had forgotten that St John would shortly arrive from Virginia. He stared at the portraits as his aunt walked up the curving stairs, her step slower and her limp more pronounced than before. A new era was about to dawn on Trevowan with St John as its master.

The old resentment flared through Adam. His brother did not

deserve Trevowan. It would lost its peace and dignity when St John invited his wastrel friends here to squander their money on gaming. The old rivalry towards his twin was rekindled. When St John returned there would be much to be accounted for.

Tamasine loved every moment of excitement that London had to offer. The diversity of people on its streets, from the beggars and street vendors to the nobles promenading in the parks or riding in their grand carriages, was a constantly changing spectacle that enthralled her. She wanted to see all the great public buildings, though the Tower of London with its grisly history daunted her. Westminster Abbey and St Paul's were the first places she visited. Rupert would doubtless be interested in their architecture and she wanted to understand something of his passion. The high-domed elegance of St Paul's did not fascinate her as much as the medieval Gothic splendour of Westminster Abbey, where so many of the Kings and Queens of England were buried in tombs displaying their painted effigies.

She shopped in the Royal Exchange with Amelia who spared no expense to outfit her in a dozen gowns and accessories that would be suitable for morning, afternoon and evening wear. Tamasine was to attend her first ball during the Christmas festivities. The pleasure of this occasion was marred when Rupert Carlton did not attend. She did not even know if he was in London yet, but every time she left the Mercers' house she prayed she would encounter him.

Another month passed and Tamasine began to despair of ever seeing him again. She was popular by now and several young men vied for her attention. She dutifully engaged them in conversation while always hoping that Rupert would appear. Margaret Mercer ignored her preoccupation and encouraged gentleman callers on the days when they were at home to visitors. But none of these men, however handsome or charming, interested Tamasine in the way that Rupert Carlton had done. She dreaded one of them offering for her. Then she would have to offend him, and also Margaret and Amelia, by her refusal.

Georganna came and sat by her in the family parlour as they waited for the rest of the family to join them for yet another musical soirée. Her tall, thin figure was displayed dramatically in a taffeta dress of broad black and white stripes worn with a scarlet sash around her waist. A high ostrich feather headdress wobbled as she walked. 'You look pensive, Tamasine. Mr Sterling and Mr Norton will attend this evening. Mr Norton seemed particularly taken with you.'

Tamasine felt quite dowdy by comparison in her gown of lemon silk. She loved bold colours but Amelia was adamant that a young unmarried woman must dress in pale modest shades. 'It is daunting being so obviously available on the marriage market. Though I do appreciate how kind Aunt Margaret has been in ensuring that I meet so many new people.'

'I hated it when men were invited to dine in order to select one of my three cousins. My uncle, Mr Lascalles, did not wish me to marry for I would bring to my husband a half-share in Lascalles Bank and they kept the knowledge of my inheritance a secret. At the time I dreaded marriage, though I hated living with my aunt and uncle too. It was at one of their dinner parties that I met Thomas. I had admired his work as a playwright for years and knew he was eager to repair the reputation and finances of Mercer's Bank after his father shot himself. In Thomas I found the perfect match. He achieved an advantageous merger with my family's bank, and through my husband I became part of the theatre and literary world that I adored.'

Tamasine was discomfited to hear Georganna state so openly that her marriage had been one of convenience.

'You and Thomas seem such a happy couple now. You do not even seem to mind that his friend Lucien Greene always accompanies you when you entertain.'

'Lucien is a mutual friend.' Georganna shrugged. 'My father too was a playwright. He hated the bank and refused to work there, though he maintained his half-share in the business. Thomas and I have so many interests in common. That was important to me in a marriage partner.'

'And to me,' Tamasine confessed. 'But I do not seem to have anything in common with Mr Norton or Mr Sterling. I could not bear to be married to a dullard, I could never love such a man.'

'Then you must trust that the right one for you will come along.

Happiness in marriage means many different things to different people. It is a lifetime commitment and too often women accept second best for the sake of security.' Georganna clamped a hand over her mouth for a moment. 'Margaret and Amelia will not thank me for speaking so frankly with you,' she confessed. 'But it is obvious you are a woman of strong spirit and few of Loveday blood have led conventional lives.'

Tamasine sighed. 'The family will wish me to wed as soon as possible. I cannot continue to be a burden on Amelia who still has not truly accepted me.'

'No one sees you as a burden,' Georganna reassured her. 'Amelia is still mourning Edward, which makes her appear sombre.'

She did not contradict Georganna but Tamasine felt that Amelia remained guarded in her company and resented the responsibility of providing for Tamasine's future.

Thomas called from the landing, 'The coach is here. Are you all ready to leave?'

Tamasine fastened her cloak and during the journey hoped that the fervent Mr Norton would not be present.

It was not until the interval when they had gone into the room set aside for supper that she saw Rupert. He was talking with their host, apparently engrossed in conversation. Seeing him again after so many weeks set her heart racing. Tamasine held back from the crush of people at the buffet table and took a glass of wine from a passing footman, sipping it slowly. She stood behind a large potted plant to avoid detection by Mr Norton who had been as difficult to remove from her side as a barnacle. From her hiding place she could watch Rupert unobserved. He was the most handsome and dashing man in the room.

'There you are, child. What are you doing hiding yourself away?' Margaret descended upon her, waving her fan in agitation. 'Mr Norton feels you have been avoiding him.'

'He can be a little tiresome in his conversation,' Tamasine defended her flight. 'He talks of nothing but his haberdasher's business.'

'A business that could keep you in style for the rest of your life, if you so chose,' her aunt responded. 'He has a fine house in

Aldwych. Is he not young and quite handsome?'

'He is dull.' Tamasine's gaze strayed to Rupert who had turned to replace his empty glass on the tray of a passing footman. At that moment he looked up and saw her. He smiled and instantly excused himself to his companion.

Tamasine felt her cheeks heat as he approached. 'Aunt Margaret, do you know Mr Rupert Carlton? He was recently in Cornwall and made the acquaintance of Peter and Uncle Joshua there. He dined with us. Mr Carlton, may I introduce Mrs Margaret Mercer, sister to my guardian, Mr Edward Loveday?'

Aunt Margaret studied him with a quick assessing gaze. She had seen Tamasine's blush and noted the quality of Mr Carlton's attire and his handsome looks. 'Do you live in London, sir, may I ask?'

'In Grosvenor Square.' He bowed to Margaret. 'It is a pleasure to meet another member of the Loveday family. Your brother and his wife made me most welcome in Cornwall. I enjoyed many pleasant conversations on architecture with Peter. It is an interest of mine.'

'And what do you do for a living, Mr Carlton?' Margaret asked.

'I have recently returned from my Grand Tour. I do not come into my trust until I am twenty-one. I am fortunate in that my allowance allows me to pursue my studies and interests.'

'Then you are a gentleman of independent means.' Margaret clearly warmed to him. 'Grosvenor Square is such a pleasant address. You must know Lord and Lady Montvillier?'

He nodded, not seeming to mind Aunt Margaret's questions though Tamasine squirmed with embarrassment that she could be so forthright and probing.

'How are you acquainted with Sir Tavistock, our host this evening, Mrs Mercer?' Rupert enquired.

'He was a friend of my late husband's and a client of our bank. You may know of my son, Thomas Mercer? He is a partner in Mercer and Lascalles. Do you bank with us, sir?'

'At the risk of offending you, I fear I am with Coutts.'

'A most worthy establishment.' Margaret smiled, showing no sign of offence.

Rupert continued, at his most charming. 'And is not Mr

305

Mercer also a playwright? I saw his play *The Admiral's Wife* last night. It was most enjoyable.'

'That was indeed my son's work. I will introduce you to him, if you wish, sir?'

Rupert nodded and later joined their party when they took their seats for the second half of the evening. Before they left, he had asked if he might call on Mrs Mercer the following morning.

Margaret was thoughtful as they drove home. 'I know nothing of this Mr Carlton, though he does seem most presentable.'

'He is much nicer than Mr Norton,' Tamasine could not stop herself from confessing.

'Then we must learn more of his family. A handsome face is all very well, but he could be a poor relation with few prospects.'

'I thought you said he was of independent means?' Tamasine pointed out.

'One can never be too careful about these matters, my dear.' Margaret settled back in her seat with a knowing smile. 'A man may say many things to impress a young lady's family. These things must be verified. Not that I think him dishonest, but it is your future security and happiness that are at stake, Tamasine.'

A lone female figure trudged along the cliff top carrying all her possessions in a small valise. The full moon trailed its beam of light across the water of the cove below and in the distance the grey stonework of the Dower House looked ghostly against the inky sky. Further inland the darker outline of Trevowan House with its tall chimneys was also visible. The only light showing from either building was in Rowena's nursery. The servants were long abed.

The woman stared grimly at the two houses. She would not be welcome here, but she did not care. The journey from London had taken her a month. She had no money to pay for a seat on a post chaise, relying on any vehicle that travelled in her direction. Some of the drivers had demanded favours from her as payment. She was past caring what men did to her. She was weak and her chest hurt as she coughed, spitting out a mouthful of blood.

Meriel dragged her weary body to the front door of Trevowan and was surprised to find that it was locked for the night. It was never locked when the family was in residence. She hesitated to ring the bell and waken the servants. She was too tired to face a confrontation.

She turned to the Dower House; no one could deny her right to sleep there. That door was also locked but she knew the catch on the parlour window was faulty and took a knife from her valise, carried for protection on the road, using it to prise open the window. The shutters inside were locked but the catches were old. She raised the valise and battered it against them several times until they opened. Meriel threw the valise inside and summoned her failing strength to haul herself over the window frame into the parlour.

Moonlight lit the room and Meriel scowled at the changes she found. Sturdier padded settles and armchairs had replaced the delicate gilded French furniture she had nagged St John to buy. The porcelain figures she had lovingly acquired had also been removed.

When she had been passing through Launceston she had made discreet enquiries about the Loveday family. On discovering that Edward was dead, and his brother William also, she had been elated. That meant St John was now Master of Trevowan and she would be its mistress. She had also learned that St John had not yet returned from his voyage to Virginia which would make it easier to establish herself here. She had kept her face hidden while staying the night before in a village ten miles away. She had not wanted to be recognised in her present condition. But a carter had bought her a tankard of ale, and after she had gone into the hayloft with him had answered her questions about the Lovedays and their neighbours. It had been a relief to learn that Amelia had left Cornwall to spend the winter in London.

She glanced around the room again, disliking the changes. But then, she would not live here; her place was now at Trevowan House.

Meriel's stomach growled with hunger. She had not eaten for two days. The carter had been willing to buy her enough ale to get her drunk and willing for a tumble but was too mean to buy her a meal. Often during her journey she had slept in barns at night, leaving before it was light. She had returned home sly as a fugitive, a ragged pauper, her looks and figure ravaged by ill health and starvation. That would all change.

She went into the kitchen but since Winnie Fraddon had prepared all the meals for St John and herself in the other house did not expect to find much food. In a clay crock in the larder she found two cinnamon cakes. Although they were stale she bit into them hungrily.

Then, swaying with exhaustion, she ascended the stairs to the bedchambers. The beds were stripped bare but Meriel did not care. She found some blankets in a chest and wrapped them around herself before falling asleep on her old bed.

Tomorrow she would be rested. Then the battle to regain her place at Trevowan would begin.

Chapter Twenty-Seven

Meriel woke later than she had intended. She had laid her plans for the day carefully and was worried lest she had ruined them. She realised that she would not be welcome here and the best way to gain entrance to the house and re-establish her position would be through Rowena. She knew that her daughter had not sailed with St John; and from the gossip she had garnered in the last few days about the family, had learned of the speculation surrounding Edward's ward and that Amelia had taken the girl with her to London. Rowena it seemed had stayed at Trevowan with only Elspeth for company.

It had not surprised Meriel how easy it had been to find out about the family; people liked to gossip, especially about those who had been struck by misfortune. Even so, she did not assume she would find it easy to reinstate herself with the family, for Elspeth was a formidable antagonist. St John's aunt had been more frightening to confront than Edward. Elspeth could not be won over by protestations or false promises, she had never liked Meriel.

None of the clocks in the Dower House had been wound and it was with relief that Meriel heard the clock in the church tower at Penruan strike ten. Elspeth was a woman of fixed routine. She would have breakfasted by now and would soon emerge with Rowena to take the child on her morning ride. Meriel hovered by the window to watch for them leaving the house. She did not have long to wait. She heard Rowena's high-pitched, excited voice even before they left the house.

Meriel swiftly opened the door of the Dower House and called to her daughter.

The little girl stopped in her tracks and shielded her eyes from the morning sun. Then she cried out, 'Mama! Mama has come home!' With arms outspread she ran across the lawn, sobbing and babbling as she was scooped into Meriel's arms.

'Put Rowena down!' Elspeth roared, stamping towards them with her cane thumping on the ground. 'How dare you show your face here?'

Meriel tossed back blonde hair that was dirty and matted. 'I have every right. I am mistress here now.'

'St John will have something to say about that!'

'But he is not here, is he?'

'Mama, come and see the cat Grandpapa brought me. His name is Bodkin and he sleeps in my room.' Rowena wriggled from her embrace. She took her mother's hand and tugged on it.

'Rowena, go to your room,' ordered Elspeth.

'Stay with your mama,' countered Meriel.

Rowena looked uncertainly from her mother to her great-aunt. Her lower lip trembled. 'Mama is home. Why are you not happy, Aunt Elspeth?'

She glared at Meriel. 'Rowena, do as you are bid.' When the girl clung closer to her mother, she shouted to summon the servants, 'Fraddon! Nance!'

'Are you going to ask them to throw me off my husband's land? Do you really want such a scandal?'

'You created the scandal when you ran off with your lover. It did not take him long to discard you, did it? It would be an affront to the family for you to live here in St John's absence. Our friends will never accept you. You have shown yourself to be a whore and my nephew has washed his hands of you.'

'But I am still St John's wife, and I will not go quietly.' Menace harshened Meriel's voice. 'The name of the Lovedays will be dragged through the mire. I have my rights. My family ...'

'Your family want nothing to do with you. Even your brothers condemned your actions.' Elspeth fixed her with a piercing stare. 'Look at you – like a tuppenny whore. You are in rags, your hair and face are dirty, and I can smell the stench of you from here. You found your true level when you ran off with Wycham – the gutter!'

Jasper Fraddon hobbled through from the stable yard. When he recognised Meriel his wrinkled face turned sour. He hawked and spat on the ground. 'Miss Elspeth, do you wish me to summon Cap'n Loveday?'

'Yes, Fraddon.' Elspeth glanced towards the Dower House. 'And you, madam, can go back inside. I will not have you in Trevowan.'

'How are you going to stop me, old lady?' Meriel made to push past her, holding tightly on to Rowena's hand.

Isaac Nance and his son Dick appeared then. Both were stocky men used to dealing with poachers or cattle rustlers on the land. Isaac folded his arms across his broad chest. 'If Miss Elspeth says you bain't to enter the house, then that be how it be.'

He blocked Meriel's passage to the main house and the cold set of his features warned her that he would not hesitate to use force.

As she hesitated Dick Nance waylaid Fraddon who was about to ride to the yard. 'I'll fetch Cap'n Loveday,' he offered. Moments later he galloped away.

'Why is everyone being so nasty to Mama?' Rowena began to cry. 'Mama, I want you to see Bodkin and my new doll.'

'This is not the time, Rowena!' Elspeth beckoned to the girl but she refused to move from her mother's side. Exasperated, Elspeth flung an accusing arm at Meriel. 'Have you not made this poor mite suffer enough? You are using her now to gain your own ends. It will not work.'

Meriel smirked and lifted the child in her arms. 'Come, Rowena, Mama would like to see your new doll. You have grown tall while I have been away.'

'Put the girl down,' ordered Elspeth.

Isaac Nance stepped towards Meriel who clasped Rowena tighter.

'You are hurting me, Mama.' She struggled but Meriel refused to loosen her grip and Rowena began to cry.

'Nance, take Rowena from her mother, she is upsetting the child.' Elspeth looked as though she would like to strike Meriel with her stick.

For a moment Meriel continued to defy them. Then Rowena

311

began to struggle and kick her legs, catching Meriel painfully on the shin.

'Why did you go away, Mama?' she wailed. 'You are hurting me. You used to hurt me before ...'

Nance snatched Rowena from her mother and gave her to Elspeth who kissed her hair and tried to calm her.

'I want Papa,' Rowena sobbed. Her pain at being abandoned by both her parents was clear on her anguished face.

'Once your papa left Trevowan, I could not stay here,' Meriel improvised, needing to gain Rowena's sympathy. This was not going as she had planned.

Rowena stared at her mother through her tears. She was an intelligent child and her eyes were accusing. 'But why did Papa not take me? He was the one who was kind to me. You were always so cross.' She wiped her eyes saying guilelessly, 'You used to be pretty, Mama. Where are your nice clothes? You are all dirty. Granny Sawle smells nicer than you, and she always smells of fish stew.'

'Insolent chit!' She raised her hand to strike her daughter and Elspeth immediately rapped her stick across Meriel's arm.

'There will be no hitting the child. You have not changed. You would use her now as you used her in the past, as a tool to get your own way. Rowena is a Loveday by blood, you are one only by deceit and treachery. We will await Adam in the Dower House.'

'I want some food. I have not eaten for days. One of Winnie's chicken pies and some wine.' Meriel's tone was arrogant. She could see that she had antagonised Elspeth and the servants but did not care. She saw arrogance as a sign of strength; to be conciliatory would be to reveal weakness. Meriel had always believed that attack was the best form of defence.

'See what Winnie has left over in the kitchen, Nance.' Elspeth glared at Meriel and did not trouble to hide her disgust. 'I would do as much for any beggar demanding food at the kitchen door.'

'I am no beggar,' she flared.

'If you want better treatment, go beg for alms at the Dolphin. Let your own family take care for you. Or did you go there to be sent away with a flea in your ear? Reuban has publicly disowned you.'

Rowena looked distressed, and to spare her further upset Elspeth ordered her back to the house.

'Go and get your new doll to show Mama,' Meriel urged Rowena, unwilling to relinquish control over her daughter. She did not believe that Elspeth would have her removed from the estate in front of the child.

'You can show Mama your doll later, my dear,' Elspeth insisted. 'Winnie is baking some fresh biscuits. Didn't you want to help her, Rowena?'

She loved the occasions when she was allowed into Winnie's kitchen. 'I will bake some for Mama.' She ran off.

Meriel scowled at Elspeth and the two servants. She knew it would be pointless to argue. She turned on her heel and flounced back into the Dower House. A maid brought some food for Meriel but Elspeth took it from her; she did not want the servants seeing the ragged and dirty state the master's wife had arrived in.

Meriel fell on the food, cramming it into her mouth.

'It did not take you long to forget your manners,' Elspeth spat.

Meriel began to cough, the deep racking sound shaking her frail figure. She put a hand to her mouth, and when the coughing finally abated the hand was streaked with blood. 'You cannot send me away,' she said faintly. 'I am sick.'

There was a spate of barking as Scamp and Faith were reunited in the gardens, heralding the arrival of Adam. Both dogs ran into the Dower House. Meriel scowled at them. She had never allowed animals in here.

Adam halted by the door, his swarthy face taut with anger. 'This is no longer your home.'

'I came to see my daughter. And you are right, this is no longer my home.' Her lips twitched into a malevolent smile. 'Trevowan House is now my home. How that must gall you, Adam. St John is master here, and you come running like a common lackey when summoned.'

'In my brother's eyes you are dead,' Adam informed her.

Meriel shrugged and leaned back in her chair, her glance assessing the contents of the parlour. 'I am very much alive. And I am not going away.'

Adam was shocked by Meriel's appearance. The once voluptuous

313

curves had vanished. She was gaunt and her voice as shrill as a fishwife's.

'You are not staying here. You made a fool of St John. Go to the Dolphin. It is for him to decide what is to be done with you when he returns.'

'I will not leave. You will have to throw me forcibly off Trevowan land. That should make a fine scandal.'

He took hold of Meriel's arm and pulled her to her feet. 'Do not defy me!'

She struggled and hit out at him, then another coughing fit bent her double, bloodied spittle flecked her cheek and she became a dead weight in his hands.

'She's swooned,' Adam ground out in exasperation.

Elspeth produced some smelling salts from a drawer where Amelia had kept them and waved them under Meriel's nose. Even they did not revive her. She moaned and Adam eased her inert body on to a chair.

'Reuban won't have her at the Dolphin,' Elspeth snapped. 'St John married the baggage for better or worse. Senara had better look at her. St John was besotted with the wench. What if we sent her away and he wanted her back?'

'Hell will freeze over before he would wish that,' Adam declared. Meriel had caused too much dissension in the family. 'But she is St John's responsibility, not ours. We can ban her from the main house for now. If St John decides differently, that is his prerogative. I suppose we have no choice but to allow her to stay in the Dower House temporarily.'

'I want nothing to do with her,' Elspeth said adamantly. 'She has brought only shame on this family.'

'She is Rowena's mother,' Adam replied. He was shocked by Meriel's condition and she was clearly ill. Lisette's and Etienne's disappearance and William's unexplained drowning had caused too much speculation already. He did not want to turn Meriel away only for her to die on the road. If Reuban would not have her at the Dolphin Inn, he doubted Clem or Harry wanted anything to do with her either.

'And little love had she shown the poor mite,' Elspeth cut across his angry thoughts. 'But I suppose she has to stay. Will

Senara tend her, or shall I send for Chegwidden?'

'St John will be paying the bill so it might as well be Chegwidden. Meriel never made any effort to accept Senara. I will not have St John say that I did not provide the best for his wife. I will send word to Sal Sawle too. If she has any feelings for her daughter she can help nurse her back to health.'

He turned away, eager to be gone from this new crisis. 'I've some details to discuss with Isaac Nance. I'll send for Chegwidden and he can examine Meriel while I am here.' Adam hoisted her over his shoulder and carried her upstairs to the main bedroom. 'She'll need cleaning up before Chegwidden sees her. Sal can do that.'

Elspeth did not trust Meriel alone in the Dower House. Sal Sawle arrived before Chegwidden but the landlady of the Dolphin Inn was far from pleased at seeing her daughter. Sal was as forthright as Elspeth and lost no time in saying what she thought of Meriel.

'She be no daughter of mine! She brought shame to your name and to ours. I only came 'cos I were told she be as dirty as a ragamuffin and looked sick unto death and needed a physician to tend her. I'll bathe her best I can. But St John would be a fool to take her back. If he pays her enough, the strumpet will go on her way. I won't have your family shamed further by a physician seeing her looking like a guttersnipe.'

Dr Chegwidden arrived before Sal had finished ministering to her daughter and Sal refused to let him into the room. It took several glasses of Edward's best brandy to placate him while he waited.

His examination took only a few minutes, his verdict tersely delivered. 'Consumption of the lungs. She is weak and I would say near to death. The finest broth must be given to her every two hours and a restorative that I will prepare and send to you. She also has the pox. The Lord's punishment for her whoring! She will need special nursing if she is to have any chance of survival, or do you want her taken to an infirmary?'

'Can you cure her?' Adam challenged him.

'Consumption has no cure. I can treat the pox, though that may well kill her in time.'

'Then do what you can for her.'

315

Chegwidden smoothed a crease from his gold brocade waist-coat. 'It is not my usual practice to treat whores. Her husband would be a fool to take her back.'

'That is for him to decide, and you would do well to remember that you are bound by an oath of confidentiality. Your wife has too free a tongue for gossip.'

The threat behind this warning was not lost on Chegwidden who blanched but retaliated, 'My fee for today is five guineas, and will be for each future visit.'

This was extortionate, but would at least ensure the physician's silence. Adam escorted Chegwidden to the door and Sal followed him. Once the doctor had climbed into his pony cart and driven away, she said heavily, 'It would be better for us all if she had died. She be tainted with evil. Can you trust Chegwidden to keep quiet about her?' Sal shook her head. 'My daughter be poxed. Reuban would've stripped her hide bare if he still had his legs. The little madam got her just deserts for running off the way she did. Your brother bain't gonna want her near him.'

'St John is the only one who can decide her future. Should I turn her out to die on the streets? And does Meriel herself know how ill she is?'

'Chegwidden took pleasure in telling her. She repaid him by screeching and railing at him like a harlot.' Sal scratched under the bulk of her large bosom. 'Since you are doing right by her, I can do no less. For all her sins she be my daughter still. If you want me to care for her, I will. The fewer people who see her the better, the state she be in.'

'Thank you, Sal.'

'I doubt St John will.' She shook her head. 'Meriel roused herself enough to announce to me it will cost her husband dear if he wants her out of his life. But even if she leaves Trevowan, St John remains shackled to her in marriage while she lives.'

Rupert Carlton called several times upon Tamasine at Amelia's London house. Amelia was delighted. Though she had thawed towards Tamasine, the presence of the girl still caused her many unhappy memories. Her duty to Edward demanded she should see Tamasine suitably wed, and the sooner the better as far as

316

Amelia was concerned. Margaret Mercer was equally keen for the match and in the first week of February Rupert was invited to dine at Mercer House with all the family.

The meal was a merry affair. Thomas was in a jovial mood and his wit was at its sharpest. To Tamasine's great pleasure Rupert returned his banter with good humour and she was encouraged to join in their repartee. Her life had been devoid of laughter for too many years. She could not have abided a man with no wit.

The meal ended and the women retired to the grand salon on the first floor of the house while Thomas and Rupert were left to their port and cigars. Rupert had hidden his nervousness all evening behind his easy humour. Now, as Thomas passed him the decanter of port, he became serious.

'I have not known Miss Loveday for very long but I have never met anyone quite like her. She is remarkable. Mr Mercer, as the head of your family in London, would it be appropriate for me to ask you for Tamasine's hand in marriage?'

Thomas rolled a cigar between his fingers before he lit it. His mother had talked of nothing else all week but the prospect of a match between Mr Carlton and Tamasine. 'My cousin Adam is now Tamasine's guardian, but I am sure that he will see no reason to discount your suit if certain questions are favourably answered. Are you yet in a position to support a wife? I understand you do not come into your inheritance for another two years?'

'Or when I marry. Though my trustee must agree to the match before funds are released. That is but a formality. He will adore Tamasine.'

Thomas knew the facts of Tamasine's birth, but should Rupert Carlton be told the truth now? It did not seem right that he should be talking of marriage without knowing her story. Thomas realised he knew little of Mr Carlton's background either.

'You are an orphan and will be independently wealthy, I understand, when you come into your trust?'

'Yes. Tamasine will lack for nothing.'

'She mentioned that you are related to the Rashleighs of Cornwall?'

'They are friends of the family. My trustee is Lord Keyne. Lady Barbara Keyne is my aunt.'

317

Thomas took a long swig of port to conceal his shock. He had not expected Rupert to be part of the Keyne family. Lord Keyne was Tamasine's half-brother. There was no blood tie to prevent the marriage but how could he give Rupert permission to marry Tamasine without him knowing her true background?

'Have you spoken to Lord Keyne of your interest in Tamasine?'

'I have not seen him for some months. The family are out of the country visiting their estate in Ireland. He returns next month.'

'And does Tamasine know the identity of your trustee?' Thomas steepled his fingers together and stared at them thoughtfully. 'Has Lord Keyne been mentioned to any of our family?'

'No, I do not believe that he has.' Rupert looked surprised at his question. 'I never spoke of him to Miss Loveday.' He leaned forward, anxious to see the serious expression on his host's face. 'Why should it be so important?' He attempted a quip. 'There is no family feud between the Lovedays and the Keynes, is there?'

Thomas was at a loss as to how to answer. This news was a tragedy for Tamasine who clearly adored Rupert.

'Not a feud exactly.' He poured a large port for his guest. 'I think you may need that. This is very difficult. Very difficult indeed.'

Thomas drained his own glass before telling Rupert the truth about Tamasine's birth, concluding bluntly, 'Lord Keyne is Tamasine's half-brother. The Keyne family refused to acknowledge her after her birth and she was sent away to a boarding school. Before she died Lady Eleanour made Edward promise that he would care for their daughter as she feared her family's censure would leave Tamasine unprovided for. My uncle became her guardian when Lady Eleanour died.'

Rupert had gone deathly pale. 'I knew nothing of such a child. I saw Lady Eleanour but rarely when I visited the family. She was a charming woman but lived quietly in her later years.'

He stared morosely at his port glass. 'From what you have said it is obvious that Lord Keyne will never condone our marriage. Even if he knew of Tamasine's existence, he would never accept her. Yet Aunt Barbara is the only family I have.'

'I would understand if you wish to withdraw your proposal, Mr Carlton.' Thomas pitied the young man and the dilemma he faced. Rupert clearly adored Tamasine.

He reared to his feet, his expression stunned. 'My feelings for Miss Loveday have not changed, but this ...' He staggered back from the table, his eyes bleak with desperation. 'In the circumstances it would not be right to bind Miss Loveday to an engagement of two years which would be necessary until I come into my majority. You have said that it is expected she should marry soon, to spare Mrs Loveday's feelings.' His voice broke and he struggled to keep his dignity and continue. 'That too is understandable. I must consider the feelings of my aunt. She has been most kind to me since the death of my parents. I cannot see any way to solve this. Your pardon, Mr Mercer. I must take my leave of you.'

He left without saying farewell to the women.

Tamasine ran into the dining room where Thomas sat staring gloomily into his empty glass. Her voice was high with alarm. 'Why did Mr Carlton leave so abruptly, without saying goodbye? That is not like him. Did you say something to upset him?'

The other women had followed her.

'The young man's behaviour is certainly most unbecoming,' said Margaret.

'He asked for Tamasine's hand.' Thomas hurried to curtail the women's squeals of pleasure. 'Unfortunately, fate is against the match. Mr Carlton's aunt is Lady Barbara Keyne. Her husband is your half-brother, Tamasine. I had to tell him the truth of your birth. Mr Carlton was naturally shocked. Any match between you would cause a family rift.'

'Then he does not love me!' wailed Tamasine. An icy hand was squeezing her heart. The pain was crippling. She could not breathe and could not bear the pity she saw in Georganna's eyes.

'You are a lovely young woman. He is not your only suitor. Many men would be proud to have you as their wife.' Margaret held out her arms to comfort her but she pushed them aside and ran into the parlour to throw herself on the settle and sob uncontrollably.

Georganna stepped forward. 'Let me talk to her. She will see this as another rejection because of her birth.'

She sat at Tamasine's feet and brushed the hair back from her

319

face. 'There will be other young men, equally handsome, equally suitable.'

'You sound just like Margaret,' she accused. Her misery was suffocating, the words wrenched out between sobs. 'I thought you understood how I felt? I love Rupert. I could never love another as I love him. Leave me alone!'

'If he loves you, he will find a way for his family to accept you.'

Tamasine shook her head, seeing no solution. He was lost to her. 'How can they? I was shut away because they were ashamed of my existence. They will never accept me as Rupert's wife. Why is life so unfair?'

'Do not despair. If Rupert loves you, he will find a way for you to be together.' Georganna was a hopeless romantic. 'Your love will be as great as Romeo and Juliet's.'

'But their love was doomed, they both died to prove it.' Tamasine sobbed harder. 'I cannot bear it, it is too unfair.'

'Then forget my silly analogy. I'm sure Rupert will stand up to his family.'

'It is too much to expect of him. Lord Keyne is a monster. And I cannot be a burden on the Lovedays forever.'

'We love you dearly, Tamasine. You are not a burden.'

'I am. Amelia wants rid of me.' Tamasine sat up and locked her arms across her chest. 'No one wants me.'

'Now you are being foolish. We have taken you into our hearts, as have Adam and Senara.'

'Why must life be so cruel?' Tamasine controlled her sobs, but her voice remained forlorn. 'I have already caused a rift between members of your family. How could I do the same to Rupert's relatives, making them takes sides? I will go away somewhere and take up a post as a governess.'

'You would hate the life,' Georganna said emphatically, and in her need to reassure Tamasine, gripped her arms. 'You are part of this family now. We all love you. There will be no talk of your going away. You can live with us.'

Tamasine dried her eyes though the pain had not eased. 'You are very kind, but I am so wretched.'

Georganna shook her friend. 'Perhaps this is for the best. You have given your heart at a young age. The family is wrong to pressurise you into an early marriage. I will talk to them. But you should also consider this. If Rupert does not stand up to his family, is he the man you thought he was? Would you want such a one as your husband?'

Tamasine sat up straight and squeezed her hands together tightly to help herself gain control of her emotions. 'You are right. My father was a man of honour and accepted me into his family. If I am worth loving then I am worth fighting for. Rupert must love me for who I am and be prepared to face the consequences of that love or it is without meaning.'

Her brave words did not fool Georganna. Tamasine's heart was breaking.

Chapter Twenty-Eight

'*Pegasus* has been sighted, Cap'n Loveday.' Ben Mumford broke the important news to Adam himself. He was inspecting the work on the lower decks of the cutter commissioned by Harry Sawle. 'She'll be alongside the dock in a few minutes, sir.'

Adam climbed through the skeleton of the cutter and ran a cursory eye over *Pegasus* as her sails were furled and the anchor lowered. His ship had weathered the voyage well and had returned without visible sign of having been damaged in a storm or attacked by the French. The relief was immense. He noted his brother by the gangplank and raised an arm in greeting. His twin looked leaner, his face reddened by the elements. St John returned the wave.

'How was the crossing?' Adam asked as soon as his brother stepped on to the dock.

'We were hit by two storms but fortunately there was no sign of any Frenchies.' St John staggered slightly and laughed. 'I need to get back my land legs.'

'Come to the house before you leave for Trevowan.' Adam's expression quickly sobered. 'There is recent news you must be made aware of.'

'I was shocked to learn about Papa. Did he suffer?'

'A bullet wound would not heal – I will tell you more of that later. There is much else we need to catch up on.' He assessed his brother's mood and sensed his impatience to reach home. 'Virginia seems to have suited you.'

St John nodded. 'What is so important that we must speak so urgently? Though I do wish to discuss the finances of the estate since Father's death.'

'I followed his usual practices.' Adam's pleasure at his twin's return faded. The antagonism was still there between them, unmellowed by their grief. 'Trevowan has not been neglected.' He lowered his voice as they walked through the yard to Mariner's House. The greetings from his family were soon over, and Adam noted the tension in his brother's face when he saw the twins.

'So you have two sons now?' St John commented sourly. 'You have been blessed.'

Senara ushered the children away so that the brothers could be alone in the parlour. Adam came straight to the point. 'Meriel is back. She broke into the Dower House some weeks ago. She is sick with consumption.'

'You should have thrown the whore out! I will not have her at Trevowan.' St John's face reddened even more with the force of his anger.

'She is dying, St John. It is for you to decide her future. Chegwidden has treated her, and we've made sure that she's stayed in the Dower House. Sal has been nursing her. Elspeth wanted nothing to do with Meriel. Amelia is in London.'

'Then Meriel can live at the Dolphin. Her family can be responsible for her,' St John snapped.

'She is too ill to be moved. And do you want Rowena to witness her mother being thrown out of Trevowan?'

At this mention of his daughter a flicker of pain crossed St John's face. 'How is Rowena?'

'She misses you. She is not allowed in the sick room with Meriel for fear she may catch the consumption herself. You might as well know the full extent of Meriel's illness. She also has the pox.'

'Just reward for her whoring!' St John gave a bitter laugh, showing no compassion for his wife. 'I hope the bitch dies soon. She gave me a cuckold's horns and made a laughing stock of me. I thought the whore was out of my life for good. She is the curse of my existence. And what of Lisette? I will not have that madcap at Trevowan either. Uncle William can provide for his own wife.'

'Uncle William drowned,' Adam announced brutally, angered by his twin's manner. St John had spent a year gaming and being entertained in Virginia whilst the rest of the family had been beset with worries and problems. 'It is possible that Lisette also drowned, but her body has not been found. She is missing and so is Etienne. He had been in England for several months.'

'I am sorry to hear about Uncle William,' St John said, calming down. 'Though we are well rid of Lisette and Etienne. This is a damnable homecoming.'

'I did what I thought best over Meriel.' Adam remained defensive. 'But the yard is in financial trouble and I have had worries of my own. I have followed the usual procedures by which Father ran the estate and will account to you when you have settled back at home. You will find all the ledgers for the estate in order. I will answer any queries but the estate is your problem now.'

St John had fallen silent and Adam poured him a brandy, adding, 'There has been much for you to take in. How were the Penhaligans when you left Virginia?'

'Garfield has made me his heir.' St John brightened. 'And once Meriel dies I shall wed Desiree Richmond. I shall be a great landowner in Virginia. Trevowan is no more than a small farm compared to the land I shall own in the old colony.' He tossed back his brandy and stood up to leave. 'But now, as you say, I have my duties as Master of Trevowan.'

When St John left Adam worked off his anger in the shaping sheds, sawing the wood to size. His brother was Master of Trevowan and it burned like molten lead in Adam's gut. His twin did not deserve Trevowan, nor did he appreciate it. He would squander its riches and employ an overseer to run the estate. The house would be shut up and neglected while he made his life in Virginia.

Captain Matthews was in his cabin stowing away the maps and ship's log when Adam boarded *Pegasus*.

'It was fortunate you did not come under enemy fire,' he observed. 'Was there any storm damage to the ship?'

'We lost the top spar on the mizzen sail, that were all. She is a fine ship. It is a pleasure to sail her.'

'Now I have the yard to run, I will not captain her again. Will you take the post, Captain Matthews? She will be doing mostly transatlantic voyages, bringing back cotton as well as tobacco.

Garfield Penhaligan has given me an introduction to a shipping agent in Washington. In the last month I have obtained contracts from merchants wishing to ship quality furnishings for sale in the American auction houses, and also to export tea and spices there.'

'You have been astute to gain such contracts. Competition is fierce.' Captain Matthews sorted through some papers on his desk. 'These are the invoices and paperwork connected with this voyage.'

He lifted a metal chest on to the table and handed Adam the money from his own investments sold in America. He could no longer afford to venture in such cargoes himself and henceforth would rely on the shipping contracts to bolster the finances of the yard.

St John pressed the horse he had borrowed from the shipyard to gallop to Trevowan. He was in a murderous rage over Meriel's return. The baggage had outwitted him, daring to return whilst he was away, though she had at least waited until his father was dead. Edward would never have countenanced her living at Trevowan. His anger was also channelled towards his brother. Adam could have ordered her from the estate before anyone was aware of her return. But Meriel had brought shame upon the Sawles too by running away with Lord Wycham, neither Reuban nor Harry would support her in the future. Reuban was too old and sick and Harry too selfish and concerned with his own future.

Now it looked as if Meriel would have to stay. Was she really dying? Or had that been a ruse to ensure she was not turned out on the streets? She was capable of such trickery.

He strode into the Dower House and startled Sal who was carrying dirty bed linen down the stairs. 'St John, you gave me a turn! I did not know you had docked. My condolences on the loss of your father. That must have been a shock.'

'As is the news that my whore of a wife thinks she can return here and expect my support and forgiveness.'

Sal hung her head. 'What she did were wrong. Very wrong. But Meriel near died when she were beaten by Lanyon and lost the child she were carrying. That can turn a woman's mind.'

'Do not make excuses for her. She had been entertaining

Wycham before Lanyon attacked her. Once a whore, always a whore! I was a fool to wed her.'

'She gave you Rowena. Is not your daughter a rare gift?'

The light of such fury glittered in St John's eyes that Sal took an involuntary step backwards as he lashed out, 'Whether she is my daughter remains debatable. Meriel told me before she ran off with Wycham that Rowena was Adam's child.'

Sal gasped and put her hand to her mouth, the laundry falling to the floor. 'That bain't true. It were a wicked thing to say. That poor, sweet, innocent child. Did Adam acknowledge Meriel's lies?'

'He denied it.'

'Then I would believe him and not Meriel,' Sal advised. 'She lied to hurt you. She would say anything to ensure that you did not stop her leaving with Lord Wycham.'

'She will tell me the truth now.' St John stepped over the bedding and took the stairs two at a time. He burst into the bedchamber and the words of hatred momentarily died on his lips with the shock of seeing his wife's condition. She was skeletal, her eyes sunken and darkly circled, her blonde hair straggly and dull. There were unsightly sores around her mouth, and fear in her eyes as she stared up at him.

'Dr Chegwidden said that I am dying. Have pity on me, St John. Do not send me away.'

'You deserve to end your days in the gutter where you belong,' he grated. He could smell the sourness of her breath and it nauseated him.

'I wronged you.' Her voice was a thin croak. 'I ask your pardon. I never meant to be a bad wife. I was so wretched after Lanyon beat me and I lost our son.' She shut her eyes and tears squeezed through her lashes. 'And you acted as though you hated me.'

'This act of contrition will not save you, Meriel.' He knew her games and failed to be moved by her show of remorse. She had returned to Trevowan simply because her latest lover had abandoned her. 'You never loved me, and I doubt you loved Wycham. He was just richer than I was. You thought he would provide more lavishly for you. How long was it before he tired of your demands?'

'You are cruel. I did love you.'

326

'You loved the fact I would one day inherit Trevowan more. But you will never be mistress here. You will never enter Trevowan House again.'

'I am your wife.' She stared at him, trying to gauge his resolve. 'I said many things I did not mean on that last day we were together. Rowena is your daughter, whatever Adam says. He has his own reasons to hate you.'

'Adam denied that you were even lovers. But if you are so desperate to convince me that Rowena is my child, I begin to wonder. She is the only reason I would keep you here, and you would heartlessly play on that.' He stared down at her with distrust. He had hardened himself against her wiles long ago but Rowena was another matter. He had been so proud of her until Meriel had thrown her parentage in his face. He did not want to admit that Adam was her father, or that Meriel had made a fool of him and he had married his brother's whore.

'Rowena is your daughter. I will swear on the Bible if that is what it takes to convince you.'

'You were never religious. Do not add blasphemy to your crimes.'

'What must I do to convince you? I am dying, St John, why should I lie? You love Rowena. I wanted to hurt you. It was stupid and thoughtless.' She covered her face with hands that were so transparently thin the veins showed through. She sobbed, 'Forgive me, St John. Rowena is your daughter.'

He felt nothing but disgust as he stared down at his wife. She looked as though she was truly dying but he felt no compassion. Pride demanded that he should believe Rowena was his daughter. He may loathe Meriel but for the child's sake he would allow her mother to die in comfort. 'Sal will tend you here, but you will never enter Trevowan House. Nor do I wish to see you again.'

He left the Dower House in haste. The smell of the sickroom clawed at his throat. He needed a large brandy. He also wanted Meriel out of his life. If she did not die he would find a way to have her locked away. He could not afford to buy her silence. While she lived, the life he had planned with Desiree would hang in jeopardy, and by whatever means he was determined to marry

327

again even if it meant that he must lead a double life with Desiree in Virginia.

Meriel turned on her side when her husband left the room. Even through her pain she smiled slyly. Chegwidden was a fool. She did not believe that she was dying. A few more weeks of good food, warmth and the best medication that money could buy and she would soon be up and on her feet again.

Through the window she could see the tall chimneys of Trevowan House. 'When I am better we will see who is Mistress of Trevowan. I will never relinquish my rights,' she vowed.

A month after St John returned Peter and Bridie were married in Trewenna church. Neither wanted a grand affair and only the family in Cornwall attended. The wedding breakfast was held at the Rabsons' farmhouse where Adam and Senara had also celebrated their wedding. Cecily and Hannah shed a tear of happiness as they watched the young couple ride away in the cart to start their new life together at Polruggan.

'How different it all was at Japhet's wedding,' Cecily could not help saying. 'I thought marriage to Gwendolyn would bring an end to his wild scrapes. How can he bear it, being locked in that dreadful place for almost a year? And Sir Gregory still has not managed to find the evidence to set him free. It cannot be long before another convoy sails to the penal colony ...'

Hannah held her mother in her arms. 'You must have faith. Japhet and Gwen are meant for each other.' She stared across the paddocks to where Japhet's mares were grazing. 'He has the horses and Gwendolyn has purchased the farm in readiness. He will be home soon. It cannot be much longer.'

'But I fear that he will be transported.'

'You mustn't worry so much. You ruin today by your fears for tomorrow.'

Cecily stared up at her daughter and saw the lines of strain in her proud face. 'You have great wisdom.'

'It comes from experience. If I allowed myself to worry about Oswald, I would never be able to enjoy the precious time we have together now.'

'He looked well today,' Cecily encouraged.

'That is because he rested all day yesterday. His chest is congested and it has affected his heart. He can do little manual work on the farm now. But I am happy that he spends so much time with the children. They will have their memories of him. I do not think he will survive another winter.'

'We thought that last year,' Cecily reminded her. 'There are only two certainties in life: death and taxes. The family is not the same without Edward, and of course William, and who knows what became of Lisette? And now there is Meriel ...' Her voice trailed off and she swiftly recovered herself. 'Such morbid talk on a wedding day. Peter and Bridie look so happy, that is what is important for now. May God bless their union.'

'I hope Peter does not curb Bridie's enthusiasm for life.' Hannah frowned. 'His piety can be hard to endure. He is over-zealous on too many matters.'

'Yet he set some of his prejudices aside to wed a woman born out of wedlock. Bridie is a calming influence on him. I cannot see her allowing him to dictate to her. I pray that they will be as happy as Adam and Senara. Did she tell you that she is expecting another child in August? Adam is determined that it will be born at Boscabel.'

Cecily smiled. 'The old rivalry is still there between Adam and St John. Did you hear them quarrelling over some work at Trevowan that St John considered Adam had neglected?'

'Now Adam has Boscabel, there should be no further cause for rivalry. It will one day be as grand as Trevowan and the estate is larger.'

'St John will not forgive him for inheriting the shipyard.' Cecily frowned. 'In the past estate and yard were bound together, one supporting the other in times of need. Separately both yard and estate will struggle to survive. St John has only the estate for income. He will have to dirty his hands by working hard on the land to subsidise the life of a gentleman. That will not please him.'

'It will be the making of him,' Hannah laughed.

'I wonder?' Cecily shook her head. 'He is so filled with anger. And now that Meriel is back at Trevowan perhaps he has cause. She has left her sick bed and is demanding she be given an allowance to match her status as his wife. St John of course refuses.'

Long Tom had finally found the information he needed to save Japhet. For weeks he had been spending his evenings heavily disguised and sitting in disreputable taverns inhabited by the criminal fraternity of London. Tonight he was disguised as a deaf-mute hunchback in a matted black wig and beard, walking with the aid of a crutch. For some weeks he had used this disguise to beg on the streets close to the rookeries where the criminals congregated and had listened for word of any highwayman who had been shot escaping capture. The underworld were suspicious of any newcomer working their territory but Long Tom had not seemed to pose a threat to them and they had gradually come to accept his presence.

He had learned much of the ways of the criminal underworld and of the hierarchy of thieves and gang leaders who ruled by brutality and terror, but the identity of the man he sought had continued to elude him until this evening. Long John had been sitting in the corner of a cockroach-infested tavern near the Thames close to St Paul's. A scrawny man in threadbare finery, one he had not seen before, entered and was greeted by several of the drinkers. The man was tall with lank dark hair hanging about his shoulders.

'So you've returned to London to seek your fortune, Dapper Lewis, me old son? Where've you been this last year – serving at His Majesty's pleasure?' a one-armed beggar sniggered.

'I've bin down Southend way. Heard a lass I once 'ad a fancy for 'ad bin widowed. 'Er husband owned a cockleboat. Thought it would be easy pickings to wed the wench and pocket her inheritance. She 'ad me working like a slave and clung on to her money tighter than a limpet. That ain't no life.'

The group ordered several more tankards of ale and drank heavily throughout the evening. Long Tom paid them no especial attention, keeping a sharp ear on all the conversations in the tavern. He was about to move on to another taproom when a loud guffaw held his attention. The group around Lewis was drunk and boisterous, ribbing the newcomer.

'So, Dapper, you've come back to enjoy the richer pickings of London. You've dropped your dandified speech. Reverted to type, ain't yer. Didn't do too well last time, I heard. Got yourself shot on 'ampstead 'eath, so Spotty Blatcher said.'

'Spotty Blatcher don't know nothing.' Dapper Lewis waved a finger belligerently in the face of his antagonist. 'I had a fortune in me 'ands that night. 'Ad the bad luck to get me 'orse shot from under me.'

'Yer always 'ad bad luck. Yer couldn't 'old up a lady's stocking, let alone a coach.'

Dapper Lewis rubbed the side of his beaked nose. 'I had rich pickings that night, I tell you. They would've seen me right for life. I could 'ave got meself a nice little inn on a coaching route. I'd've been set up fine and dandy.'

'I've 'eard it all afore. You were a piss-poor tobyman.'

Lewis lurched to his feet and caught his antagonist by the man's dirty linen stock. 'I tell you, I had a fine haul. Me 'orse got shot and I 'ad me loot stolen by the cur I tried to get another 'orse from. Me saddle bag were full of jewels. The bugger shot me. I put a bullet through 'im but it didn't do no good. The bastard stole me loot. It were some lord I held up, I tell you. I didn't hang around. I were shot bad so I laid low then went down to Southend. They got the bugger who shot me, though.' He tittered. 'A cove by the name of Gentleman James.'

Long Tom slunk outside the tavern to wait for Dapper Lewis to leave. An hour later he followed Lewis to his digs. Once he knew where the highwayman lived, Long Tom sent word to three accomplices. In the middle of the night Lewis's room was broken into and he was knocked unconscious and taken to an old warehouse. Long Tom interrogated him through the night and finally got the confession he needed to clear Japhet's name.

Chapter Twenty-Nine

The sulphurous smog that had hung over London lifted and on the first sunny day for weeks Tamasine and Georganna rode their mares along Rotten Row in Hyde Park, Amelia and Margaret accompanying them to the park in an open carriage. Most of the gentry in London also took advantage of the fine day to be seen parading in their finery.

'The park is a poor substitute for a good gallop across open fields,' Tamasine said wistfully. 'A brisk trot is the best you can manage amid so many riders.'

'We ride to see and be seen,' Georganna replied. 'London is a place where every moment counts and who you are seen with is of paramount importance.'

Several of the male acquaintances that Tamasine had made during her visit doffed their hats to the ladies and stopped to talk. She was restless. Most of these men bored her with their compliments. Her heart ached from missing Rupert and her smile was false and never reached her eyes. When she saw Mr Norton approaching, she groaned. 'I do not wish to speak to him. Aunt Margaret means well but she keeps encouraging him. Look, she is waving to him and beckoning him over. Let us ride to the far side of the park.'

'Margaret and Amelia will not like us disappearing, but the day is too nice to waste.' Georganna grinned conspiratorially. 'A military band is playing in the bandstand. We will ride over to listen. It is not right for Margaret to encourage Mr Norton if you are not interested in his attentions.'

Suddenly Tamasine reined in her mare. 'We must turn back. There is Rupert with a party of friends.' She stared at him transfixed, misery shadowing her lovely face. He turned to talk to a man on his left and, as he did so, raised his eyes and saw her. He visibly started but looked away without acknowledging her.

Tamasine was devastated. 'I have to leave. I cannot stay now.'

'Do not let him see how upset you are. Engage Mr Norton in conversation. You may make Mr Carlton jealous,' Georganna suggested.

'That seems so petty,' Tamasine groaned. 'Why can I not forget him? He does not love me. It is a month since he walked out of the house without a word.'

'Then he needs to be shown how popular you are.' Georganna glared at the group among whom Rupert now stood with his back to them. 'And on cue Mr Norton is approaching. He is very persistent as an ardent lover should be. Forget Rupert. He is not worthy of you if he can ignore you so easily.'

Tamasine tossed back her head, her chin tilted in defiance. 'You are right. He will not ruin this lovely morning. We have been confined in the house too long when the weather was miserable.'

Though her smile of greeting was false, Mr Norton simpered and blushed as he offered to accompany the two ladies to the bandstand. His friend Mr Partridge joined them. He was a short man and something of a buffoon, but his silly quips made the women laugh. Tamasine saw Rupert on the far side of the bandstand, watching her. Though it took every ounce of her willpower she looked away, ignoring him as he had earlier ignored her. When the band paused in their playing, Georganna suggested that they should leave. Two more of Mr Norton's friends had joined them, one flirting outrageously with Tamasine. They bade the gentlemen good day and Margaret was flushed with pleasure when they returned to the carriage.

'It is not only Mr Norton who enjoys your company. Was that not Mr Banks flirting with you? He was widowed last year and is an eminent lawyer. I am surprised he is not at his practice. But then, he employs several clerks and now only takes on the most prestigious clients.'

Tamasine fell silent as they rode back to the Strand. She had prayed to see Rupert again but it had only increased her pain and misery. That afternoon she shut herself in her room at Amelia's house. They had quarrelled. Amelia was impatient that Tamasine showed no interest in the men to whom she was introduced.

'Be grateful that gentlemen with such fine prospects seek your company. Mr Norton would make an offer, I am sure. Edward would have considered him most suitable as a husband for you. Is this how you repay my efforts in bringing you to London? You are being selfish. If you return to Cornwall, there will be constant questions about your background. I would find that too distressing.'

'Do you intend to return without me?' Tamasine was appalled. She had hoped that Amelia was becoming less antagonistic towards her when clearly she wanted Tamasine not only married but living as far from the family in Cornwall as possible.

'My duty to Edward is at an end when you marry. You would be a fool not to take your opportunities when they are presented to you.'

Tamasine threw herself on to her bed where the sobs she had tried so valiantly to hold back engulfed her until she fell into an exhausted sleep. Her dreams were disturbed by images of Rupert but when she ran to him he disappeared into a shrouding mist.

A voice calling her name and a hand gently shaking her shoulder roused her. The sun was low in the sky, turning the walls of her room amber. Shadows from the bed hangings lay purple across the floor.

'Miss Tamasine, wake up,' the maid insisted. 'You have a caller. Mrs Loveday has received him in the red drawing room.'

'I do not wish to see anyone.'

'It is Mr Carlton.'

Tamasine swung her legs from the bed, her hands going to her hair in alarm. It was in tangled disarray and her dress was crumpled.

'I must change, I look a fright.'

'There is no time. The conversation has been quite heated. Mrs Loveday was reluctant to receive him.'

Tamasine ran to her dressing mirror and smoothed down the folds of her primrose-coloured silk gown. Hastily she pinned up several loose curls. 'She must not send him away.'

Her heart hammered in her breast. Amelia had been uncompromising in her views on Mr Carlton once she had learned of his family connections. If she did not wish Tamasine to return to Cornwall, she would be even less inclined for her to become linked with the Keynes.

With undignified haste she sped down the stairs. She could hear Amelia's voice, strident and angry, and Rupert's answering, politely cool.

'Mr Carlton, this is a surprise,' Tamasine said as she stood in the doorway. The sight of him was enough to make her feel faint. She did not trust her legs to carry her across the room.

'Miss Loveday, Tamasine ...' The pain in his voice made her catch her breath expectantly. 'I could not stay away. Forgive me, I have behaved abominably.'

'And you continue to do so,' Amelia declared. 'This talk of defying your guardian is hardly conducive to ...'

Rupert cut through Amelia's reproach, his anguished gaze upon Tamasine. 'Lord Keyne will not agree to our marriage. He will not receive you. And when I come of age, if I were to wed you, I would no longer be welcome in his home.'

'Then there is no hope for us,' she groaned. 'Thank you for explaining how matters stand to me. I have no wish to meet Lord Keyne. He treated my mother abysmally and so did his pompous father.'

Rupert crossed the room to take her hand and raise it to his lips. 'I do not care what he says. I will marry you if you will have me? Though we must wait two years, I cannot support a wife on my allowance.'

'I would wait until the end of the earth to marry you,' Tamasine sighed, her fingers curling around his hand. 'I thought you had come to hate me.'

'I could never hate you. I love you.'

'It is not acceptable for our family to support Tamasine for two years, sir,' Amelia snapped. 'We have tolerated her presence because circumstances made it impossible for us to do otherwise. She is expected to marry, and to marry soon.'

'But I love Rupert.' Tamasine stared at Amelia with horror.

'You are too young to know the meaning of love. You have thrown yourself at the first handsome man who has sought your company.'

'That is not true!' Tamasine was outraged. She had not thought Amelia could be so cruel. 'My father wanted me to be happy. I love Mr Carlton. We can live off my dowry until he comes into his inheritance.'

'No honourable man would agree to such an arrangement. You cannot marry him. I will hear no more on the subject.' Amelia rose. 'Please leave, sir.'

'I will wed no other but Mr Carlton,' Tamasine defied her.

'You are sixteen and while under the guardianship of our family, young lady, you will do as you are told.' Anger reddened Amelia's cheeks. 'Such a marriage is impossible. As Mr Carlton will agree when he has had more time to consider the consequences. Family ties are important.'

Rupert paled, a muscle pulsing along his jaw. He bowed curtly to Tamasine. 'I will not live upon your dowry. I should not have come.' He marched from the room.

She ran after him, ignoring Amelia's order for her to remain in the drawing room. 'Do not let her drive you away, Rupert!'

He slowed his step. 'Mrs Loveday is right. I would wait two years for you, but your family is impatient for you to be wed.'

'Then I will run away. We could elope.'

He shook his head. 'I will cause no further scandal to be attached to your name. I do not wish to be cruel, but you are a reminder of a side of your father's and mother's pasts that our families would rather not have to acknowledge.'

'But Adam would not force me to marry. My father would have agreed to my marrying you.'

'How can you know that for sure?' Rupert stroked a tress of her hair. His expression was tortured. 'Would your father have wished to be reminded all his life of a past indiscretion that caused so much pain to your mother?'

'He was a greater man than that. A man of honour.'

'Then we must work towards winning the consent of both our families if we are to be truly happy.'

'I will ask Mrs Mercer if I can stay with them. She was eager for a match between us. Then I will be able to see you in London.'

'It will not be easy. Lord Keyne has returned to the capital. I am expected to live with them if my allowance is to continue. But there must be a way ...'

'Tamasine, go to your room.' Amelia bore down upon them. 'I forbid you to see Mr Carlton. And you, sir, please leave my house, or must I call the servants to have you removed?'

'I would not put you to such inconvenience, Mrs Loveday.' He raised Tamasine's hand to his lips. 'Promise you will wait for me, my love? I shall never forsake you, no matter what barriers my family would put between us. We shall be wed.'

'I will wait for you, Rupert. I give my word as a Loveday.'

'No gentleman would take your word when he knows such a marriage is not possible,' Amelia fumed. 'If you love Tamasine, you will not bind her to an agreement that can only lead to unhappiness.'

'I bind myself freely,' she declared. 'I consider myself to be betrothed to Mr Carlton, if that is his wish?'

Rupert's eyes blazed with admiration. 'I will be true to my word, my love.'

'Then you are both fools!' Amelia declared. 'Much can happen in your young lives in two years.'

Gwendolyn paced the morning room at the Mercers' house. She was alone with her visitor; the rest of the family had been summoned to Amelia's house to discuss Tamasine's defiance.

'Today is the anniversary of my wedding and I spend it alone. Sir Gregory, how can a year have passed without Japhet gaining his pardon? You got a confession from the highwayman who held up Lord Sefton's coach and he was arrested. So why has Japhet not been freed?'

'The wheels of the law grind slowly. It could be months before the evidence is brought before a court. We need the King's pardon for Japhet to be released more quickly.' Long Tom forced an encouraging smile, but he was worried that unless he obtained an audience with the King in the next day or so, a pardon would come too late. A new transportation fleet was preparing to sail to the Australian penal colony.

'Why is fate conspiring against Japhet? I know hundreds of people try to petition His Majesty every week, but this is a miscarriage of justice that could cost my husband his life.' Gwendolyn placed her fingers on her brow, trying to ease the pressure of a nagging headache that had been with her for weeks.

Sir Gregory did not answer. Gwendolyn's distress was difficult for him to witness as it was caused by his own failure.

She spun round to face him. 'I put my faith in my godfather obtaining a pardon for Japhet once we gave him our proof, but Craigsmoor fell foul of the Prince of Wales's set who turned several of the King's ministers against him. It was a great blow to his pride after two decades as a loyal courtier. He suffered a seizure and left London to recuperate on his country estate. I will come with you to court tomorrow. Perhaps with two of us petitioning it will make a difference.'

For two weeks Gwendolyn and Sir Gregory spent long hours sitting in draughty corridors, waiting for a summons to the King's presence. The press of other people all with righteous pleas for justice was oppressing and demoralising. Many had been waiting for months. Long Tom had also requested an audience with Mr Pitt, the Prime Minister. But even though Pitt had been highly congratulatory of the work Sir Gregory had performed for the government during his years in France, the progress of the war kept the Prime Minister continually occupied in cabinet meetings.

After another day of frustration and failure, Sir Gregory declared, 'I will call upon Mr Pitt in person, trusting that this time he will receive me.' He was determined to waylay the Prime Minister at his home if all else failed. Fortunately that did not prove necessary. This time when he gave his card to the Prime Minister's secretary he was informed he might have an audience, but that Mr Pitt may not be free for some hours. Sir Gregory sat down and composed himself for a long wait. A mere four hours later, the secretary summoned him to the Prime Minister's presence.

It took but ten minutes of Mr Pitt's valuable time to study the confession and the evidence that Sir Gregory had gathered in support of Japhet's innocence. The pardon was penned by the Prime Minister's own hand.

'I regret this matter has taken so long, Sir Gregory,' he said. 'Matters of state take all my time, but you have been a good servant of the government. I am glad to be of service to your friend's family. A miscarriage of justice cannot be allowed to rob a man of his freedom.'

Though the hour was late Sir Gregory went immediately to Gwendolyn to inform her of his success. He found her still dressed and writing a letter to Japhet in the parlour. The fire had died low and she had pulled a paisley shawl around her shoulders. Thomas and Georganna were at a reading given by Lucien Greene and were not expected to return to the house until the early hours of the morning.

Sir Gregory grinned as he hurried to her side and waved the pardon. 'At last your husband will be free!'

'Praise God.' She leaped to her feet and flung her arms around Sir Gregory's neck. 'Thank you so much. You have given Japhet back his life. We are eternally grateful.'

'I shall call at Newgate tomorrow ...' Sir Gregory began.

'No, it must be now. Japhet should not spend a moment longer in that dreadful place than is necessary.'

'But it is almost midnight.'

'It must be now. I still have a feeling that something dreadful will happen to him.'

'One more night will make no difference. You have the rest of your lives to be together.'

An irrational panic filled Gwendolyn. 'We must go tonight. That this is the anniversary of our wedding makes it even more appropriate. And I would not be able to sleep. Please, Sir Gregory, what if after so long something happened to Japhet tonight? How could we live with that?'

She remained distraught when he had thought she would be joyful. There was no understanding a woman's mind. Her body shook from reaction to the news.

'Please, take me to Newgate tonight or I shall go alone and demand the release of my husband.'

Sir Gregory suppressed an inward groan. Gwendolyn's face was awash with tears and he knew that she was capable of carrying out her madcap scheme. He sighed. 'As you are so distressed I will go tonight. You must remain here. Newgate is a dangerous place at night, far worse than during the day, for most of the inmates who can buy drink will be drunk, abusive and unruly.'

She shook her head. 'The waiting will be more than I can bear. I will stay in the carriage if you insist.'

Reluctantly he agreed and within half an hour the coach had pulled up outside the dark and sinister walls of the prison.

'Please, make haste,' Gwendolyn urged. She knew it was foolish and irrational but she was still gripped by an indefinable fear that fate was conspiring to keep her and Japhet apart.

The Keeper of Newgate had to be roused from his bed and was in a surly mood. He appeared wearing a scarlet nightcap and a threadbare robe over his nightshirt. 'You're too late, Loveday is no longer an inmate of this prison. He were taken to the prison ship three days ago.'

'Why was his family not notified?' Sir Gregory demanded.

'He were condemned and his sentence duly carried out.' The man was truculent and Sir Gregory suspected that something was not right about the haste and secrecy of Japhet's removal.

'Where is the fleet to sail from?'

'He were taken to Rotherhithe with fifty other prisoners.'

'When do they sail?'

The Keeper shrugged. 'As soon as all prisoners are boarded, I reckon. They're no longer my responsibility once they leave here.'

When Sir Gregory left the Keeper he was seething with fury. Outside the office he heard his name called softly from a dark and mildewed corridor.

'Sir, if you've been asking after Loveday, he were taken three days ago.' A turnkey with a bull-terrier face and shifty eyes edged closer. The smell of him was as foul as a sewer. ''E didn't go natural like, if yer get me meaning.'

'What exactly are you implying?'

The turnkey rubbed the lobe of his ear. 'Such information 'as a price. I know you've paid dear to bring Loveday his luxuries. It'll cost yer five guineas.'

'If what you have to say is relevant you shall have your money. If not you'll get nothing.'

'Show us yer money,' the turnkey demanded.

Sir Gregory was eager to leave the prison; he could afford no delays in getting to the ship. He pulled a purse from his pocket. 'Tell me and be quick about it.'

'Loveday were dragged out of the prison. He was unconscious. I heard two of the turnkeys sniggering that he'd got his come-uppance and not before time. I reckon he were drugged. Loveday had a visitor just after Dapper Lewis was brought in, a flash cove name of Osgood. They had words, so I heard. Man name of Billings took Loveday away. Billings ain't bin seen since.'

Long Tom handed over the money convinced that Sir Pettigrew Osgood was behind Japhet's hasty removal from the prison. When he returned to the carriage he could not meet Gwendolyn's eye.

'Where is he?' she said with a note of hysteria.

'He has been taken to a ship. There is something wrong about the haste of his removal, but I doubt the ship will yet have sailed.'

'Then we must go straight to the dock.' Fear made her body tremble with violent reaction. 'Let us not delay.'

As the carriage sped through the streets, Gwendolyn battled against her fears. Please God, let the fleet not have sailed! The blinds of the carriage were pulled down but as they passed through a rough area of the city, Gwendolyn recognised a woman's shrill voice and, though consumed by fear for her husband, lifted the blind aside to look.

Two women were fighting over a bottle of gin; one of them was Celestine Yorke. Both were drunk and they tugged at each other's hair, screaming abuse.

'Get your hands off me!' Celestine roared, landing a punch on her opponent's eye. 'Bugger off! Don't call *me* a whore. I'm the Darling of London. I've bedded lords and politicians and they showered me with jewels to win my favours. I am the Darling of London, I am. This is my gin and you ain't having it.'

'More like the Hag of London! You looked in a glass lately?' her drunken companion tittered. 'No man would give more than tuppence to get into your stinking bed.'

Gwen turned away, disgusted by the scene. 'That is the woman who cost Japhet his freedom.'

'She was his Nemesis but she should be pitied now,' Sir Gregory reasoned. 'Having witnessed her evil, Japhet came to realise how precious you were to him. You are his salvation.'

'But she is so worthless. How could so low a woman bring Japhet to ruin?'

'Lust can strip a man of reason. Was he not suppressing his feelings for you, believing that you deserved better than him? The Yorke woman manipulated men of wealth and power. Japhet gave her nothing but himself. Perhaps that was a balm to his battered pride. And she has not prospered from her evil in denouncing him.'

Sir Gregory spoke more to take Gwendolyn's mind from the ordeal ahead than from conviction. The manner in which Japhet had been taken from the prison made him fear the ship had already sailed. Osgood would not have risked so much to have Japhet taken aboard a vessel that would remain in dock. He continued in a scathing tone, 'The Yorke woman has not worked on the stage for half a year. She could have retired and lived a genteel life for she had the income from several properties. But her rich lovers deserted her and she took to the bottle. She could not abide no longer being in the limelight.'

When they arrived at Rotherhithe the pale moonlight showed the masts of scores of ships anchored in the river. The Thames was filled with vessels; some would be moored mid-channel for weeks awaiting a berth to unload their cargo.

'I will find out what I can,' Sir Gregory said. 'Again, I must ask you to wait here. Do not leave the carriage. Drunken seamen are a threat to a woman alone. The coachman has a blunderbuss to protect you. I will be as quick as I can.'

Gwendolyn huddled in her furs oblivious to the cold. The ship could not have sailed. Fate would not part her from Japhet now. It could not be so cruel. She hugged that faith close to her heart. To think otherwise would be to put a jinx on Japhet's luck. Tonight they would be reunited. The thought rang like a litany through her mind and she ignored the feeling of cold dread clutching her stomach.

She had no idea of time as she waited for Sir Gregory to return with her husband. Occasionally a church clock chimed and there were shouts and the sounds of revelry from the waterside taverns. Each thud of her heart felt like an hour, every shuddering breath an eternity.

The door opened and Gwendolyn held her breath, peering into the darkness. The short figure of Sir Gregory climbed inside. 'I am so sorry, my dear. The ship sailed two days ago on the early tide. Osgood timed his vengeance well.'

Gwendolyn sat frozen with fear.

'Will it not be docking at other ports to collect more prisoners? There are prison hulks at Plymouth.'

'The ship is full. They will be joined by others from Rochester and Plymouth to form a convoy. They will not risk putting into port with so desperate a cargo. I am sorry, my dear.'

She shook her head. 'I cannot allow this to happen. Japhet has been pardoned. I will myself sail to Australia and deliver the pardon, if I can find a passage on a ship that takes the same route. We may intercept the transport ship and gain him his freedom before we reach the other side of the world.'

'You cannot embark on so hazardous a venture. You have a young son.' Sir Gregory was shocked at her proposal. 'Your family would not permit it.'

'I am no longer answerable to them. My duty is to my husband. I would follow him to the ends of the earth to be at his side. Now we have his pardon he cannot be subjected to the misery of a prison ship and face the horrors of a penal colony. Will you help me to find a passage, Sir Gregory? I have no one else to turn to.'

Sir Gregory admired her courage. 'If you are determined on this then I will offer my services as your companion. You cannot journey alone.'

'I could not expect so much from you, Sir Gregory. You have been a loyal friend, but such a journey will take many months before we may return to England.'

'I am a vagabond at heart. I have toured Europe, and learned much during my voyage with Adam to Virginia. I always had a mind to venture to the Orient and even beyond.'

'I would be forever indebted to you, Sir Gregory.'

'You could of course trust me to take Japhet's pardon to the penal colony? There would be no need for you to undergo the rigours of the voyage.'

Gwendolyn shook her head. 'I have been parted from my husband too long. I cannot spend months worrying myself into a frenzy at home. My destiny lies with him. I am not afraid.'

'Then God be with us all. I have seen the faith the Lovedays put in loyalty and honour. Fate has played its hand in their fortunes. Trials and scandals have not diminished their strength. Honour has sustained them through some turbulent years.'

'It is all a matter of pride, and we are a proud family.' Gwendolyn squared her shoulders, preparing to meet this new challenge.

'Where will that pride take you?' Sir Gregory responded. 'In these uncertain times, only further uncertainty can lie ahead.'

'Then so be it. Tamasine has vowed to be true to Mr Carlton. I will not forsake my husband. Honour demands it of me.'

SOUTH LANARKSHIRE LIBRARIES

<u>HOUSEBOUND SERVICE</u>

225	166	89
98	75	
198	200	
580	177	
880	54	
	150	
	253	
	115	
	115	